Stain of
the Berry

Also by the author

Amuse Bouche
Flight of Aquavit
Tapas on the Ramblas
Sundowner Ubuntu
Aloha, Candy Hearts
Date with a Sheesha
Dos Equis

Stain of the Berry

the Berry

A Russell Quant Mystery

Anthony Bidulka

INSOMNIAC PRESS

Library and Archives Canada Cataloguing in Publication
Bidulka, Anthony, 1962-
Stain of the berry / Anthony Bidulka.

(A Russell Quant mystery)
ISBN 978-1-55483-088-6

I. Title. II. Series: Bidulka, Anthony, 1962- . Russell
Quant mystery.

PS8553.I319S73 2012   C813'.6   C2012-905397-X

The publisher gratefully acknowledges the support of the Canada
Council, the Ontario Arts Council and the Department of Canadian
Heritage through the Canada Book Fund.

Printed and bound in Canada

Insomniac Press, 520 Princess Ave.
London, Ontario, Canada, N6B 2B8
www.insomniacpress.com

THE CANADA COUNCIL | LE CONSEIL DES ARTS
FOR THE ARTS | DU CANADA
SINCE 1957 | DEPUIS 1957

Canada

ONTARIO ARTS COUNCIL
CONSEIL DES ARTS DE L'ONTARIO

a word for every year

Trout
Kuhio
Mocha
Oia
House
Bali
Gong
Zihua
Gites
Drivethrough
Rainbow
Silversea
Amuse
Halekulani
Mashatu

Happy 15th, Herb

and one more
Love

Acknowledgements

Writing the acknowledgements section for each book is one of my favourite things to do because I am continuously grateful to so many people who make up the world I live in as a writer. It's also one of the most difficult tasks because there is no way I can possibly mention everyone I should. Included in that list are the people who sit in the audience when I appear at bookstores and other venues. It astounds me that you show up. I hope you know that your presence is a very special gift. And then there are the letters, cards, emails, the wonderful folks who write to me via my website and many other gifts and kindnesses that buoy my spirit and inspire me to write more, write better, just write. My thanks.

I have the opportunity with each book to travel to many different cities in Canada and the United States. Every visit is an exciting, unique, wonderful adventure. Thank you to all the booksellers, store managers and employees, event coordinators and festival, conference and award show organizers for all that you do. These have been some of the best times of my career.

To the people of the worlds of print, radio, the web and TV, thank you for paying attention and sharing your time and talent, air time and column space. You continue to make a difference. Your support means a great deal to me.

Special thanks to: Aden Bowman Collegiate students and teachers for including me in your fantastic literary morning; book club participants for your interest and humour, excellent questions and fine hospitality; the talented writers it has been my honour to share a stage with over the past year, including Robert Taylor, Craig Hickman, Gene Kahn, Guy Vanderhaeghe, Sharon Butala, Gail Bowen, Pride Week Coffeehouse participants, Gary Ryan, Murray J. Malcolm, Anne Metikosh, Patricia Nell Warren, Jeff Mann and Ellen Hart; Katherine & NeWest for the Magical Mystery Tour and more; the talented children of St. Michael's School—I loved your performances; Terri for the fantastic flamenco; Prairie Ink for superb tapas and sangria; Deneen for coming back; October 20 in Saskatoon—you people rock! David and Dick for making honest men out of each other at last; James for Tree; Frances—you are forever my Captain Giovanna Bagnato—the store, the window, the sangria, the food, the crowd—you're #1; Keith and Martin, there is nothing common about your hospitality; Blossoms for knowing just when to brighten a day with flowers; the curiously enterprising Paul and Jan for Greek tapas, Korean onion rings and killer dinner parties; Taylor and Bugger because I couldn't not; Pat and Lynne for Victoria treats and mojitos on the beach; Kit—you are never invisible; Dori for pillow talk; George (aka Birch) for always putting me on your Reading List; Ross for unknowingly inspiring the Arctic locale; Kell for help with Moose Jaw street names; Huw for the best poster ever; Kevin Hogarth for great photos and teaching me about face powder; Farewell, Kenny; Holly and Jim for curry at the Bengal; Bob and Eleanor for the South African feast; CnC for 15th escargot and meat; Kathryn M. for blowing bubbles in wine; Richard (Linklater!)—jazz & blues=good, eighties pop=bad! Nowell for Atlanta welcome package; my fellow GWRs; Hi, Moo and E! My sisters and their marvellous clans; and Mom: ta da!!! Stardust memories.

Andrew Frape of TechGuys created a killer website, a marvellous home for Russell Quant and all his stuff. Way to go, Code Monkey.

Insomniac Press—Mike and staff—you make magic. With appreciation.

Michele Karlsberg—peddling my prairie detective to foreign airline employees while holidaying on a cruise ship—wow, you are *GOOD!*

Excerpts from an editor's letter: "...I circled a

great many ellipses...I did find the placement of the conversation a bit unusual...if you change the day of death...there are too many 'dudes' in this section...I know that it is difficult to explore such issues...loved the farting—hilarious...I did note that the pigs do sound like sheep...that is an excellent scene, by the way...not quite getting where you want it to be...I was very much drawn into your thought-provoking portrayals of fear and childhood...you revel in your smaller characters...we never hear her speak and yet obtain an amazing sense of who she is...you need to lighten it...please revisit this...Saskatoon has its own character...these are harsh consequences for Russell...I think you should check on this...detach yourself a bit...a complete and complex novel...the multitude of links are so subtle I almost missed some of them...my intention is to support you and your writing to the best of my abilities..." *And I feel that from you every day. Thank you, Catherine.*

A book is nothing without you, the reader.
And Herb.

Chapter 1

I awoke startled, my heart playing a spicy salsa beat within the cavity of my chest. Perspiration stuck to me like shrink wrap, yet the room was cool as a tomb. I was unaccountably frightened, disoriented, not fully conscious really, struggling to identify the source of my discomfort. Was it a dream? A nightmare? Someone was chasing me. A hand was reaching out for me, almost touching me. But no, it wasn't me the hand was reaching for, it was someone else, someone familiar, and I was watching from afar, helpless. Then the image was gone, replaced by a jarring clamour assaulting my fuzzy brain. My left arm shot out for the phone on the bedside table, knocking it to the floor. Thankfully, the action brought to an end the unsettling din, but then came something much worse. A deliberate, dark voice invaded my addled brain: *The boogeyman is gonna get you.* My eyes flew open, searching the empty space for what or who was haunting my room. I heard it again: a voice, disembodied. I rolled onto my side to the edge of the bed and reached down, fumbling for the phone's receiver. I pulled the handset to my ear.

"What? What? What!" I called into the phone, loud enough to wake the two schnauzers at the foot of my bed, both completely hidden beneath the bedcovers I'd wrestled off myself sometime during the night.

"What?" a voice repeated back, sounding not at all like the Grim Reaper in my head but rather more like a frightened woman.

"I'm sorry, I'm sorry," I answered back, for some reason relying on repetition to propel me further into this unexpected conversation. "I was sleeping." Bet she was surprised. Through slitted eyes I saw that the clock on my bedside table read 2:37. "Did you say something about a boogeyman?" I asked.

"Oh God, I'm sorry…you're gonna think I'm crazy." Her voice sat in the lower registers but was no doubt feminine. Then, more to herself, "Maybe I am crazy."

Well, I don't know who you are, but yup, I pretty much don't think too highly of you so far. " I think you have the wrong number," I growled, instinctively pulling at the bedsheet to cover myself. Barbra and Brutus, my mutts, growled their own displeasure at the rude awakening. "Oh be quiet," I said to them.

"What?" this from the woman.

"Not you." Well, maybe. "Wrong number," I told her again and was about to hang up when I heard her call my name. Huh? "Excuse me? Do I know you? Who is this?"

"Russell Quant?" she repeated, haltingly.

I debated a lie. "Yuh-huh," I answered, my tongue still thick and eraser-like with sleep.

"He...he's coming to get me...I don't know why...but I can't take it anymore!"

A ripple of shivers surged over me and I sat up in bed, focusing on the caller's voice, which was trembling like an aspen leaf in a breeze. She was definitely scared, not hysterical, but close. My shift in position caused Brutus to hop off the bed in search of a quieter resting place on the floor. His sister Barbra sighed greatly but stayed where she was. "Are you okay, miss? What's your name?"

"He won't leave me alone. He wants to hurt me."

I was more confused. "Listen, is something happening right now? Are you in danger?" My voice sounded anxious. I had to do something about that; it wouldn't do my caller any good if I sounded more scared than she was.

She said nothing for a moment, but I could hear a sort of whimpering as she considered the answer to my question.

"Should I call the police? Tell me exactly what's happening." I felt like a 911 operator. "Is there someone there with you right now?"

And then—dial tone.

It was turning out to be one of those mythical Saskatchewan summers. The days long and hot and dry, often punctuated by nameless winds born of the same capricious airstreams that give rise to the gentle Mediterranean zephyr, the dust-laden Saharan sirocco, the insistent French mistral, the dry Egyptian khamsin, the Rocky Mountain chinook and the indefatigable African harmattan.

Our summer nights come late on a rising moon of many colours. And when it's hot enough and conditions are exactly right, careless skies unleash a fury so powerful it's as if the whole world is under the unpredictable control of Seth, the ancient Egyptian god of storms. These are wild, crazy storms that blow like hurricanes across the prairies, fracture the sky with kilometre-long, jagged fingers of lightning and deposit enough water to float an ark. After minutes or hours—one can never be sure which—the storm passes, leaving behind rainbows so perfect they might have been drawn by a child, fields of diamonds born of water droplets and the sweet, sweet aromas of everything that is fresh and new.

Yet as much as prairie folk pray for rain to bolster crops (whether you're a farmer or not does not really matter), they also need hot and dry conditions to turn thin green stalks into fat golden ones. So thankfully, in between these glorious bursts of wet, most of our Saskatchewan summer days are bone dry. And as dry as the weather was, so too was my business.

My name is Russell Quant. A few years back I decided to leave my stable, scheduled, regular-cheque-every-month job as a police constable for the Canadian prairie city of Saskatoon, Saskatchewan, and hang my shingle as a private detective. Saskatoon's population is somewhere over the 200,000 mark and growing, with a large network of towns, villages and farming communities surrounding it. So, there's stuff for a detective to do, just not always. And not always interesting.

My cases have run the gamut from The Case of the Stolen Perogy Recipe to murder—with emphasis on the perogy side of the scale. And lately, business had been bad. My resume of recent cases was looking pretty sparse and my bank account even more so. I had reached a point where I'd begun to think I'd never work again and would have to sell the family jewels—which consist of a green-tinged, silver ID bracelet from my first high school boyfriend (well, I pretended he was my boyfriend) and a pair of cufflinks (one broken) that had belonged to my late father but which he'd never used.

You see, every year, sometime in June, the population of Saskatchewan slips into a comatose state of inactivity that lasts for the duration of our short but sultry summer months. People go to lakes. They golf. They camp. They have celebratory barbecues for no apparent reason. They eat copious amounts of tiger-tiger and grape-flavoured ice cream. They attend a plethora of summertime festivals and go for long walks. They do just about anything but work. And apparently, troublemakers—the people who keep me in business—have the same routine. But come September, with the first whiff of cooler evening air, the populace grudgingly slough off their sloppy sandals and loose-fitting shorts and slip on their most rigorous dress shoes and slick business suits, at the ready for action. Kids are back in school. University hallways are packed. Committees are formed. Boards return from hiatus. Decisions are made. Hobbies are reborn. Business is done and, thankfully, evil-doers get back to doing evil. I could hardly wait. Until then, I was relegated to long mornings at home before schlepping to work to stare at the phone, rearrange files and hope for something interesting in the mail, like a flyer for two-for-one geranium plants at my favourite greenhouse.

My office is on Spadina Crescent, just out of downtown, in an old character house that used to be called the Professional Womyn's Centre. Several years ago a young lawyer, Errall Strane, purchased the property, did some remodelling and, in deference to a piece of history, renamed it the PWC Building. After renovations, PWC was left with four office spaces. Errall runs her law practice out of the largest suite on the main floor, the balance of which is rented to Beverly Chaney, a psychiatrist. Two smaller offices on the second floor belong to Alberta Lougheed, a psychic, and me. Mine is the smallest, but the only one with a balcony and a view that more than makes up for its size. From the small deck I can gaze across Spadina Crescent at beautiful Riverside Park and the South Saskatchewan River.

Because of the disturbing phone call, which had kept me tossing and turning the rest of the night, it was close to eleven a.m., later than usual (really) when I pulled into the gravel lot behind PWC. I hustled up the metal staircase that hugs the rear of the building and takes me directly to the second floor. I think at one time it was meant to be a fire escape, but now the ancient railings are so unstable I'm the only one who dares to use it. Stepping indoors, I heard the unexpected; it was the sound of...what was that noise? It sounded distantly familiar. It was activity—maybe even bustle? I peered over the banister of the stairs that lead down to the main floor. The PWC reception area is dominated by a massive circular desk which divides the space into two: a waiting area for Errall's clients to the right and one to the left for all the rest of our clients. The spot of honour behind the desk is home to our ever-cheerful group receptionist, Lilly. As I looked down, all appeared as usual, except for the fact that there were a number of people milling about, sitting in chairs, drinking coffee, chatting with Lilly. Who were these people? They appeared to be...clients. Some were for Errall (these were easily distinguishable by their serious manners and clothes to match). The others were for Beverly and...could it be...some for Alberta too? I glanced at Alberta's office door, decked out with a never-before-seen, handwritten sign that said in quite serious-looking print: Spirits At Work—Do Not Disturb!!! This Means You!

Holy cow. Even Alberta was busier than I was. Could it be that it was just me suffering from summer doldrums? I looked down at my business attire, which over the past few weeks of heat wave and inactivity had slowly but surely deteriorated to

consist solely of wrinkled khaki shorts, one of my
collection of diva concert Ts (Cher, Shania, Whitney)
and a pair of flip-flops that had seen better days. I
backed away from the banister as if beyond it was
the Twilight Zone and scooted into my office,
shutting the door soundly behind me.

Shit. This didn't feel good. Everyone else was
busy. What was wrong with me? My last paying
client had been Bohdan Mazurchewich, who paid
me less than four hundred bucks two weeks ago to
find out what his wife did while he was out of town
on business. Turns out she ordered-in, rented Meg
Ryan movies, drank daiquiris and banana milkshakes,
hung with girlfriends, laughed a lot and in general
enjoyed life. Something she apparently didn't do
while Mr. Mazurchewich was at home. This was
definitely information he needed to know. I should
have charged him more.

I selected a Diet Pepsi out of the mini bar fridge
that holds up one end of my desk and took a seat,
pulling my Daytimer front and centre to study its
contents. What was on my schedule? Lunch today
with Anthony. Next week was Darrell and Nick's
seventh anniversary—I had to remember to send a
card—and Brutus was due for a dental exam at the
end of August. Today was July fifteenth. I sipped
my drink and stared at the phone.

Fringe Festivals, with their culturally diverse, mind challenging—and sometimes boggling—array of live theatre and off-the-wall entertainment, occur annually in cities across the continent, and Saskatoon's version is reputedly one of the best, maybe not for its size, but certainly for its heart and energy. Everything takes place in a handful of venues and blocks in the historically rich Broadway/Nutana area of the city, and it was along these busker-lined, poster-plastered, sun-drenched streets that I meandered until it was time to meet Anthony for a late lunch.

Owner of several high-end menswear stores carrying his surname (with a small "g") gatt, Anthony is a man of indeterminate age (far beyond his forties and maybe even his fifties?), immeasurable means (lots of dough) and unquestionable breeding (speaks with a smooth English-accented flourish), all topped off with a dashing Robert Redford/Jay Gatsby handsomeness. He and his partner, Jared Lowe, are in the vanguard of the Saskatoon society set. Anthony is wise in the ways of the world, gay and straight, and determined to make me so as well, taking his role as my friend/instructor/occasional pain-in-the-ass very seriously. If I didn't love him so much, I'd hate him.

"You cannot be serious," Anthony said a little too loudly as he strode towards me, wearing exquisitely tailored pants just this side of white, a shirt of orange and pink that defied the odds by looking just right on him and a pair of white leather shoes that were making a comeback that week.

I looked at him questioningly, pretending I didn't know what he was talking about when of course I did. Anthony can be a bit of a snob, and as much as he tries to mentor me, insisting that I hold wineglasses properly by their stem and keep my elbows moisturized, I also have a role to play in his life in teaching him how to loosen up and get a little down and dirty.

"You really don't expect me to eat meat that's been marinating in sun and flies since six a.m. off a stick, do you?" He'd obviously caught sight of some of the wares being offered by food vendors who were lining the streets selling everything from corn on the cob to sushi to deep-fried Mars bars. "And without a seat or a glass of wine to choke it all down with? Barbarous!"

I nudged him forward with my right arm, me in my messy flip-flops and him clip-clopping in his fancy shoes next to me. "Anthony, you haven't even given it a try. This is what you do at the Fringe."

"No, this is what you do if you live in a Third World country and have vultures eating carrion in your backyard. Seeing as that fate has yet to befall us, I have a better idea."

"You said I could pick the restaurant."

He shot me a disgusted look above the rim of

his Maui Jims. "That is correct. And, even without consulting my *Oxford*, I can tell you that the definition of restaurant includes tables and chairs, handsome servers, menus listing outrageous prices and suggestions for jaunty aperitifs and..."

"Okay, okay, I give up." I knew my friend well enough to have mentally given up five minutes before.

"Suspecting your treachery, I took the liberty of calling ahead," he told me as he ably manoeuvred me by the elbow across the street toward one of his favourite local dining establishments.

In the bustling game of restaurant roulette, Calories is one of Saskatoon's better established players. And in a city—apparently one of many—that purports to have more restaurants per capita than any other in North America, its chances of continued survival and thriving success are surprisingly good. For whereas the city is rife with Asian, Greek and Italian (i.e. pizza) establishments, Calories is one of only a handful of Saskatoon restaurants that offers a truly gourmet dining experience and one of considerably less than half a handful that are listed as "French" in the Saskatoon phonebook. From a menu pasted behind a window near the front entrance, I could see that today's offerings included a vegetarian special of herb ragout in a Taleggio cream sauce, sautéed frog legs and asparagus tips *persillade* with a tapenade drizzle and raw arugula, along with a towering blah-blah-blah of blah-blah-blah infused with blah-blah-blah that sounded absolutely irresistible. Not a pepperoni, avgolemeno soup or bowl of special fried rice in sight.

Anthony yammered on. "...And I was able to secure one of the outdoor tables so we both can have our way. You can still be out in nature amongst the odours of beef jerky and unchanged infants while I get to keep my nose over a glass of chilled rosé. How's that?" We pulled up to a scant collection of blue, bistro-style metal tables pressed tightly against the restaurant's façade and roped off from the maddening crowd by a row of black metal poles with chain strung between them. Indeed one of the tables had a Reserved sign on it. A pretty girl with a sweating pitcher of cold water swooped down and removed it as soon as she caught sight of Anthony.

We sat down; Anthony discussed the menu with our cute, shaved-headed server, consulted me and then ordered.

"So tell me what's been going on," Anthony asked with knowing eyes and concern in his voice. "You strike me as a bit melancholy."

"Nah, I just really wanted some of that meat on a stick," I answered back in full smart-ass mode.

"It's Sereena."

I looked away, making a show of being busy drinking my water and watching a fire-eater perform on the median. Sereena is my neighbour—that is she *was* my neighbour until she disappeared last year...or rather, never came back from a Mediterranean cruise. Her house went up for sale (still was) and I've not heard from her. I don't know why I was so surprised. Sereena Orion Smith has always been an enigma to me and to most people. When people ask me about her, I tell them to listen to that song from the early eighties "I've Never Been to Me" by Charlene. Like the gal in that song, I have no doubt that indeed Sereena has been "undressed by kings...and seen some things that a woman ain't s'posed to see." That is the easy answer, the answer I give because really, despite all the time we've spent together, she remains elusive, shrouded in mystery, parts of her forever unknowable to me. Yet I *do* know her; I feel an undeniable and intimate connection with her. The question for me isn't "Who is Sereena Orion Smith?" but rather "Who *was* Sereena Orion Smith?" There is something guarded about her, as if protecting a past she never wants fully revealed. Still, there were times she'd tossed about names of places she'd been and people she'd known, adventures she'd had, not to gloat or boast, but in loving memory of a life lived well (and perhaps a bit raunchily). Yet somehow, the reality of what she was before she came into our lives remains illusory, like some fantasy story that is never told the same way twice.

"Actually," I said off-handedly, "I've pretty much given up on her."

It was a bit of a lie. Or maybe not, I wasn't sure yet. I'd spent considerable time and energy attempting to track down my ex-neighbour over the past few months. And money. Truth be told, my investigation into her disappearance was a big reason why my bank account was about to file for social assistance. As a detective—and Sereena's friend—I felt a responsibility to find her and guilt when I continually failed to uncover even a sliver of a hint as to where she'd gone. In indomitable Sereena fashion, she'd pulled off the perfect disappearing act. All I or anyone else had to go on were bits and scraps that added up to...*bubkes*.

"I don't believe you," Anthony stated. "But I know you're discouraged. We all are. We miss her, and we're worried about her."

I nodded and was glad to see our wine arrive.

"But that's not all, is it?"

Ah geez, here it comes.

"Someone is turning thirty-five in about ten days," Anthony said after he'd tasted and approved of the wine. "And not embracing the idea I take it?"

"Y'know," I said, leaning in towards Anthony, suddenly wanting to talk about this. "I wouldn't mind the age thing so much if there weren't so many reminders. I was paying for gas the other day and this young dude behind the counter complimented my wallet and asked where I got it. I thought, hey, a hip young guy thinks I have a hip young wallet. I told him it came from Birks. And do you know what he said to me?"

Anthony winced in anticipation.

"He said, 'Great, that'll make a perfect gift for my dad's birthday'! His *dad!* Anthony, I have a *dad's* wallet!"

"Nonsense. I've seen your wallet and it is a stylish, sophisticated accoutrement. And it should be," he sniffed. "I gave it to you."

I kept on with my barrage of woes. "Sometimes the best I can do on the treadmill at the gym is a fast walk instead of a run, I found a white chest hair and…aw shit, Anthony… the other night…my wonderpants felt tight around the waist."

My wonderpants. Everyone has a pair. They're black, never wrinkle, I've owned them forever yet they're always in style, and, most importantly, I've been told they make my ass look great. The whole point of wonderpants is that they always look good and always fit—even if you did eat a bag of Doritos the night before. But now, I had to face the very real and undesirable possibility that my ass had outgrown their otherworldly powers.

Anthony sipped his wine contemplatively, then said, "It's much too soon for a mid-life crisis, puppy. You're a six-foot-one, fresh-faced, sandy-haired Adonis for goodness' sake, so don't rush out for a barbwire tat around your bicep or an age-inappropriate wardrobe from Abercrombie & Fitch. This isn't about aching traps or greying hair."

I gulped at my wine, hopeful for good news. "It isn't?"

"You just need a really good date."

Crap. Wrong answer. "I date."

"I'm not talking about random crushes followed by randy sex. I'm talking about meeting a man who gets your heart and head and blood racing."

"But—"

He shushed me. "Just wait, Russell, I'm not done. I'm not talking about marriage. I'm not talking about a move-in-set-up-house-get-a-crystal-pattern relationship. I respect your judgment on when and if that's right for you. I'm talking about at least opening yourself up to meeting some guys who might...shall we say, befuddle you enough to at least momentarily sway your judgment...regardless of the final outcome."

With sun reflecting off his shiny pate, the server delivered our food with quiet efficiency. For once I was hoping for a chatty waiter. I looked down at our plates. Somehow Anthony had ended up with a beautifully arranged but inconsequential salad of frilly greens whereas I sat before a pile of meat smothered in sauce. No wonder my pants were beginning to revolt.

"I don't understand a word of what you just

said," I told my friend.

"No," Anthony said with a wicked smile. "I wouldn't imagine that you would. Therefore I've taken the liberty of arranging a birthday present for you that will explain everything."

"Oh?" Suspicion.

"His name is Doug Poitras."

Jiminy Cricket crack house cracker! and other curse-filled cusses raced through my head but not quite out of my mouth. "You got me a man?" I asked in astonishment. "You got me a real, live, breathing man for my birthday?"

Anthony gave me a look drier than crust. "He can be returned, Russell."

"How about we cancel the order altogether?" I suggested with little humour left in my voice. I did not want this. "I'll make the call. Where did you get him? The Hudson Gay Company? Boyfriends-R-Us?"

He ignored that. "Even Errall is getting back in the game. She's bringing the new woman in her life to your surprise birthday party."

Whoa. Too much new information at once. How did I—a detective, no less—not know about any of this? "Errall is dating? I'm having a surprise birthday party?"

"I know little else about Errall's guest, so don't ask. And I tell you about the party only because no one should be surprised by a social gathering in their honour. Ever. Especially you. The chances of your showing up in…well, in something as disastrous as your current costume, are much too high to risk. I'll send something over from the store of course."

I slumped into my plate of meat. "Now I really am melancholy."

"Ah, it never rains but it pours," he responded, nibbling on his delightful wee salad.

"Spouting overused clichés, Anthony? So unlike you." I had more wine. I usually don't go for rosés—a *Château de Sours* Bordeaux from France—but this one wasn't bad and I needed the thirteen per cent sustenance.

Anthony delivered his next line with his smile awry. "In addition to Mr. Poitras, you seem to have another admirer." He nodded to somewhere over my shoulder.

I surveyed the street crowd but saw no such admirer. I gave Anthony an inquiring look.

"Over there," he said. "She's loitering near the Bulk Cheese Warehouse. Rather menacing looking really, a fetching Grace Jones meets the Terminator type. Staring daggers into you."

How could I miss that? I moved my gaze to the two-storey, grey brick building across the street and just caught the tail feathers of a tall, black woman with wide shoulders and a storm trooper gait before she disappeared around a corner.

She must be one of the street performers, I

thought to myself. The Fringe brings out all kinds of characters into the streets. But something in the back of my mind warned me that I was horribly wrong.

The officious rapping on my front door came at the crack of dawn—not quite nine a.m.—Thursday morning. I was just out of bed and barely dressed (a pair of loose, threadbare, grey cotton, U of S sweatpants) and a bit grumpy (no coffee yet).

My house is on a large lot at the dead end of a quiet, little-travelled street; a grove of towering aspen and thick spruce neatly hide it from view of the casual passerby. Inside, the house is a unique mix of open, airy rooms and tiny, cozy spaces, each appealing to me depending upon my mood. A six-foot-high fence encircles the backyard and at the rear of the lot, accessible by way of a back alley, is a two-car garage with a handy second storey I use for storage. My home is my castle, a place where I re-energize and take refuge from the world and expect to have my morning coffee in peace. So enough with the knocking!

I pulled open the front door, ready to berate the devil in a blue dress behind it. Darren Kirsch may not exactly be the devil, and as a Criminal Investigations Division detective he doesn't wear a blue uniform anymore, but close enough.

"Ever hear of calling before making an early morning raid?" I greeted him with a scowl. "Do you have the phone number for the police complaints department? You must know it off by heart. I'm sure you must give it out often enough." Low blow I know, but no coffee is no coffee.

Darren Kirsch is the archetypical City of Saskatoon policeman—six feet plus with a top-heavy, muscular body; short, dark hair; neat, dark moustache; deep-set, stern eyes and a snarly nose, but that particular combination on this particular big lug is actually pretty darn cute. Cute and as heterosexual as wearing socks with ugly sandals in the summer. He looked me over, from the freak show that was my morning hair, down my bare chest all the way to my unshod feet. He shoved the rolled up, plastic-wrapped copy of the morning paper that had been lying at my front gate into my abdomen and pushed past me, barking the command, "Read it."

I closed the door and watched the warm reception given this intruder into my morning by Barbra and Brutus. Turncoats. "Don't you need a warrant to barge in here like this?"

He crouched down to schnauzer level to scruff up the erogenous zones behind their ears. "These two don't seem to mind. Now read the paper, Quant. Page A-five, the local news column." He stood up and headed toward my kitchen. The dogs and I followed.

I figured out pretty early on that to make a go of being a private detective in this city, I needed a contact in the police department. Kirsch is mine. We're still working on figuring out where the line is that we shouldn't cross, and we most definitely are still working on deciding whether we even like one another, but we help each other out when we can. Although I suspect him to be a closet homophobe and he suspects me of suspecting him, it works for us.

By the time I freed the *StarPhoenix* from its protective packaging, flopped onto a stool at my kitchen island, found the page Darren directed me to and read the news column, he'd managed to find the makings for coffee, set it to perk and let the dogs out the back to enjoy the start of what looked to be another bright, shiny day.

I felt Darren hovering over me and his thick arm brushed my bare shoulder as he pointed to one of the brief articles. "This one," he said hoarsely.

I read the four or five lines again while he watched. It was about an apparent suicide during the early hours of Wednesday morning. A young woman, name not yet released, jumped from an eighth-floor balcony of a building on the corner of University Drive and Broadway Avenue. I had walked right by that building on my way to meet Anthony for lunch at the Fringe. Even so, other than a sense of sadness at the loss of life, the story meant nothing to me. I looked up at Darren questioningly.

"Where are your mugs?"

I pointed to a cupboard and watched in idle fascination as super-hunk-cop served me up my morning java. What was going on? Why was he here?

"Do you know anything about this?" Darren asked, placing his butt on a stool opposite my own.

"No. Should I?"

He didn't immediately answer, instead watching my face as if trying to decide something. "The woman who jumped, her name was Tanya Culinare." Another pause. When I didn't react one way or the other, he asked, "Does that name mean anything to you?"

"No, Kirsch, it doesn't. But I'm getting the feeling you think it should. Why don't you stop with the games and tell me what's going on?" My near nakedness—even though I was in the kitchen of my own home—was making me feel inferior to Kirsch in his bland but serious-looking suit and tie, and I wasn't liking the sensation much.

"We searched Miss Culinare's apartment, looking for a suicide note..."

Uh-huh.

"We found a note. Next to the phone."

Okay, you got me. Morbid curiosity. "What did it say?"

"Only two things. Your name. And your phone number."

Chapter 2

Nothing had come out of my recent visit from Constable Darren Kirsch. Yes, the dead woman had a scrap of paper with my name and phone number on it, but I had no idea who she was—other than the faint suspicion that she was the mysterious after-midnight caller who'd hung up on me several days earlier. Curious, but ultimately it led nowhere, which left me with absolutely nothing to do. Professionally speaking, that is.

I'm the kind of person who has little problem filling time one way or the other. I love my work, but in its absence I can always find a million things that need doing or ways to entertain myself. And so I found myself playing Mr. Butch around PWC for the next couple of days, doing those tasks that Errall as landlord would hire someone else to do but to which I offered myself as a confident expert. I replaced a cracked window pane in Beverly's office, cleaned out the eavestroughs, sprayed recalcitrant thistles in our parking lot with weed killer and made an ill-fated attempt at fixing a leaky kitchen faucet. At the end of the week I presented Errall with a healthy bill for my services, which she paid with a cutting barb: something about believing *I* should pay *her* for giving me the opportunity to exercise my flagging masculinity.

So after all that manly-man toil, I was happy to spend Saturday getting my hair cut, nails manicured and aching muscles massaged in preparation for a boys night out with my friend Jared, Anthony Gatt's long-term partner. Jared's successful career as a fashion and runway model had all but ground to a halt since he'd recently turned the model-death-knell age of thirty-five…see, it is a cursed age… and he was in a state of flux as he figured out just what it was he was going to do with the rest of his life. This was lucky for me because I was in the mood to play and he had all the time in the world. Our plan was to meet for drinks on Earl's deck, one of the best in town, follow that with a late curry dinner at the Taj Mahal, then maybe a few more drinks and some dancing at Divas.

Jared was already there when I was shown to our table next to the firepit on the ivy-covered deck that hangs off one side of the Earl's building on 2nd Avenue. It was a busy night with the young, beautiful staff showing off toned and tanned legs and arms while serving up pitchers of mixed drinks and frothy mugs of beer to rowdy patrons wearing their trendy best. Jared was in a gauzy, peach, striped shirt with light-coloured slacks, a combination that looked ridiculously good against his suntanned-bronze skin and head full of relaxed copper curls.

"You look fantastic," he enthused with his heart-shaped smile as I took my seat.

Jared was generous with compliments that never seemed insincere. I regarded my tan, short-sleeved sweater and matching pants, thought it might look okay and hoped the outrageously expensive belt from gatt helped to hold in what I, in this den of youthful physical perfection, couldn't help but feel was an ever-expanding paunch. We ordered dirty martinis and made juvenile comments more suitable to horny high school boys about our cute waiter until he returned with our drinks.

"Have you heard anything?" Jared asked for about the zillionth time since Sereena had pulled her vanishing act.

He knew I'd know exactly what he was talking

about. But I sometimes like to play coy. "About what?"

His expression remained admirably unchanged while he sipped his cocktail and said nothing.

"Why do you ask?"

"You look a little gloomy."

I frowned at him. "I thought you just said I looked fantastic."

"Gloomily fantastic."

"You've been talking to Anthony."

"We are partners. We do that sometimes."

"She's disappeared, Jared," I said to him, sounding matter-of-fact to cover the real jolt of pain I felt each time I thought about it. "She's just gone." I guzzled my drink and wondered how soon I could order another.

"You know, even though I've known Sereena since she moved in next door to you," Jared said, leaning into me across the table, "I've wondered these last months since she's been gone whether maybe I never really knew her very well at all. Where was she born? Does she have family? How did she get that scar on her chin?"

He flipped an olive into his mouth and after a quick chew continued on. "I know some of the stories—or are they rumours?—about how she dated this king or that prime minister, how she once had a house in Belize and an apartment in Venice, gambled away fortunes, and we all know her story about

Mick Jagger and the pineapple—you know some other stories. Anthony does too, but put them all together and we still have…nothing. Her life before Saskatoon is this colourful movie that has kept us entertained for years, but now that she's gone I've been getting this feeling—you know the one—where you've left the theatre and suddenly can't remember the plot of the movie you've just seen? How can that be? Wasn't I paying attention?"

I took a deep whiff of summer air lightly singed with the cloying aroma of annual forest fires burning hundreds of kilometres north of the city. I knew what he meant. I'd felt it too. It was surprise and confusion mixed with a lingering guilt that we'd somehow had this superstar character living amongst us but, as with real superstars about whom one reads endless details in tabloids and newspapers, we really knew nothing of substance about her. But I was done with guilt.

"You know what I think, Jared?" I asked, feeling the heady effects of the cloudy gin. "Our relationship with Sereena and hers with us was just as she wanted it, just as she manipulated it to be. She had this way about her that made it feel as if she'd pulled us close, but really she kept us at a distance that felt safe to her. She was a genius at it.

"Sereena really gets to know the people around her, who they are, what they do, what they love and hate, what makes them interesting. She knows that given the slightest opening, people love to talk about themselves; I've done it, you've done it, we all have. But her ability to have people reveal themselves to her without reciprocating is also her way of hiding from them, like some kind of protective barrier."

Jared nodded thoughtfully. "So while we're self-importantly gushing on about ourselves and our lives, all we've managed to learn about her are the snippets of gossip and anecdotes she's judiciously meted out."

"All of them insignificantly small pieces of a big life," I said, "none of which come even close to revealing the bigger picture. And, unfortunately, that fact has made it virtually impossible for me to find her. I've been such a lousy detective when it comes to this, Jared. Over the years there've been clues about her cloudy past that I noticed but did nothing about: the elevator operator in New York City who called her Mrs. Ashbourne; the mysterious man aboard the yacht whom she refused to identify or even acknowledge existed. Her initials are SOS, for Pete's sake!"

"Mysterious man on a yacht?"

I slugged back the last drops of my martini. "You know, the last time I saw Sereena was on a yacht—the *Kismet*—in the Mediterranean. I noticed a man, really just an indistinct character in the shadows, but he seemed intent on watching me.

Yet, when I confronted Sereena about him, she acted as if I were seeing things. Later, when I researched the ownership of the boat, I found it was registered to the A&W Corporation. When I dug further I discovered that A&W stands for Ashbourne and Wistonchuk."

Jared's brow furrowed. "Ashbourne…the name the man in New York called her."

"Yes, and Wistonchuk is my mother's maiden name!"

"What? How…what does it mean?"

I shook my head like a dog with stick-on fleas. "Who knows!" My months-old exasperation was beginning to show. "Sereena, or Mrs. Ashbourne, or whatever her real name is, is gone and my mother claims ignorance…which I tend to buy; she's about as mysterious as a bowl of mashed potatoes. Since then, all my investigations have run into solid dead ends. Every time I think I've found a lead, it dries up like a dandelion and blows away. It's as if the whole world is in cahoots in hiding her from me. And I'm not good enough to find her, too stupid to figure this whole thing out!"

Jared reached across the table and laid his hand over mine and through sheer force of will urged my eyes to meet his. "Russell, you know that isn't true, don't you? None of this is your fault. Not finding her is not your fault. We've all seen what you've gone through these past months trying to find her.

You think we haven't noticed, but we have. You have tried to move mountains to find her, all at the expense of your own time and money and career. Sereena hasn't been found because she doesn't want to be found. She wasn't stolen away; she's not some helpless damsel locked away in some tower, awaiting your rescue.

"She's our friend—she's one of your best friends—so it hurts that she's not here, that you can't do anything to bring her back, but it's not through lack of trying. It's not because you're not good enough or smart enough. It's because this is the way she wants things to be. And as much as I hate it too—we all do—we have to respect that. We have to accept it and move on. You have to accept it."

"Have you?" I asked him.

He waited for a moment before answering, then, "I have. But only because I really feel she'll be back." He ran his fingers gently over the bumps of my knuckles. "She'll be back, Russell. Some day."

I wasn't so sure.

I woke up late Sunday morning, with some whisker burn (obtained long after Jared went home to Anthony) and a nice big smile on my face. I spent the afternoon in my yard, cutting grass, pulling weeds and trimming dead branches off mock orange bushes that hadn't wintered well for some unknown reason. I deadheaded flowers, played with the dogs and downed gallons of diet iced tea. Around four p.m. I had a quick shower, prepared tapas and a pitcher of margaritas and fell onto a sun lounger in a gloriously exhausted state and napped and sipped and ate and napped and slurped and ate and read Ellen Hart's latest until the sun set, sometime around ten. A proper day off.

Monday morning appeared mere hours later and I was up unusually early (despite the margaritas). By nine-thirty I was heading for the office in my Mazda, top down, freshly washed hair drying in the wind, whistling a happy tune. The cure for summer blahs? Get laid. It puts a definite bounce in one's step. And yet, somewhere in the back of my mind, I could hear Anthony's voice: "I'm not talking about random crushes followed by randy sex."

I strode into PWC, by all appearances the successful private investigator, even having set aside my wrinkled cotton shorts and flip-flops in favour of a pair of sharply pressed black dress shorts, a fitted, white, short-sleeved shirt and a pair of closed-toe (but open-heel) black sandals; a summer-y yet put-together look, I thought. Anthony would be proud; I was learning a thing or two. There were several people on Errall's side of the room, and a couple others on the other—obviously clients of Beverly's because they were much too conservative looking for Alberta. I threw Lilly a smile and wink and headed for the stairs. She smiled back and waved me over.

Lilly is a blond Snow White—several years post-fairy-tale-wedding—whose Prince Charming-hockey-playing-beer-drinking husband finally agreed to her working outside the home. Perhaps he'd come to understand that she was more than just a pretty face, and singing with birds and picking daisies in the forest were not nearly challenging enough for her.

"Good weekend?" I asked as I approached her desk.

"Oh, terrific. You too?"

"Uh-huh. Hey, your cheeks look a little rosy." Rosier than normal I should have said. "You were out in the sun, eh?"

Lilly's big blues, the type you see on day-old babies, made a swing over to the waiting room and back. "Those people are here to see you."

Ahhhhhhh…what? I glanced over my shoulder and saw a nearly middle-aged man with two elderly people, another man and a woman. They were staring at me with expectant looks on their faces. I turned back to Lilly and whispered, "Who are they?"

"The younger man is Mr. Warren Culinare. He's here with his parents."

Culinare? Could they be relatives of Tanya Culinare, the woman who'd committed suicide?

I thanked Lilly and went to greet my unexpected visitors. We shook hands and introduced ourselves (the parents were Anne and Mike Culinare) They all turned down coffee, and I led them upstairs to my office, which I hoped I hadn't left too messy.

"How can I help you?" I asked once we were settled around my desk.

Anne and Mike, a stout, grey, wrinkle-faced couple nearing their seventies, remained silent and looked at their son as if only he could explain.

"We were sent here—or rather it was suggested that we come here—by Officer Kirsch of the Saskatoon police," Warren Culinare said. He was forty, and despite stylish clothing, careful grooming and a gym membership, he couldn't deny genetics. In thirty years he would be his father; already his belly was expanding over his belt line and youth was melting off his face. "He was the officer who looked after things when Tanya, my sister, died."

I gave them a sympathetic nod. "I heard about Tanya's suicide. I'm sorry for your loss." I wondered what Kirsch thought I could do for these people. Did he think I'd been lying to him? Did he think I'd tell *them* why their sister and daughter had my phone number with her when she died?

"That's not true!" Anne Culinare spoke for the first time. "She didn't commit suicide." Her light accent was hard to place. Polish maybe.

"Mom," her son warned her off. "Let me handle

this. I'm sorry, Mr. Quant, we're all just, well, very upset. You see, we buried Tanya on Saturday."

I nodded. I'd seen the obituary in the paper.

"But Mom is right. We don't believe Tanya killed herself."

The mother shook her head but said nothing. The father's sad eyes travelled from wife to son and back again but never looked directly at me.

"I don't understand," I told the family. "Did Constable Kirsch say something…?"

"No, not really. He said the investigation pointed toward suicide. I got the feeling they weren't going to be looking into things any further. I told him there was no way Tanya would have done that to herself. Never. She wasn't that kind of girl. He said there was nothing the police could do unless we had some proof."

"And do you?"

He hesitated before admitting, "No."

"My Tanya did not do this thing," Mrs. Culinare told me again, but she seemed to have little else to add to the statement of what she believed to be fact.

"Before we left the police station that day," Warren continued, "the officer took me aside, told me your name and said that maybe you could help us."

Really? Darren Kirsch had never referred me to a client before. Most cops never would, unless they thought the police couldn't help any longer. Was that the case here? Did Darren believe there might be something more to find out even though the police were ruling Tanya's death a suicide? He'd obviously not told the Culinares about the paper with my name and phone number on it. But he must still think there might be some connection between me and Tanya Culinare, even if I didn't know what it was myself.

"What kind of help are you looking for?" I asked.

"My parents live in Kindersley, a few hours away by car, and I live in the States, in Washington. There's no other family in Saskatoon, no one who can tell us more about Tanya. You see, our family… well, I hate to admit it, but we didn't know Tanya very well any more. We all ended up living so very far apart; my parents are getting old, and my sister and I are twelve years apart in age and…oh well, I guess there are no good excuses…we always just thought there'd be plenty of time—some other time—to get together. We didn't even spend Christmas together for the last couple of years. We won't make that mistake again." He shared a meaningful look with his parents. "Other things always seemed more important at the time. But, as always, that's a stupid mistake to make in life. Stupid." He stopped there to swallow hard, then continued. "You're probably wondering why, if we didn't know Tanya well, we're so sure she didn't kill herself."

I was.

"To be blunt, Mr. Quant, I'm not sure." He shot his parents a meek look.

Anne Culinare drew in a sharp, shocked breath. "No, Warren!" she berated her son.

He tried to ignore his mother and kept on. "I'm not as convinced as my parents, but even so, I can't accept a terse, one-line statement from the police as the last word on my sister's life. I need something more than that. I need—we need an explanation. Even if she did kill herself."

Mrs. Culinare began to weep into a wadded ball of Kleenex and her husband placed a gnarled hand on her round stomach, patting it as if it were a cat.

"Mom...Mama," Warren said, reaching over his father to put a hand on her shaking arm. "Mama, I'm sorry. I'm not saying Tanya did kill herself, but I want to know the truth. If she did do that to herself, I want to know why, if she didn't, then I want to know how she really died." He turned back to me, his eyes red-rimmed. "Mr. Quant, we are serious about this. If Tanya died some other way... well, we can't let that rest. You understand?"

"I do." I picked up a pen and pulled a pad of paper in front of me to indicate I was ready to do business. "You understand that I may not be able to get any more out of the police than you did, so I'll need all the information you can give me on Tanya: where she worked, where she lived, who her friends were. What she did for fun, what enemies she might have had, what worried her, that sort of thing. Can you help me with any of that?"

Warren looked down at his hands, embarrassed. He named the place she worked, gave me her address and phone number and then stopped. He leaned forward and slid a set of keys across my desk. "These are Tanya's keys. For her apartment and car and that sort of thing, I guess. I'm not exactly sure what they're all for. You can use them to…to find out the rest."

Boy, when he said they didn't know her, they really didn't know her.

"I'm flying back to Seattle on Wednesday after I get my parents settled in back at home." He slid a business card towards me. "But you can call me any time at the numbers on there. I'd like to help in any way I can… I just can't think how, other than to hire you."

I nodded mutely and stared at the nearly bare page on the pad in front of me. Not much to go on. We spent the next few minutes going over the business part of hiring a PI; son and parents bickered briefly over who would pay me until I mentioned my hourly rate and then the parents soundlessly backed off. After that, we were done and I showed them out.

"Kirsch," came Darren's standard barked telephone greeting.

"Quant," I woofed back and immediately heard him groan. "I just had a visit from the Culinares. Wanna tell me what that's about?"

"Whatsamatter? You not accepting new clients these days? It looked like you had plenty of time on your hands the other day, sitting around in your panties and sleeping till noon." A standard Kirsch slam.

"Ever hear of someone taking a vacation?" I retorted.

"Ever hear of boxer shorts?"

Oooo, that pinched. Bastard. "Ever hear of nose hair clippers?"

"What do you want?" He always gives up so easily. "I ain't got all day here, y'know."

"Not that I don't appreciate the business, Darren, but what's up with the Culinares? Did you send them my way because of the note or because you felt sorry for them or because you think there's something more to the case than a simple suicide?"

"Isn't that your job to find out? Isn't that what the 'I' in PI stands for?"

"Don't jerk me around. You obviously want me to help these people or else you wouldn't have given them my name. So help me help them."

"There's not much I can tell you, Quant," he said, his voice settling into a more businesslike tone. "As far as we're concerned, Tanya Culinare committed suicide. There was no sign of a struggle or anyone else in her apartment at the time of her jump or anything else to suggest foul play."

"Then why send the Culinares to me if you believe that?"

He was quiet.

"It's the note, isn't it? The one with my name and number."

"It's the only thing that doesn't quite fit the picture, Quant. Otherwise I would have told the Culinares to save their money rather than spend it on a detective. Which, by the way, was their idea in the first place, not mine. But when they asked if I knew of anyone, well, given the note and all, I thought you might be the right choice." The Culinares and Kirsch didn't have the exact same story, but I decided to let it go for the moment.

"Is there anything else you found that might help me get started?"

"No."

"Can I see the police file?"

"No."

"Can I—"

"G'bye, Quant." And he hung up. That is pretty much how the majority of our calls end up. The "g'bye" part was a new twist.

I stared again at the nearly blank paper that contained everything I knew about my new case, then ran my hands over my face and through my hair. As I often do at times like these when I need to think, I got up from my desk, threw open the doors to the balcony and stepped outside for a breath of fresh air and, hopefully, some good ideas of what to do next.

The morning had grown hot, already in the low thirties, and the park was dotted with mothers and children and small groups of summer session students on break from their classes at the U of S. The ash trees that line the street were fat and green with leaves that hung limp in the heavy heat. Cars were vastly outnumbered by bicycles, joggers, ice-cream carts and scooters and I could hear the rowdy calls of a nearby group of Hackey Sack players. Parking was only permitted on our side of the street and the majority of metered spots in front of our building were filled with shimmering, metallic-hued, over-priced SUV's (Errall's clients), sensible sedans (Beverley's clients) and beat-up VW bugs (Alberta's clients). I was about to pull back from the balustrade and take a seat in a Muskoka chair when I noticed something unusual. In stark contrast to the scantily clad people in the park was a figure in a serious brown suit. He was standing next to a dark blue Envoy with an Avis car rental sticker on the front bumper. None of that by itself was unusual; this part of town is jam-packed with business towers full of lawyers and doctors and chartered accountants and entrepreneurs of many varieties who often stroll down to the park for a stretch or a spouse-disapproved hot dog. What *was* unusual was that this guy had binoculars hanging from his neck. As I watched, he took good care to look both ways before crossing the street to the wide walkway that lined the park. He walked a bit further, stopped, then brought the binoculars up to his eyes. But instead of directing them at the more scenic South Saskatchewan River, he was staring straight at the business side of the street...at the buildings...at PWC...at...me.

Chapter 3

Tanya Culinare's apartment was in the Broadway Condominiums building at the top of the Broadway Bridge. The location is infamous for a once-upon-a-time five-way intersection known as Five Corners (until Saskatoon residents got fed up with figuring out confusing light signals, merging bridge traffic and right-of-way). So now it's down to three, but for many it will always be known as Five Corners. The Broadway Condos building has a speckled past including vociferous protest campaigns by local residents who felt the high-rise would obstruct their panoramic view of downtown (which it does) and the rumoured involvement of shady foreign investors (never screw with a guy named Yuri). Construction started, stopped, started, stopped, started, stopped and finally was completed sometime in the late eighties or early nineties. It's a twelve-storey building with stunning views of the South Saskatchewan River to the north, Broadway Avenue to the south and everything in between. In addition to regular residential units, the building also offers something called Premiere Suites—luxury furnished one- and two-bedroom condominiums for rent on a daily, weekly or monthly basis—and on its lower floors are a number of businesses including a popular gym called Fitness Corner (I bet the owners are glad they didn't call it Fitness Five Corners).

Tanya's brother had left me the key to her apartment, giving me complete access, at least until the end of the month when a moving crew he'd hired would clean up the place and remove all of Tanya's things in preparation for the next tenant. I wondered where everything would go. Into storage? Her parent's basement? Did anyone care? And to top it off, a complete stranger—me—was given free rein to rifle though her personal belongings. The whole thing made me sad. How would Tanya Culinare feel about this invasion of privacy, about how easily her life could be boxed up and dispensed with?

I must admit I was a trifle disappointed not to

have to finagle my way into Tanya's apartment building using subterfuge and/or chicanery. Sometimes that's the most fun part of my job: figuring out how to get into someplace I'm not *supposed* to get into. But the keys on Tanya's ring allowed me unchallenged entrance to the building and her eighth-floor apartment, and that's where I found myself late Monday morning.

As I slipped the correct key into the lock of apartment 863, I noticed something strange. I ran my hand over the surface of the wooden door. It was smooth and dusty and discoloured, as if it had recently been sanded in preparation for re-staining. I pulled back to see if the same could be said of the other doors on the floor, but they all seemed to be in normal, un-sanded shape. I filed that under 'C' for curious and entered the apartment. The air smelled stale in the way typical of places where no one had lived for a while, or where someone had died. Tanya'd been gone less than a week, but her home was already letting her go.

I took a quick preliminary look around: nothing out of the ordinary. Just a regular apartment, probably a little nicer than some. I strode over to the living room drapes, pushed them aside and opened the sliding doors to let in some much needed light and fresh air.

I gingerly stepped outside onto the balcony and into the space where Tanya Culinare ended her young life. Her body had been found on the sidewalk near the front entrance of the Fitness Corner gym. I leaned against the balcony's narrow, black metal railing and peered straight down. To land where she did, Tanya would have had to climb up onto the rail ledge and take a flying leap. I shuddered at the image.

Tanya had a corner suite and the balcony wrapped around, giving her unimpeded views in two directions. Her apartment faced southwest, and from it I could see Broadway Avenue with its ongoing Fringe festivities (somewhat slack in energy on a hot Monday morning) and beyond that, tree-topped 8th Street and the older suburban areas of Nutana, Haultain, Queen Elizabeth and Avalon. Nice enough, but sad that there was no final glimpse of ocean, mountain or stunning sunset before Tanya took that fatal jump into nothingness. She was thirty-one.

It was like an oven on the balcony. I spotted several potted plants; a couple stalky, pink geraniums still flourished, enjoying the stress of abandonment, but everything else had withered and dried into brittle sticks of brown. I stepped back into the apartment and closed the door behind me.

I began an in-depth search of the place, starting with the back rooms—two bedrooms and a bathroom—progressing to the front—living room and kitchen/dining room area. Even though I knew everything was destined for a box or the garbage, I still tried to be neat about my work, leaving things where I found them, which isn't as easy as it sounds when you're fingering every piece of clothing, handling every piece of paper, looking in and under every spot conceivable including the refrigerator, toilet tank and garbage cans. I'm good at searching; I'm methodical and I take mental notes.

It took me just over an hour to finish. I came up with four things of interest. First was an abundance of pictures of Tanya with another girl, about the same age. They were similar in many ways, both tall, lean, athletic looking with angular, attractive features and short hair styles. Tanya, however, was blond, with slanted, sharp eyes the colour of chestnuts—cat's eyes. The other girl's hair was softer looking, tar-black, and she wore a wide, generous smile in most of the pictures whereas Tanya's mouth stayed a straight, serious line above a pointed chin. On the back of one of the photos was a notation: Tanya and Moxie. I was betting Moxie was Tanya's best friend. Best friends are a detective's best friend when trying to find stuff out. I'd need to find Moxie.

The second thing was Tanya's address book. She either wasn't very good about recording phone numbers and addresses for family and friends or else she simply didn't have very many people in her life that fell into those categories. But it did include information for a Moxie Banyon, so I stuck the address book and one of the photographs in my shorts pocket for later use.

The third and fourth interesting things were sort of related. One was under her bed: a baseball bat. The other was a fifty-by-sixty-five, centimetre impression on the carpet in front of the front door, as if something very heavy had sat in that unlikely spot either for a long time or very recently or both. Not far from the front door was a battered piece of wooden furniture, about waist high, which looked about the right size and shape. I tried to move it and was stopped by its great weight. I supposed I could have moved it if I'd really wanted to, but not without plenty of effort. I knelt down in front of the thing, opened the cabinet doors and found inside an upside-down, antique sewing machine. I knew the type: my mother had one at home. You open the doors, flip up the machine, swing out some hidden drawers and voila: a sewing machine, the kind with a foot pedal and torture-chamber-looking pulleys and thingamabobs. The sucker weighed a ton, yet Tanya Culinare, who as far as I knew was not a heavyweight wrestler, had, at least once, moved the beast in front of her door. But why? Why the bat, why the barricade against her door? Sure, I know different people take different precautions depending on who they are, where they live, if they live alone, if they're male or female, but in an eighth-floor, cushy apartment in a safe part of town? Did it make sense? Was Tanya Culinare frightened of something or someone in particular? Or just paranoid?

I closed the curtains, took one last look around and left.

I knew given the time of day that my chance of finding neighbours to talk to was not great, but I gave it a whirl anyway. And indeed all the eighth-floor doors I knocked on were answered with silence until the last.

"Who is it?" came a faint man's voice.

"Hullo?" I called through the door. "My name is Russell Quant. I'm investigating Tanya Culinare's death—your neighbour? I was wondering if I could ask you a few questions."

A second or two, then, "Just one moment please."

And indeed I waited an entire moment. What was he doing in there? Laying carpet?

The door creeped open ever so slowly with a bit of a creak and finally produced the apartment's resident, a slender man in his seventies, with a black, pencil moustache and silver hair severely greased back à la Clark Gable (although he more closely resembled Mr. Furley, the Don Knotts character from *Three's Company*). He wore a paisley, black-collared smoking jacket over a white shirt, black pinstriped pants and gently worn house slippers.

I held out my hand. "I'm Russell Quant."

The man arched a thin eyebrow astonishingly

high on his forehead, tipped his head to one side and slightly forward and pursed his freshly Blistexed lips all at the same time. He offered me his hand, palm down as if he wanted me to kiss the large ruby ring on it, and said, "My, my, yes you are. Welcome to my home, Mr. Quant."

I shook the hand—passed on the ring-kissing—and gave him a smile. "Thank you. May I come in?" I wasn't sure if I really wanted to anymore. I smelled something off about this guy.

"Where are my manners?" he said with a blush but still did not step aside. "Of course you may enter. My name is Furberry, Newton Furberry. Good afternoon."

I looked down at my watch. It was nearing twelve-thirty. "Oh my gosh, Mr. Furberry, I didn't realize the time. I must be interrupting your lunch. I can come back another time."

He chuckled a practised chuckle. "No, no, my dear boy. I don't sit for lunch until two. We've plenty of time. Please," and now he stepped aside, "come in."

I brushed by Mr. Furberry, getting a healthy dose of freshly spritzed aftershave—barbershop quality.

"Please, just down the hall and to your left."

I followed the instructions and found myself in a world of...well, I wasn't sure what it was meant to be...perhaps a mix between old world grandeur and garage sale kitsch. Other than a small television in one corner of the room, it looked as if Mr. Furberry hadn't been shopping in several decades. Not that anything looked particularly worn or dirty or ruined, just...old. The walls were covered in a velvet-flocked wallpaper of deep, ruby colours and sepia-toned portraits of distinguished-looking people. The floor was hidden beneath thinning Oriental area rugs and heavy, dark wood furniture. Every surface was littered with books, photographs (some in albums, some just lying about) and tchotchkes of glass and bronze and crystal. On the ceiling was a chandelier that could have used dusting, and mottled light came through windows muted by layers of silk and organza. There were no fewer than three fresh flower arrangements in great vases throughout the room, and next to a grandly stuffed armchair was a trolley on which was a bud vase with a single red rose, a half-eaten plate of chocolates and a recently used tea service. This must have been where Mr. Furberry had been sitting in repose when I'd come a-calling. The room smelled of mint and mothballs and was so dim it was hard to believe that on the other side of the wall was bright summer sunshine. In the background I could just hear the strains of some foreign language opera from a... CD? Radio? Gramophone? All in all, the atmosphere wasn't unpleasant, just...peculiar.

"Please, take a seat over here," Mr. Furberry

told me in his quiet, gently nasal voice, indicating a low slung couch covered in rich, burgundy velvet. "I'll return shortly. If you'll excuse me." And with that he left the room, rolling the tea trolley in front of him.

After a couple minutes I contemplated either leaving or snooping. I can usually be counted on to do the latter, so the debate was short-lived. I stood up, feeling a bit like a bull in a china shop, stretched and began to look around. All of Mr. Furberry's things were aged but fine and well taken care of, possibly cherished keepsakes passed down from ancestors. I flipped through some photos, mostly grainy black and whites, but they meant little to me. I checked out one of the bookcases and found the contents curious and indicative of an eclectic taste in literature. Mr. Furberry enjoyed non-fiction— biographies mostly—of silver screen legends, political heroes and infamous criminals. He also read travel books, adventure tales and historical accounts on a wide variety of subjects. There was not a paperback amongst the bunch. I heard the trolley's wiggle-waggling wheels and plopped myself back on the sofa just in time.

"Did you enjoy looking at my things while I was away?" the man said lightly as he began to pour tea, his expressive eyebrow once again perched high on his head.

Whoops. Busted. But how? Did he have one of

those paintings with the eyes that move? I looked around for one and picked out a couple that easily fit the bill. "I'm sorry, I didn't mean to…"

"No, no, my good fellow, I didn't mean you shouldn't; I meant I hoped you did. You see, that is why I've collected and display my fine things: to share with guests and companions."

Er, okay. I thought a comment on his "fine things" was called for, especially if I expected any help out of the guy. "The portraits on the wall are lovely. Are they of your relatives?"

He gave me a hard-to-read look as he handed me a delicate china cup three-quarters full of tea and answered simply, "No."

Newton Furberry lowered himself onto an upholstered straight-back chair next to the tea trolley and across from me. He made a production of offering me lemon or milk for my tea—I took neither—and dripped a few squirts of lemon into his own.

"I sometimes take milk in the evening, but during the day it seems too much, don't you think?"

Huh? Was this a scene from *Pride and Prejudice*? "Mr. Furberry, did you know Ms. Culinare well?"

"Oh yes, of course, I suppose we must get right down to business," he said in a scolding tone that told me I'd failed in my social graces. But hey, I'm on a clock.

"Thank you, yes. Did you know her well?"

He thought on that a moment, sipping at his tea then carefully placing it with its matching saucer down on a wee table next to him, not on the trolley, which apparently was for service purposes only. "Indeed, Mr. Quant. Ms. Culinare and I had a relationship." He stopped there and did the eyebrow thing again, staring at me as if waiting to register my shock. I disappointed him again. "No, no, it's not what you think. My goodness, she was just a child and…well, my tastes run a little more to the… shall we say, exotic and," more eyebrow action, "decadent."

"I see. Can you tell me about the relationship you did have with Ms. Culinare?"

"Sandwich?"

And indeed, on a tray was a concentric patterned mound of delicate "sandwiches," or rather what I'd call sandwich wannabes. These so-called sandwiches were two slivers of paper thin white bread without crust between which were even thinner slices of cucumber. This guy was really into the high tea thing. And I'm all for it too if I'm at the Empress Hotel in Victoria on a dull, wet day, but not today.

"No, thank you. They look lovely though."

He sniffed and daintily helped himself.

I waited for him to nibble the thing to nothingness, which took all of one point five seconds and asked again, "About Tanya Culinare?"

Furberry sighed enough to raise his bird-like

chest and said, "We played chess. Sunday afternoons this past winter. She wasn't very good, but I was instructing her and she was improving. I was disappointed when she gave it up."

"I'd be interested in anything you can tell me about her."

He gave me a quizzical look. "You said you were investigating her death? Oh my, I've just realized I've allowed into my home a complete stranger. Mr. Quant, just who is it that you are? I assumed you were with the police, but now I think not."

"I'm not with the police," I said in my most reassuring voice. "I'm a private investigator."

I thought I saw a hint of a smile beneath the man's Grecian Formula'd moustache.

"Really? How fascinating. More tea?" he offered, visibly thrilling to the intrigue factor of having a detective in for an afternoon sip.

"No, thank you."

"Who is it that's hired you?"

"Tanya's parents," I told him. "They're uncomfortable with the ruling of her death as a suicide. I'm investigating the possibility of there being something more to it."

Another questioning look with the eyebrow at its zenith. "Yet you ask *me* to tell you about her? Wouldn't her family be able to give you the best information in that regard?"

I thought about how to respond and finally went with, "I'm afraid not."

Mr. Furberry's face visibly fell. He tsked a few times. "I see. My, how sad, how truly sad." He looked away for a second, dabbing the tip of his nose with a hanky he'd pulled from a breast pocket, then returned his gaze to me. "How can I help?"

Ahhhhhhhrrrrrgggggggg! "Can you tell me what kind of person Tanya Culinare was?"

"She was not what I, or most other people I would imagine, would call a warm person. I got the distinct sense that she did not allow people to get close to her very easily. Getting to know her would not be a simple thing. She was direct, opinionated, no nonsense." He hesitated for a moment as if in thought, then added, "And fragile. Yes, in many ways she was a fragile young woman. Beneath it all she was kind and helpful. That's how we first became acquainted, you see. I'd come home from a book-buying sojourn, laden down with heavy packages, and I'd misplaced my keys. Ms. Culinare happened by and took care of everything. She invited me to rest in her home while she called the building superintendent and arranged to have me let into my apartment. She even went so far as to arrange a new set of keys to be made for me and then picked them up and delivered them to me. She was a very capable woman. At some point she noticed and mentioned my chess set—which I always have set up—do you play, Mr. Quant? Oh never mind that now—and I offered to teach her in exchange for her help that day." He took a deep breath. "I was very saddened by her untimely death."

"Were you surprised by it, Mr. Furberry? Did anything you and Tanya talk about during your chess lessons ever lead you to believe that she might commit suicide?"

The man absent-mindedly tossed two cucumber sandwiches into his mouth like peanuts, momentarily forgetting his genteel manners while he considered my question.

"I was about to answer no to that question, Mr. Quant. As I've already told you, she was a very capable person. I'd have a hard time imagining what could possibly drive her to such an act of desperation. However…"

Yeeeesssssssss?

"However, beneath her protective armour I sensed a woman of heightened emotions. Although I never really witnessed it, I could believe that when she was angry, she would be livid; when she was sad, she'd be desperately so. This is fully speculation on my part, Mr. Quant, I've nothing to support my words, you understand?"

I nodded. And what the heck, I tried a cucumber thingy. "You said Tanya gave up her chess lessons with you. Why did she do that? And when?"

Again he gave the questions some thought before

answering. "I suppose we played three maybe four times in all, between November of last year and March of this. I invited her two more times after the last, both times she turned me down without reason and I stopped pursuing it at that point. Which, I think, was justifiable on my part, wouldn't you agree?"

He carried on without my response. "I don't really know why she stopped. The last time we played she seemed distracted, a trifle pricklier than normal. I recall asking her if there was something bothering her, but she passed it off as being in a bad mood. Perhaps she'd simply lost interest, in me, the game, I don't know. I spoke to her only once on the phone after that—a conversation in which she gave me short shrift—and I never really spoke to her again after that. These apartment buildings seem so small, you'd think one would run into neighbours every day, at least in the hallways or lifts, but in truth, that rarely happens."

Interesting. I wondered if something of import happened to Tanya Culinare in March, something that might have led to her eventual demise four months later, something that had required a bat under her bed. "What about other people coming and going from her apartment? Did you meet any of her friends?"

"No…er, well, now just a moment…there was one girl. I cau…met her as she was letting herself into Tanya's apartment one day. She obviously had her own key or had borrowed it. She said she was a good friend of Tanya's."

"When was this?"

He narrowed his eyes in thought. "Around Christmas, possibly."

"Do you remember what she looked like? Her name?"

"Dark hair," he answered slowly. "Very pleasant smile as I recall. That's all though. No name."

I wondered if he was talking about Moxie. I pulled out the picture I found in Tanya's apartment and showed it to him. "Is this the girl with the key to Tanya's apartment?"

He nodded. "Yes, that's her. Nice smile, wouldn't you agree? Who is she?"

I ignored his questions. "Mr. Furberry, this is important. Did you, in all the time you spent with Tanya, ever get the sense that she was afraid?"

"Afraid?" he asked as if he'd just now heard the word for the first time.

I shrugged. "Of someone? Of having her apartment broken into? Of...of...of anything?" I was reaching here.

He raised his cup of tea to his lips and took a slow sip. "Afraid," he repeated. "Well, Mr. Quant, I have a passing acquaintance with fear. Generally I would say that Ms. Culinare was not afraid, but now that you mention it...that final phone call...

yes, I suppose so. I suppose her manner could be described as someone who was afraid of whoever might be on the other end of the phone line." He let out a chuckle. "But she certainly could not have been afraid of me...do you think?"

I shrugged. I decided I'd gotten all I could from Furberry, at least for the moment, and rose to leave. "Thank you for your time. I appreciate it."

"Mr. Quant, you asked if any of the people in these portraits on my walls are family." He stood too and crossed over to an armoire and selected a heavy, bound photo album. "I want to show you something."

I joined him and looked down at the album. He turned to a page that displayed a crumbling but carefully preserved picture of a rather rugged-looking couple next to some kind of plough. "My parents," he said quietly. He turned the page to a picture of a young fellow who looked like one of those miner guys who sing in Rita MacNeil's choir when she does that song "Working Man"—what're they called? Men of the Deeps?—except a lot dirtier and a lot sadder looking. "This is Vilmer Kaufmann," Furberry told me using a faraway voice. "Every day this man lowered himself into the ground, into the dirt and choking dust of a potash mine, emerging only after many hours of bone-cracking labour looking like dirt himself. He hated every moment of it. He was often scared too."

I nodded, not sure what to make of this. "This is your relative then? Your father? Brother?"

"Me," he said, turning to look at me with one last raise of his mighty eyebrow.

I looked back at the face of the man in the picture, obscured by black grime and misery. Vilmer Kaufmann and Newton Furberry were indeed the same person.

I glanced questioningly at the portraits.

"Strangers," he said.

I nodded.

"I lived with my parents until they died. I lived a frugal life. I saved every cent so that the day I retired I could scour the grease and dirt from my skin, from my hair, from under my fingernails, change my name and buy myself the genteel life I'd always lusted after. I wanted to become a fine gentleman. I wanted people to believe the people in these portraits could have been my relatives." He closed the album and stared at its cover. "I just...I just wanted you to know that."

I reached for his hand and shook it warmly. Looking deep into his eyes, I said, "I suspect you've always been a fine gentleman, Mr. Kaufmann."

He smiled and held my hand a bit longer.

"Hello, my name is Warren Culinare. My sister was Tanya Culinare," I said to the woman I'd been directed to, having changed my persona on the elevator ride down from the peculiarity of Newton Furberry's apartment to the Gatorade-PowerBar-infused Fitness Corner gym.

"Oh my god," Donna Littlechild said with a surprised look on her face. "I'm so sorry. About Tanya I mean. It was terrible what happened to her. I can't believe it. I'm so glad someone else…" She stopped there. I guessed she was about to say she was glad someone else found Tanya. After all, she had landed near the front doors of this facility, and as the gym's manager, Donna Littlechild could very well have been the one to discover her if it hadn't been for an early morning jogger who beat her to it.

"Did you know Tanya very well?" I asked.

She shook her head, setting her dark ponytail swinging back and forth at the nape of her neck. "You know, I'm sorry, I really didn't. I knew she lived in the building, and she did have a membership here, but she pretty much came in, worked out and kept to herself. She was in good shape, knew what she was doing. She didn't need my help or the help of any of our instructors."

"I see. I was wondering if you could let me into her locker, to get her things."

"Oh, gosh, yeah, I didn't even think about that. I wouldn't have noticed until her locker rent came due. Do you have the key? Otherwise we'll have to break in."

I presented Donna with Tanya's key ring. "I'm not sure. Do any of these look right to you?"

She didn't take the ring, instead she turned on her heel and marched back to the front desk, consulted a binder—probably a listing of lockers and who was renting them—then led me deeper into the long, narrow facility. The place was empty except for an impressively fit fellow in his late sixties who, judging by his unfortunate wardrobe, really liked the Olivia-Newton-John-"Let's Get Physical"-headband look. "We'll have to see. Let me check if there's anyone in the woman's locker room, and if not you can come in with me. Y'know, I think she had one of those cheap locks with a key, not a combination lock. I remember because the one time I did have something to do with Tanya was when her locker was broken into. I told her to get a better lock."

Boing! "Her locker was broken into? Is that common around here?"

"Actually no," she said as I followed her around a corner. "I know you'd expect me to say that, but it's true. Until Tanya's break-in, some time in the spring I think it was, we hadn't had a locker broken into for over a year. It was unusual. That's why I remember it."

We'd gotten to the door of the women's locker room and Donna excused herself to check it out. She was back in a flash with an apologetic look on her face. "Sorry. There is someone in there. We could wait a bit, or I could see if I can open it myself."

She looked trustworthy enough. I gave her the key ring and slumped against a wall to wait, watch Oliver Fig-Newton John and think about when I'd get a chance to go to the gym myself that day. I was determined to get back into my wonderpants without wincing.

Donna emerged with her hands full. "Yup, got it right off. It was this tiny key here. I see she didn't take my advice after the break-in about using a stronger lock." She handed me a small pile of Tanya's effects, mostly toiletries and a fresh towel. Nothing of much use to me.

"Do you remember what was taken when Tanya's locker was broken into?"

Donna nodded slowly. "That was the other weird thing. She said nothing was missing. She seemed pretty shaken up by it though. Maybe she noticed something later and I didn't hear about it."

"Were the police called in to investigate?"

Donna shrugged her shoulders, deep caramel brown against the white of her tank top. "Investigate what? A broken lock? Nothing was stolen. Didn't seem like a big deal really. I even wondered if it wasn't a mistake. You know, someone goes to the wrong locker, the key doesn't seem to work, so they break the lock off, realize their mistake but are too embarrassed to admit to it. It happens."

I nodded. "I s'pose." I was not entirely convinced.

Riversdale is one of Saskatoon's founding communities, amalgamated in 1905 with the village of Nutana and the town of Saskatoon. This sometimes seedy, sometimes charming area is a culturally rich enclave of the city's Chinese, Ukrainian, German, Vietnamese, Aboriginal, Hong Kong Chinese and Filipino populations. I've spent many happy Saturday afternoons traipsing the aging blocks of infamous 20th Street, where one can find one-chair barbers with nary a blow-dryer in sight, confectioners and grocers that stock hard-to-identify foreign goods and second-hand stores and pawn shops that deal in anything you can imagine (and more). There are clothiers, art galleries, sex shops, take-your-life-in-your-own-hands beer parlours and specialty restaurants serving mouth-wateringly good and plate-heapingly plentiful meals at wallet-shockingly low prices. If you want to drink till dawn and stagger home with others who do it for a living; if you want to sit in a booth and watch pornographic videos; if you want to buy a cheap couch; if you want to taste the best dim sum; if you want to attend a prayer meeting; if you want, well, if you want anything that a typical shopping mall is too prim and proper to provide, anything just off the edge of propriety, anything exploding with sensation, 20th Street is the place to go in Saskatoon. Except after dark. Then you're just being reckless with your life.

I found V. Madison Steel Products Inc.—where Tanya had worked in shipping and receiving—a couple blocks from 20th (with daylight to spare). It was just off 18th Street West on the 400 block of Avenue M, a curious part of town that time seems to have, if not forgotten, at least misplaced. As I made a right turn at the southeast corner of the incongruously named Optimist Park, I was surprised to find myself on a gravel road. Had the city crews simply run out of asphalt and neglected to come back? Did the neighbourhood forget to pay its taxes? Was city council mad at these people for some reason?

I passed by a strip of businesses housed in those one-storey, circa 1950, squat, square, spare buildings, their exteriors matching the dull pallor of the gravel road. The street was littered with broken-down half-ton trucks and cars with doors, trunk hoods and side panels spray-painted colours that did not match. In the distance I could see the impressive domes of St. George's Church, the odd New Life Feeds building that looked like a giant 24-pack of Scott Towels and overhead a crazy criss-cross pattern of countless power lines. And every so often, amongst the dingy buildings of this mostly industrial community, I spied a rat-trap house squatting behind bushy-leaved trees and high fences, as if in hiding.

I nose-in parked—as was the local custom—in front of a building near the dead end of a railroad track. I got out of the car and was surprised by the quiet. It was like the main drag of some western town right before the big shootout between the sheriff and a villain in a black cowboy hat. And there was me without my spurs and chaps.

While I waited in the mouldy, stifling hot reception area for someone to answer the door chime I'd set off, I glanced through a company brochure from a Plexiglas holder on the front counter. Apparently V. Madison was "Reinforcing the Steel Industry" with their product lines, which included steel beams, teleposts, rebar, wire mesh, epoxy rebar, carbon plates, quenched and tempered plates, water well casings, tie wire, loop ties, redi rod and a partridge in a pear tree (I added that last bit myself).

"What can I do ya for?" a big-bellied man who really needed to visit a laundromat asked me as he shoved his way through a swinging door on the other side of the counter from where I was standing.

"I'm Warren Culinare," I said. I have no problem reusing a good disguise.

"Good fer you," he answered, sort of snarly, sort of impatient. I guessed I was interrupting his afternoon coffee break, and since I probably didn't look anything like the people who usually set foot into V. Madison Steel, he took me for someone who was either lost or a salesman, but certainly not a paying customer, and therefore expendable or suitable for some good old-fashioned rudeness.

"I'm Tanya's brother." Take that.

"Oh shit, man," he said, realization dawning on him rather slowly. "You're Tanya's brother. Oh shit. We're real sorry she died, right?"

Was that a question? "I was wondering if I could talk to someone here who knew Tanya."

"Why?"

Heh heh. I like it when people catch me with a surprise question. "Well, as you probably know, I live in the States, and Tanya and I hadn't spent much time together lately. I just wanted to talk with someone who might, you know, tell me about her." I did my best to look almost weepy.

He looked confused for a moment, then said, "Jus a sec." And he disappeared behind the swinging door. A full minute later the door opened again and out came a woman so skinny and grey I thought she might be a tube of steel herself.

"I'm Stella. You're Tanya's brother then?" she asked in a permanently hoarse voice. From the smell of her, I guessed a two-pack-a-day habit.

"Yes. Were you a friend of hers?"

Her bony shoulders hunched up a bit. "I don't

know if I'd say that. We pretty much alls just come in here and does our jobs and go home, you know. We don't have time to make friends or nothing."

"You didn't socialize after work or go out for lunch together or something?"

She scrunched up her face. "This ain't no salon or someplace like that, mister. This place is open from seven o'clock in the morning till three-thirty. No coffee breaks hardly, ten minutes for lunch at our desks or wherever, then we go home, take care of our homes and kids and yard work and alls that, you know."

"Perhaps there is someone else?" I asked, hoping but doubting it.

"Ain't no one else really. The guys certainly don't hang out and chit-chat, not with us anyways. And there's only Tanya and me in the office anyways. Now it's jus' me till the boss hires again. Left me a bunch of work. Sorry to says, I know she was your sister and alls, but alls I'm saying is that it's hard doing work for two, you know. She was okay though, Tanya was. She did her work; I did mine. We weren't friends, but we got along fine. A little sensitive maybe, fragile like, you know?" She seemed pleased with her use of a word she'd not had many opportunities to use before. "Yeah, fragile, like she might just as soon break in half as anything else if youse said the wrong thing to her. 'Specially lately." Stella couldn't take it any longer and dug a cigarette out of a packet she had been grasping in her bony left hand. She lit up like a pro and stared at me through the resultant haze with the content eyes of an addict meeting her fix.

"And why was that, Stella? Do you know why she was so fragile? Problems at home? At work? Boyfriend problems? Anything like that?"

Scrawny shoulder shrug. "Hard to say. Didn't talk to each other much, as I says already. She jus' wasn't real stable, that's all. Lotsa women are like that."

A real feminist, this Stella. "I see. Well, maybe I could clean out her desk? Did she have a desk? Or work area?"

"Oh sure. C'mon back."

I followed Stella through the swinging doors into a large warehouse space with row after row of two-storey, tall, metal shelves stacked with V. Madison Steel product. Powerful fluorescents tried their best to lighten up the place, but with all the tall shelving and grungy-coloured steel, the alleyways between the shelves remained depressingly dim. We followed a maze-like path to get to the far left side of the warehouse where in one corner sat two face-to-face desks surrounded by several scratched-up, dented file cabinets.

"I do the accounting 'round here," she said, pointing to one desk. "But now I do shipping and receiving too since Tanya left." Okay, okay I got it.

Tanya's death left you in a lurch. "Anything Tanya left behind that was hers and not the company's would be in that there desk." She nodded toward the other one. "Here's a box," she croaked, holding aloft a cardboard container about the size of a boot box that she'd grabbed from a nearby receptacle.

I accepted the box and sat down on a metal folding chair (definitely not an ergonomically savvy office environment here) in front of Tanya's desk and gazed at the piles of paper trail for steel products. "Thanks."

As Stella slid behind her own desk, she lit up another cigarette and watched me. I began opening drawers in search of personal items. Even if they didn't relate to my case, somebody needed to do this, and it might as well be me. I could leave whatever I found here in Tanya's apartment to be boxed up at the end of the month with the rest of her things.

There wasn't much. Just a fake-suede-covered folder full of personal stuff like sales receipts from McNally Robinson, Audio Warehouse and some local area restaurants, a copy of her most recent tax return (I guessed she must have used her work computer to complete it) and some miscellaneous correspondence. I didn't want to go through them with the grey ghost watching over me, so I just stuffed the folder in the box. On the desktop was a Daytimer opened to the day before Tanya's death—just as she'd left it. I flipped back and forth and found that it was more of a manifest for shipping and receiving deadlines for various products and follow-up customer calls she'd planned to make. The only personal item I found in the pages I scanned was a notation about a month earlier for a haircut. I threw it into the box anyhow. There was a hand mirror, some cuticle scissors and hand lotion and that was about it. I decided to leave the pens and erasers, half-used pads of yellow stickies and calculator for the next lucky gump who landed this job—or long-suffering Stella—whoever it ended up being.

"I can show myself out," I told Stella as I rose from the desk.

"Okay, then," the words came out aloft a puff of tobacco smoke.

I gave her a smile, tucked the box under my arm and headed for the front door. I heard the chime again as I exited the building and was enjoying a much needed lungful of fresh air when a wall of brute force slammed into me from behind and knocked it right out of me.

Chapter 4

I literally flew through the air in one direction while the box of Tanya's things that I'd just collected from her work desk headed in another. I landed atop the hood of my Mazda, my lower belly taking most of the brunt of the collision. Everything happened so fast I didn't even have time to turn around to face my aggressor before I felt a huge weight fall on top of me. We flailed in that position for several seconds as the man tried to grab my arms and pin them behind me. By the pillow-soft cushioning I felt between me and him and a rather distinct scent of old sweat mixed with sausage and onion pizza, I was pretty certain my attacker was the Weight-Watchers-'before'-picture, "What can I do you fer" guy who'd greeted me so warmly when I'd first arrived. Knowing that tummies full of sausage and onion pizza don't like to get hit, I arched up my shoulders as far as I could (with three hundred extra pounds on me), positioned my elbows into sharp angles and jacked them back, aiming for bloated central. When I met my mark, the fella let out a painful "whoooof" and fell back just enough to give me room to turn around and get in a doozy of a right-fisted punch to the face, which landed square on his nose. He looked at me, startled, and put his hands to his face just in time to stem the flow of blood that started to burble from his left nostril.

"That's enough," crowed someone from my right.

I swivelled to face the voice, fists at the ready.

"Ed, you go inside and get cleaned up," the woman said, and big Ed complied without a backward look. I think he was feeling rather sheepish having been beat by a guy half his size. I was about to shout out that I'm gay too, but I decided to contain myself.

"Now tell me who the hell you are!" the woman bellowed at me. She wasn't much lighter than Ed and had an almost perfectly round face topped with

Anthony Bidulka

a mop of short, curly brown hair. Her eyes were chocolate-covered almonds under knitted brows, and her nostrils were flaring wide.

"Why?" I answered back, now a bit surly myself. "Because you got me just where you want me?" I crossed my arms over my puffed-out chest and leaned back against my car, striking a pose that exuded more confidence than I actually felt. Shit... was that a rip in my shirt? "You should get your bodyguard better training."

"He's not a bodyguard. That's just Ed; he works the forklift around here."

"Forklift operator and attack dog, nice for the resume."

"Who are you?" she asked again, this time with a little less hostility.

"Who are *you*?" Me not quite giving up on the hostility yet.

"I'm Vicky Madison. I own this place of business."

Oh.

"And I know you're not Tanya's brother. I met Tanya's brother at her funeral and you're not him."

Oops.

"Now tell me who you are and why you're stealing Tanya's things."

Finally someone who seemed to give a damn. "I'm Tanya's other broth..."

She spit to the side then turned back to me with

a look that said she wasn't buying what I was selling. "Give me a break, jerk-off. I know damn well Tanya only had one brother."

Well, it was worth a try. I had one more trick up my sleeve—the truth. "My name is Russell Quant. I'm a private detective. Warren Culinare hired me to look into Tanya's death."

Vicky's face changed. Her nostrils returned to normal size, the throbbing at her temples subsided and her eyes miraculously turned from dark brown to a pleasant, almost hazel shade. How'd she do that? "What do you mean 'look into'? We were told Tanya killed herself. Isn't that right?"

I nodded, taking a less aggressive pose as well. "That's what the police say, yes."

"Then…?"

"Her family wants to know if Tanya did kill herself, why she did it."

"*If* she killed herself? You think there's a chance she didn't?"

I shrugged and watched her face closely. "What do you think?"

Vicky raised her hands in the air, palms out towards me. "Hey, I'm just her employer."

"I…the family would be grateful for anything you could tell me about Tanya."

Vicky's eyes narrowed as she thought about this and looked me over, as if deciding whether or not to trust me. "I got nothing to say to you." I guess the answer was not.

We stood there for a few seconds, regarding each other, assessing what more could come of our interaction. I broke the stalemate and handed the woman a card. "This is my business card. If you think of anything I should know…" I stopped there, thought of something and added, "I promise to keep anything you tell me confidential, even from the family, unless you indicate otherwise."

She looked at me hard, stuck the card in her workshirt breast pocket and stomped off.

I was feeling light-headed as I directed my convertible out of Riversdale toward Idylwyld, and it wasn't from my do-si-do with big Ed. The dashboard clock told me it was almost five, and I hadn't had a bite to eat since breakfast. I zoomed up Idylwyld to Circle Drive—the freeway that's supposed to circle the city but is neither a circle nor a freeway—and headed for Tong's Wok. Two hours later I was home, had taken Barbra and Brutus for a jog at the dog run and was microwaving a heaping plate of Singapore noodles, *wei* won ton, Tong's Wok special mixed vegetables and mushroom egg *foo yung* all atop a hillock of steamed rice. When the micro beeped that my meal was ready, I prepped a tray with my food, soy sauce, utensils, napkins and a can of Kokanee. With a glass of water for me and bowl of water for the pooches, I carried my bounty outdoors to the table on the backyard deck. After winching up the patio umbrella and setting everything out, I went back inside to retrieve the box of Tanya's things I'd collected at V. Madison Steel. Once settled, I spent a few minutes satisfying my growling gut, shovelling food into it like a human garburator—not good for me, I know, but momentarily satisfying. After a bit, I slowed down and took some time to sip my drinks and watch Brutus root around in a bush of spent peonies. Barbra was content to sit at my feet and watch as well, it being too hot by far for her to be anywhere but under the shade of an umbrella.

Sufficiently sated to continue my meal at a more leisurely pace, I opened the box of goodies from Tanya's desk and pulled out the suede folder. Piece by piece I assessed each item for its usefulness to my case. The pile of "useless" grew quickly, and the pile of "useful" was discouragingly barren, until I came upon an envelope stuffed into the inside flap of the folder. It was a standard size envelope with Tanya's name and c/o work address typed on the front. No return address. Inside was a single sheet of paper with a single word of text on it:

BOO!

I drew in a quick breath, taken aback by the jarring simplicity of the word, loaded with as much striking power as an unexpected slap to the face. A million obvious questions jumped to mind, not least of all which was: Who would send her such a thing?

So Tanya did have at least one enemy. Is this why she barricaded her apartment door? Kept a bat under her bed? Who was she protecting herself from? Why didn't anyone seem to know anything about her? Were they just unwilling to talk to me? Or was I talking to the wrong people? The two people who did have an opinion about Tanya— Newton Furberry and Stella—thought she was fragile and possibly unstable. Were they right?

I pushed aside my plate, downed the rest of my beer and reached for Tanya's Daytimer. I began in January and studied each entry for anything that would give me some clue about this woman. Other than obvious work-related notes, she was very concise in her entries, often relying on only one or two words to jog her memory. By the time I reached July only two things stuck out. She'd made very few notations for the time period outside working hours—other than a couple of haircut appointments—except for the letter "M" which was always followed by a time in early evening, such as "M – 7 p.m." or "M – 5:15." After March, the M's disappeared. The second thing I noted was a noon-hour appointment, every two weeks, with someone called Dr. D.

I had to put some thought into how I could possibly track down a Dr. D amongst all the possible doctors with a D beginning their first or last name in Saskatoon. So I focused on the hopefully easier M clue and began to recite M possibilities to myself: "Mom…call Mom? Milk? Money…Madison…could it be her boss? Was she meeting her boss at night for some reason? What else? M…m…mmmmmustard?" There was one more obvious option. I ran inside the house and came back seconds later with the address book I'd found in Tanya's apartment. I flipped to the "B's" and saw the entry for Moxie Banyon, the girl in the photo, the same one who Newton Furberry saw entering Tanya's apartment with her own set of keys.

I ran back in for the cordless phone. When I returned, Barbra lifted her head from the cool deck floor and gave me a questioning look, but she was nowhere near inquisitive enough to actually get up. Brutus came loping over for a head pat and slumped down next to his sister, having gallantly rid the yard of all dragons. I punched in the numbers next to Moxie's name.

"The number you have dialled is a long-distance number—"

I hung up and looked at Moxie's address. Chestnut Avenue. I hadn't heard of such a street in Saskatoon, but then again I hadn't heard of a lot of streets in Saskatoon, especially in some of the newer suburban areas that seemed to be spreading like wildfire on the outskirts of town. The first three numbers of her phone number were six-nine-two. These sounded even less familiar. Well, as long as the number was somewhere in Saskatchewan I should still be able to reach her without much trouble. I keyed in the number with the three-zero-six Saskatchewan area code prefix.

Bingo. It rang, then, "We're sorry, the number you have dialled is no longer in service, please—"

I hung up. Crap. I dialled four-one-one for the operator.

"This is Brenda with Sasktel. How can I help you?"

"Brenda, I have a Saskatchewan number beginning with six-nine-two. Can you tell me where that number is located?"

Silence, some clicking in the background, then, "Six-nine-two is a Moose Jaw, Saskatchewan, number, sir. Can I direct your call?"

"Yes. The number I have seems to be out of service. Do you have a number in Moose Jaw for Moxie Banyon?" I spelled both names.

More clicking. "I'm sorry, sir, I only have an R. Banyon listed. The number you're looking for may be unlisted."

Was that a hint? I've always wondered if phone operators really know unlisted numbers but just won't give them out. "Is the R. Banyon on Chestnut Avenue?"

"Yes, sir. May I direct your call?"

"No. Thank you, Brenda. You've been very helpful."

"You're welcome."

I disconnected the call and set the phone back on the table while I mulled over an idea in my head. I absent-mindedly pulled a half-soggy Wei Wonton from my dinner plate and popped it into my mouth. Chewing helps me think.

Moxie is not a common name, so I was willing to bet that the Moxie Banyon in Tanya's address book was the Moxie in the picture I found in her apartment, who was the same woman Newton Furberry saw entering the apartment with her own key and more than likely the "M" in Tanya's Daytimer. She was also my best…my only current hope of finding out more about Tanya's personal life. Since her phone number was disconnected, there was a chance Moxie had left Moose Jaw, but there was also a chance she'd simply gotten an unlisted number or was resident at the R. Banyon address…R being a husband or other relative's initial. I mentally considered my Tuesday schedule. Yep, empty. Tomorrow's forecast was for another day of clear blue skies and temps in the mid-thirties. I hadn't had the RX7 out on the road for quite a while. Don't they say highway driving is good for a car—cleans out the carburetor or some such macho nonsense? Although Moose Jaw is a good two-and-a-half hour drive from Saskatoon, I've found in my line of business that whenever I snoop in person, the results come out much better. It was decided. Time for a road trip.

I was definitely getting a bad case of convertible-hair and a touch of windburn as I followed Highway 2 dotted with potash mine signs toward Moose Jaw. There is nothing quite as exhilarating as driving fast on a hot summer day with tunes blaring, the top down and your shirt off. When I reached the outskirts of town, I pulled into an Esso station for gas, time in front of a bathroom mirror and directions. By eleven I was rolling up in front of a decent-looking little house on Chestnut Avenue. It appeared to be freshly painted in earthy colours and was surrounded by a honeycomb wire fence heavy with newly blossomed sweet peas in purple, lavender, maroon, pink and white, and thick stalks of hollyhocks reaching for the sky. The front gate, centred with the house's front door, was beneath a homemade wooden arbour that I guessed would've collapsed were it not for the support of the wiry tendrils of a sturdy grapevine that crawled up each side. Beyond the gate was a crumbling cement sidewalk that led to the house's entrance and separated the tidy front lawn into two halves. Each side was identical except for another arbour on the left side of the house, which likely led to a backyard; on the right was an above-ground kiddie swimming pool.

I stopped at the gate and observed a woman kneeling next to the pool, smiling at a child, a girl of about four or five I thought, frolicking in the pool wearing bright pink bathing suit bottoms. The woman turned when she sensed my presence and looked at me. I was right. It was Moxie Banyon. Or at least it was the same woman as the one in the photograph from Tanya's apartment.

"Can I help you?" she asked, sounding friendly but not getting up to greet me. She gave me the smile, the one that looked so easy in the picture.

"Good day for it," I said, nodding at the pool. "Are you Moxie Banyon?"

The woman's face fell. Uh-oh.

"Who are you?" she asked, less friendly now and trying to keep a close eye on me and the little girl at the same time.

"My name is Russell Quant. I'm a private detective from Saskatoon. I drove up here today to ask you a few questions. It shouldn't take long."

"I'm afraid you've come a long way for nothing, Mr. Quant."

I regarded her dark features, shiny hair glistening in the sun, summer skin several shades browner than in the picture, melted milk-chocolate eyes. "Can you tell me why?"

Moxie stood up and held out her hands to the girl. "Maya, come on, it's time to get out of the pool."

"Noooooooooo, Mama," the youngster whined. "It's too hot to go inside. You said we could swim."

"And we will," Moxie told her daughter. "We'll swim some more later. I promise. But right now I need to talk to this man, and I can't watch you at the same time."

"I wanna stay outside."

"Okay. Just not in the pool, okay, Maya?"

Maya, a miniature version of her mother, slogged through the water as if it were wet cement and allowed herself to be hauled out and into a waiting towel. Moxie wrapped the towel around the girl and told her to see if she could find the ladybug they'd apparently spied earlier that same morning.

"She's a good girl," I said. And I could tell that Moxie was an exceedingly good mother too. "Thank you for talking to me. I'll try not to take too much of your time."

Moxie straightened herself and faced me with one hand on a rounded hip. "Can I get you something to drink? Coffee? Water or something?" she offered, indicating for me to take a seat in one of three lawn chairs set up near the pool.

I gazed uncertainly at the chair. It was one of those with the criss-crossing strands of some sort of plasticized material, the kind I've fallen through on more than one occasion. But I gave it a go and it seemed willing to hold my weight. "No, thank you. I'm fine, Moxie."

"I'm not Moxie," she told me, lowering herself into the chair across from mine and watching my reaction.

"Oh, my, I...I...I'm sorry," I sputtered. "I just assumed...I just...you are a friend of Tanya Culinare, though?"

"No. I'm not. Why do you ask that?"

I pulled out the photo that showed this woman next to Tanya and handed it to her. I wondered how she was going to get out of this one. I instinctually liked Moxie, so I disliked having to put her in this uncomfortable situation, but she did just lie to me.

Moxie stared at the picture with intense interest, almost longingly. "Where did you get this?"

"In Tanya's apartment." I waited for a few seconds, and when it seemed she wasn't about to come clean, I asked, "Do you remember when this was taken?"

After another second she broke her concentration from the picture and gazed up at me. "I don't. This isn't me. As I told you, Mr. Quant, I'm not Moxie."

Crazy lady? Forgetful? Trying to mislead me? What?

"I'm Missy, Moxie's twin sister."

Okay. Was not expecting that. Missy glanced over at her wandering daughter and asked her how she was doing. I used the time for the brief exchange between mother and daughter to rethink my line of questioning.

"I'm sorry," I said again. "I didn't know. Can you tell me where I might find Moxie?"

"You're probably wondering why I didn't tell you that first off," Missy said, eyeing me with care.

Welllllllllll, yep, uh-huh.

"I wanted to know who you were first, and what you wanted with Moxie."

I nodded. The protective sister. "Of course. I can provide you with identification if you'd like, before I meet Moxie."

"There's no need, Mr. Quant. You see, Moxie is dead."

Not wanting to discuss the matter further in front of her young daughter, Missy asked if I would come back later that evening after Maya was asleep and her husband was home. Was it simple coincidence that two young women who knew each other—at least well enough to be in a picture together—were now dead? I couldn't be certain, but I sensed there was important information to be had in Moose Jaw, so I accepted the invitation and headed downtown to find a hotel room.

I was a child the last time I'd spent any time in Moose Jaw, visiting some relative I don't remember, so the quirky little city with its North and South Hill, urban forest, meandering stream, European-inspired public park, creative architecture and banquet of playful, building-size murals was a pleasant re-discovery. I'd heard rumours of a fantastically suc-cessful hotel-spa-casino complex that had sprung up several years earlier, spurring this sleepy com-munity back to the vigour it once enjoyed as the prairie headquarters for the Canadian Pacific Railway and home to a renowned training centre for wartime fliers. After securing a room at the Temple Gardens Mineral Spa & Hotel and some *meing com* and *geal kob* at Nit's, a Thai restaurant I'd heard good things about, I had time to kill and decided to participate in the activity Moose Jaw is best known for: cor-ruption.

During the era of Prohibition, Moose Jaw had a direct pipeline to Chicago via the Soo Line that runs southeast through Minneapolis. The booze trade primed the town and it blossomed like a flow-ering stinkweed. With it came hoodlums and gamblers, graft and prostitution, and the construction of a warren of underground caves and tunnels through which flowed illicit booze and shady characters in-cluding, so the legend goes, Al Capone himself.

As I passed by River Street, the area once ripe with seedy flophouses, rambunctious gin joints and smoky gambling dens, I was oddly disappointed by the current sanitized version, yet something about the place still reeked of mischief and my mind was a barren field ready for seeding by the time I reached the Tunnels of Moose Jaw tour office. I spent the afternoon, along with several other tourists, immersed in the colourful version of history, well preserved, beneath the seemingly innocent prairie city streets of Moose Jaw, Saskatchewan.

It was as if Moxie Banyon's twin sister, Missy, had decided to throw me a party. As I pulled up to the house on Chestnut Avenue that night, the lights inside were burning bright and several other cars were parked nearby. The door was answered by a brown-haired man of medium height with a pleasant face and wrestler's body. He reached out for a shake and introduced himself as Shane Ollenberger, Missy's husband.

"We're in the back," he said, stepping aside to allow me into the house. "Can I get you a beer?"

"Ah, no thanks, I'm okay. But, Shane, I'm curious. The way I tracked down your wife was by a phone number listed to an R. Banyon?"

The man guffawed. "You're gonna bring that up, are ya?" he said good-naturedly. "R. Banyon is Robert, Missy's grandpa. This used to be his house, and our phone number was his phone number. After we moved in to take care of him, we never bothered to change it, even after he passed on. Nothing like a bit of procrastination, eh?"

I smiled and nodded. "But Moxie, your wife's sister, had a phone number registered to this address?"

"Oh yeah. When she moved back to town and in here with us, she wanted her own phone line. So the bills wouldn't get all mixed up, y'know." His mouth turned downwards as he added, "Disconnected now."

I followed Shane down a narrow hallway that dissected the modest house in two equal halves and led to the back door. He let me out onto a small, un-stained wooden deck, which, based on the woodsy scent of fresh sawdust, I guessed was newly con-structed. Besides Shane, there were four other people on the deck, sitting in a semi-circle of lawn chairs similar to the one I'd used earlier in the front yard and facing out toward a neat square of grass. The only face I recognized was Missy's.

"Have a seat, man," Shane said, indicating an empty spot in the middle of the others.

I wiggled into the chair, feeling a little on display, and nodded a hello to Missy on my right. "Thanks for seeing me."

"When I told Mom and Dad that you were asking about Moxie, they wanted to come over to hear what you had to say."

I smiled at the couple seated to my left, both in their late fifties, and except for hints of grey in their hair, they were dark-featured like their daughters. They told me their names were John and Marion.

"And this is my brother," Missy said, motioning toward a younger man, surprisingly blond as Madonna, who sat a little off from the others and to the right of his sister. "Cameron."

"Hello, Cameron," I said.

He answered back with an unfriendly glare.

"Thank you for coming out to talk with me," I said to the group in general. "I hope I haven't interrupted anything you had planned for tonight."

"Shane," Marion Banyon spoke up, "didn't you offer Mr. Quant something to drink? It's so hot tonight."

"He did," I quickly assured her. "I'm fine, thank you."

She looked doubtful. "Okay then, if you're sure. Just ask if you want something though."

I smiled at her hospitality. "Thank you, I will. As I explained earlier to Missy, the reason I came to Moose Jaw looking for Moxie is that I'm a private detective looking into the death of a woman named Tanya Culinare. Tanya had in her possession a picture of herself with Moxie, and I..."

Missy nodded. "Well, of course she would. They were close friends. Well, much more than that, really, but that was over before Moxie came home. It's just so sad about Tanya—she was a nice girl. Kept to herself mostly, but very nice I thought. Didn't you, Shane?" She turned to her husband, who'd now lowered his bulk into a chair next to her. "Didn't you think she was nice? I can't believe she's dead too. Was it really suicide or...I suppose that's what you're looking into, is it, Mr. Quant?"

"Errrr...did you say they were more than friends?"

"Moxie and Tanya dated for a few months...not long...ah..." she turned to Shane again. "What would you say, about four, five months, last year was it?"

He nodded as he thought. "Yeah," he agreed. "I think they broke up around March, was it? That's right. Right before she moved back here."

"And then..." Missy began, faltering as her throat choked up. "And then she died in April."

"I am so sorry about that," I told the family. "I didn't know until Missy told me this afternoon."

"It's hardly been four months," Mrs. Banyon said quietly over the hush that covered the deck. "We're nowhere near over it yet. And now to hear about Tanya. This is so tragic. Two such beautiful young women. Too young for death. Too young for a lot of things."

I was momentarily speechless. How to proceed? This was a family still grieving for their lost daughter and sister, and I needed to respect that.

I twisted a bit in my seat to face Missy Ollenberger face on. "Do you think Tanya's suicide might be related to her breakup with your sister?" Nice one, Quant. By the uneasy look that passed quickly over Moxie's sister's face I knew I'd blundered. But I couldn't take it back.

I sat silent, remonstrating with myself, while

Missy thought about what I'd asked. She looked at her husband, at her brother, then back at me. "I don't know if I can answer that, Mr. Quant. Moxie and I were very close. We talked about everything, over the phone when she and her friend Duncan moved to Saskatoon, and all the time when she moved back in here. She was pretty serious about Tanya pretty quick. They talked about moving in together. They never did, but Moxie spent most of her time over at Tanya's place anyway." That would explain her having a key. "And they really seemed to get along well at first."

"At first?"

"Moxie was…well, Moxie was going through some stuff…and I think it really took a toll on the relationship."

"What kind of stuff?"

Missy began to get that look people get when they think they've said too much but can't help themselves. "She just…she was having some problems, you know?"

Well, actually I didn't. I stayed quiet and stared intently at the woman.

"It's hard to explain, but part of it was that she was becoming paranoid about stuff going on around her."

Psychological problems? "I'm sorry," I said. "I don't think I understand. What sort of stuff?"

"Moxie told me…" Missy began, then shot an

uncertain glance in her parents' direction, as if hoping she could shield them from what she was about to say. I was guessing I was about to hear something that had been a matter of consternation and disagreement amongst the Banyon/Ollenberger family members for some time. "You see, Mr. Quant," she falteringly began again, "Moxie told me that…that the boogeyman was after her. And that he was trying to scare her to death."

Chapter 5

The mood on the deck grew dark despite an evening sky tinged with the blues and golds of a long summer night's dusk.

"Boogeyman?" I repeated. The word chilled my skin. Why did it keep popping up? I had a squirrelly memory of a voice in my head, from the night Tanya Culinare died, warning me: *The boogeyman is gonna get you*. And then the note in Tanya's desk that read: Boo. What the hell was going on?

"It's my fault," John Banyon told me in his low smoker's voice. "She got that nonsense from when the girls were just small. Marion here," he said with a side nod indicating his wife, "was a nurse in those days. She sometimes worked night shifts, which meant I had to get the girls to sleep. I wasn't very good at it, and to keep 'em quiet when I finally got 'em fed, cleaned up and into bed, I used to tell 'em that if they weren't good girls, if they didn't stay quiet and go right to sleep, the boogeyman would come and get 'em." He unsuccessfully tried to lighten the story with a half-hearted chuckle that curdled on his lips. He said, "I'm sure your mama or papa told you the same thing, it was jus' the sorta thing we said in those days."

"Daddy, it wasn't your fault," Missy said charitably to her father. "You told me the same thing and I'm okay. I think there was stuff going on with Moxie that maybe we don't understand."

"Did Moxie tell you who this boogeyman was or what he was doing to scare her?" I asked the twin.

Missy gave me an odd look, as if surprised I was even considering Moxie might not have been off her rocker and that her story about a boogeyman coming to get her might be true. She shook her head. "Not really, nothing that made sense anyway. You see, Mr. Quant, Moxie was going through a tough time. That's the reason she moved back here, back home, to get her head back together."

"And was she? Getting her head back together?"

"She was jus' fine," John Banyon answered. "There was nothin' wrong with Moxie. She jus' got a little spooked by the big city. Not everyone's cut out for that type of life. Moose Jaw is a lot smaller than Saskatoon, see. People are friendlier here. What you see is what you get. Not always the case in bigger cities. Once Moxie got back here she was jus' fine."

Uhhhh, but she's dead. I looked around the room to see if the others concurred with Moxie's father's assessment. I got nothing. The faces were blank. Somebody wasn't saying something—I just couldn't figure out who or what. "I'm sorry if this is uncomfortable, but could you tell me how Moxie died?" I threw the awkward question out there for anyone to answer.

"She drowned," Shane finally responded once it became apparent that none of the others had it in them. "She got an admin job at one of the public pools here in town. She often stayed after closing hours to finish up stuff; she was a real hard worker, dedicated-like. It was an accident. They think she must have gotten a cramp or something, panicked and...well..." He let the sentence die off.

I stared at Shane, then at Missy. "So she drowned in the pool when no one else was around?"

Nods.

"Was she in the habit of going for a swim after she finished work? Was she a good swimmer?"

At first there was quiet, then Missy said, "She wasn't swimming."

I must have missed something in the story. I raised my eyebrows to indicate my confusion.

"From where her office is—was—Moxie had to pass by the pool area to leave the building. She must have slipped on some water. You know how the floor around a pool can get all slick-like. And she fell in."

Another chill. "She was found in the pool with her clothes on?"

Nods.

"She was pretty athletic, especially baseball; she loved baseball," Shane told me. "But swimming she just couldn't get. She tried but never got the hang of it. It was funny. We even joked about it when she got the job at the pool. We…" He stopped there, realizing nothing was very funny anymore.

I didn't understand how Moxie's family wasn't jumping to the same conclusion I was. This smelled so fishy I could've used some tartar sauce. But then again, their lives were those of ordinary Saskatchewan folk, where the reality of murder rarely occurs off the TV screen. It wasn't my job to incite unsubstantiated suspicion, so I left it alone. For now.

"You mentioned something about someone named Duncan who lived with Moxie in Saskatoon?"

"They didn't live together," Missy told me. "But they were friends since grade school and they moved to Saskatoon at the same time, when they were in their twenties. It was an adventure. They were inseparable for years. But you know, people change and mature and all that, and I think they had drifted apart before Moxie moved back to Moose Jaw. At least she didn't talk about him much anyway. I don't know where he is now."

I asked for Duncan's full name and the last contact information they had for him. It was getting late and I could tell the family was feeling the strain of discussing a sad part of their lives that was in many ways still as raw and painful as the day it happened. It was time for me to go.

After a quick clean up in my hotel room, I headed across the street with a pocket full of cash I was pretty sure I wouldn't return with. The casino is small, like a taste-test version of Las Vegas, but it has all the right bells and whistles and glitz, complete with gaudy carpet and close-to-sexy servers in tawdry outfits. I settled in front of a pleasingly mind-numbing, button-pushing terminal that featured dancing cowboy boots and was well into a second twenty-dollar bill when my cellphone rang.

"Hello," I answered as quietly as the ching-ching, ching-ching cacophony around me allowed. I'm not fond of people who use cellphones in public places—as if everyone else around them would like nothing better than to hear their conversations—but when I'm on a case, well, I've been known to use double standards to my advantage.

"Is this Russell Quant?" a man's voice said. He sounded young.

"Yes. Who am I speaking with?"

"This is Roger Hannotte. I'm the maintenance manager for the Broadway Condominium building. I got a message here saying you wanted me to call you 'bout something?"

"Yes, yes, that's right," I said, getting up and walking away from the bank of legal bandits to what I hoped was a quieter location near the glass doors of the front entrance. "Thank you for calling back, Mr. Hannotte. As you must know, one of your building's tenants committed suicide last week."

"Yeah, eight sixty-three."

I guess Tanya was just an apartment number to him. I put on my best detective-pretending-to-be-a-cop voice. "Due to the nature of the death, we're doing some investigating and I had a question for you."

"Sure, officer, whatever."

Sure was noisy in that casino, barely heard what he called me. Oh well, whatever. "When we searched Ms. Culinare's apartment, I noticed her front door looked as if it had been sanded down. Had you been doing repairs to it recently?"

"Uh, yeah," Roger said. "It was weird. Vandalism

I guess."

"Did someone write something on the door? Graffiti maybe?" A threat?

"Graffiti? Uh, no. Like I say, it was weird. Graffiti I could sorta understand, but this was some whacked-out stuff."

He had my attention. "Why, Mr. Hannotte? What was it?"

"The door was covered with scratches," he said. "Deep scratches. It was like some kind of animal or something was trying to get into that apartment."

An unbidden shudder ran through me. The boogeyman. I was beginning to form an image in my mind of what he might actually look like. It wasn't a pleasant picture.

After hanging up from my conversation with Roger Hannotte, I stood for a moment staring at nothing, thinking about what he'd told me, feeling a little spooked. What could possibly have made those marks on Tanya Culinare's door? A neighbour's dog? A really aggressive Avon representative? When I'd asked Mr. Hannotte what Tanya had told him when she reported the damage, he'd said she'd told him she didn't know how it had happened.

Through the glass of the casino doors I could see that it was dark outside, very dark, and lurking

somewhere out there I could imagine a creature…
oh blast it! I admonished myself; I do not believe in
the boogeyman. I was about to head back to my
hotel room when my eye caught something just outside the front doors and part way down the block.

No way.

Couldn't be.

A dark blue Envoy. It had an Avis sticker on the
front bumper.

I'd last seen the exact same vehicle in Saskatoon,
parked outside my office. Only that time it had
been accompanied by a man looking at me through
a pair of binoculars.

I pushed my way through a gaggle of grey-
haired women who'd just been dropped off at the
casino entrance by a harried-looking man driving a
van—possibly the sole widower amongst a group
of energetic widows from the local care home. Just
as I stepped outdoors onto the pavement, I heard
the squeal of tires and watched the blue vehicle pull
away from its spot. Damn. I decided to give chase
on foot, thinking maybe I'd get lucky and catch up
with the SUV at the nearest red light or at least get
close enough to get a peek at the driver or the plate
number. Fate, however, had a different plan for me.

I was getting up a good head of steam, repeating
the mantra, "I know I can, I know I can," when an
arm shot out from the shadowed depths of a doorway.
The forearm caught me right at the Adam's apple

and pulled me up short, leaving me stunned and staggering. The force of the unexpected impact had spun me around and I narrowly avoided a fast trip to the sidewalk. As I fought to catch my breath, I saw a man closing in on me.

"Are you okay?" he asked in a surprisingly sincere voice, even though he'd come this close to decapitating me (well, not really, but I was in the mood for overdramatization).

"Are you crazy?" I queried the man as if he just might be. My voice was a raspy, smoker's, hard-drinker's version of its normal self. Now that I knew this wasn't an attack and the Envoy was long gone, I lowered my hackles and took some time to regulate my breathing, keeping myself slightly stooped over, hands on my thighs. "Ever try getting someone's attention with a simple 'Hey you'?" I asked the man, who I had come to think of Mr. Asshole Jerk in my head.

"I'm sorry, Mr. Quant, it's just that you were running away and I wanted to talk to you."

Hey! How'd he know my name? I swivelled my head to look up at him then straightened to my full height, flexing a muscle or two (just in case he needed convincing that, despite recent events, I was no pushover).

Wait a sec. I recognized this dude. It was Cameron Banyon, Moxie and Missy's younger brother. He was mid-twenties, blond hair long and scraggly—

which was in vogue for people his age who weren't suit-wearers—and the skin on his face was pocked from too much scratching during a case of childhood measles. He gave off a friendlier vibe than he had back at his sister's house, but then again, he had just tried to sever my vocal chords.

"So talk," I said, massaging my throat where his arm had nearly guillotined me. "Because I am momentarily speechless."

"Moxie wasn't paranoid," Cameron said, sounding a bit out of breath himself. "And she wasn't going crazy like Missy made it sound. Missy, and my mom and dad, don't like to admit it. They don't want to believe it or can't believe it, I guess. But those things, Mr. Quant, the things she talked about, they were really happening."

I stopped rubbing my bruised throat and studied the man. "You know this for sure?"

He nodded and stared at me with some kind of hope in his eyes. Hope for what?

"Can you tell me what kinds of things were happening to Moxie?"

Cameron nodded and for the next couple minutes, on that dark Moose Jaw street, he laid before me a gruesome tale, all in a fast-paced, jittery manner as if he couldn't get it out of his mouth fast enough. "He was hounding her, Mr. Quant. He would call her over and over and over again, at all times of the day and night, and then always hang up. At work.

At home. She'd change her number, but he always found it out somehow. He'd leave her stuff, like... like...like one time she found a pile of dog turd in front of her apartment door, and her building didn't allow dogs, so it couldn't have been an accident. He was always watching her. She could tell. She could just feel his eyes wherever she went.

"And one time, he must have called nine-one-one and sent the cops over, saying that someone in the apartment was being strangled to death, as if... as if...as if that's what he really wanted to do to her. Moxie really loved her car—an old convertible—and he musta known it 'cause he would do things like spray-paint her headlights black or pound nails into the tires. She had nowhere else to park it except on the street. She'd report the damage to the police, but there was nothing they could do. One morning, she found it with the driver's side window smashed and the car was filled with gross rotting garbage. She finally had to sell the car. She cried so hard about that. And sometimes she'd find these notes stuffed in her purse or a coat pocket or a drawer at work. She'd get bills in the mail for stuff she never bought. He was driving her mental. She couldn't take it anymore."

My ears did a little twitch. "Notes? Do you know what these notes said?"

Cameron nodded again. "The one she told me about, it said, 'Boo.'"

Hello Kitty. I had in my possession another note, the one I found in Tanya's desk with the same chillingly solitary word written on it. What was happening here? Was this some bizarre coincidence? A cruel joke gone wrong? Or were the deaths of these two women—once a couple—somehow tied together by this boogeyman?

"Missy thinks Moxie told her everything, but she didn't, not after she realized Missy stopped believing her. I believed her," Cameron told me. "I believed her and she told me stuff."

"Do you think Moxie and Tanya broke up because of what was happening? Maybe Tanya didn't believe her either?"

He thought about his answer for a few seconds. "Sorta, but not really. She and Tanya talked a lot about what was going on. I think at first Tanya wanted to believe it was just a string of bad luck. Who wouldn't? But I think little things started happening to her too. They were getting really freaked out. Dad was right about one thing. Moxie did want to get out of Saskatoon. She was scared there. She thought it was dangerous to stay in Saskatoon. She thought if she came home she'd be safe. Tanya couldn't understand that, and besides, she didn't want to come live in Moose Jaw. She didn't know anyone here or have a job or family here." The young man gave me a meaningful look. "I don't know if they split up so much as fear drove them apart."

"Did Moxie have any idea who was doing this to her?"

He shook his head. "No, and that's what was driving her 'round the bend. She couldn't think of who or why or how they were doing all this shit to her. Moxie was a really nice person. She was a really good sister." He stopped for a second to swallow a lump in his throat. "Everybody else liked her too. I can't think of who'd want to do this to her either. She was really scared, Mr. Quant."

I nodded my sympathy. "So she broke up with Tanya in March and moved back to Moose Jaw, in with your sister and brother-in-law?"

"Yeah."

"Do you know if she experienced any more harassment after she returned to Moose Jaw?"

He pasted his sorrowful eyes onto mine. "She's dead, isn't she?"

I was back in Saskatoon and in my office by eleven on Wednesday morning, busily labelling and filling file folders. For each of my cases, I have a billing folder, a correspondence folder, a suspect folder and, my personal favourite, a herrings folder. In the herrings folder I place information I have yet to follow up on or don't really know what to do with. Generally these are the bits and pieces I pick up or hear about during a case that usually end up meaning absolutely nothing, but instead of allowing them to burrow around in my brain, I put them in the Herrings file, knowing I've put them someplace safe where I can revisit them whenever I need to (if ever). I was adding a few notes to the Culinare herrings file when I decided to call upon Constable Darren Kirsch for a little help.

"Why do ya keep calling me?" Darren asked with a crumbly edge to his deep voice. "Don't ya know there are other police officers who could take your call?"

"I've grown accustomed to the sound of your voice," I drooled flirtatiously, just the way he hates it. I could almost hear his cheeks grow red over the phone line. "And I like to check in to see how you're doing from time to time."

"Well, I don't have time for girlfriend chatter, Quant, so you better have a crime to report—or better yet, a change of address, let's say to Timbuktu. If not, I'm hanging up."

I chuckled. I love Darren's wan attempts at keeping up with me in terms of caustic humour and sarcastic wit. The rigid, stick-up-the ass gene he got saddled with at birth, however, ensures he must always fail. But I like that he keeps trying.

"Do you have any buddies in the Moose Jaw Police?" I asked, ready for business. "I'm wondering about a Moose Jaw woman, formerly a resident of Saskatoon, who drowned in the local pool."

"Sad story, but why do I care?" Darren shot back, playing the tough-nosed cop that I suspected he really wasn't. I could hear him rustling papers. Ah, the never-ending paperwork of a cop. I missed it not.

"I'm wondering if maybe it wasn't an accident."

That stopped him. He took a deep breath and asked carefully, "Why do you wonder that?"

"The victim had just moved back home to live with her sister because she'd been having some harassment problems in Saskatoon. And her ex-lover just committed suicide. Her ex-lover…" I slowed the pace of my voice here; I knew this would get him. After all, he was the one who got me involved in this case in the first place. "…was Tanya Culinare."

"The jumper from last week."

"Yuh-huh. The same."

He was silent, thinking. "I don't get it, Quant," he finally said. "Other than the two of them being friends once—"

I interrupted. "Lovers, Kirsch. These two women were a couple."

"Yeah, okay, I get it, lovers. But why do you think the drowning wasn't an accident? Do you think the jum…Tanya killed her ex, then felt all guilty and offed herself?"

I wagged my head from side to side considering the theory. Not bad, but it somehow didn't sound right. Something, something… "You know, Darren, I'm not sure. It just seems suspicious is all. Call it intuition. These were two healthy young women. They were connected. They were both experiencing some level of harassment." I didn't think the time was right to bring up the whole boogeyman thing. I did want his help after all, not to be laughed out of town. "And now they're both dead under abnormal circumstances. That just doesn't happen every day in Saskatchewan. I think it's worth some questions. I think it'd be a good thing if you talked to some of the blues in Moose Jaw and see what they can tell you about the investigation into Moxie's death, if there even was one. She'd just broken up with her lover, she'd moved back to Moose Jaw to escape harassment; she was fully dressed and all alone when she drowned; if I were a cop on the case, I'd have a million questions. Any scrap of informa—"

"Yeah, yeah, I know the drill, Quant. I'm a detective too."

"So you'll do it?" I didn't want to play the "you got me into this" card quite yet.

"We'll see. Anything else?" he snapped.

"Did you want any gift suggestions for my upcoming surprise twenty-ninth birthday party?" My nose grew.

He hung up before I could give him my list.

Taking the chance that Alberta might actually be in her office, although she seldom is during regular working hours, I made the short trip from mine to hers with little hope of finding her there and a not-quite-formulated question on my mind. I was in dubious luck. Alberta, a plucky, plump, personality-plus brunette with a thousand faces, was in and open for business.

"Russell, sit down," she called out even before I'd reached the doorway of her one-room office. Her space is only slightly larger than mine but looks considerably smaller, what with all the crates and steamer trunks and decades-old hat boxes and upright wardrobe containers that fill every nook and cranny of the place like actors waiting to go onstage. I had no idea what was in them, and I had the feeling I wouldn't want to know. The room was dim, relying on the flickering artificial light from several antique floor lamps and one glowing crystal ball, which commanded a place of honour at the centre of a heavy, dark oak table that took up much of the free floor space. The air was thick and smelled of incense and ginseng tea. Incongruously, Alberta was made up as a modern-day Carmen Miranda, replete with a fruit-adorned turban and a brightly coloured, spangle-trimmed getup that was just a bit too tight for her curvy figure. Why? Why? Why? I want to ask that of Alberta whenever I see her bizarre never-the-same-thing-twice attire, but instead I content myself with enjoying the always-entertaining view.

I did as I was told, choosing a chair meant for

clients near the table, which was draped with a colourful collection of silky throws and across from where our resident psychic was seated, intently contemplating the shimmering crystal ball. I wondered if she had it wired for satellite TV.

"You want to know about something?" she asked, her breathy, deep, feminine voice sounding surprisingly normal in the paranormal atmosphere of her office.

"Well, yes, I…I'm not sure what I'm really looking for with this, but it's something that's come up a few times in a case I'm working on and I thought you might know something about it."

"Of course," she replied, showing no impatience with my go-nowhere prattle. "Go on."

"Have you ever…have you…" I rearranged my butt in the chair. "Do you know anything about…well…about…the boogeyman?"

Alberta's round cheeks flattened against her face and one eyebrow, plucked into a sharp arch, moved up her forehead near a bunch of Concord grapes dangling there. "Of course. Doesn't everyone?"

She stared into the depths of the crystal ball for a few seconds while it sat there mutely, glowing its otherwordly (or, more likely, Eveready-powered) glow. This is exactly the kind of psychic stuff she does that makes me squirm; I just don't know enough about her world and so it makes me uncomfortable, but I always try to be—well almost always—ready to listen with an open mind.

"It's...it's just something that's crossed my path a few times lately..."

"He's like that," she said.

Oh gawd, there actually is a boogeyman and Alberta knows him.

"When he's skulking around, preparing for his attack, readying himself to frighten you, to drive you insane, that's usually the first thing he does," she told me matter-of-factly. "He enters your mind like a burrowing worm: at first it seems like it's a dream or a nightmare, but actually it's more of a warning." Her black eyes pinned me down. "And when he's done with that, with all the teasing, well, then you better watch out."

I gulped like a ten-year-old around a campfire. Pass the s'mores, please. "Watch out? Why? For what?"

She heaved her shoulders as if to say: If things have gotten to that point, it's already too late. "Once he has you," she told me, "he doesn't let go easily."

"You said he'll attack, scare you, but will he...kill you?"

"If you let him."

Okay. End of story time. "You're speaking in abstractions, right, Alberta?"

"Albert Fish," she replied.

I shook my head to indicate I had no idea who or what she was talking about.

"He was an American serial killer and cannibal who boasted about eating children in the nineteen-thirties. He was often referred to as the Boogeyman, but the name itself is much older and universal. A boogeyman can be a woman, but it's usually a guy if it's human," she said with a snort. "Or a boogeyman can be an animal, like a werewolf or monster under the bed. Or a thing, like anthrax or al Qaeda."

"So what you're saying," I said, desperately trying to apply logic to illogic, "is that the boogeyman can be any idea or figment of imagination that conjures up feelings of fear."

"Sure." Ah. Good. "Sometimes." Oh crap. "People like to put a face on what they fear, but the more they fear it, the closer it comes, ready to get them, hiding in the closet or under the bed or on the other side of the door."

"But it's not real. It's imagination," I insisted.

She shrugged. "Albert Fish wasn't imaginary. It's true, Russell, some boogeyman are abstractions, but others, I'm afraid, most definitely are not."

This is what I was afraid of. I never believed in the boogeyman as a child, and now I was having trouble believing that some boogeyman character was responsible for what happened to Tanya Culinare and Moxie Banyon. Bad luck, coincidence, sure, but the boogeyman? Nah. Yet if Alberta was right, there really could have been a boogeyman after Tanya and Moxie.

I asked the question I most wanted answered. "Why does the boogeyman come after someone in the first place?" If I knew why, I could find out who.

"Lots of reasons. Fear. Anger. Retribution. And sometimes," she said with a glint in her eye, "just for the fun of it."

There was nothing fun about what had happened to Tanya and Moxie. Not for them, anyway.

"Anyone is susceptible to the boogeyman, Russell," Alberta added, petting the side of the crystal ball with a plump finger, the back of her ring making a languid sound as it slid over the glass surface.

I frowned at her. "What are you talking about?"

"You should be worried about more than your clients."

The air in the space around us seemed to disappear as Alberta's glittering eyes moved toward the crystal ball.

"What are you saying?"

"He's here, Russell. The boogeyman is in this room."

I felt my cheeks grow suddenly hot. "What's he doing in your office?" I asked, keeping my voice— and hopefully the mood—light.

"He came in with you."

Chapter 6

To shake the image of the boogeyman out of my head, I decided to walk the several blocks to Colourful Mary's, Saskatoon's only openly gay-owned and -run restaurant-slash-bookstore. It's owned by my friends Mary Quail and Marushka Yabadochka. Mary is half Cree, half Irish and Marushka is Ukrainian—a combination which makes for unique choices in terms of reading material and menu selection. I wanted two things from my visit: lunch and information.

Now that I knew Tanya and Moxie had been

lovers, I had a new direction for my investigation. My clients wanted to know why Tanya died. Suicide or not, I had to wonder if it had something to do with her relationship with Moxie Banyon or, more likely, the systematic harassment the two women had in common.

I was greeted at the front entrance by Mary, whose beautiful oval face lit up the entire eatery. It was busy, as usual, with no room left on the desirable outside deck, so Mary took my hand and led me inside to a small wooden table painted bright purple and situated on the invisible barrier that separates restaurant from bookstore. I took a seat on the sunflower-yellow chair she pulled out for me and accepted her recommendation of a garden tomato salad with strips of hot, spiced bison and a glass of iced tea.

While she placed my order, I surveyed the room; Colourful Mary's is always a people-watcher's delight. There were the little old ladies with portable oxygen tanks and walkers who'd made the short trek from a nearby senior's high-rise; the downtown business-suit types grateful for an hour in a place where it was safe to loosen their ties and pantyhose; and of course the foodies who were drawn in by the aromas wafting out to the street from Marushka's kitchen. At any given time, there is always an assortment of patrons from both the Aboriginal and LGBT communities, which are a mainstay of the customer base, and, of late, an inexplicable influx of politicians and city officials. If Mary and Marushka weren't careful, they'd soon have to expand their popular eatery, but that always seems to be the kiss of death for this type of restaurant, the kind that relies on ambiance, homemade food and unassuming charm to lure repeat customers.

When Mary returned with my meal, she plopped herself down in the berry-blue chair across from me and let out a breath. "Phew. What a day. What a summer. It's been like a zoo in here every day since May. What's going on in this city? Somebody finally put us on the map or what?" she said with a smile. "How you doing, sweetheart?"

"I know you're busy, but do you have time for a question or two?"

"Oh sure, for you, anytime is a good time. Besides, the girls and boys have the floor covered. My job is to seat people and make nice. But since you got the last table, I think I got a minute or two. What's up? Wondering what to have for dessert? Marushka made up a batch of her mom's *nalehsnikeh*—they're rolled-up crepes with peach or strawberry or prune inside, served hot and sprinkled with cinnamon."

"Watching the waistline," I said sadly. Damn, I hated having to say that. It sounded old. I speared a piece of tomato and chewed on it dejectedly. "Actually, it's about a case I'm on. Since you two are in the know in the lesbian community, I was wondering if you or Marushka know anything about two women: Tanya Culinare and Moxie Banyon. They were a couple a while back, like until March or so. Late twenties, early thirties. Tanya worked shipping and receiving for V. Madison Steel, Moxie hung out with a guy named Duncan Sikorsky until she moved back to Moose Jaw in late March, early April."

Mary was nodding with her beautiful dark-clay eyes never leaving mine. "Yeah, yeah, I think I know who you're talking about. Not so much the Tanya girl, but Moxie and Duncan, I'm sure they used to hang out here a bit. Haven't seen them in a long time though, but I think that's because they used to come in when Butterfly worked here. Butterfly and Duncan had a thing going for a while."

Perfect. "Butterfly's not here anymore?"

"No. He went back to school and needed night shifts, which I couldn't give him at the time. I think he picked up some hours at the Victorian though."

Butterfly Missaskquahtoomina—according to the Saskatoon phone book—lived in the basement suite of a house on Lansdowne Avenue. Unless Butterfly was taking summer session classes, university was out until fall, and since he was a nighttime waiter, I was hoping I'd catch him at home.

"Yeah," a bleary-eyed twentysomething mumbled from the space he'd created when he opened the apartment door in response to my knock. He was bare-chested and wearing baggy blue boxers that rode very low on slim hips. His shoulder-length hair was luxuriously black and needed a comb-through.

I resisted the urge to look at my wristwatch, which I knew would tell me it was after one o'clock. I wasn't being judgmental, just jealous, desirous of a sleep-till-noon-day and non-existent hips for myself. "Are you Butterfly?" I asked.

"Yeah."

"I'm looking for a friend of yours, Duncan Sikorsky. Is he here by any chance?"

"Duncan? Noooo, he's not here. He's in Vancouver, man." He was rubbing his eyes, making the skin around them turn a fiery crimson. "What you want him for? Hey, who are you, dude?"

"I'm a friend of a friend. We're just kinda looking for him." How's that for a detailed response? "Can you give me his phone number or something?" I was trying for the laid-back approach.

Butterfly was suddenly very still. He was now fully awake, his soulful, dark eyes alert, and with something other than cobwebs filling his head. He looked at me strangely. "Hey, I don't think that's a good idea. I don't know you. And Duncan wanted to get away from his shit here. I gotta go, man." He began to pull back and close the door.

Why were all these people so spooked?

"Hey, hey, hey," I said hurriedly, shoving a foot against the door to keep it from slamming into my face. "This friend of ours, she died," I said in a serious tone. "That's why I want to get in touch with Duncan. To tell him." A lie, but at least it stopped him from shutting me out.

"Oh shit, man," he said, distress pouring over the comely blunt edges of his young face like syrup over ice cream. More eye rubbing. "That's brutal. Who is it? I can maybe call and tell him."

Oh no you don't. "The family would rather I do it in person. You know how it is."

He looked confused. "Uh, yeah, I guess. I suppose I could give you his number...but, like, don't give it to anyone else. Really, man, you have to promise. Duncan had some shit going on down here and he needs his privacy, y'know?"

I was desperate to ask what kind of shit he was talking about, but I thought the question might be answered with a door splinter in my nose. "Sure, of course. Thanks, Butterfly."

"Hold on."

As Butterfly stepped away from the door, I saw why I wasn't getting an invitation inside. On a couch, barely covered by a sleeping bag, was an obviously naked man. And stumbling down the hall, like a barely conscious, newly born colt, probably off to the bathroom, was another. I smiled at Butterfly when he returned with a paper on which he'd written

Duncan's phone number, and wished him a very good day. Ah, to be a university student again.

"Hi. Is this Duncan?" I was on the balcony off my office, standing at the railing, watching a foursome of eighteen-year-olds playing a late afternoon game of Frisbee in the park.

"Who is this?" the man on the other end of the phone line answered back. Not very friendly for an ex-Saskatonian.

"My name is Russell Quant..."

"Are you the guy who visited Butterfly today?" Good news travels fast.

"Yes, that's right. Butterfly gave me your number."

"Who are you really? What do you want with me?"

"Moxie Banyon—"

"I know. She's dead. You didn't have to tell me that. I was at the funeral."

If only this guy would let me finish a sentence. "And Tanya Culinare—"

"What about Tanya?"

"Do you know she's dead too?" It wasn't the most empathetic way of breaking the news, but he wasn't giving me a chance.

There was silence. Then a sob. "Fuck you, man! Fuck you! She is not! You're a fucking liar!"

"I'm sorry, Duncan. I didn't know if you knew."

"How...why...oh shit! Oh Shit! Did you kill 'er, man? Is that what this is about?"

Whoa! My heart skipped a beat and my cheeks flamed. I'd certainly accused others of murder in my day, but I'd never been the one being accused. It was not a pleasant experience, especially coming directly out of left field. What was this guy thinking? "Duncan, hold on a second..."

"Don't you ever call me again! Do you hear me? Leave me alone! I don't ever wanna see you or hear from you! Do you understand? Leave me alone! You just leave me the fuck alone!"

The line went dead.

I had the distinct feeling that Duncan Sikorsky had run away from Saskatoon to hide from something or someone. But why? And why did he immediately assume Tanya had been murdered—by me—when I told him she was dead? Had he suspected his good friend Moxie had been murdered too? Is that why he left Saskatoon? I had my work cut out for me. After consulting with my client via a phone call to his office in Seattle and arranging for Barbra and Brutus to sleep over at Errall's, I booked myself on an early morning flight to Vancouver. I had just hung up with the rental car company when Lilly called me from downstairs to tell me I had a visitor—Victoria Madison of V. Madison Steel. Interesting what seeps out of the woodwork if you just give it time.

I had Lilly show Tanya's former boss up to my office, and after the social niceties were out of the way, Vicky and I sat down and regarded one another carefully across the cluttered surface of my desk.

"I'm surprised to see you," I told her with a hint of a smile, "seeing as the last time we met you had Bluto deliver your kind regards."

"I'm sorry about that," she said, readjusting her bulk in the chair. "But I knew you weren't who you said you were. I was just looking out for Tanya's best interests, that's all. You can understand that."

I could. "Have you thought of something you think I should know, Ms. Madison?"

"Vicky. Call me Vicky, everyone does. And yeah, Mr. Quant, I do want to tell you something. But I'd wanted to check you out first, make sure you really were who you said you were. After all, you *did* lie to me about your identity when we first met."

All right already, I lied to you. Detectives do that sometimes, get over it.

"You see, it was me who told Tanya to call you in the first place."

A surprise. "Excuse me?"

"I don't know if she ever did it, but I'm the one who told Tanya to call you."

Tanya *had* called me. At two-thirty a.m. on the day she died. I just didn't know it was her at the time.

"You see, Tanya didn't have a lot of friends, but she and I, we got along. I was her friend, even though I was her boss. She reminded me of myself when I was her age. She was young, not too comfortable with her sexuality, having trouble keeping relationships going…with friends, family, lovers, anybody. When she first came to work for me, she was a real closet-case, 'scared of her dyke shadow' I used to call it. I kinda figured she was a lesbian when I hired her, but we never really talked about it until we ran into each other at a women's dance some months later. I ended up taking her under my wing I guess, tried to guide her, help her. My girlfriend thought she was a hopeless cause, thought it was like me taking in a stray cat that was too far gone to ever housebreak, but I didn't think so. Eventually she started to do okay, I think. I encouraged her to get more involved in the community, join a choir, do some sports, try to make some friends, become more social, that kind of thing.

"Then she met Moxie. Moxie was good for her. Tanya was quiet, withdrawn at times, too serious. Moxie was just the opposite. Then Moxie got kinda weird on her and left town."

"Kinda weird how?" I thought I knew the answer, but it never hurt to get substantiation.

"I don't really know. Maybe that's just my view of things. Tanya didn't like talking about it much. She just said Moxie was getting harassed or something like that and had to leave town for a while. That really upset Tanya. She kind of went into a tailspin after that, started having problems of her own. It was almost as if..." She stopped there with a look on her face as if she'd just thought of something.

"As if what, Vicky?"

She looked at me, her tiny cocoa eyes opened wide above her mounded cherry cheeks. "It was almost as if she thought she was experiencing the same harassment that drove Moxie away."

"You didn't believe her?" There was something about the way she said it.

"People calling her and sending her threatening notes and stuff... I don't know, it sounded kind of incredible and so much like what Moxie had complained about. I didn't know if it was true, but I told her that if it was, she needed to get some help. She didn't know who to call, so I asked around. Eventually your name came up, and with your being gay and all, I thought it'd be easier for Tanya to deal with you than some macho bull-dick detective."

I'm not macho?

So that's how Tanya ended up with my number. But she hadn't used it...until it was too late. I tried to piece together the strands of information I had collected so far. Vicky's story didn't sound exactly like the one I'd heard from Cameron Banyon, Moxie's brother, but close enough. Moxie started getting harassed and she told her girlfriend, Tanya, about it. Tanya sort of believed it (according to Cameron), or maybe not (according to Vicky). Around February, Tanya quit playing chess with her neighbour and began acting weird and, according to Moxie's brother, started getting harassed herself. Moxie moved away (and they broke up?) in March. Tanya continued to get harassed, maybe even bad enough to talk to Vicky about it. Moxie drowned in April. Tanya died (suicide?) in July.

"I don't know if she ever called you. I suppose not. She was so shy about stuff like that. And, to be totally honest, Mr. Quant, she wasn't the most stable girl around." Same opinion as Stella, another stellar V. Madison Steel employee. Boy, their Christmas parties must be a real hoot.

"So I just came to tell you that, about me giving her your number, in case it ever came up or you were wondering about that. And to tell you that if there's anything I can do to help you, or the family, I'd gladly do it. I liked Tanya. She was a good gal. She shouldn't be dead."

We agreed on that. "Is there anything else you can tell me about Tanya, about her life, friends, anything that might point to why she'd commit suicide?"

"Like I said, I don't think she had many friends."

"What about the harassment she talked about?

Did she give you any idea who she thought might have been doing it?"

She shook her head, the clump of brown hair on top of it moving with it. "But whoever it was, he was doing a damn good job. Every day, Tanya became more and more jittery and nervous. I hated to see her like that, but I didn't know what else to do for her."

"Did you know Moxie Banyon well?"

Another shake. "Nope. Met her once."

"What about someone called Dr. D?" I thought I'd throw that in for good measure.

Vicky hesitated, then decided to answer. "I guess it can't hurt to tell now. Dr. D is Dr. Dubrowski, Tanya's therapist. I suggested him to her as well."

My, Vicky Madison was certainly a fountain of referrals. "What sort of doctor is he?"

She gave her noggin a few taps.

Dr. Uno Dubrowski was listed in a *Yellow Pages* ad as a psychologist who offered treatment for mental, emotional, spiritual and relational health issues, specializing in abuse, depression/anxiety, disordered eating, transitions/change and career/workplace. His office was on College Drive, right across the street from the University of Saskatchewan campus and the Royal University Hospital (better known as RUH). I knew the chances weren't great that the doc would share any secrets about his client, Tanya Culinare, even though she was dead, but I still had to try.

To up the likelihood that I'd even get in to see him without an appointment, I showed up at Dr. Dubrowski's office—which was actually a converted bungalow—toward the end of his work day, which I guessed to be around four or four-thirty. Really, how much longer than that can anyone listen to people's problems? I entered through the front door and found myself in a Costco-furnished sitting area: maroon leather couch, a couple of swivel chairs better suited for behind a desk, a faux-oak coffee table and several peaceful-looking prints on the wall. A small table against a far wall held an empty coffee urn, a half-full pitcher of lukewarm water and a briefcase-sized stereo playing Yanni. I glanced around for a fishbowl but saw none. There was no receptionist's desk, only a short hall with a bathroom on one side and a closed door opposite it, which I took to be the good doctor's office. Since that door was closed and the front one wasn't locked, I supposed he was in but with a client, so I settled in to wait it out.

About fifteen minutes passed before the office door opened. Out walked a sombre-looking woman with a mohawk and nose ring and a pair of jeans that barely made it around her waist. She was about forty-five and grossly overweight. When she saw me, her face registered surprise then quickly moved to scowl. I smiled politely as my eyes followed her to the exit then, once she was gone, zoomed right back to the door of Dr. Dubrowski's office. It remained open, but the man himself did not emerge. I decided to give him a few minutes, in case he needed time to write up notes about the client session he'd just completed. I wondered if he writing the words, "Contact *Extreme Makeover* team immediately." I was contemplating what else the doctor might be jotting down when a diminutive man in a crumpled blue shirt, knitted tie and grey pleated slacks exited the office, letting loose a shrill chord of flatulence followed by a rumbling burp.

Dr. Dubrowski almost fell off his soft-soled shoes when he caught sight of me, obviously assuming the waiting room would be empty at day's end. The first thing I noticed about his face was that so much of it seemed to be covered by eyebrow, one long, blackish, furry one, below which were a pair of oversized round spectacles, a pointy nose and smallish mouth, which was now pursed into a perfect "O." And I thought mohawk woman was surprised to see me.

"Hello, Dr. Dubrowski," I greeted, standing up and stretching out my hand, hoping he'd welcome the diversion away from his shocking lack of waiting room decorum. "My name is Russell Quant."

"I-I-I don't believe we have an appointment,"

he stuttered. "D-d-d-do we?" And with that he let loose another sonorous bit of gas and his eyes began to twitch. "Oh my, dear, dear, I'm sorry for that. You've startled me. You really have." His stomach growled.

This guy was a mental health care professional?

"I don't have an appointment, and I'm sorry to have disturbed you," I said, at my most charming and polite. "But I was wondering if I could take a few minutes of your time."

Assuming I was a potential patient in need of one of his specialties, Dr. Dubrowski's face morphed into one of unbridled compassion. He laid a gentle hand on my shoulder and directed me into his office. "Of course, of course, Russell, please come into my office. I'd be happy to spend a few minutes with you."

I was impressed with his immediate empathy and professional concern for a bloke who'd blundered into his work place, demanding some time. As I allowed myself to be led—or was I being pushed?—into the inner sanctum of Dr. Dubrowski's world, an inexplicable feeling of comfort and safety settled over me like a warm blanket. And what a unique world it was, unlike any therapist's office I've ever seen in real life or on TV or in the movies. This was nothing like the office belonging to Beverley Chaney just downstairs from my own office at PWC, or that of Bob Newhart, or Babs in *The Prince of Tides* or

Niles Crane on *Frasier*; this was more like…*Sesame Street*.

First of all, there was no desk, only couches and armchairs, a futon, a papasan chair, a couple of rocking chairs and a beanbag chair. There were stuffed animals everywhere, a fully operational train set that wound its way around a mini-Mayberry-looking town and a very fat cat—live, curled up on a pillow—that barely had enough energy to open its eyes in recognition of my presence. Here were the fish bowls, tanks actually, several of them, many gallons full, alive with the brightest collection of fish I'd seen since *Finding Nemo*. The bulbs from the fish tanks threw the room into a soft, dreamy kind of light. It was just this side of too warm in the office, but as I sank into a cotton-candy-soft armchair, it seemed to me to be just right. Everything was ju-uusst right. *The better to psychoanalyze you with…*

"How can I help you today?" the slight doctor asked, handing me a tall, narrow glass of chilled apple juice I had not asked for. It tasted just right.

I looked at him, the twitching and farting and stomach growling all gone, as if I'd imagined them, the man before me seemingly no more capable of doing such things than would Donald Trump in a business meeting. "I'm looking for some information about a client of yours: Tanya Culinare. I'm a detective and I was hired by her family to investigate her death."

For a moment he was silent, and I detected a slight eye twitch before he finally spoke. "I see. The loss of Tanya was greatly distressing to me, so I can only imagine what her family must be going through, although I never met any of them."

"Oh? Not a close family?" I played dumb and tried to lead the doctor on, hoping to get him talking before he decided not to.

"Of course you know I cannot reveal anything from my sessions with Tanya." Damnation! "I'm sure you understand, Russell?"

I nodded, trying to keep the disappointment from my face. "Of course."

"It must be difficult for you, dealing with death, crime, jealousies, mistrust, as you must do on a daily basis in your line of work?" He laid out the words before me like a buffet from which I could choose to eat. Or not.

"Yes, it's not always easy." I replied.

"Do you find that you take the day's worries home with you?"

"Sometimes."

"How does that make you feel?"

Psycho talk. The indomitable Dr. Dubrowski was trying to make a patient out of me, and, I must admit, the pull was great. I'd never been in any kind of therapy before, and the idea of having someone whose job it was to listen to me and talk things out with me without judgment or condemnation was very attractive. And Dr. Dubrowski, who'd appeared almost comical in the light of the real world outside this room, was, in the syrupy, warm ambiance of his chummy, cozy office, someone who inspired confidence and the desire to share. I could see myself hugging this little man. I thought then that I just might have to look into this psychoanalysis thing…but not today.

"Well…" I let the word roll off my tongue. "For instance, in my dealings with my current case, I must admit to feeling frustrated, and in general, the ultimate futility of what I do can really get to me, especially when I don't have all the facts." Hint, hint.

"But people come to you for help," he said, "oftentimes in the midst of living through their darkest days. Being in a helping profession, such as you are, must ultimately be extremely rewarding. You must not lose sight of that."

Yeah, uh-huh, but… "Take Tanya Culinare for instance. I so want to help her family, her brother, her poor mother and father. They knew so little of her in life—always thinking they had more time—now they want to know her in death. They deserve to know why she died. If she killed herself, they deserve to know why. If it was some other cause…" I let that one hang.

The doctor choked up a bit of spit and lowered his eyebrow until the hair was hanging over his bug-eye glasses. "Yes, yes, that is a mighty respon-sibility you have."

"And Tanya would have wanted this too, don't you think?" C'mon! Tell me something! Anything! Why was she seeing you? Did she tell you about the harassment? Was she mentally stable or was she making it up? If she was being harassed, do you know who was doing it? "Do you?" Oops, I said that last bit out loud.

"Do I what, Russell?"

"Do you think you could help me out? Tell me anything?" Nice recovery, Quant.

Dr. Dubrowski rose from his seat. Screech. "I'm sorry, Russell. I'd love to help you. I really would. I just cannot. I know you understand."

I stood up too, headed for the door, stopped and turned around. "One question, Doctor. Do you think Tanya Culinare killed herself?"

He looked at me for what seemed like a very long time. I watched his watery eyes and found it dizzying to concentrate on them through the thick lenses of his spectacles. Eventually he approached me and placed a hand on my shoulder to direct me out of his office, just as he had directed me in. As he gave me one final shove across the threshold into the waiting room, he said, "Yes, I do." And with that he shut the door in my astounded face.

As it poked through an omnipresent layer of clouds, my plane made a neat U-turn over the Pacific Ocean on its approach into the Vancouver airport. The North Shore mountains dominate the city's landscape, and from my side of the plane I even thought I could just make out the dormant, snow-capped volcano, Mount Baker, in the state of Washington to the southeast.

I've been to Vancouver (and Vancouver Island, a short hop-skip-and-jump across the Strait of Georgia) on numerous occasions, for mini-getaway vacations or on layovers to some further destination. If the weather is on your side, it's a fabulous walking city, and even when it's not, there is always a lot going on to entertain visitors. Some of the city's attractions might be guessed at from its numerous nicknames: Lotus Land (a reference to the mythical island of Lotus trees and Vancouver's easygoing lifestyle), Hollywood North (because of the booming film industry) and Vansterdam (due to rather liberal drug enforcement policies).

Over the years, I've done the touristy things everyone should do at least once: the Capilano Suspension Bridge (scary, never again), Stanley Park (big ass park), Granville Island (scrumptious seafood), Gastown (trinkets-for-tourists heaven) and hanging out in neighbourhoods such as Punjabi Market, Little Italy, Greektown, Japantown and a whole series of Koreatowns. Now when I visit, my time is spent a little more leisurely, as I'm usually escaping a hectic pace or the cold of a prairie winter. I love to spend mornings drinking lattes, reading the papers and people-watching at outdoor coffee shops situated on sunny street corners. Afternoons are for shopping, eating and having wine with lunch. Come evening, I select a restaurant from the scores of choices (usually somewhere that offers fresh seafood—something we rarely get in Saskatchewan) and settle in (with more wine). With its mild, rain-forest-like climate, stunning scenery, year-round outdoor activities, lively cultural scene and laid-back attitude, Vancouver consistently ranks at or near the top of the best cities in the world in which to live. And it's a pretty darn nice place to visit too.

It was noon the day after my encounter with Dr. Dubrowski when I was sitting in a rental car outside Duncan Sikorsky's apartment on Nicola Street in the city's West End. (I had gotten the address from his mother via Moxie and Missy Banyon's moth-er—mothers love me.) Judging by our less than affable telephone conversation the day before, I was pretty sure Duncan wasn't about to invite me into his apartment for bubble tea, but he couldn't stay in there forever. After I arrived, I'd called his number using my cellphone and hung up when he answered, so I knew he was in there. Eventually he'd have to come out into the world. I'd confront him someplace where I couldn't be refused entry or thrown out. Until then, I was in for a couple of butt-numbing hours.

As with many who set up house there, the mouse in my game of cat and mouse lived the entirety of his life of concealment within a fourteen-block radius centered around the West End. He lived there, worked there, ate there, socialized there, grocery shopped there; he had no need for a car. And ultimately, neither did I. When Duncan finally came out of his apartment just after three p.m., he hoofed it down Nicola towards Davie. So out I got, took a deep whiff of the pleasant moist air and followed suit. Duncan was tall and lanky with bad posture and spiky dark hair styled into a faux hawk that needed a touch-up. He wore a pair of rugged-looking, low-rise, boot-cut Ansil jeans with a wallet chain hanging to mid-knee, and a hoodie over a white T to keep himself warm on the chilly, overcast day. On Davie, he made a left and followed the street to Starbucks, where he purchased a grande latte. Then, after crossing to the other side of the street, he continued on, passing Burrard, Hornby, Howe, Granville, Seymour and stopping just before Richards Street where he disappeared through a doorway.

Once he was inside, I hurriedly made my way to the door and saw that it was an entrance to a small art gallery called Black Canvass. By the look of the product displayed in the single window facing the street, this wasn't a cheap print and reproduction place but rather a serious gallery that handled a small number of original pieces by local artists—none of whose names I recognized—with one thing in common: they liked the colour black. Each of the three large pieces featured in the window had black as the pre-dominant colour with only a few other tints at the dingy, near-black end of the pigment scale thrown in for contrast. The subject matter was gothic, brooding, overwhelmingly morose: wan-looking people in poses of regret, remorse or restriction by way of bondage; nonsensical scenes depicting wild swirls that reminded me of black holes and jagged, ragged buildings that looked like the kind of places where acts of crazed violence would regularly be committed. Each 36" x 48" canvas was given a name like *Vortex of Hell* or *Death Dream*. I guess they'd look all right in the right kind of room—like maybe a dungeon or torture chamber. *Why don't you help yourself to some dip; it's right over there on the table next to the* Schism of Damnation.

Because of the movable wall on which the paint-ings were hung, it was impossible to see inside the store, but as I stood there, trying to appear as if I belonged, a group of six tourists pushed their way past me and into the gallery; I guess they were in the market for a portrait of hellish black death. I saw by a sign on the door that the gallery was open from ten a.m. to nine p.m., checked my watch and debated going in. Duncan had obviously taken the late shift and would be there until closing. Now that I knew where he was, I thought it best to give him time to do some work before I ruined his day. Besides, I was starving. I'd sat in that car for several hours without so much as a cup of coffee. So, after committing the gallery's address to memory, I headed back up Davie and then to Duncan's apartment building to retrieve my car. I left it in the parking lot of my Davie Street hotel, Opus. Feeling like I needed some exercise and fresh air, I took a quick jaunt down to English Bay Beach at the end of Davie for a glimpse of water (as a prairie boy must) then headed for the Oasis Pub for a snack and a beer. Everything handily within a fourteen-block radius.

I decided the best time to return to Black Canvass would be an hour or so before closing, with the hope that most customers would have cleared out by then and Duncan would be relaxed, readying to close up and head for home. The day had remained overcast and grey, and by eight p.m., as I made my way down Davie toward the gallery, the streets were dim and gloomy but bustling with late night shoppers and diners, revellers departing from Thursday night happy hours, coffee gangs high on gossip and caffeine and the always-present parade of street urchins. I wove my way amongst the maddening crowd and was just passing Marquis Wine Cellars when something caught my eye on the opposite side of the street.

There is very little that looks out of place on Davie Street, but a six-foot-five dark Amazon with a nearly bald pate except for a stripe of blue dissecting it into two perfect halves, wearing a Janet-Jackson-circa-*Rhythm-Nation* uniform and massive gold hoop earrings—two in each ear and one in her nose—qualifies. She looked like…Grace Jones. Could it be the same woman Anthony had spied eyeing me up on Broadway Avenue in Saskatoon last week? Naaaaaaah. But could there be more than two (other than the original of course)? What the…?

I decided to test my theory. I made an about-face and headed back in the direction I'd just come: past Genesis Nutrition, the Suntanning Centre, the Dish restaurant, up toward Denny's. I crossed Thurlow before tossing a look over my shoulder and across the street to see if I'd grown a tail. Nothing…nothing…then, oh yeah, there she was, her shiny, blue-striped head bobbing inches above all others. Her gleaming eyes were drilling a hole into my back, creating an easy entrance for the chill of apprehension that began creeping its way up my spine. Who was she? Had she followed me all the way from Saskatoon? What did she want with me?

There was only one question I didn't need an answer to; I just knew it in my bones: This woman was dangerous.

I picked up my pace and whizzed by the Samurai restaurant, Gay Mart, Stepho's and Fresgo Inn and was bearing down on the Parkhill Hotel when I dared another look behind me. Was she gone? Had I been imagining things? Nope. There she was, making long-legged strides, crossing to my side of the street. So I did the same in reverse. Crossing at mid-street, I dodged intermittent traffic and, once safely on the other side, headed directly into the Pump Jack, hoping the dark, crowded pub would offer me safe refuge. The place was hopping, the music loud, and the atmosphere, although going for leather-and-studs-rough-and-toughness, was more convivial and jovial with its preponderance of teddy bear daddies and the boys who love 'em having a laugh over a couple pints of brew and games of pool. I was perhaps a little out of place in my off-white khakis, purple T and a distressed look on my face, but I tried my best to blend in. I chose a spot about midway down the long, narrow room from where I could keep an eye on whoever came in through the front entrance.

"Can I buy you a beer?" a portly gentleman in a black leather vest that barely reached half-way around his hairy torso asked me in a surprisingly refined voice.

"Ah shit," I answered to his bewildered, mustachioed face.

"Huh?"

Behind his bulk, I'd caught sight of Grace. She'd just stepped into the place and her beady, bright eyes were covering the crowd with the intensity of laser beams. She wasn't giving up easily. I pushed my face into that of my leather-clad gnome admirer and asked, "Is there a back way out of this place?" Certainly a place like this would know the importance of a handy back door.

"Sure, sweetheart, but don't you want a drink first?" Was I moving too fast for him?

"I gotta take a rain check on the drink," I told him in some haste. "Right now, I really gotta get out of here."

Nobody loves drama more than a guy in a gay bar. Without further prompting, my new best friend took my hand and together we scrambled away under the cover of the carousing crowd toward the rear of the bar. With a sure-footedness that belied his ungainly shape and size, the man led me through a maze of people and corridors until we came to a door with an exit sign above it. Hallelujah. We burst through it as if we'd just been released from prison...or a Billy Graham crusade. "What's your name?" I asked my companion.

"Rufus."

I gave Rufus a big slurpy one on the lips and

took off like a jackrabbit. Eventually I came to a street called Broughton. I wasn't familiar with it, but I knew it was heading away from Davie, which was just what I wanted, and began hoofing it. After some minutes, I reached Robson. If anything, I knew that Robson Street, with its eclectic mix of retailers to meet the varying tastes of everyone from tacky tourist to serious shopper, would be even more crowded than Davie and easier to get lost on if Ms. Tall Thang was still onto me. I turned right onto Robson and allowed myself to be swallowed whole by the swarms of people, like a minnow caught in a school of spawning salmon. I kept going, regularly checking my back. The crowd thinned the further I got until eventually I reached Richards, the cross street for Black Canvass. Only then, not having seen my tracker since the Pump Jack, did I deem it safe to return to Davie.

I'd spent a lot of time eluding Grace Jones and it was nearing nine p.m.—closing time for the gallery—and getting dark out when I popped my head into Black Canvass, setting off a door chime. The entire gallery was no bigger than my hotel room (not big). The walls were roughed-up plaster painted the colour of dirt—all the better to show off the sunless, murky canvases hanging like giant, sleeping bats from wires attached to the dark grey ceiling. Near the rear of the store was an unmanned, waist-high counter and behind it a curtained doorway that likely led to a back area used for storage, bathroom and probably not much else. The room was heavy with silence, no radio or street sounds, and the air smelled vaguely of curry and marijuana. After a brief wait, the heavy fabric at the doorway parted and out stepped Duncan Sikorsky, chewing on something that he was trying to swallow at the same time.

"Hi. How are you today?" he mouthed the words, managing not even a single expression across his long, narrow, almost-handsome face.

I would have loved to play the polite customer for a while, but that wasn't going to get me anywhere. I'd already wasted too much time allowing him his work day and then playing hide-and-seek with Matilda the Hun. "Duncan, I'm Russell Quant. We talked on the phone yesterday."

I saw the thin face stiffen and his fetching dark eyes grow immediately wary under a furrowed brow. I saw now that he had a nose ring and a silver stud implanted below his bottom lip. It looked good on him. The fear did not.

"Wh...why are you here?" he stammered, taking a step back toward the curtain. "What do you want?"

He was terrified. What on earth happened to this guy to make him so scared? Did he still think I was somehow responsible for Tanya's death? I wondered if there was a back door and if he was frightened enough to use it, leaving me alone with all these paintings of the damned. What was he so terrified of? Little ol' me? Was I *his* boogeyman?

"I just want to talk to you. About Tanya."

"She's dead for real, isn't she?"

I nodded. "I'm afraid so."

His face was crumbling and his eyes were moist when he uttered the word, "You?"

"Me?" Me what? "Duncan, I—"

"Did you kill her?"

Aw man, jeepers. "No, of course not," I told him in a soft un-murderer type voice. "She committed suicide. Last week. I'm a private investigator hired by her family to find out why."

This seemed to calm him some, but not much. He stopped edging backwards and his shoulders lost some of their rigidity. "Suicide? Suicide?" he repeated more to himself than me. He looked at me, pleadingly. "Are you sure? Are you sure it was suicide?"

I hesitated. That was all he needed.

"You're not, are you? That's why the family hired you. They don't think so either, do they? It wasn't an accident, not Tanya. Moxie's death was no accident either."

"Duncan, if you can calm down a bit and tell me what's going on, maybe I can help. What do you think happened to Tanya and Moxie? Why are you so scared?"

The young man seemed to gain resolve, some

heretofore hidden resource of strength, as he straightened up to his full height, passed by me to the front door and turned the lock. He returned to his original spot behind the counter and said, "I'll show you why."

Once stunning works of art had become works of horror. Duncan had led me into the back room behind the curtain where indeed the gallery stored a small inventory of unhung pieces: old pieces from a recent installation not yet retrieved by the artists, sold pieces not yet picked up by the purchasers and new pieces waiting for wall space. Amongst them, in the dim, murky confines of the rear storage room, were three more. Three vandalized, disfigured, destroyed pieces. But there was nothing random about the mutilation. It was planned. It was grotesque. It was meant to send a message.

These canvases, in sharp contrast to the pieces currently on display, were once joyful representations of children picking berries on beautiful, sun-dappled summer days. Now each bore a symbol corroded onto its ruined surface by splashes of turpentine or low-grade acid. The first was branded with a *B*, the next two each with an *O*.

Oh hell. The same cryptic message Tanya and Moxie received. Right before they died.

I looked up at Duncan's tortured face, the area

under his eyes seemingly growing darker with each passing minute.

"They were mine," he said. "I painted these, to remind me of home when I was a kid. Whenever there was room in the gallery, I'd put them up, hoping to get some exposure. I don't even know when it happened. I just found them like this one day when I was closing up a few weeks ago." His voice was tremulous as he told me, "He did it. I know he did it."

"Who, Duncan? Who did this?"

A rattling noise came from the front of the gallery. The door. Someone was trying to get in.

We both turned and stared at the curtain as if we could see through it. Sudden choking fear filled the space like smog.

"Oh God," Duncan whispered hoarsely. "Oh God, he's here."

Chapter 7

Again the rattling. This time more insistent.

Duncan looked at me accusingly. "Who is that? Did you bring someone with you?" He began to back away from me.

"Duncan, no," I insisted. But in the back of my mind I wasn't so sure. Maybe I had, inadvertently, brought danger to Duncan Sikorsky's doorstep…in the form of a six-and-a-half-foot-tall Amazon. "I'm here to help you," I told him. "You have to believe me. I want to help you."

"I-I-I don't know you."

"Is there a back way out of here?" I asked, noting that my very survival that day seemed to hinge on the existence of back doors.

"Yeah, yeah," he said, nodding towards the back of the dimly lit storage area. "Over there. Leads into a back alley."

"Come on!"

We raced for the door, conspirators in our shared desire to escape whatever was behind the front door. I watched impatiently as Duncan pulled and yanked at a series of deadbolts and locks. When he finally drew open the door, his scream was so loud the blast of it pushed me away. Standing in the doorway was a tall shadow wearing a dark raincoat; an arm came at us brandishing something long with a sharp tip. Duncan fell back into my arms as the threatening figure moved towards us.

"I didn't mean to scare you," the man said as he lowered his umbrella and stepped into a dull circle of light. "I know I'm a few minutes late, but I really wanted to pick up my painting before the weekend." He had the sense to look a trifle sheepish when he saw the look of horror pasted on our pale faces. "Gosh, I'm sorry. I tried the front, but when it was locked I came back here hoping someone was still around. I'm really sorry."

For a second I'd've just as soon popped him one than accept his paltry apology, but propriety won out. It took our heart rates a full thirty seconds to return to something approximating normal.

"I have to deal with this," Duncan said to me, obviously recognizing the customer and doing his best to pull himself together.

"Can we meet later?" I asked. "I'd like to ask you some questions."

Duncan looked at the man, then me, then back at the man and back at me. "Uhhhh…not tonight. I got something going. Uhhh…tomorrow?"

I nodded. "Sure. Absolutely. Where? When? I'll be there." Mr. Flexible.

"Fountainhead," he named a restaurant a few blocks away. "Noon?" And with that he galumphed into the front with umbrella man, who was no doubt anxious to get his painting and get the heck outta there.

I took another look at the three ruined paintings with the letters B-O-O written across them, then followed. "Noon at the Fountainhead," I confirmed with Duncan as I passed by him and the man on the way to the front exit.

He looked up from where he was hoisting a plastic-wrapped, framed canvas from a pile of similarly wrapped paintings leaning against the wall behind the counter and nodded. I left.

It was Friday, July twenty-fourth—my birthday. When I'd first left Black Canvass the night before, my noon-next-day meeting with Duncan Sikorsky seemed oh so far away. The shoppers had retreated from Davie Street to Robson Street, the tourists to Gastown, the hawkers and stalkers to Granville, leaving the youngsters and hipsters, yuppies and guppies, gaybes and wannabes all fresh on the street from crumpled-sheeted beds, rowdy loft parties, martini-infused happy hours and early movies. It was time to party in Vancouver, and since I was still in my *early* thirties—I would not admit defeat to thirty-five until the next day—I was damn well gonna join in.

After a pit stop at my hotel room for a shower, a spritz of Bvlgari and a new outfit: an El Barrio T over red and gray patterned Etro pants with a two-button close and Le Coq Sportif shoes, all topped off with a navy skullcap, I was ready to go. My first stop was the long, elevated bar at Glowbal Grill and Satay on Mainland Street in Yaletown, a mere hop, skip and jump from Opus. I filled up on marinated seafood on skewers and dirty martinis and watched the pumped-up and primped-up crowd who were there to be seen (or to talk animatedly on near invisible cellphones rather than to each other). When I was done with that, I made my slightly inebriated way (by this point I actually was hopping, skipping and jumping) to Odyssey nightclub on Howe where I danced and flirted and until three a.m. Even later I found myself in a hotel room that wasn't my own.

Dumbass.

I woke up on Friday feeling every second of every day of all of my thirty-five years.

Double dumbass.

But I'm nothing if not professional—even if I had been busy sublimating the fact that I didn't want to be thirty-five. Regardless, by the time I swung open the door to the Fountainhead Pub I was perky, fully caffeinated and ready to detect.

I waited for an hour, becoming much less perky as time passed by at the speed of a Celine Dion lullaby, hoping that perhaps I'd heard noon when actually he'd said one. But that wasn't it and I knew it. Duncan Sikorsky had stood me up.

Giving up, I dashed out of the restaurant and galloped the several blocks down Davie Street to Black Canvass. I threw open the door and startled a Pippi-Longstocking-fallen-on-hard-times type character. I asked where Duncan was and she told me that his shift didn't start until three-thirty. I ran out of there, back the way I came, up to Nicola Street, all the way to Duncan's building. I was certainly working off (and paying for) the dregs of my night of debauchery. I clumped up the steps to his second-floor apartment and banged on the door with my fist. I waited an unrespectable amount of time before pulling out my set of lock picks from the back pocket of my jeans and made short work of Duncan's knob.

And of course he was gone. As were most of his clothing and personal effects.

Whatever other things Duncan Sikorsky was hiding from, I was now one of them.

It was a dejected Russell Quant who walked those ten-kilometre-long blocks back to Opus that day. Had I screwed up? Should I have waited Duncan out, refusing to leave the gallery last night until he told me all he knew? Should I have approached him differently in the first place? He knew something important about all of this, about why Tanya and Moxie were so scared...possibly about why they died the way they did. I should have done whatever it took to get it out of him when I had him. Now he was gone, who knew where?

All three of them, Tanya, Moxie and Duncan, had received the same eerie message: Boo. And now two of them were dead. I couldn't blame Duncan for being petrified. But who was doing this to them? My best hope of finding the answer had just taken a powder. I'd never find him in this city—if he was even in Vancouver any longer. He might have caught a ferry to Seattle or a flight to Zimbabwe for all I knew. There was nothing else for me to do but go home and hope to catch a fresh lead there.

After I showered to wash off all the running-around sweat, and confirmed my flight with Air Canada—another connector through Calgary—I packed my bags and headed for the lobby to check out. To my surprise, with my bill came a package. The hotel clerk told me it had been delivered for me, by a man, at noon. I paid and then rolled my suitcase to a relatively quiet corner of the lobby. The package was a large, brown envelope with my name hand-written on the front. No note accompanied the package, but I knew it was from Duncan. He'd delivered it himself when he knew I'd be away from the hotel, waiting for him at the restaurant.

Inside the envelope was a single sheet, an 8 x 10 glossy photograph. It was a picture of about a dozen people, arranged like a class photo or some other such related group. The background was an off-white wall with oak wainscotting, unremarkable and unidentifiable (at least by me). I searched the faces. I recognized three: Duncan, Tanya, Moxie.

And then one more.

It never fails to impress me, the seeming ease with which one can make the transition from mountain and oceans to prairie flatland and countless lakes in under two hours. The Air Canada jet touched down just as the yellow ball that was the sun plopped itself into a blanket of neon pink, blazing orange and raspberry-jam crimson almost too extraordinary to believe. After collecting my luggage, I retrieved the Mazda from long-term parking and headed for home, restless and worried. And thirty-five years old.

Anthony had told me about my surprise birthday party. Although today was my actual birth date, the soiree was planned for tomorrow night, Saturday, and I was glad for it. I was definitely not in a party mood and wanted nothing more than to hit the mattress of my own bed for as many uninterrupted hours of sleep as I could string together.

So I wasn't thrilled to find my house being watched.

Most of my neighbours have garages and, even in the summer months, we tend to park indoors rather than on the street. So as I drove past my street, heading for the back alley that led to my garage, the unfamiliar white car stuck out like a drag queen at a monster truck rally. Not because there weren't any other vehicles unfamiliar to me parked on the street—I'm no Gladys Kravitz—but this one had a man sitting behind the steering wheel. I suppose the fella could have been waiting for a friend or lost and consulting a map, but as a detective, I'm naturally suspicious. Besides, I had a pretty good idea who he was.

Instead of making for my garage, I spun a noisy U-ball, sped down my usually peaceful nighttime suburban street and pulled up about half a centimetre behind the white vehicle with a threatening screech. I stepped out, pulled my wardrobe bag from the passenger seat, tossed it over my shoulder and began a slow sashay toward my front yard gate as if nothing unusual was going on. About half way there I stopped, turned and stared at the man in the car, whose face—although it was dark so I couldn't tell for sure—must have been registering surprise.

I nonchalantly walked back toward the car as if I'd just noticed it by happenstance and rapped my knuckles against the driver's window. I heard a little motor whir as the window came down, revealing...wowee, quite the face; Anthony had outdone himself.

"You're Doug, I presume?" Doing my best Rhett-Butler-Frankly-Scarlett-I-Don't-Give-A-Damn routine.

"Yes," a bass voice confirmed after an understandable hesitation.

That Anthony. The bugger couldn't wait for tomorrow but had to have my "gift" delivered on my actual birthday. I stared at the man. He certainly didn't look desperate for a date. Yet here he was, sitting outside my house, waiting for me, like a puppy with a red ribbon tied around its neck. Well, maybe not a puppy...more like a black lab/husky mix, un-spayed and fully mature.

Although I was fatigued, hot and vexed with my friend for putting me in this awkward situation, the eyes and hands had me. Doug Poitras had striking eyes, the colour of freshly roasted cocoa beans, surrounded by thick fringes of brunette lashes, crowned by gently curving brows, giving him a slightly mischievous yet intelligent look. One of his hands was resting on the steering wheel, the other in his lap. I don't know why I like hands so much… whether it's the thought of what they can do, how they can touch, feel or make me feel, or perhaps it's the knowledge of how effortlessly these daily-used instruments can move from swinging a hammer, signing a business document or maneuvering a jet, to caressing a lover's body, driving him to brinks of indescribable joy. It's the shape, the strength, the texture: it was Doug Poitras' hands that got me. Touch me! God, I was tired. But not that tired. I invited him in.

The house was deadly quiet without Barbra and Brutus bounding about, and I was sorry they weren't there to give me their first impressions of this man. I knew he was tall, six-three at least, dark and handsome, but do dogs like him? Always an important question to get an answer to.

Despite the lateness of the hour, it was still tinderbox hot outside, so I directed Doug to the backyard deck, asked him to light a few citronella candles in case any mosquitoes were still awake and excused myself to get out of my airplane clothes—not my idea of first date attire. I hustled to the bedroom, stripped and debated a quick shower but knew that was just silly. Instead I threw some cold water over my face and chest, threw on a pair of knee-length, cotton walking shorts and a tight T—I'm not beyond showing off once in a while—and some scent, and I was back in the kitchen in a jiffy. I stuck my head out the back door and asked, "Beer or wine?"

He was sitting rather rigidly in a deck chair next to the patio table. He looked up, hesitated and answered, "Er...a beer would be great, thanks."

I noticed he was wearing a long-sleeved shirt and a pair of pants that were obviously the bottom half of a conservative suit. Weird thing to wear on a blind date in the middle of summer, especially since he'd no doubt had Anthony's famously intrusive wardrobe guidance. If he could resist that, well, then he couldn't be all bad. I stifled a grin, thinking he looked like a Jehovah's Witness gone bad.

I found two Blues in the bar fridge in the living room and joined my very own *Bachelor* contestant on the deck, taking the chair across from his so I could look directly at him. He looked even better in the candlelight, his skin a burnished gold, the strong features of his face falling in and out of flickering shadow.

"Do you want to get more comfortable?" I asked. He looked startled.

I laughed. "No, I mean the shirt. You must be hot."

He smirked, put down his beer and unbuttoned his cuffs and several front buttons to the centre of his torso. Ripped.

"So how did he make you do this?" I asked after a couple seconds of silence—uncomfortable for him; me, I was having fun.

The face hardened and he shifted his head to one side. "Excuse me?"

"Anthony," I said. "How did he get you to do this: sitting outside my house in wait, delivering yourself as my birthday present. He must have something really good on you. Or maybe he promised you a new wardrobe from gatt?"

The man tilted his impressive dimpled chin in an "I'll never tell" fashion and gave me a smile.

"Oh, come on. This can't be any fun for you."

"Maybe it is," he responded, his wonderful deep voice rolling over me like molten molasses over ice cream.

"Okay," I relented. "So you're a man who keeps his secrets. Tell me about yourself. Why might we be right for one another?" It wasn't a question I'd normally ask a date—although, not a bad idea—but this wasn't a normal date and my brain was still a little googly from my trip. I didn't have the energy or inclination to play demure.

His lips twitched with internal mirth; he was looking much more at ease with the situation now. "I think we'd look great together on one of those greeting cards we'd send all our friends and family at Christmastime to wish them a happy holiday but really to show off how perfect our relationship is," he answered, an enigmatic sparkle in his eye.

Swoon.

"So, Mr. Poitras, exactly who are you?"

I thought I saw him stiffen, but then he shrugged and looked out into the darkness of the backyard. He murmured, "Not a very interesting story."

"Oh I doubt that. Anthony doesn't know uninteresting people. I know by your clothes that you're probably a businessman. Lawyer? Accountant? Am I right?"

He shook his head, letting a strand of dark hair fall attractively over one eye. "No, nothing like that."

I gave him a look telling him I wasn't about to let him off the hook that easy.

"I, ah...I'm in security."

"Oh." Most of my experience with security guards was of the eighty-eight-year-old variety who stroll the university campus or man airport parking lot booths. "What do you secure?"

"Valuables."

"You're a bodyguard then?" That would explain the rocking bod.

"In a way."

Not very talkative. I sat silent, a trick I've learned over the years to demand more information without actually seeming demanding.

He fell for it. "My firm arranges security for people who need it for...well, for a variety of reasons."

"You mean like famous people?"

"Like that. And what about you?"

Was I done with him? Apparently so. "I'm sure Anthony has filled you in."

"You're a detective."

I nodded.

"Are you working on anything interesting right now?"

"Yes, actually. There's this guy I'm investigating. I'm interested in finding out more about him, but he doesn't say much and I don't even have his phone number."

"I should go," Doug said, abruptly rising from his chair, his bulk throwing a dark shadow over me. "It's late."

I got up too, bringing us nose to nose. "Thanks for stopping by," I said, my voice a register lower than normal. I was surprised at my brashness, it wasn't like me—as far as dating-type situations—but there was something about this guy. I was surprised to realize—I wanted him to stay.

"Thanks for the beer."

I looked down and saw he hadn't touched a drop. "You're welcome."

"I'll see you soon." And with that he stepped

out of the personal space I usually reserve for myself and special others.

I wordlessly led him back into the house, through to the front foyer and out the front door. On the front landing we stopped and looked at one another. It had been an odd encounter. Neither of us seemed prepared for it. Was this still a silly birthday prank or had something more happened here? This had gone far beyond flamingos on the lawn or a stripper in a cake. But what was it? I didn't know. And by the look on Doug's face, neither did he.

Doug held out his beautiful hand. "It was nice to meet you, M...Russell."

I grasped it and nodded a "likewise."

I watched him make long, purposeful strides down my front walk and out the gate to the street. I still didn't have his phone number.

Chapter 8

For my thirty-fifth birthday party, Errall was supplying
the backyard, but the arrangements were all Anthony
and Jared. It was supposed to be a wiener roast in
homage to my beloved childhood memories. But a
wiener roast Anthony-style. This meant there'd be
an open firepit in the centre of Errall's backyard
around which the guests would gather, but that was
about the end of any resemblance to the smoky,
bug-infested, burnt-marshmallow, ash-tree-switch,
hickory-flavoured, Kool-Aid-soused events I remember from my childhood.

Waaaaaaay back then, my father would pile my mother, my two siblings, Bill and Joanne, and me into the Fargo quarter ton on sunny Sunday afternoons and haul us to the pasture. The truck would buckle and jump over dirt paths created by years of plodding cow hooves until we'd finally reach our destination, a favourite family spot about a mile or so (not kilometres back then) from the farmstead: it was a secluded grassy meadow between two groves of trees that met at a comely slough filled with tadpoles and leeches and other creatures, endlessly interesting to a curious young boy like myself. Mom would spread out old blankets, and while we kids drank hi-cal Kool-Aid and busied ourselves making daisy chains or pictures out of clouds, she would pull the makings of a feast from the special-occasion wicker basket. After lunch of tuna or chicken salad sandwiches, chunks of sausage and hard-boiled eggs, seeded grapes, ripe peaches and sweet strawberries and usually finished off with some sticky-icinged cake, Dad would haul out the baseball mitts and ball that were black with age and farm living, and the five of us would play catch for what seemed like hours in that sun-dappled field of wild grasses.

It wasn't until the afternoon grew old that it was time for the main event—the wiener roast, the thing that we were really there for. Dad and Bill would build the fire from sticks and lightning-cracked logs that Joanne and I had scrounged from the woods.

Mom would pre-butter a dozen hot dog buns and mix together the ingredients for her spectacular homemade potato salad, which she'd kept cool all afternoon by immersing them in the shaded waters of the slough in watertight Tupperware containers. The most fun was finding the wiener roast sticks, the ash and birch switches that had to have just enough heft to hold a wiener aloft above the fire without drooping, yet not be too thick to properly impale the slender pink tubes of mm-mm goodness without splitting them in half.

Dad would have a Pilsner beer—also slough-cooled—while we roasted his wieners and ours. Mom would pour the rest of us tall plastic glasses full of frothy, homemade root beer, her mother's recipe, and hand out paper plates—the only time she ever allowed their use—with healthy dollops of the potato salad already in place. And then, when the wieners were bursting at the seams and dripping their juices into the fire, we'd plop them into waiting buns, squirt ketchup and relish and bright yellow mustard all over them and dine al fresco, prairie style. It was absolutely, excruciatingly glorious.

Moving ahead a quarter century, things had changed considerably. Anthony detested wieners and, despite my protestations to the contrary, refused to believe that I, and every adult the world over, did not as well. To give him credit, I was told (by Jared) that he did try his best to accommodate my childhood experience. He spent significant time researching gourmet wiener options, but alas, finding none which met his high standards, my birthday wiener roast became a pig roast. I'd only seen such a thing in pictures of Hawaiian luaus—a crispy-brown pig, slowly turning on a spit above a fire—but I had no doubt that if Anthony put his mind to it, he'd find a way to duplicate it in Saskatchewan.

In addition to the pig, Anthony insisted on an abundant collection of skewered foods, which in his mind, what with the whole meat-on-a-stick theme, seemed a fine alternative to hot dogs. There'd be marinated shrimp and scallops, spicy beef and smoked porks, plump mushrooms and onions and a wide selection of succulent vegetables in a medley of summer colours. To balance out the menu, tortes and cobblers replaced sticky-icinged cake, and Kool-Aid and root beer and Pilsner were supplanted by Veuve Clicquot and frozen gin served in silver-plated flasks for that authentic out-in-the-woods feeling I so fondly remember.

Also under Anthony's careful tutelage, Errall's backyard was transformed into the Tribal Council area from *Survivor*. Just in case the actual outdoors didn't sound real enough, a series of specially burned CDs would fill the air with realistic outdoor sounds. You know how it is with hoot owls, burbling brooks and chirping blue jays, you can never rely on their sense of timing.

"You're not surprised," Errall complained when she opened her front door and caught the look on my face.

"I think you're supposed to wait to say that until you've led me to the backyard and everyone jumps up and yells happy birthday," I replied matter-of-factly.

"It was Anthony, wasn't it?" she said, pulling me into the house with her left hand—the other was holding a near empty bottle of Boh. What a lesbian.

"He really thought it was more important that I show up tonight appropriately dressed to entertain guests, rather than in dirt-encrusted jeans and un-combed hair like I usually do when invited for dinner at your house." I was being only half-sarcastic. Unless you've been in a wind storm or something, just how many times a day do you need to comb your hair? "Which, by the way, would have given it away anyhow."

"Whaddaya mean?" She frowned at me.

"You never invite me over for dinner."

"True. He's probably right anyway. You look nice."

Compliments were something new Errall and I were trying out with one another. It usually went better when at least one of us was drinking. I was wearing a pair of black linen, wide-leg pants that reached mid-calf and a loose, black, cable-knit, summer-weight sweater with a deep V-neck. She looked good too in a petunia print, sleeveless frock, her dark mane in a sassy bob that swished just below her sharp jaw line, but I decided to keep that to myself until I saw just how fun this party really was.

As we made our way through the house toward my backyard surprise that wasn't a surprise at all, I needn't have fretted, for little did I know that this night would bring me more than my fair share of honest-to-goodness surprises.

When we reached the back door off the kitchen, the unusual silence that only occurs at surprise parties and never in real life was palpable. My smugness at being in on the whole deal was suddenly being replaced by something else, something that was gurgling in my tummy and feeding my brain endorphins. Was it excitement or trepidation? I wasn't sure. I looked at Errall, waiting for her to make the first move by opening the door.

"There's something I have to tell you before we go out there," Errall whispered breathlessly.

Uhhhh, yeah, I know, surprise party ahead. I gave her one of those "duh" looks.

"Not that, idiot. I have a date with me tonight."

Gulp. Anthony had warned me, but I didn't believe it until now. Errall had had one or two dalliances since her break-up with her long-term partner, Kelly, a couple of years ago, but not with anyone she'd referred to as a "date." What did this mean?

Leaving no time for reaction, Errall placed her slender hand on the doorknob, mouthed the words "happy birthday" to me and threw open the door to a chorus of screams from the assembled guests revealed. On cue, someone plugged in multiple strings of festive patio lanterns, lit the tiki torches and started the music. I felt the palm of Errall's hand push me into the melee and then she disappeared.

Although I'd been experiencing some—shall we say, discomfort—about the whole turning thirty-five thing, I have to say, every now and again, having a big ol' birthday party like your mama used to throw you when you were a kid is not to be underrated. For the first several minutes as I took in the collection of familiar, smiling faces, all there to be with me, to celebrate with me, wishing me well, I experienced a gushing fountain of oochy-koochy emotion stuff that I was unprepared for. I hugged and kissed and tickled and giggled and perfected a mock-shock look when asked if I was truly surprised. About half the people bought it. Beverly and Lilly from PWC were there with husbands and kids in tow, Alberta too, with a new beau, a guy who claimed to be training to pilot the first commercial space flight to Mars in 2009—I was guessing he'd already been to the moon—and by day was a librarian. There were Anthony and Jared, Marushka and Mary, a host of other friends, neighbours and even my mother, who'd made the trek from her little farm an hour away to surprise her "Sonsyou" (little son). But there was a glaring empty spot in the crowd, a space that, although she was physically small, seemed immensely huge in her absence.

"You're thinking about Sereena." It was Jared, looking ridiculously perfect in gauzy white.

He'd caught me staring into space as I was waiting at the tiki bar for my margarita from a bartender dressed as a hula dancer. Maybe this was the guy who delivered the pig from the islands. We shared a look. I missed her. What can I say?

"Ohhhhhhh, Keeeeeee-rist!" This from someone who'd just bellied up to the bar.

I looked over, expecting—as had been the custom for the night—some new attack on my age, virility or ability to navigate without a motorized scooter. Instead I saw surprise number two—and it was none too pleasant.

"What the hell are you doin' here, bub?" Jane Cross asked with an exaggerated snarl on her cute-but-gnomelike face.

My head swivelled to and fro, looking in vain for the hidden *Candid Camera*. Or maybe this was for a new show entitled *World's Cruellest Home Videos*. I couldn't believe it. If my life were set in medieval times or lived as an intergalactic space fantasy, Jane Cross might be referred to as my arch-enemy or nemesis, but I simply like to think of her as pain in the butt number one. Well, not really. She's not that bad I suppose. She just gets under my skin—like a case of the Itch after a swim in Pike Lake.

Jane Cross lives in Regina, almost three hours away for Pete's sake—so why did I keep on finding her in my life?—and she is a colleague, another of that rare breed: the Saskatchewan sleuth. In our short history together she's attacked me in a hotel room, sprayed me in the face with Herbal Essence hairspray and scared my mother out of her wits. Who would ever think to invite *her* to *my* birthday party?

"Whassamatter?" she snorted, accepting a beer from the bartender. "No disco parties to shake your booty at tonight?"

No fair. I accepted her homosexual slurs before as pure ignorance…that is until I'd recently found out she is the type of woman who is overly fond of plaid shirts, big dogs, tool belts as accessories and other women, and should therefore damn well know better. "Is there a Birkenstock warehouse sale in town this weekend?" I shot back.

Jane's button nose expanded and steam came out; she couldn't help but look down at her feet. Yup, Birkenstocks with wool socks. It was thirty-two degrees in the shade for crumb's sakes.

"It's a big party," she grumbled at me. "You find your corner and I'll find mine."

Errall sidled up next to Jared, threading a thin arm through his thick one, and looked back and forth between me and Little Bo Bleep. "I see you've met," she said with an air of relief.

"You know this guy?" Jane said to Errall.

"This 'guy' is the birthday boy," Errall responded with a forced smile, sensing all was not right.

"You know this gal?" I mimicked.

Errall shot me a warning look before saying, "Jane is my date, Russell. Remember, I was telling you?"

Bomb.

I plastered on my own fake smile and, with a hand on Jared's elbow, said, "You'll excuse us, right? I have something to discuss with Jared."

Jane scowled; Errall looked blank. As we walked away I heard my mother approach the two women. I debated waiting to overhear the conversation: given the players, it would be a goodie. But I truly did have something to talk to Jared about and I didn't want to spend any more time with Jane Cross than I absolutely had to. The last thing I heard was my Ukrainian mother saying to Errall—R's in full roll—"Hello, Carol. Tank you for inviting me for party. Very nice den, uh huh."

"I take it you don't like Errall's new squeeze?" Jared got out once I'd manoeuvred him into a relatively quiet corner of the yard next to a crabapple tree heavy with fruit and released his elbow.

"When the hell did that happen? How did those two even meet?" I was incredulous.

Jared shrugged. "I just met her tonight too, so I'm guessing it's pretty new."

I could think of a million jabs and barbs, but what was the point? "Listen, Jared, I hate to do this right now, but I have something important to talk to you about. I wouldn't do it tonight, but it might be urgent."

"Sure, of course," he said, immediately concerned. His emerald eyes searched mine and were filled with the desire to help in whatever way he could. He is just that kind of guy.

I pulled out a folded-over copy I'd made of the photograph Duncan Sikorsky had left me and handed it to Jared. I knew he'd recognize it. He was one of the twelve people in it.

Jared looked at the photo and registered surprise. "Wow. Where did you get this?"

"From Duncan Sikorsky."

"Duncan, yeah, okay, I know him, but…why? Why do you have this? Why did he give it to you?"

I ignored the questions for now. "What can you tell me about the picture? Who are these people?"

"Well, that's easy," he said brushing a stray

golden lock off his forehead and sipping his drink. "It's the Pink Gophers."

I searched the bowl of my own drink for any sign of hallucinogens. My face told the rest.

"The Pink Gophers," Jared explained patiently, "is a Saskatoon-based, LGBT-friendly chorus. I'm a member. We're on hiatus until the fall."

"You can give me the names of all these people?"

"I can do better than that. I can give you our contact list with names, phone numbers and emails if you want."

Jackpot. "I do want."

"Russell, what's this all about?"

"It's a case I'm working on. I can't tell you much." No need to tell him I really didn't know what this was all about. Yet.

"Of course. I understand. But…well, is someone in trouble?"

"Tanya Culinare and Moxie Banyon."

"Yeah?"

He hadn't heard. I suppose he wouldn't have unless they were good friends who'd kept in touch during hiatus. Moxie died in Moose Jaw and Tanya's death was recent and coverage in the Saskatoon paper had been sparse.

"They're dead," I told him, laying a comforting hand on his arm.

His eyes grew humongous and his jaw slackened.

"Oh no, Russell, what happened? When?"

I gave him a brief overview. He listened attentively, every so often letting out a moan of sympathy.

"I wish I'd known," he said when I was done. "We didn't know each other outside the chorus, but I'd have certainly gone to the funerals to offer my condolences to their families."

"Jared, I visited Duncan in Vancouver. He's a man scared out of his wits. Tanya and Moxie were scared too. I think all of this might be related. Can you think of anything, other than being friends, these three might have in common, why they'd be getting threats?"

"Getting threats? They were scared? Of what?" Jared was trying to keep up with an admittedly complex story.

I humped my shoulders. "I don't know. The boogeyman?"

Jared stayed silent for a moment, as if mulling something over. "Ah, Russell…"

"Yeah?"

"You know, I haven't really given it too much thought, but I had something weird happen to me about a week ago. I only mention it because you brought up the boogeyman. And that's exactly what I thought of when it happened."

My back stiffened and my *Barnaby Jones*-Buddy Ebsen (I was thirty-five, after all) sense went on full alert. "Tell me."

"Anthony was away in Boston on a buying trip, so I was home alone. I'd gone to bed early with a stack of trash magazines and a bowl of popcorn—a guilty pleasure when he's away—and fallen asleep. I remember waking up hearing a low, almost rhythmic thumping, like drums in the distance. I finally realized it was coming from the front door of the apartment, but when I looked through the peephole, there was no one there. Half hour later, same thing. That time I opened the door, but the hallway was empty."

Jared and Anthony live in a downtown penthouse suite where panhandlers, random acts by mischief makers or even kids selling chocolate-covered almonds so their class can visit the legislature buildings in Regina aren't regular occurrences.

"It happened once more," he told me, "and then the phone started ringing with hang-ups."

"Call display show anything?"

"Unknown number, so probably a cellphone or pay phone."

"Has this ever happened before, Jared?"

"Never. And maybe it's all just a weird one-time thing, some mistake or something, but it spooked me. You know how the mind can work overtime in situations like that: home by yourself, your loved one away, dark, lonely night; you start hearing squeaks and creaks that are probably always there but you've just never paid attention before."

I was alarmed and my voice showed it. "Jared, this is more than just a few squeaks and creaks. Someone had to be there, at your door, on the other end of the phone line."

"Yeah," he said, not quite sharing my concern. "But it could have been a wrong address, wrong number type thing. Hasn't happened since."

I wasn't so sure. "I'd like to get that contact list as soon as possible. And if you can think of any reasons those three and you might be the target of scare tactics…"

"Sure, of course. I'll let you know."

"Okay you two!" I could hear Anthony's cultured British voice booming over the music and party chatter as he approached us with a trio of shooter glasses in one hand and lime wedges and a salt shaker in the other. "Enough canoodling. The boyfriend is back."

Anthony distributed the lime and glasses of gold tequila with a wolfish smile. "And speaking of which…"

I was in trouble.

"My gift to you has just arrived," Anthony announced, raising his glass in salute and leading us in the traditional preparatory lick between thumb and forefinger and salting of our skin.

I was surprised to feel a jolt of electricity surge from my nether regions at the mention of Doug

Poitras. Normally I abhor anyone's undoubtedly good intentions at fixing me up. I'm single. I like it. Deal with it. But Doug had spiked my interest, heated my blood to a slow boil, set the tiny hairs at my neck on fire. I was delighted with the thought of seeing him again.

"Happy birthday, Russell," Anthony and Jared saluted. We licked the salt, threw back our shots and bit down on the sour lime. Yum.

"Bring him on," I called out with a tequila-fueled knavery that felt good.

After a round of salty lip kisses, Anthony moved aside and pulled close a man who'd been standing a few feet away, his back to us. "Russell, I'd like you to meet Doug Poitras."

My heart plummeted and all playful puckishness was quickly forgotten as I stared at a man who was a complete stranger to me.

If this was the real Doug Poitras, then who was the man I'd invited into my home last night?

Chapter 9

I had thought the days of having my mother drive me home from a party because I'd had a bit too much to drink were long past me. But who could blame me for imbibing like an eighteen-year-old on his first visit to a cocktail bar? What with turning thirty-five, learning Errall was dating again, finding out her date of choice was the pugnacious Jane Cross, worrying Jared might somehow be tied up in my current case and in danger and having a potential Mr. Right turn into Mr. Who?

The man Anthony introduced to me as Doug

Poitras was pleasant enough, both in looks and demeanour, but after the sizzle and sparkle of *my* Doug Poitras, he barely registered. And he quickly vanished from the scene when my indifference became wholly apparent. Or maybe it was because the first thing I asked him was to get me a double rye and Coke.

So who was my Doug Poitras? Anthony denied any knowledge of arranging for a man—any man—to await my return from Vancouver the previous evening. My detailed description drew blank stares and, I believe, some doubt as to my probity, which of course infuriated me further and drove me deeper into a bottomless bottle of Canadian Club.

My mother had planned to stay in the city at my house for the balance of the weekend and therefore was going my way at night's end anyway, so it all worked out. As she ferried me home, I quickly recalled how there is nothing quite as discomfiting as the silence of a mother driving home her inebriated son. Not that I had made a fool of myself, or was slobbering on my bib and tucker, but, I have to admit, my world was a wee bit out of focus. As I slouched in the passenger seat with my ma behind the wheel, I couldn't help but think that a strongly worded lecture would have almost been preferable, for in the quiet I could most clearly hear what that stout, bespectacled, Ukrainian woman was surely thinking: "But you ver vonce a policeman, for shame."

She was over it the next day. I can't say as much for me. It was Sunday, a day of rest, but not with Kay Quant (nee Wistonchuk) around. She had me and the pooches up and out of bed by eight a.m., at which time she fed me hole'n'one eggs (she takes a piece of mushy white bread and pinches a hole in the centre, lathers butter on both sides, slides it into a pan of bubbling hot butter, and as it toasts, she cracks a farm-fresh, yellow-bellied egg into the hole and does what she loves best—fries it) as well as a heap of bacon, instant coffee and a deep-fried *pyroshki* filled with prunes for dessert. Barbra and Brutus had to make do with small, round, brown kibble. But only because I insisted. Nevertheless, I think I saw some prune around Barbra's mouth; even my mother is capable of rebellion against what she thinks is just plain wrong, like not feeding people food to animals. After that we showered and dressed and headed out to church.

Just my luck: the service that morning was led by Father Len Oburkevich, a former client's dead partner's twin brother (long story) on whom I'd once had a wee crush.* It wasn't until after a lunch of borscht and breaded beef cutlets and cucumbers in a mayonnaise and white onion sauce that Mom allowed me to beg off for a nap—and only if I promised to play cards with her later. I headed for my private kingdom—also known as my den—

---

* *Amuse Bouche*

where I prefer to nap because the sofa is as soft as marshmallow and for some reason I love to fall asleep surrounded by my bookshelves and travel knick-knacks and framed photos of loved ones. It took my brain a while to settle into rest mode though, with random thoughts about the case of Tanya Culinare's death whizzing through my head like pinballs looking for a hole to land in. But eventually sweet sleep overcame me to the gentle tune of two dogs snoring.

When later came, I felt a second wind, and pleased to have it, decided upon an alternate plan. My mother and father had been farmers who came into "the city" only when they needed something they absolutely could not obtain from a local small town store or their own land, barn or chicken coop. As a result, many of the things city folk take for granted Mom had never before experienced, and our annual fair, the Saskatoon Prairieland Exhibition (the Ex) was one of them. That evening was the last night of the six-day event that features death-defying rides, win-defying games of chance, SuperDogs, a kick-ass petting zoo, beer at the Prairie Patio, an ugly hat contest, spudnuts, thick slices of fresh-out-of-the-oven Doukhobor bread slathered with chunky strawberry jam, chuckwagon races and a grandstand where one could rock out to classic bands such as Prism and Trooper.

I have a longstanding agreement with my friend

Doreen that during exhibition week I can park in her nearby back alley parking spot just off Lorne Avenue instead of spending endless minutes trying to find a bootleg spot that would cost me big bucks. In return I always bring her back an elephant ear and a corn dog, the only two reasons she would ever visit the fair herself. It works out well for both of us. So that evening, about seven-ish, Mom and I pulled into Doreen's backyard, walked the half block to the entrance on the corner of Lorne and Ruth Streets, paid our nine bucks, idly wondered just who Lorne and Ruth were to rank streets named after them and entered the rambunctious, colourful, lit-up-like-a-Las-Vegas-wedding-chapel, wonderfully seedy world of a prairie fairground.

Things were going well: delicious, church-basement ice cream and souvlaki on a bun were being consumed, Mom shocked the teenyboppers around her (and the roadie running the show) by showing off remarkable marksmanship at a game that required shooting water at a target to power a racehorse— she won, quite handily, six times in a row and came away with a ridiculously huge panda bear. We fed Styrofoam cupfuls of sunflower seeds to baby goats at the petting zoo. Then things turned ugly. Namely, we ran into Jane Cross. With Errall.

The conversation was awkward and stilted, Jane and I unable to enjoy our usual verbal bantering in front of my mother because it generally contained a liberal sprinkling of innovative swear words, which left us with little to say to one another except, "How 'bout that weather?" Mom had known Errall's ex, Kelly, because Kelly had been a school chum of mine, and although Mom wasn't quite wise to the lesbian thing, she instinctively knew something wasn't quite right with Errall (or, as she called her, Carol) showing up every place with a new "goot friend." So we dumped them as quickly as we could, begging off to catch one more Slingshot-Killer-Upsy-Daisy-Curlicue-Upchuck-slam-o-rama ride, or whatever it's called, before the fireworks, which were slated to begin at 10:40 p.m. (not 10:30, not even 10:45, but 10:40 on the dot).

We, of course, went nowhere near the midway ride lineups; Mom had no interest and I'm not a fan either. Something about the up and down, round and round, side to side, all at the same time just doesn't sit right with me or my stomach. I like to watch, but Mom had other ideas, and with not-quite-subtle manoeuvrings, both physical and verbal, she got us back to the shooting gallery games and proceeded to procure a menagerie of stuffed animals. If this were Vegas, they'd have comped her a room and front row seats for Cirque du Soleil...or took her for a little "ride" into the desert.

As 10:40 approached, I pried Mom away from her water gun so we could find a good spot from which to watch the fireworks display. And still I could not catch a break, for despite all our efforts and the thousands of strangers who walk through the Exhibition gates every day, who should end up next to us but Jane and Errall.

In a way it was okay, seeing as they were willing to take a load off me by offering to hold some of Mom's furry winnings, which somehow I'd ended up with while she, completely unencumbered, chewed the buttery niblets off a cob of corn.

The first firework sprayed high into the black velvet sky like a spatter of phosphorescent paint. All together now: Ooooo. Ahhhhh. Ohhhhhhh. Ayyyyyyy.

And so the pyrotechnics progressed. I wasn't paying full attention, I have to admit. My eye kept dropping from the sky onto that other little firecracker in town known as Jane Cross, and my mind kept asking the same question: What does Errall see in her? Sure, I suppose she is cute enough when she isn't scowling. And I suppose there is that whole rough and tumble bravado that appeals to lesbians of a certain ilk. But did Errall know that this woman had once sprayed me in the face with hairspray? And that she calls me "bub" even though I've asked her politely not to?

And it was over Jane's cabbage-shaped head, which was closer to the ground than most around her, that I caught sight of something even less appealing: a set of eyes fastened upon me with heated intensity. Crikey. I was getting a bit fed up with being watched. Was this the same guy I'd caught peeking at me through a set of binoculars at PWC? Or the fellow in the rental outside the Moose Jaw casino? Maybe another fake Doug Poitras? Or a friend of Grace Jones?

Well, it was time I found out.

I whispered in my mom's ear to stay with Errall until I came back from the washroom, shoved a walrus and two monkeys into her arms and took off toward the eyes.

The Ex fireworks display happens on an empty slip of land that separates Kidsville (where they keep the short people rides, clowns and the best candy apples) from the main midway, and it was into the latter that Mr. Sneaky Eyes disappeared. I didn't have much to go on, but in the kaleidoscope light of a nearby, whizzing ride called the Zipper, I caught a quick glimpse of who I was after: a slight guy of middling height with a red baseball cap worn slightly askew. Better than nothing.

If anything, the temperature had risen since sunset and the flashing lights and swirling machines of the Ex appeared grandly dramatic against the charcoal backdrop of the prairie night sky and helped light my way. For several minutes I dodged in and out between the swooshing rides with calliope tunes, root beer and candy floss booths and lineups for tokens, almost catching up with the guy several times but never quite. I'd see the red hat bobbing up and down amongst the throngs of fairgoers and merchandise hawkers and I'd push them aside as politely as I could, but I always found myself a few too many seconds behind.

Eventually we ran out of midway. The demarcation line between fair and no fair was as clear as white to black and there was no doubt I'd entered no man's land, an end-of-the-line, nothing-here-to-see-folks kind of place, completely cut off from the supersonic light, clanging noise and frantic activity of the fairground. In the sudden darkness I nearly tripped over a writhing mass of electrical cables as I raced past the last hot dog stand and a portable bathroom.

From the blackness came: "Get him, boys."

Not exactly the words you want to hear in a situation like that.

There were three of them. Red Cap was among them and seemed to be the leader. They surrounded me like the hyenas from *The Lion King*. Now where's that "Hakuna Matata" spirit when you need it? I didn't have much time to consider the answer as the goons jumped on me like retirees on a $4.95 all-you-can-eat buffet.

They weren't pros or anything, and I quickly got the sense their hearts weren't really in it. They just wanted to scare me.

Mission accomplished.

Red Cap's buddies were wearing skullcaps pulled low (more for disguise than style, I think) and jeans pulled lower, but that was about all I saw of them as they wrestled me to the ground. The next thing I knew Red Cap had his face in mine, so close I could barely make out his features. I could feel hot breath and spittle on my skin as he spoke, his voice seething with anger. "You leave us alone! Do you hear me? Leave us alone!"

And then came the howler monkey.

Jane Cross landed on the back of one of my assailants (not Red Cap) with the precision of a four-year-old playing leapfrog. It did the trick. Not expecting someone to attack them, the boys quickly got off me and the one with the tiny, screaming broad attached to his neck tried to swipe her off as if an icky, creepy-crawly spider had just fallen on him. He twirled around and did a jig, but she wasn't giving up her hold so easily, or her yammering. Red Cap grabbed hold of Jane's shirttail and yanked as hard as he could. She gave him a donkey kick that sent him flying. By this time I was up and ready to join the fracas. Even though it was still three-to-two for the bad guys, this was not at all the scene they were expecting, and with an extra powerful buck Jane's victim dumped her unceremoniously onto the rough ground and took off into the shadows of night, quickly followed by the other two.

I rushed to Jane's side and knelt down beside her.

"You okay, Jane? Are you hurt?"

She looked up at me, wounded...in pride but not physically. "Ahhhh, shit, man, what was that about, bub? And why'n hell am I always having to run to your rescue?"

I did a double take. "Huh? Just when exactly have you ever rescued me before?"

Jane brushed off my helping hand and popped into a standing position like a Weeble that wobbles but won't fall down and busied herself flattening down her short dark hair. "Whatever," she mumbled. "So who were those guys? I can tell trouble when I see it."

"Oh really?" I said standing up and checking my own hair. "What was your first clue? The flying fists or the verbal threats?"

"Or maybe it was you screaming like a girl and covering your face so they wouldn't mess your makeup," she shot back.

I had to laugh at that. She joined in.

"Mom?" I asked.

"With Errall. She's okay. I saw you take off after that guy and guessed the only thing you were cruising for was a bruising."

"Suppose you were wrong?"

She ignored that. "So what's up, Quant? You got troubles you can't handle?"

"I can handle them just fine."

She turned serious. "Quant, you were just jumped by three guys. They weren't about to give you a chance to fight back. They meant business."

I nodded my agreement. But I'm a lone wolf. Awwwhhhhooooooooooo! I work alone. "I'm okay. I got it covered."

She eyed me with undisguised doubt. "Uh-huh. Whatever, bub."

Rescuer or not, I still wasn't fond of her calling me bub.

I tried to sleep, but my body was having none of it. Random spots of pain, compliments of my fairground wrassle, dotted my body like blips on a radar screen. Finally I could ignore it no longer and got up. Barbra and Brutus registered the disturbance with disapproving, half-lidded stares but moved nary a centimetre from their warm, soft spots at the foot of the bed. I shuffled over to the full-length mirror next to my walk-in closet and surveyed my naked body. Sure, maybe the Badstreet Boys weren't intent on doing me serious damage, but they'd done enough. The skin around my ribs, chest and thighs was beginning to show telltale bruises. I turned around and stared at the small scar, just above my buttocks, from a knife wound I'd suffered last year.* God, what kind of life was I leading? Becoming a

---

* *Tapas on the Ramblas*

detective was supposed to be a dream come true, a dream of living a carefree, I'm-my-own-boss-on-my-own-terms kind of life. I hadn't counted on the people-beating-me-up-and-stabbing-me part. Or had I? Wasn't that part and parcel of being a PI? Did something about me get off on the violence, or at least the threat of it? Was this my version of playing extreme sports or being an astronaut or riding a Ferris wheel?

With Jane's help I'd hidden what had happened from my mother, so she was peacefully asleep in the guest bedroom at the other end of the house. No need to worry her. She'd go home tomorrow none the wiser and that was for the best. I knew sleep was not an immediate option for me, so I threw on a lightweight, tartan housecoat, tiptoed into the kitchen for a glass of water and retired to my office. The dogs skipped the kitchen trek but joined up with me in the office, looking as if they'd been awakened from a thousand-year sleep, thought I was insane and were solely interested in the nearest soft spot in which to curl up in and get back to it. I slipped into the chair behind my desk and the schnauzers cuddled up on the rug in front of the unlit fireplace.

I couldn't decide between a game of Internet backgammon or checking out eBay art auctions and in the end settled on checking my email. The inbox contained a promise of increased size from Kristy

Cream, a few happy birthday greetings including one from my friend Christopher (I call him Kit) Egan in Minneapolis and a message with an attachment from Jared. It was the Pink Gopher Chorus contact list. I opened it and printed it off. Eleven names with phone numbers and addresses. Finally something to go on: my investigation was up and running once again.

Monday morning, after another barnyard-animal-heavy breakfast, my mother got in her van and headed for home and I got on the horn to Darren Kirsch. After promising to never call him again (with my fingers crossed behind my back), I forwarded him Jared's email with the Pink Gopher contact names and he agreed to run a check on them for priors with the police department. That done, and with Jared's list, Duncan's group photo, a map of Saskatoon, a to-go mug full of coffee and a litre of water in hand, I hopped into the Mazda and set out to attack the list from an entirely different angle. I call it the personal touch. Better known as: knocking on doors.

My first stop was a house on Elliot Street, where two of the choir members, presumably a couple, lived. An elderly man with a hacking cough and cigarette-stained fingers answered the door. He told me he bought the house for a steal in March when the previous residents, "two lezzies," decided to up and move to New Zealand. According to him they hadn't been back since. Scratch.

As I made my way to the next address in Pacific Heights on the west end of town (quite a distance from the Pacific Ocean or anything higher than a beaver dam), I attached the earpiece of my hands-free carphone to my ear and dialled Jared's number. There was something that didn't add up. He agreed to pick me up at my office near noon and we'd have lunch.

"I'm Jinny. *Who* are *you*?"

Jin Chau was very thin, his shoulders scrawny under a well-worn, pink B.U.M. Equipment T-shirt that just barely reached the top of a pair of waist-squeezingly tight, black jeans. He wore no socks and his narrow feet were noticeably paler than his face. At first I thought it was a no sunblock thing… until I looked closer and saw that Jin was wearing makeup: concealer to even out the ochre tones of his elongated face, mascara to make his dark eyes pop, eye shadow, a hint of lipstick and a pinch of pink on high but sallow cheeks. His once black hair (roots were showing) had been dyed red but ended up a faded, pinky-orange hue and was styled into a feathered puff that dominated the crown of his head, reminiscent of the Bay City Rollers.

"I'm Russell Quant," I told him, feeling rather unglamorous.

"Yeeeesssssss you are," he purred, placing a hand on a hip in a gesture that was meant to be sexy. I noticed his nails were long and shone with clear polish and he wore a multitude of rings. "What can I dooooooooo for yooooouuuuuuu."

"I'm a private detective and I was wondering if I could ask you a couple of questions."

The sultry come-hither look dropped off his face faster than a shrimp turns pink in boiling water. Jin stomped away from the door into his living room, which, given the size of the suite, was about two stomps away. I took it as an invitation to enter, so I closed the door behind me and followed him in.

"Is this about Stephanie?" he crowed, his feminine, singsong voice now nasally. He leaned against a large, flat-screen TV. The only other pieces of furniture in the room were a red leather couch and two armchairs, each oriented towards the television.

"No, it's not," I quickly reassured him.

"'Cause if it is, I don't want to talk about that bitch."

I took a quick gander around the place: a kitchen and smallish dining room were attached to the living room; down a short hallway were two closed doors likely for a single bedroom and a bathroom. The windows were covered with red, plastic Venetian blinds and the floor was a nondescript, beige carpet. In the kitchen the few surfaces that weren't littered with magazines and newspapers were crammed with non-perishable (I hope) foodstuffs and goodies in cellophane packages with writing on them I could not read. The eating area, by comparison, was rather tidy; sitting atop a black wooden table was an unlit candle, a plate with condiments including soy and hot chili pepper sauce and a pile of red, plastic placemats.

"It's a dump," Jim commented, his eyes following mine. "This place is my uncle's. My parents put me here. My uncle and aunt and grandparents live on the main floor, and most of the other apartments in the building belong to relatives too. Of course no one wants to live with me, not even my parents." He shot me a challenging look as if waiting for me to agree with them. "Lucky for me. I don't want to live with them either."

"It's not so bad," I said. It really wasn't.

"So this isn't about Stephanie?"

"No."

"What do you want with me then?"

I took a deep breath and soldiered on. "You're a member of the Pink Gophers?"

"Yeah. So what? I'm not even sure if I'll go back this year. They have practices every Thursday night. *Every Thursday night all winter long.* Who can show up *every* Thursday night? Excuse me, I got a life, sisters." He said it like he was Beyoncé.

I nodded, wondering if his membership in the chorus was some sort of court-ordered thing, kind of like community service. "Jin, some of the members of the choir have been having troubles over the past few months, weird, unexplained things, harassment. I was wondering if you've been experiencing anything like that?"

His eyes narrowed as he considered this. "Since when? We stopped singing after Christmas. Didn't even have a spring concert this year. Haven't seen them since. We'll start up again in September, I suppose." His words came out quick and precise, clipped at the end like he either didn't want to spend much time talking or didn't want to spend much time talking to me.

I didn't know the answer. When did the boogey-man start coming around? All the witnesses were either dead or not talking to me. "Since Christmas." It was a shot.

Jin shrugged. "Life is weird. Always weird shit happening."

"Nothing out of the ordinary?"

"My bike got trashed. Really made me mad too. A girl's gotta have wheels, you know." Jin's face took on a new look, one manufactured through sporadic practice to appear soft. Although he kept talking, I could feel his wanting eyes roam up and down my body with a message all their own. He pulled away from the TV and stepped nearer to me. I held my ground.

"And someone egged my windows." He fingered his plume of hair, ensuring every discoloured strand was perfectly erect. "I wish I could live on the top floor, or in another building—maybe something fancy like a penthouse or something. But this is all my parents will pay for." His eyes turned to flint as he told me this. "My uncle is robbing them blind as it is. He's charging them six hundred a month. Six hundred! Can you believe it? For this dump!" His arms and hands fluttered about the space around him. Can an apartment with a flat-screen television still be a dump?

"He tells them he's giving them the special family rate, and they believe him. They're stupid; so that's what they get for being so stupid and wanting me out of the house." His shoulders rose and fell with an emphatic gesture à la Bette Davis. "I don't care. I'll get out of here myself one day. I'm working part-time at my cousin's garage and part-time at my other cousin's hair salon. That's pretty good money when you don't have to pay rent. So I'm getting some extra money together. Maybe in a couple months I can move.

"Oh," he added as an afterthought, "I had to change my number once because some asshole kept calling me late at night and hanging up. Probably wanted to get some of this…" He swivelled non-existent hips.

"...but was afraid to ask for it. I don't have time for that, mister sister, no way. Except for the right man." He waited a beat, then, "But other than that, nothing really weird or out of the ordinary."

Life for Jin Chau was a very different adventure from my own. I gave him a card and left.

When I got back to PWC a minute or two after noon, Jared was already waiting for me in his Jeep Cherokee. I'd tracked down three more of the names on the choir list and, with slight personal differences, each had experienced some form of harassment but nothing severe enough to warrant more than a nuisance complaint to the police. Nine down, two to go.

Jared surprised me with an outing to the Berry Barn, a U-Pick/restaurant/craft shop/greenhouse combo located several kilometres south of the city in the middle of a twenty-seven acre plot of saskatoon berry bushes. It was a beautiful day for a drive down Valley Road with its gentle curves, mounding hills and postcard views. I regretted not taking the Mazda so that we could drive with the top down and bask in the sweet scents of Saskatchewan summer that meld so perfectly in this valley: the rich, green freshness of newly sprouted grass at the Instanturf farm; the swirling flavours of chocolate, vanilla and butter pecan from What's the Scoop ice cream shop; the flowery scent of rose bushes, honeysuckle vines and million bell petunias for sale at Floral Acres greenhouse; the hot haystack aroma of canola and flax ripening in surrounding farmer's fields; and the wafts of sweetness from the U-Pick Strawberry Ranch.

We were lucky to land the last two-seater on the restaurant's deck overlooking the South Saskatchewan river and made short work of the menu, each of us ordering cream soup served in a hollowed-out, round loaf of whole wheat bread, iced tea and, of course, a slice of saskatoon berry pie. So busy were we enjoying the ambiance and our idle chit-chat that it wasn't until we got to dessert that I finally tackled some business.

"I've been working on the Pink Gopher contact list you emailed," I said. "Thanks for that, by the way."

He smiled, and I smiled back noticing a hint of purple staining his lower lip.

"What do you call that shade of lipstick?" I asked innocently. "Plum? Lavender? Amethyst?"

"Oh man," he said with a boyish grin, wiping at his chin with a napkin. "Is it all over my face?"

"Nah," I told him. "Just on your lips. It looks good actually."

He raised an eyebrow as if uncertain whether to believe me but kept on eating.

"But there's someone missing," I told him.

"Missing? What do you mean?"

"Your list had eleven names. The photo I showed you was of twelve people."

He cocked his head to the side and narrowed his golden eyes as if concentrating. After a short bit of head counting, he said, "Nope, that's right. There were only eleven of us in the choir this year. Who's the twelfth person in the picture?"

I pulled the photo out of my pocket and laid it on the table top. "Moxie Banyon. Did her name not make the list for some reason?" I asked, expecting to hear that she'd joined the group late or simply never gave her contact information to whoever had put the list together.

"That's right," Jared said as if just remembering a forgotten fact. "Moxie was there, but she wasn't a member of the Pink Gophers."

I raised my eyebrows at that one. "But she's in the choir photo."

Jared tapped the photo. "This isn't an official choir photo or anything like that, Russell. It's just a picture we took when we were all together. If I remember it right, this was taken in December. Tanya and Moxie had just gotten together like the month before. Tanya was a member of the group; Moxie paid her own way and came along with us just so she and Tanya could be together that weekend. You know how it is with new love." He reached over the table. "Hey, you've got some berry on you." With his thumb he wiped away the offending piece of fruit from my chin.

"Came along with you? Where was this photo taken?"

Jared laughed his easy, breezy laugh. "Crazy story actually. It was December, first part of the month I think, and the Pink Gophers had been in Regina competing in a multi-provincial gay chorus competition. It was a lot of fun. There were choirs from Manitoba and Alberta and BC and even one all the way from Nova Scotia."

"So this picture was taken at some hotel in Regina?"

"Better than that. It was taken at a motel in Davidson!"

I was chewing on the last of my pie and accepted a refill of my iced tea from a grandmotherly waitress. "You've lost me."

"We were stranded on the way back to Saskatoon after the competition. It was one of those freak storms that forecasters don't know about until it arrives. We were only halfway home when we realized we were in trouble: the highway was all but invisible. We were over an hour away from Regina and over an hour away from home, so we had to stop because the roads were quickly becoming impassable; the first town we got to was Davidson. We were lucky to find even a handful of motel rooms left to share—everyone was getting off the roads—and we stayed the night. We took the photo to commemorate the experience.

The next morning we drove home."

I was chewing on this new information, my eyes idly following the course of a group of kayakers on the nearby river when I heard Jared ask, "Are you okay? You're frowning."

"This changes things a little, that's all."

"What do you mean?"

"I was beginning to suspect that if there was something suspicious about Tanya and Moxie's deaths, the answer could be found in this group tied together by one thing in common: The Pink Gophers."

"Couldn't that still be true?"

I shook my head. "Not really. Not if Moxie wasn't a member of the choir. Whatever is happening to these people isn't happening because they were members of the Pink Gophers," I explained, "it's happening because they were in this specific picture on this specific day."

Jared nodded slowly.

I glared at the seemingly innocent faces in the picture, twelve people, all with jubilant smiles on their faces, safe from a raging blizzard, having fun, not a care in the world. I knew of or had met some of them: Jared, Tanya, Moxie, Duncan, Jin. Was one of these twelve the boogeyman? If so, what was it about this day, the moments and hours leading up to and/or following the taking of this snapshot, that drove one of them to such drastic measures?

"What can you tell me about that day, Jared?

Anything strange happen? Was anyone acting out of character? Did anyone have an argument, anything like that?"

"Gosh, Russell, I'm going to have to think about that. If I had to answer now, I'd say no, nothing happened. There was a storm. We stayed the night. The next day the storm cleared and we went home. That's it."

After paying the bill and a quick stop in the greenhouse where Jared picked up a hanging basket of blue lobelia, we headed for the parking lot.

We both saw it at the same time.

A startled breath escaped Jared's lips as the flowers splattered on the ground.

Chapter 10

The sickly sweetness of fruit sitting too long in the sun assaulted our nostrils as we beheld the windshield of Jared's Jeep Cherokee, awash in the purple pulp of countless splattered saskatoon berries.

It took some doing to convince Jared to call the police and make a report about the vandalism. Sure, a bunch of squished saskatoon berries on a windshield is more of a messy inconvenience than real damage, but I wanted what happened on record, just in case this turned out to be related to the harassment being experienced by the other members of the Pink

Gopher chorus. I stopped short when Jared suggested that I, as a recent occupant of the vehicle, might just as easily have been the target.

By late afternoon we were done with the authorities, had eaten a complimentary piece of saskatoon berry cheesecake offered by the apologetic and sympathetic management of the Berry Barn, had cleaned off Jared's truck at a U-Wash and Jared had dropped me off at PWC. I stood outside the building and studied the cerulean sky growing dark at horizon's edge. The hot air from earlier in the day, which had wrung a melody of sweet scents from every flower in the city, had grown heavy and still. Something was afoot. A weighty humidity smelling of electricity hinted at the possibility of a dazzling summer storm, a sure remedy for keeping our prairie landscape from sizzling away into so many acres of dry husks of crop and desiccated chunks of earth.

Instead of zipping up to my office to check on email and phone messages as I'd planned, I jumped into the Mazda and decided my time would be better spent checking out the final two Pink Gophers before the weather got rough. But my luck had run out. Neither Kim Pelluchi nor Richie Caplan was to be found. I snooped around their homes a bit, debated breaking in, resisted. Instead I tried a few neighbours' doors, to see if anyone could tell me where to find them. After a few information-dry conversations, and with a threatening sky painting itself above the city, I gave up for the day and made for home.

Barbra and Brutus were both fidgety when I opened the door, no doubt in reaction to the low grumbles of brown-black clouds beginning their pre-storm song and dance. I let them out to run off their jitters while I battened down the hatches (a radio newscast I listened to on the way home had confirmed my suspicions and warned that the city was in for a doozy). I toured the house, checking all the windows and doors, then headed into the backyard to lower patio umbrellas and stack plastic chairs that might take flight should the winds come swooping in. In the time it took me to do this, the storm was almost upon us, announcing itself in grand fashion with whipping gusts that shook the trees in my yard as if demanding an early leaf fall. Craggy bolts of lightning stretched across the sunless sky like thorn bush branches on fire, followed by impressive bass booms of thunder.

I love a good storm, particularly if I'm safe and sound in my little nest looking out at it. There is something very cozy about witnessing the power of nature, knowing you and yours are in the protective embrace of home and not in peril, privileged enough to watch it as pure entertainment. And to that end, as I pulled a crazily swinging bird feeder off its pole, placing it for safekeeping on the ground, I called out for the dogs. I was surprised they weren't underfoot as they normally would be at a time like this, not-so-subtly trying to nose me in the direction of the house where they'd rather be—but not without me. Yet they were nowhere to be seen. I called out again, thinking they must be in some bush or other, rooting around for truffles or gold bullion or enjoying some other such hopelessly futile but nose-worthy activity. No response. Thinking they couldn't hear me over the growing howls of wind, I set out in search for them.

My yard is large, a warren of charming sitting areas and little out-of-the-way hiding spots, criss-crossed by bricked pathways that lead to and fro and ultimately dead-end at the edge of my property, which is encircled by a tall fence—a handy way to keep dogs in and other things out. Many dogs have an inbred fear of storms, and whereas Barbra had only just begun to demonstrate discomfort with them in the last couple of years, Brutus has been a bona fide chicken since day one. Brutus used to belong to Errall and her ex, Kelly, but while that relationship was ending, Brutus had come to live with us and never went back. I jokingly (sort of) blame Brutus' lack of courage during storms on the lack of male role models during his formative years. Errall then shoots back with how Brutus occasionally squats to pee ever since he's come to live with me. Which is a pretty good retort since it's true. Why *does* he do that?

I was running out of hiding spots when I noticed with considerable chagrin that the backyard gate was wide open, swinging wildly in the wind. Oh crap, I thought to myself, they've left the yard. I gave the sky an assessing look and felt the first fat plop of rain anoint my cheek. I debated going back inside for a jacket but was betting the dogs hadn't gone far, and if I ran after them now I'd have a better chance of catching them before they got disoriented in the storm. I quickly checked the gate's latch. It seemed fine. I wondered how it had come undone since keeping it shut is something I am very careful about, but there was no time to think about it then. I pushed the gate aside and stepped into the back alley.

Outside my property to the right is a dead end, so I headed left. I barely made it two steps when the wind, speeding down the tunnel of the alley like a five o'clock train, almost bowled me over. Suddenly, like a wet blanket being tossed over me, I felt the cover of rain, thoroughly drenching me from head to toe in less than five seconds. Bugger. Where the hell are those damn dogs? If I was wet, they'd be wet, and that meant wet dog smell. I began to yell out for the schnauzers, not knowing if my voice was loud enough to cut through the noise of the storm. I made it to the cross street at the end of the alley. No dogs. Where could they have gone? It is very unlike them to go off without me. Unless they were chasing something.

Or someone?

I loped down the cross avenue to the street my house is on and started toward my front yard, noticing an eerie lack of activity on the street. Everyone was inside—as anyone in their right mind should be—waiting for the storm to blow over. I fell into an uneasy jog, tossing my head right to left, seeking any signs of the animals, calling their names, getting a little pissed off and worried about them at the same time. When I reached my front yard, I noticed that gate too was swinging open. What the heck is going on here? I knew the fingers of wind were strong, but I didn't think they were dexterous enough to unhook gate latches.

I nearly jumped out of my skin and, I must admit, let out a little yip when from behind me I heard the warning honk of a car horn. I swung around, fists clenched. A car. Where did that come from? The rain was now alternating between brief showers of droplets sharp as pinpricks and flashes of rushing water that ran over me like a carwash, and yet I knew the storm-master was only playing with us: we'd seen nothing yet. I wiped the water from my brow and peered at the vehicle that had stopped a few metres away. The driver's side window slowly descended, but from the angle where I stood I still could not make out who was inside. I approached slowly, no doubt looking like the Creature from the Drowned Lagoon. As I came nearer, a particularly sharp crack of lightning shot across the sky, throwing the car and its inhabitant into a million-watt glow. That was when I first caught sight of the driver, his face in scary-movie downlighting that made the most (or worst) of the heavy dark brow that dominated his forehead. It was Dr. Uno Dubrowski.

I was startled to see him, of all people, driving down my street in the middle of a summer howler, his jagged eyebrow riding low on his face, looking not entirely unlike a geeky Frankenstein.

"Are you all right?" he called out to me, no doubt wondering what I was doing taking a shower outdoors while fully dressed.

"I'm fine," I called back, collecting my wits enough to approach the car and lean down to speak to him. "It's just my dogs. They've run off in the storm and I can't find them."

He nodded but said nothing.

"What are you doing here?" I bluntly asked.

He looked down and away then produced a plastic Sears shopping bag. "I brought you this."

Fortunately the wind and rain were taking a momentary breather, making it easier for me to continue with this…whatever it was. I accepted the bag and looked inside. Frowning, I pulled out a three-pack of Calvin Klein underwear. What in the name of Helen Keller was this about? Was Dr. D giving me a gift? Was this some kind of sexual offering… game…perversion? Did he want me to model these for him? I decided to respond with a blank look (which wasn't difficult).

"Y-y-y-you left them," he explained, seeing my confusion. "In my w-w-w-waiting room? When you came to see me the other day? I thought…I thought you'd want…I didn't want to…well, here they are." I think he followed that up with a little gas, but with all the other competing wind it was hard to tell for sure.

"These aren't mine."

"Oh." His pale face grew a rosy shade of pink. "Oh d-d-dear, d-d-dear me, that is…I'm so sorry. I apologize. You were the only man who'd been in that day. What a dilemma; I assumed they were yours."

I shook my head and handed the package back through the window. Finding a three-pack of skivvies is a dilemma? I regarded Dr. D's odd-looking face, fogged up spectacles and curling lips and concluded that, maybe, for him, it was. This was a man who didn't live easily in the real world beyond his safe, warm office. Or was there something more to all this? Had he really come all this way in a thunderstorm to deliver a pair of underwear?

"Was there something you needed to tell me, Dr. Dubrowski?"

His pupils lolled around in the pool of his

eyeglasses, and for a moment I thought he was about to say something, trying to form words but couldn't quite do it. Instead he just shrugged his shoulders and let out a wheeze.

I felt a fresh assault of rain droplets against my back and pulled myself away from the car. "I'm sorry you had to come all this way for nothing." Behind my back I could hear a high-pitched bark. An unhappy Barbra. "I really must go, Dr. Dubrowski."

"Of course. Thank y-y-you for everything." He burped.

Uh, okay. "Perhaps you'd like to come in?" I said, giving him one more chance should he have something salient to get off his chest: something about Tanya Culinare or Vicky Madison or Calvin Klein.

"No. That won't be necessary."

The car pulled away just as another flash of lightning darted across the heavens, quickly followed by a bang of thunder. I darted into my front yard. Barbra and Brutus were on their hind legs, up against the front door of the house, pawing at it furiously, demanding to be let in. Barbra was yipping her "I'm not happy, how can you leave me out here?" bark. Now I could imagine that something, perhaps a neighbourhood cat, might have lured them from the backyard and eventually they found their way to the street and recognized the front yard from our many walks, but when had they learned to work gate latches? When they saw me coming, they high-tailed it over to me, their back ends wagging with such enthusiasm they might have fallen off if they weren't connected so well. En masse, we rushed for the front door in search of safety from the building storm. Locked, of course.

I led the pack down the side of the house, through a connecting gate (this one unopened) and into the backyard. We entered the house through the deck doors into our wonderfully warm and dry kitchen. When we were all inside, I fell to my knees and we played nuzzle the snouts for a few seconds as I asked them where they'd been and why they'd taken off like that. After that, I instructed them to stay on the welcome mat while I found a towel to dry them off. Once that was done, I handed them each a bacon-flavoured, low-fat treat (if I was on a diet, they were on a diet), and together we retreated to the master bedroom and a comfy seat (the bed) from which to observe the storm.

Just as we were settled, the phone rang. I debated picking it up, trying to recall whether the danger of talking on the phone during an electrical storm was true or just an old wives' tale.

"Hello?" I answered regardless.

"Mr. Quant?"

"Yes."

"It's Warren Culinare. From Seattle." Tanya's brother. "I hope you don't mind my calling you at home. I was just wondering if you'd made any progress on my sister's death?"

"Of course I don't mind, Mr. Culinare. Call me Russell."

"Warren."

"As I told you, you or your parents should feel free to call me any time. I know you must be anxious to hear any news about Tanya." I wasn't expecting the call and had yet to think through what I should or shouldn't tell Tanya's family. For instance, do I out her to them? They certainly hadn't told me she was a lesbian, which I knew didn't necessarily mean they didn't know. And what about her relationship with Moxie Banyon and Moxie's death? Her visits with a psychotherapist? The harassment she'd been suffering? The possible tie to her involvement with the Pink Gophers? Some of the people I'd talked to thought Tanya Culinare was unstable. Her doctor thought it likely that she had ended her own life. None of this was what her family wanted to hear. But who was I to decide what they should or shouldn't hear? They were my clients; they'd asked me to dig up any information about their sister and daughter that might have contributed to her death, accidental, contemplated or otherwise. The problem was that all I had thus far were theories, nothing concrete. I didn't want to raise or dash their hopes either way.

Warren Culinare knew a minimum of what I'd

been up to. I'd gotten clearance from him to make the trip to Vancouver—it was his dime after all—but when I'd reached him he was at work and seemed too preoccupied to ask many questions. His primary concern was finding out why his sister had died, the price tag was secondary. But now he wanted more. So I spent the next few minutes filling him in. At the end there was silence. "Warren, are you still there?"

"Yes, yes, I am."

"We're having a storm here. I was worried it had somehow severed our connection." At that moment the room was thrown into unnatural brightness as dancing thunderbolts lit up the sky followed by the requisite thunder. Brutus whined and shifted his position on the bed to be closer to me. Barbra snuffled at his shanks as if to comfort him.

"You've given me a lot of information, Russell. A lot to think about. I just…I just can't believe how little I knew my own sister and what she was going through. I know you say you still don't know anything for sure, but…well, in your gut, Russell, do you think my sister killed herself or did someone do this to her?"

I knew what he wanted me to say. But I couldn't. "I'm sorry, Warren. I just don't know enough yet."

We ended the conversation with my promise to keep on working on his family's behalf and his thanks.

I scrunched down into the softness of the pillows and dog fur around me and watched the wildness outside my bedroom window, contemplating Warren Culinare's question. Had Tanya really killed herself or did someone do it for her and make it look like suicide? Some time later as the power faltered and flickered, my eyes grew heavy and my head fell next to Brutus' hind leg. I fell asleep.

When I came to, it was dark as a nightmare. I was sprawled across my bed, fully clothed, and it took me a second to remember why. The room was alive with noises, the loudest of them sounding like the clattering of a precarious stack of china about to topple. I searched for the source and found it was the windows of the bedroom being buffeted by a howling wind. A million tiny hooves clip-clopped above my head as a driving rain continued to paint the roof wet. Either the storm had raged on unabated while I'd slept or one system had passed by only to be replaced by another. According to my bedside clock—nope, the power had cut out—according to my wristwatch, which read 7:48, I'd been asleep for over two hours. That was weird. I have been known to enjoy a good nap, but rarely at that time of day, and rarely for that long. I guessed it was the combination of storm, warm doggie fur and a long hot day of detecting that had conspired to put me out at length.

Speaking of doggies, I realized they were no longer on the bed. I slowly pulled myself up on one elbow and looked around the room. My eyes widened when I saw them.

Instead of watching the storm or cuddling on the rug, Barbra and Brutus were on their haunches, facing the closed bedroom door. And now, in addition to the yowling of the outdoor tempest, I could make out a low rumbling issuing from somewhere deep within their chests. I know these dogs well. They were on alert. They'd heard something, something other than storm noises, something that was unfamiliar to them, something unsettling and frightening to them. I sat up and called their names gently. Brutus ignored me, but Barbra tilted her head in my direction, giving me a liquid look of warning, but remained at her station. I tried to concentrate my own ears. What was it they could hear?

What...? What was that? Banging? Knocking?

My heart did a backflip and my cheeks flushed with the rush you get when you're all alone and you hear something that doesn't quite fit. I hopped off the bed and approached the bedroom door. Was there someone behind it? I slowly pulled it open. The dogs rushed out and down the hallway. Oh gawd. Where were they going? Did I need a weapon? My gun was safely locked away...in a box in the garage. This wasn't due so much to thoughtlessness on my part as to a deep-rooted belief that it's best to first try to solve problems without firepower if at all possible. But I needed something. I scoured the room for a weapon, and in one corner of the room, I saw a collection of bamboo poles I'd artfully arranged there. Aw well, not exactly a baseball bat but better than nothing. I retrieved the sturdiest of the bunch and prepared to face whatever was out there.

As I made my way down the murky hallway, bamboo in hand, I cocked my head to listen for a repeat of the banging noise I thought I'd heard before and wondered where the heck those doggone dogs had gone. The power was still out, immersing my surroundings in the colour of dim. Every room I passed had the distinct possibility of being a Fun House of Horror and I tiptoed by each with escalating trepidation.

Bark! Bark!

Brutus. Another bad sign. Schnauzers aren't given to barking unless they have a very logical reason. Where was he? Front door? Back? At a window? What was he seeing? Sensing? Was someone in the house? A momentous crack of thunder sounded overhead with such force that I felt the floorboards rumble. The lights flickered on—yay—faded up—hooray—then blackened out again—crapola. A fresh deluge of rain backed by gale-force winds slammed against the house. And then came the banging.

Forsaking fear, I rushed to the front door and

threw it open. I was hit with a punch of weather, wet and sticky and stinging and hot all at the same time. That was it. Nobody there. I took a step outside onto the front landing and searched the expanse of the front yard, relentlessly dark under the cover of a turbulent night. As best I could make out, there was no one there. I debated rushing out to the street. It was invisible from my front door because of a thick growth of poplar and pine trees I encourage for the sake of privacy—something I wasn't quite so interested in at a time like this. I desperately wished I could see a neighbour, any neighbour, the comforting view of another person, a friendly face, I wished...I wished Sereena was back, next door, thirty seconds away.

I slammed the door closed and marched determinedly toward the kitchen. When I got there I stopped on a dime. Why was I being such a scaredy-cat? I remonstrated with myself; it wasn't like me. Maybe it was from being awakened too quickly from my nap. Maybe it was because I'd slept too long. Maybe it was all the weird electricity in the air from the storm. Or maybe it was because I entered the kitchen and found the dogs growling at the back doors.

I stared through the windows of the doors. Even though it was still early on a July evening that would, under regular weather conditions, remain light until well after nine p.m., outside was every shade of black and grey, and I could barely discern a mock orange bush from a clay pot in the unnatural dusk. I tried to settle the dogs—and myself—with a calming voice, but it did little good. There was something or someone out there that shouldn't be.

The banging again.

What the…! I could see nothing. I reached for the handle and slowly slid the door open. The dogs hesitated, upped their growling, then took tentative steps onto the back deck, suspicious noses sniffing at the air, as did I (growling and sniffing included).

"Who's out there?" I called.

More banging. Another step. Nothing. No one. I shuffled across the deck, my eyes dancing wildly over the little I could make out of the yard. *Nada*. Down the steps I went, onto the lawn, the wind and rain having their way with me. I noticed the dogs were not at my side. I looked back: They had decided to remain near the door, their eyes looking worried. Afraid to get wet or just a couple of mewling kitty cats?

Banging.

I moved forward, tightening my grip on the bamboo.

And there it was: the door to my garage, at the back end of the lot, wide open, the wind having a heyday tossing it back and forth like some kind of toy.

"It's just the door," I yelled back at the pooches but mostly for my own reassurance.

I dropped the bamboo and galloped down the length of the yard toward the garage. I reached for the door to rescue it from the violent embrace of the wind. A hand shot out from the darkness, grasped my arm and pulled me in.

I responded with force. As did Barbra and Brutus. Within seconds they were at my side, lunging at the dark figure that had grabbed hold of me from the unseeable depths of the garage. He had me by the left forearm, so with my right hand I reached blindly into the darkness from whence the offending hand came. I felt flesh, took hold of it and pulled with all my might. The intruder tumbled out of his hiding place and slammed into me hard, throwing us both down onto the soggy ground. The dogs were on top of us, snapping and growling but thankfully refraining from actual biting. I rolled atop the attacker and landed a punch squarely on his jaw. He pushed up with his hips and threw me off balance, at the same time reaching up to throttle me around the throat. He was yelling. It sounded like, "Bus stop hustle!" but I wasn't in the mood to ask him to repeat the message.

Somehow we struggled to our feet, each of us trying to get good purchase on the other guy, upset schnauzers nipping at our calves.

"Stop it, Russell, stop it!"

This time I heard him, the familiarity of my name echoing in my ears. This guy knew me. Bunching up my arm muscles, I heaved against him and shoved him against the side of the garage. As he fell back he voluntarily let go of my neck.

Yup. He knew me. I knew him.

Even in the dark with rivulets of rain threatening to wash away his chiselled features, I could tell it was Doug Poitras. Or rather, the fake Doug Poitras.

"Who the hell are you?" I screamed at him, not bothering to restrain Barbra and Brutus, who, along with me, had formed a menacing semi-circle around the man. "And don't bother lying. I know you're not Doug Poitras."

"Russell, my name is Alex Canyon," he said, careful to make no move indicating a planned getaway attempt. He'd obviously dealt with pissed-off schnauzers before.

I shook my head with disgust. "What do you want with me?"

"I can't answer that in a sentence," he told me after allowing another roll of thunder to die away. "But if you give me a chance…Russell, you have to trust me."

I guffawed at that one. "Oh yeah, sure, I'm a real sucker for trusting guys who lie to me, pretend to be someone they're not, break into my garage and who knows what else."

"I didn't break in, I just…well, I was just trying

− 233 −

to keep out of the storm until…well… Can we go inside?"

We stared at each other for several seconds. Me because I was trying to see something in his face, something to allow me to accurately assess the level of danger he represented, and he because it was either look at me or down the snouts of two rather unhappy schnauzers who were anxious to protect their master.

"Only if you promise to tell the truth. No song and dance." It was a stupid request, I suppose. If he was a liar, there was nothing I could do about it. But it couldn't hurt to ask, and really, what else was I suppose to do with him? Leave him in my garage?

Alex Canyon trotted after me and the dogs into the house.

"Hold on," I said once we were inside and out of the inclement weather conditions. "Power's out and we're soaking. I'll get some candles and towels."

When I returned to the kitchen, Alex had doffed his shirt and was using a tea towel to dry his hair. The dogs were at his feet, guarding (or maybe ogling) the grade A slab of beefcake. With opposable thumbs, they'd have taken photos.

He looked up at me and held forth the now sodden tea towel. "Sorry," he said. "I was dripping on the floor and…"

I nodded and wordlessly tossed him a bath towel. I lit a trio of tapers I'd found under the bar in the living room and, after setting them into holders, took off my own shirt. Sure, he was Adonis material, and maybe I wasn't thrilled about being in my mid-thirties, but I'm still no Peewee Herman. Besides, this wasn't a competition. We were wet and getting chilled. Right?

I left one of the candles on the kitchen island, kept one for myself and handed the last one to Alex Canyon. "Why'n't you take that and follow me."

If this were a tale of gothic romance, I'd have led him directly into my boudoir, loosened his flowing hair from its ponytail bondage and pulled off his pantaloons with my bare teeth. But this was current day Saskatchewan and, as far as I knew, neither of us was named Fabio, so instead I took him into the living room and proceeded to set up logs in the fireplace. I offered him a seat, but no drink, and, once the fire was blazing, faced him squarely in the eye.

"So?" I said. "Spill it, Alex Canyon."

"First I want to apologize for impersonating Doug Poitras the other night, for lying to you."

"Why did you?"

"I wasn't expecting to speak with you that soon. I wasn't ready."

Ready? "Ready for what? Who are you? And why have you been following me? Why did you set those goons on me at the Ex?" I was going for broke and planned to blame him for everything I could think of that had gone wrong in the last few days, including the fact that my wonderpants were tight at the waist.

"I have been following you," he admitted with a straight face. "I followed you to Moose Jaw. I've been watching your office and home. But I had nothing to do with any goons at...what did you call it...the Ex?"

I gave him a doubting look. "You promised you wouldn't lie. Are you telling me you weren't watching me at the fairgrounds? You weren't the one who ordered those assholes to attack me?"

He shook his head. "Russell, I did not order anyone to beat you up." He said it in a way that made me think I could either choose to believe him or not, it was no hair off his chest. There was something about his manner, the tone of his voice, which told me he wasn't lying. But if it wasn't Alex Canyon behind the attack, then who?

"I don't know who attacked you, and I'm sorry about that, but I had nothing to do with it," he repeated.

"Oh yeah," I said, pretending I wasn't exactly convinced. "So you're telling me you'd never do such a thing."

For a second he hesitated, no doubt judging how honest his reply should be. "I didn't say that," he said. "I just didn't do it this particular time."

Ahhhh, a tough guy. Well, so am I. "Are you

going to tell me what this is all about, or are we just wasting our time here? If so, I'll give you your shirt and you can buzz off." I was hoping he'd stay. And keep his shirt off.

The next words out of his mouth threw me into a spin.

"Russell," he began carefully. "I know you've been searching for Sereena Orion Smith. I'm here to stop you."

Chapter 11

I was desperately trying to make enough saliva in my mouth to swallow. The words Alex Canyon was saying to me made no sense. How could this man, this stranger, know about my search for Sereena and now be prepared to stop me?

Why? Why would he want me to stop?

Who was he really?

How would he know about any of this?

Where was she? He had to know where she was if he was so desperate to keep her hidden…or imprisoned?

Little did Mr. Canyon know that I had already begun to conclude for myself that the search for my missing friend was futile. Over the past months I'd tried everything, talked to everyone, travelled everywhere I thought she might be, all to no avail: plenty of expense and time and heartache for nothing. She was gone. Maybe forever. I believed, somewhere in my soul, that her disappearance wasn't foul play but rather that Sereena had masterfully orchestrated her own disappearance. Like a ghost. Poof. Gone. She just didn't want to be here anymore.

But none of that made it any easier. I missed my friend. I worried about her…when I wasn't pissed off that she'd left without so much as a goodbye wave. All that remained of her was that blasted For Sale sign on her lawn. Having drinks and witty repartee with a cardboard sign isn't nearly as pleasant. Even so, the time was coming when I knew I'd have to give it all up. I had to let her go. I had to believe she would come back when she was ready—if ever.

But now…this changed everything.

"Where is she?" I hammered him with a steely gaze and hard words. "Tell me."

"No," he said simply.

I stood up from where I'd been crouching by the fireplace and glared down at him. "So then why are you here? Why have you been watching me?"

He wasn't much for being stared down at, so up he came, our noses inches apart. "I wanted to get an idea of what you were up to."

"What are you talking about? Why? You're not telling me anything, Mr. Canyon."

"Alex."

"You're not telling me anything, Aaaaaaalex." The bitchy me.

He grinned but said nothing more.

Another faceoff. Finally I stiffened my chin, curled my lip and told him, "I won't do it. I won't stop looking for her." So there!

He looked at the flickering fire as it grasped at charred logs with its hungry fingers, then back at me. There was a burning glint in his eye but nary a smile as he licked his lips. "Something about you, that first night we met...well, I didn't think you would."

"So now what?" I goaded. "Come on, you gonna pull a gun? Silence me? Do it now, buddy, just try it." Apparently a little nap really puts the piss and vinegar in me.

Instead of any of my suggestions, Alex Canyon calmly said, "I'll take my shirt back now."

The power was still out, so I hadn't tossed the sopping shirt into the dryer, and I hadn't thought of hanging it up in front of the fire. "It'll still be wet," I told him. What a putz I am sometimes. Like that was going to stop him from leaving and encourage him to tell all.

He turned heel and headed for the kitchen. The

dogs looked up from where they'd taken root by the fire, close but not as close as they get to the gas fireplace in my office, which burns even hotter, but without the risk of flying sparks that might singe their precious fur coats. With looks that urged us to reconsider, they stayed put until I too headed off.

By the time I arrived in the kitchen, Alex had buttoned up the front of his shirt and was tucking it into the waistband of his jeans.

"Thanks for the towel," he said, brushing his fingers through wavy hair, eyeing me with those Kahlua eyes.

I was at a loss for words. I couldn't get a grasp on this guy's game.

I watched as he reached behind him. Was this it? Was he pulling out a weapon? I hadn't seen one in his back pocket and I certainly had checked him out, stem to stern. It wasn't. It was an envelope. He handed it to me. It felt damp. The front was blank, without address or any other marking.

"What's this?" I asked.

"Just be careful, Mr. Quant," he told me. "Be very careful."

Alex Canyon left and the rain dissipated, leaving behind a scent of heaven and slivers of sun poking through the spaces where clouds were breaking up. It had gone from night to day, and, in an hour or so, it would be night again. I fingered the envelope he'd given me and slowly peeled back the flap. Inside was a letter of instructions. At the end, Alex had handwritten a request: "Trust Me" followed by his name. I dialled Errall's number. I'd need someone to look after Barbra and Brutus.

It was very early on a late July Tuesday morning when I stepped out of my life and into a dream, a dream that would last for the next thirty-six hours. I would leave behind Saskatoon, my current case and, in some ways, all that I knew to be sane and real. There was no way I could have known as I began that day how much my world would be shaken.

The sun in Saskatchewan was forecast to rise at 6:01 that morning, and as I turned off Thayer Avenue onto Wayne Marks Lane, it was still two hours off. Between two pond-size puddles compliments of the previous night's rain, I found a parking spot near Hangar 10. The West Wind Aviation Aerocentre is within visual distance of Saskatoon's commercial airport but wholly removed from the main terminal. I locked the Mazda and headed inside. Surprisingly someone was waiting for me, processed me through, and within minutes I was walking down a brightly lit tarmac gleaming with early morning dampness toward a Cessna Citation 560 Ultra, engines running.

I was almost upon it when I saw a figure standing beside the plane's right wing. A jolt ran through my chest and I stopped in mid-stride.

I'd been hoodwinked.

This wasn't about Sereena at all. I had stupidly allowed myself to fall into a trap, with the promise of Sereena as bait, for there, next to the Cessna, was Pepé le Bleu, all six-foot-five of her, skin gleaming black and that crazy stripe of blue blazing atop her head, like some punk rooster. She of the golden nose ring and Mr. "Trust Me," Alex Canyon, were obviously in cahoots. She'd tailed me on Broadway Avenue and to Vancouver, Alex everywhere else. And now they had me.

Or did they? I swivelled my head right to left and debated my chances for a clean getaway on the deserted tarmac. They weren't good. Flights out of the main airport hadn't begun for the day, so the chances of getting someone's attention over there wasn't likely and, as far as I knew, everyone in Hangar 10 was in on this with Alex and his pet, Godzilla. Still, I wasn't about to stand there and be abducted or threatened or killed or maimed or whatever they had in mind for me, so I was preparing to bolt when it spoke: "Get on the plane." Her voice was as deep and cold as a coal mine and sounded kind of Arnold Schwarzenegger-ish.

"I'm not going anywhere with you," I told the Incredible She-Hulk. "I agreed to meet Alex Canyon here. Alex, not you. I'm not going anywhere in that plane and certainly not with you." I think I made my intentions clear.

A new voice: "Russell." It was Alex. He appeared from nowhere and was now standing next to the gleaming white, unmarked jet. He was wearing a lightweight, knee-length jacket to protect himself from the morning chill and a wind that whipped locks of dark hair over his forehead.

I hesitated, decided to hell with it and moved forward slowly, stopping in front of him. We didn't shake hands. "I can only assume you've decided to whisk me away to a deserted island where we'll romp naked on the beach, after which you'll profess your love for me," I said, my tone more serious than the words.

His eyes were dark slits as they searched mine. For a fleeting second there was some kind of connection, then it was gone. Without a word, his thick jaw moved up and over, indicating the steps and that I should use them. The strong silent type, I guess. Last night he'd instructed me to trust him. It was now or never. But how could I? I glared at the big woman next to him.

"Grette Gauntlus," he said by way of introduction. "She's with me."

In for a penny…I did as instructed and mounted the steps, bowing my head as I entered the cabin of the eight-passenger jet. The lighting was dim, but I could see enough to tell this wasn't just an everyday corporate junket type of aircraft. It had leather seats that looked like sofas, a fully stocked bar and entertainment centre, plush carpet and obviously expensive artwork fastened to the rounded walls. I was betting I was in for more than pretzels and plastic utensils.

At first I thought the cabin of the plane was empty...but then...I saw a sole inhabitant, someone sitting with their back to me. My heart began an erratic pitter-patter. Sereena. Perhaps this aircraft wasn't going anywhere at all. Maybe this happened to be the most convenient place and time for a meeting with my long-elusive neighbour. Maybe...

I inched down the aisle, my eyes never wavering from the back of the chair. I stopped less than a metre behind it and waited. I wasn't sure if I was ready to face this.

"Please," the voice said, "won't you join me?"

When I sat in the seat opposite my host, I studied his unfamiliar face. He was dark, with liquid black eyes, jet-black hair—dyed maybe, and beginning to recede—and beautifully shaped, thick lips. The skin beneath his jaw and over his eyes was beginning to loosen; he was nearing seventy, and a strikingly handsome man.

"My name is Maheesh Ganesh," he told me in his polished Indian accent. "Will you have some coffee? Or perhaps juice of some sort?" But then he must have thought better of it. "But maybe not yet. We've a long way to go and you must return home the sooner the better, yes?"

I nodded. I guess I'm taking a jet plane ride this morning after all, I said to myself, still debating whether I should make a run for it.

"Of course then." He picked up a small portable device that looked like a miniature cellphone and spoke into it. I understood none of the words but imagined he told a pilot to get us underway. "You'll like to fasten your seat belt device now, yes?"

In surprisingly short order, the jet was hurtling down a runway and was off into the silky dark sky. I wasn't even certain which direction we were flying in or whether Grette Gauntlus and Alex Canyon had boarded the plane or stayed on the ground.

A button on a console lit up with a musical bing, and Maheesh Ganesh told me it was safe for us to release our seat belts, which we both did.

"And now, Mr. Quant? Some coffee? Something else for you?"

I accepted coffee, which he poured from a handy carafe he plucked from where it had been fastened in a nearby alcove made just for that purpose. As we sat across from one another, the Cessna zipping through the sky, we regarded each other as friendly strangers. Strangers about to get to know one another a whole lot better.

"Who are you?" I asked the man.

He laughed. "You are direct. I like this."

I nodded but said nothing. Was he stalling?

"As I've already said to you, my name is Maheesh Ganesh, and I am the very close friend of Candace Batten."

I gave him a blank look. I'd never heard of the woman.

"And Darlene Krimpky." His heavy left eyebrow rose high on his forehead as he added the last name, "And Sereena Orion Smith."

"Obviously you know that I know Sereena. But who are these other women?"

"They are all the same woman," he told me. "You see, Darlene Krimpky sometime in her early teens became Candace Clark...or, should I say Candace Clark Doerkson Chapell Ashbourne Batten...who eventually became the woman you know as Sereena Orion Smith."

For a brief second I wanted to tell the man that he was a crazed maniac and demand that the plane be turned around and I be returned to Saskatoon. But only for a brief second, a brief second during which I wanted to hold onto Sereena's mystery. I knew that once I had the truth there was no turning back. My jaw tightened and I winced as I waited to hear. After all these years, after all this time knowing only parts of this woman, I was about to have the whole of Sereena's life revealed to me. Or, at least, what this man—whoever he was—knew of it. I knew it was possible that he knew little more than I did, or that he was preparing to lie to me, but something told me that this was not the case.

"Where are we going?" I asked, wanting even for a few seconds more to halt the inevitable. "Are we going to see Sereena?"

"Can you wait to learn that if I ask you to?" the man said in his strange way.

Jeepers. I nodded. I sipped the good coffee. It was time. "Tell me."

And so it began.

"Your friend, the woman you know as Sereena, was born Darlene Krimpky. She was raised in a small village, I believe not far from where I just met with you. A place called Smuts." I knew it. It was not even a village, maybe not even a hamlet, but a one-cow dust bowl about an hour's drive out of Saskatoon. "She was the only child of dirt poor parents who subsisted on the kindness of others— that and cigarettes and alcohol. They died as people of that sort do, much too young, and within a year of each other. Darlene was thirteen at the time. She ran from this Smuts and, sadly, there was no one to run after her. Not even the police bothered to search for her.

"She ended up in California where the weather was warm and a beautiful child—especially a smart one—had options. Like any young girl, she dreamed of money and men and fame and fortune, but, being wise, she intended on earning them on her terms and somehow escaped the trap that many runaways fall into. She watched as her peers became prostitutes and drug addicts and alcoholics in order to dull the pain of their dingy lives. She herself knew there was no such thing as...well, as free lunch. She wanted to pay for her lunch...and leave a big tip as well.

"The morality of a beautiful and desirable young girl faces many challenges, and over the years some she won, some she did not. In order to achieve her goals, she learned to lie. She lied about everything—where she was from, what her skills were, how old she was—in order to get jobs that did not involve giving away sex when she did not wish to and allowed her to pay for rent, food and clothing. Bad jobs led to sad jobs, which led to better jobs and eventually jobs that paid well enough to allow her time to go to school at night and complete her education."

"What were these jobs?" I asked.

"Mostly modelling. A fourteen-year-old pretending to be an eighteen-year-old who looked like a thirteen-year-old proved to be very popular, especially with the sorts of men and magazines that don't bother to check personal statistics too closely. Eventually she became an actress in commercials. She also enrolled herself in every beauty pageant she qualified for. If they wanted her to be a Southern belle, that's what she became. If they wanted her to be an innocent, that's what she became. You understand, yes?"

I did.

"Of course, not being a U.S. citizen—that being the one thing she could not easily fake—Darlene Krimpky, now Candace Clark, could not enter most of the very big, important pageants, but, being a dazzling beauty, she won many low-grade affairs and thus captured the attention of many," he paused, "interesting people."

"What sort of interesting people?"

"People who could further her lofty goals and ambitions. I'm sure many of these, mostly men at first, assumed they were taking advantage of her, but the opposite was more often true.

"By the time Candace turned twenty, she was a minor player in a 'C' list, jet-set crowd that consisted of low-level royals, high-level studio executives, also-ran movie actors and musicians, celebrities-for-hire and the almost-rich-enoughs who could afford to rent the good life but not purchase it. In such a group of people, Mr. Quant, there are never enough stars to go around, and a woman like Candace, a woman with uncommon grace, sharp wit and smouldering sexuality, is always a fine alternative and very welcome."

I turned my head away from Maheesh and stared out at the strange, steel-blue sky outside my window.

I tried to picture Sereena doing everything he was describing and found it easy to do. Maheesh must have recognized my need for reflection and remained quiet. After a moment I looked at him and asked him to continue.

"For the next decade, Candace met with greater and greater success in furthering her plan: escaping the world of Darlene Krimpky and the cold and dirty streets of Smuts. And, I do not think she would deny it, she had a considerably good time doing so. With every diamond-encrusted brooch she was given, with every king and sultan she bedded, with every couture gown or chinchilla coat she draped across her shoulders, with every wealthy husband, she strove for that alluring prize which, frustratingly, always seemed to move just out of her reach. That place, that thing, that finish line…whatever it was… I don't think she ever truly knew what it was… eluded her."

Diamonds, sultans, chinchilla…gawd, Sereena *is* the woman from that song.

"By thirty-five she'd made her way through many preposterously rich men and divorced two of them with little more than a blink of her eye. She left them both with many fabulous memories and much less money, property and jewels than they had before they met her. But, really, she'd taken little of *real* value from them. She began to search for something more, although, once again, I don't know if she knew what it was until she found it.

"Her third husband was Arthur Ashbourne. He was fifteen years her senior. Of course he was very rich, travelled in the highest social circles, but that meant little to her. By this point Candace had been on every yacht, seen every tropical island, breakfasted in Paris, lunched in Madrid, supped in Kiev, all that nonsense. She had titles and prestige and famous friends and homes she never visited. But it was what she didn't have that she found with Arthur, a very kind and wise man. Quite simply, Mr. Quant, she found love."

I smiled like an idiot, as if I were watching a Sunday afternoon Danielle Steel movie of the week. Sereena was played by Lindsay Wagner or Jacqueline Bisset or Jaclyn Smith, and Arthur Ashbourne was Efrem Zimbalist Jr. or Perry King. I'm a sap for happy endings. But something told me Maheesh wasn't done with me yet. I wanted him to stop right there. I wanted to have this happy-at-last ghost of Sereena's past live on in this fairytale setting Maheesh had described. For a little while, I got my wish, for about then a stewardess, who had been hidden until then, approached us and asked what we'd like for breakfast. Maheesh had kippers and scrambled eggs and tea with milk. Very British, I thought. I opted for toast, unbuttered, and coffee with skim milk.

Over our meal, Maheesh kept the conversation

light, veering off the subject of Sereena or Candace or Darlene or whatever her name really was, preferring instead to ask me about myself. Our conversation was as mundane as talk between two strangers on a jet heading for who knows where can be. I was grateful for the respite, for as I ate, my mind was busy enough. Part of me wanted to dash away, escape this crazy man and his hefty henchmen who'd abducted me in the middle of the night (sort of) and put me on a flight to nowhere, filling me with incredible tales that might not be true.

I was also worried about my case. I had made a promise to the family of Tanya Culinare that I would find out why she died. I was worried about Jared and how he might be tied up in what was turning out to be a complicated mess. Was he in danger from this boogeyman character that Tanya and everyone around her had come to fear? Was I in danger? Was Maheesh Ganesh my boogeyman and I hadn't even recognized him? Who was he really? Why had he come to get me? That's what I asked him next as we sipped on the remains of our beverages.

In response to my question, Maheesh moved to adjust his body in his seat, grimacing with the effort, a sign that this was not a young man. We paused through a jag of turbulence then continued our talk. "After a great deal of time and effort, Candace and Arthur conceived a much wanted child," he told me. "This was not the first pregnancy for Candace, and it was not easy for her. There were risks. She was in her late thirties by this time. She lost that baby."

I pulled in a breath and felt sad for my friend.

"Another pregnancy the following year went to full term."

Hope.

"Tragically, the child was stillborn."

Dashed.

"Arthur…" Maheesh hesitated and shifted his eyes to the ice blue outside. Finally he turned back to me. "You'll excuse me. This next thing is difficult to speak of.

"Only days after the death of the child, Arthur was felled by a massive stroke and died in Candace's arms. Her own body and mind were still traumatized by the loss of their child." More silence, then, "A short time later, Candace attempted to take her own life."

I was stunned. Not only by Sereena's sad story but also by the harsh reality that life had once conspired to steal her away. I would never have known her if she had been successful in her suicide attempt. I wanted to ask how it all happened, who saved her, but decided not to. This was Maheesh's story to tell in his own way.

"It took Candace years to pull herself together. Many tried to be good friends to her, including myself, but, I'm afraid, we fell painfully short. She wallowed in depression for some time, but her spirit was too strong to sustain that. She eventually turned to overindulgence once more and with greater verve than before. Drugs, alcohol, frivolity, all masks for her pain." He shook his head then, pursing his lips in great consternation, and, if it was possible, his dark eyes turned even more sorrowful. "For the next part, I blame myself. And for this I am ashamed."

I accepted more coffee from the stewardess and kept my silence.

"I thought it would be good for her, you see. I thought she needed a new place, new things, new people, new air to breath, something to pull her from the path of destruction I believed her to be on. You see, I was returning to India for several months, to attend to family business, and asked...or rather, cajoled...Candace to join me. Whether she would remain for all or part of the trip didn't matter, and I told her she could decide once she got there."

In the back of my suspicious detective's mind I wondered if this was Maheesh's romantic play for the lonely, lovely, wealthy widow, but I kept the uncharitable thought to myself. For now.

"And that was when I made a most dreadful mistake. I introduced her to one of my colleagues, Akhilesh Batten. He came from a traditional but well-to-do family. He was well-educated in America. His name, Akhilesh, means Lord of the Universe. Candace liked this. And so, in time, she and Akkie were married."

Oh dear.

"Candace accepted her new life with great aplomb and responsibility. She'd had lives in New York and Munich and Rome, and now it was time for her Indian life. Another grand adventure in her life story. To make matters even better, Candace immediately became pregnant and gave birth to a healthy daughter."

I smiled. Oh my goodness. My Sereena is a mother.

"They named the girl Sangita, which means music. Candace's life was full of new joys. Her husband was attentive and lavish with gifts. He was also…a child molester."

Would this never stop? My heart fell to the soles of my feet as I steeled myself for what was coming next, and Maheesh, anxious to be rid of this horrible tale as fast as possible, thankfully made short work of it.

"We believe Akhilesh began molesting his daughter at less than one year old. He was clever in hiding his deeds, but Candace was too good a mother not to notice the changes in her daughter. She began to keep a very close eye on her child, becoming upset if Sangita and Akkie were left alone together for too long. Candace just knew something was not right. She had no proof, but something about how the child had changed gnawed at her and told her that all was not as it should be.

"As she became more suspicious, Akhilesh began to tell people, his family, his friends, me, that he feared Candace was becoming mentally unstable and that *he* doubted *her* ability to care for Sangita. There was a tension growing between them that all of us could feel. But we had no idea what was really happening. Candace did her best, but ultimately she failed. One night…" He stopped with a choke in his throat. "In an attempt at intercourse with the child, Akkie killed…our dear, sweet baby…our Sangita died." Maheesh stood up then, for the first time since I'd laid eyes on him. "It was the most ghastly, ghastly thing." His tortured voice sounded like the ripping of paper. "I know. I was a guest in their home that night."

I looked up at the older man and saw the horror etched clearly on his face, even so many years after the event. "And Sereena?" I asked softly. "What about her? Was she there too?"

"Oh yes," Maheesh whispered. "She murdered Akhilesh Batten."

After the stunning revelation that Sereena, *aka* Candace, had killed the husband who'd molested and murdered their daughter, Maheesh begged to be excused and stumbled off to the washroom. I was glad of it, for I had no idea how to react to the information. For a moment I thought I might give way to hysteria. Was this some sort of sick, hallucinogenic dream I was in? What the hell was going on? How did I get on this plane? Where were we going?

When Maheesh returned, he sat in a different seat, away from me, saying he needed some time alone and that we would talk more later. I used the time to mull over the story Maheesh had told me, formulating a million questions as I did. It didn't seem like much time had passed when I felt the Citation point down and begin its descent into... well, I still didn't know where we were. All I could be certain of, because of my clever knowledge of where the sun rises and sets, was that we'd gone north and maybe a little west.

Once we were on the ground, the jet taxied to a stop and I saw a sign welcoming us to Yellowknife. We were in the Northwest Territories! Good God, I thought to myself, what had I gotten myself into? But I didn't have much time to dwell on that. After a short stop, the plane rushed back into the sky, heading northeast this time.

We arrived at our final destination, a private landing strip somewhere on Somerset Island, Nunavut, at just after two p.m. We were in the frickin' Arctic! If I spit I could probably hit the North Pole. During that last twenty minutes of the flight, the pilot, more talkative the farther into no man's land we got, pointed out that we were flying across the legendary Northwest Passage. We flew low enough so that when I glanced out of my window I could clearly see seals and whales in their home environment. The light here was different somehow. Maybe all the ice and water we were flying over grabbed hold of the sun's beams and supercharged them, filling them with an almost gem-like glow. Stunning. And yet I knew I wasn't feeling the exuberant joy I usually experience when faced with such natural splendour. My mind and heart were heavy with the story I had heard on the trip and with deep concern for Sereena.

Like many others, I know precious little about the Arctic. I know the Arctic Circle is invisible and marks the southern limit of the area where the sun doesn't rise on the winter solstice or set on the summer solstice. The pilot told me the Arctic includes the Arctic Ocean, thousands of islands and the northern parts of Europe, Asia and North America including regions of Alaska, Canada, Greenland, Iceland, Scandinavia, Siberia and Russia's Far East. Millions of acres of wilderness forest are set aside for parks, military reserves and wildlife refuges.

Even though it was late July, part of me still expected to deplane into a winter tundra environment with growling polar bears and tusky walruses in the not too far off distance. Instead it was a beautiful day, the temperature in the comfortable teens, with dazzling sun reflecting brightly off the water we'd just crossed. The Hummer that awaited us tried hard to look rough and tough in a rough and tough environment with roll bars and some dirt and dust caked to its underbelly, but it was still a Hummer. I was surprised to find Alex Canyon sitting behind the wheel when Maheesh and I climbed into the back seat. He said nothing and started driving. No sign of Grette the Giant—which was fine with me.

We didn't have far to go. Obviously the airstrip had been built for convenience by whoever owned the property we were on. And in this case convenience meant: build me a place to land my plane that's not too far away from my humongous, cedar lodge getaway perched attractively over an Arctic river valley. I've always thought of getaway homes as ironic; in general, the people who can afford them really have very little to get away from.

The Hummer did its best to give us a luxuriously bumpy ride and in short order delivered us to the lodge, where it parked under a portico at the front entrance. Maheesh led me out, and Alex stayed in the vehicle. We made it up three steps onto the front porch and then entered the rustic-by-design maw of the house. I was, shamelessly, impressed. I'm not much of a cabin/lake person, but if I were, this would be the ultimate.

The comfort and luxury of the place enveloped me like a blanket as soon as I entered. There were oversized fireplaces, intricate tapestries flowing down high walls, works of art that were "country" but not mawkishly so, thick carpets, dark, polished woods and tall, wide windows that took advantage of every possible scenic view surrounding the place, inviting nature in and making it part of the décor. Somehow it worked, and if I hadn't known better, I would have believed this house had grown from a seed right alongside the indigenous berry bushes and shrubs and had blossomed into this perfection. Well, a seed propagated by one or two of the fellas from *Queer Eye for the Straight Guy*.

"There is someone who would very much like to see you," Maheesh said, once we were fully inside and my eyes had returned to their normal size.

At the sound of his words my pulse began to thread wildly; I could feel it at my wrist and neck like a wee racehorse under my skin.

Sereena.

I was going to see Sereena. I was finally going to find out what the hell was really going on. For, despite Maheesh's story on the flight over here, I still had no idea why she'd suddenly disappeared.

Maheesh patted me lightly on the back and regarded me with an uncomplicated kindness in his eyes. "Please follow me?"

With my host leading, we walked through a cavernous sitting room that faced a massive outdoor wooden deck over water. He opened one of the glass doors, politely allowing me to go before him.

And that was when the world stopped making sense.

There was someone waiting for me.

Someone with a face that stopped my heart cold.

Chapter 12

He looked pretty good.

For a dead guy.

I've heard people talk about having their mind play tricks on them. I've never figured that one out, never quite believed it...except if drugs were involved. But unless Maheesh Ganesh slipped something into my coffee on the plane, I wasn't under the influence of anything stronger than pure shock and disbelief. The man standing in front of me had died six years ago in a skiing accident. My mother's brother, my friend Anthony's ex-lover, my uncle:

Lawrence Wistonchuk. Yet there he was, older certainly, thinner than I remembered, holding out two shaking hands towards me, a tremulous smile on his face.

"My God," were the first words from his lips. "How I've wished for this moment."

Although the feeling was mutual, I was far from being able to express it in words.

When I first came to the big city from small town Saskatchewan to attend university, my mother's brother, Lawrence, took me under his mighty wing. It was not, however, through any sense of duty or responsibility for his sister's kid, for in actuality I hardly knew him before then. He and my mother did not get along. Lawrence helped me out because, as I later learned, he saw in me a younger version of himself. I don't know how accurate he was, but I've always been honoured he thought so.

Lawrence and Anthony, couple extraordinaire, hosted these extravagant dinners and parties, populated with bizarre and interesting people, and I was always invited. My uncle Lawrence defined what it meant to be larger than life. He was attractive, well-mannered, well-educated and well-heeled. I wanted to be him. When he travelled, which was often, I was given the keys to the house, the cars and the impossibly bountiful lifestyle that went with them. It was almost too much for a nineteen-year-old farm-boy. I'll never know why, but he trusted me implicitly with all of it.

Tragically, Lawrence did not return from his last trip. He was fifty-one at the time.

In his will, Uncle Lawrence left me a sum of money with one simple instruction: Buy a Dream. I was a Saskatoon police constable when Lawrence died. I wasn't completely unhappy with my job, but I wasn't thrilled with it either. I liked the work, but I just wasn't cut out to wear a uniform or drive a car with a bubble. I knew becoming a private detective in a small Canadian city was a risk, career-wise and financially, but in all other ways it promised freedom. It was the money from Lawrence that allowed me to quit my steady police job, pay off the mortgage on my house and survive the first months of my new life. As instructed, I had bought a dream.

And now, in this unknown land near the top of the world, standing before the ghost of my uncle, feeling alone, bewildered…frankly, freaked out…I felt as if I was living in a dream. And I couldn't decide if it was a good one or a bad one.

"Russell," his soft voice reached out for me through the haze of my confusion. "I know this is a surprise. I'm hoping a pleasant one. Please, won't you come closer?"

I realized I hadn't moved a centimetre since first setting eyes on my uncle's face. I remained cemented to the floor just outside the doors that led onto the mighty deck that hung over a bay of water fed by a trickling river. I was blind to the extravagance of nature laid out before us. It was like nothing I'd ever seen before, but I couldn't see it now. I turned my pale face to the sky, gulped at the fresh air and begged for the sun's warm fingers to massage the blood back into it.

"Perhaps a walk?" the man suggested, taking a step closer.

I looked at him. My uncle. Uncle Lawrence. The last time I'd seen him I'd dropped him off at the Saskatoon airport and was more interested in getting back to the shiny new Jag he was letting me drive in his absence than in long goodbyes. More and more over the previous several years he'd been going off on his "jaunts"—as he called them—slyly intimating he was off to rendezvous with another in a long list of mystery lovers he never identified. He and Anthony had broken off their relationship years before, but I suspected my uncle had never quite found the same intensity with a partner again and used his jaunts as the remedy...or perhaps ointment for an unhealed wound. That particular trip he was off to ski some impossibly glamorous mountain in some impossibly glamorous European principality with impossibly glamorous friends and promised to return in several weeks. But he never did. He'd been buried in an avalanche and we never saw him again.

The man before me now certainly resembled that person. He was, what?...fifty seven now...yet he looked older, thin, gaunt. Uncle Lawrence had been a robust man with a healthy appetite for everything life had to offer; he had dark, wild hair that sprung from his head like curly tentacles and eyes full of mischief that sparkled when he laughed his uproarious laugh. But now his shoulders were narrower, his chest deflated, his hair grey and thinning, and his eyes had dimmed to that of a normal, mortal man. And God how I still loved him.

I fell into my uncle's arms and he into mine and we remained that way for many minutes, no words required. I am not a man given easily to tears, but if they didn't fall they certainly welled up in great pools about my eyes. I could feel his fingers burrow into the muscle of my back and the bristle of his cheek against my own. We'd been through so much together; he'd taught me so many great things, even in death. I could not believe my grand fortune of having him back. Even if this did turn out to be a dream, it was, I now knew, a damn good one.

Finally we pulled away from one another and took another minute to hold each other at arm's length, studying the other's features.

"Come," he eventually said. "I've a snack and water packed up for us. Let's take a hike."

I had no idea what time it was, and I'd never be able to tell by the sun, which seemed happily nestled in the sky for the duration of the summer. It looked early, but was likely late afternoon. Yet as big a day as it had already been, I was nowhere near ready for a rest and gladly accepted my uncle's invitation. He gathered up a backpack, threw a light sweater over his shoulders and offered me one, and off we went, down a steep set of steps off the deck to ground level at the rear of the massive house.

Surrounding us was topography unlike any I'd seen before: vast plateaus of limestone and sandstone bedrock, intricate webbings of deep river valleys and dramatic hill-like structures formed by eons of erosion. I let my uncle set the direction and pace while I tried to take in the strangeness of my surroundings and companion. For several minutes we just walked. No talking. At one point my uncle reached into his pack and pulled out two apples and handed me one. It was huge, so big in fact that for the first few bites I had to hold onto it with both hands, like I remember doing as a young boy eating an apple half this size, with hands twice as small. It tasted fresh, just the right amount of tart to invigorate my taste buds, juicy and sweet. We listened to each other's satisfied crunches and smiled at one another. I was certain we had once done this exact same thing together in another place, another time. When we were both finished, I thought I was ready to speak. I'd have to start slow.

"Where are we exactly?"

"We're near the northeast coast of Somerset Island, north of what's known as the Arctic Circle.

Prince of Wales Island is to the west of us, Baffin Island to the east, the Queen Elizabeth Islands are to the north, not much else after that. The only permanent settlement on Somerset is Fort Ross, an old trading post quite a ways south from here." He was filling the empty space between us with details.

I nodded and kept my eyes where they'd be safe, on our vivid surroundings of every shade of gray and green and blue. We veered off from the river, the terrain barren, craggy, scrubby with wild flowers and alive with fowl: snow buntings, sandpipers and rough-legged hawks. "Is this where you've been all this time?" I asked.

"No," he said with a weary shake of his head. "I'm only a visitor here, like you. This lodge belongs to an acquaintance of ours. He's been kind enough to allow us to meet here. This place is only habitable a couple months each year, if that. The middle of last month they still had massive snow drifts in this area. And last year the first snow of the winter was August eighteenth." He kept on, "They tell me the ice was late breaking up this year; it kept the belugas out of Cunningham Inlet until a couple of weeks ago. They'll leave again sometime in August."

"And you with them?"

He let out a soft laugh. "Ah, no, my boy. By then I'll be long gone."

I came to a stop and put a hand on my uncle's forearm, turning him so we were face to face. I'd had enough banter. I wanted—needed—facts. "What is going on, Uncle Lawrence? What happened to you? How can you still be alive? Where have you been all these years? Who are you? Who is Maheesh Ganesh? Who is Alex Canyon? Where is Sereena?"

He nodded toward a grouping of rocks that would make for decent seating and we each found a spot.

"Oh, my dear Russell," he began. "As lovely as it is to sit here with you in the sun and see your face again, hear your voice, ruffle your hair, I'd truly hoped it wouldn't come to this."

Nice.

"And, although it was wholly innocent on your behalf, it was you who forced us into this."

My temper felt a spike in temperature. "Me? What did I do? I didn't put myself on that plane this morning. I didn't…" And then I thought better of it. There was so much more going on here, more than I was anywhere near to comprehending. Perhaps I needed to shut up for a bit. "I just want to understand," I told my uncle. "I want to know what I should feel about seeing you alive. Should I be happy, angry… suspicious? Do I have you back for good, Uncle Lawrence?"

"I'll answer your questions, Russell. As best as I'm able. Please be patient."

Patience. Not my strong suit. "I can only try."

He laughed again. "That's my boy. So much

like me. Curious as they come, exuberant, lively. Perhaps…" He stopped there and studied my face. "…perhaps I did manage to teach you a thing or two after all." He chuckled lightly. "But even I have learned to police my tongue, if not my brain, at times." He stopped for a sip of water then started talking, as if from a fresh page of text. "Maheesh is my spouse. Alex Canyon is our security officer. Ms. Gauntlus works with Alex. I instructed Alex to send Grette to watch you, several months ago."

"Months?" I was startled by the news. How had I missed her for that long?

"I wanted to see what you were up to, my boy."

"You could have just asked," I said, a little crankiness sneaking into my tone.

My uncle simply lolled his head to one side in response to my suggestion. "Eventually it became necessary to send Alex to check on the situation and dissuade you from looking any further into Candace…Sereena's disappearance. Knowing you as I do, however, I suspected he would fail. Then I sent Maheesh to bring you to me."

"I don't understand," I said plaintively.

"Sereena Orion Smith was first known to me several years ago as Candace Ashbourne. Arthur Ashbourne and I were best friends. When they were married, Sereena and I immediately liked each other, especially once we discovered our shared Saskatchewan past. Arthur and I had met years earlier at business school in London; he was a professor and I was the young colt intent on becoming a man of power and influence." He chuckled, and as he recalled this time in his life the deep lines in his face seemed to soften and disappear.

"I came away with more than high education and ideals; I came away with a lifelong friend, despite the difference in our ages. This friendship saw us through all the extraordinary highs and lows of lives well lived. When Arthur and Candace were married, I was their witness. Although many in Arthur's circle were suspicious of Candace, I approved. She and I saw the world the same way. And there is an immediate—oh, what to call it?—connection I would say, between two people who care for the same person. I saw it in her, she saw it in me. We both loved Arthur very much. Don't mistake me, I didn't hope to love him as a man—I knew that was impossible—but I cherished him as the best friend a man could ever wish for. He was so dear."

"Maheesh told me about Sereena's travails. I'm glad she had a friend in you," I said, still trying to believe that these two people, both so important to me at completely different times, knew each other.

He looked at me with hooded eyes. "And she always will have.

"After the horror of losing the babies and then Arthur, Sereena fell into a great malaise followed by great extravagances meant to blunt her depthless depression. I lived through it with her, or at least I tried. It was around that time that we bought the Kismet together. In what must have been a drunken state of euphoria, we decided to purchase a luxury yacht and spend the rest of our time on this marvellous earth sailing the seas and sampling only the ripest fruits offered at each exotic port." I saw a hint of smile as he remembered those halcyon days.

"Sounds wonderful."

He nodded. "But wholly unrealistic and, in the end, barely a Band-Aid for the gaping wound that was Candace's heart. Maheesh and I had been playing on the outskirts of a burgeoning relationship during these years and he also developed a close relationship with Sereena. He suggested the extended trip to India, and, as it turned out, that decision changed all our lives forever."

I nodded, already knowing some of what came next...except for how my uncle was involved.

"Russell," he said with a hand on my thigh, "it's become a bit chill. Let's head back. You must be exhausted and starving too."

"I want to know what happened next," I said in a voice that sounded a little like an order. "I want to know what happened to you and to Sereena after the murder of her husband."

My uncle gave me a disapproving look. I don't know why I felt I could speak to him that way. It was not at all indicative of our former relationship—the one before he was dead. I cherished my uncle, looked up to him, respected him. Maybe…maybe it was simply that I wasn't quite convinced that this man before me was really him. But of course it was. This wasn't an afternoon soap opera or a hanky-a-minute movie of the-week.

"I'm cold now," he stated and, with some effort, raised himself into a standing position.

As we headed back, my uncle spoke of little but the fine weather we were experiencing. He pointed out a tiny fox scampering in the distance and suggested I hike to Triple Waterfalls, a nearby five-storey torrent of free-falling water. When we reached the lodge, he directed me to my room, a large suite on the second floor, and excused himself with the promise to meet again over dinner at eight.

After a brief nap, I was surprisingly refreshed and decided to investigate my surroundings. I left by the front door and took a moment to study the sky, still bright with a sun that looked like an egg yolk diluted in a pool of clear gelatin. I circled the building and found myself at the edge of the river over which the house was perched and near where my uncle and I had begun our walk. I pointed myself in the direction opposite to the one we had taken and followed the river's lead. Although seem-ingly flat, like an endless desert of stone, I soon found that this land was capable of great deception; arctic plain could become dangerously craggy with alarming suddenness where erosion had created strange hidden gullies of dramatic proportion. It was at the bottom of one of these lesser gullies that I discovered a pristine-looking basin of water, one of countless I'd glimpsed on our descent into Somerset Island. It looked so inviting, but the weather was hardly warm enough for swimming, so I resisted the urge to jump in. However, someone else had not.

I might have missed him had it not been for the pile of clothing I almost tripped over. I scanned the water's surface, shiny and silvery like a fish belly, and after a few seconds witnessed a head then shoulders rise up from beneath it and make for shore. It was Alex Canyon. As he came closer and the water sluiced off his finely molded body, it became boldly apparent that the man was completely naked. He couldn't help but see me where I stood my ground, protecting his clothes from the possibility of an attack by a marauding bear. (Well, you never know.)

Watching him approach, I felt myself grow weak at the knees. This was a man whose job required him to keep his body in top physical condition, which he'd accomplished with resounding success. As for those physical items over which he'd had no control, well, he just lucked out. This was most readily apparent even after emerging from water that must have been frigidly cold. You see, when it comes to men and their finest of appendages, there are two distinct categories: showers and growers. Growers require certain stimulation and a consummate situation to reveal their ultimate potential (I'd been fooled before), whereas showers are always already more than halfway there. Alex Canyon was most definitely a shower.

"Mr. Quant," he addressed me when he arrived, doing nothing to cover himself and showing no signs of consternation at my finding him in the alto-gether.

"The water looks a little chilly," I commented.

"It was fine," he answered matter-of-factly, prob-ably lying through his chattering teeth.

Now that I knew a little more about Alex Canyon and his role as a security officer for my uncle and Maheesh, I had something to work with in terms of getting a conversation going with the big lug. "Shouldn't you be patrolling the grounds or some-thing?"

"Gauntlus has that well in hand for now."

Ah yes, the Amazon. "She's quite the woman."

"That she is."

"Are you and she…?"

He gave me a look as if he didn't understand my meaning, when of course he did.

"Are you a couple then?" he forced me to ask,

every word coming out sounding awkward.

His face broke into a playful grin. It was one of those rare grins that by its mere presence will cause a face to transform. Suddenly granite became clay, impenetrable wall became an open door, Alex Canyon was a beautiful boy when he smiled. "No, Russell," he told me, my name slipping sensually through his lips. "My type falls more into the category of someone like you."

Gulp.

Did I hear right?

He was the one without clothing, yet I was feeling naked.

Alex Canyon bent low to retrieve his underwear, which he pulled up over muscular calves and ham hock thighs to where they belonged, sitting low over narrow hips. He worked on his socks, then pants and shirt. Not a stitch of modesty from this guy. As is my habit with direct pronouncements of attraction, I did my best to throw it off track. Don't know why. Just my way. "Why do my uncle and Maheesh Ganesh require protection? Why do they need you and Dauntless Gauntlus?"

"She hates when you call her names," Alex answered with a cocked eyebrow, as if on to my game. He slipped on shoes that had tractor-tire grip. "She knows that you do."

"The question stands," I persisted.

"Mr. Wistonchuk will answer all your questions

about that. Is that all? Is there anything else you'd like to say to me?"

"I wished you'd warned me that Grette was your playmate."

"There was no need."

"It would have saved me a heart attack this morning when I arrived at the plane."

"Anything else?"

"Uh, I guess not." What a loser. I could have said something encouraging like, you're my type too, handsome.

"Dinner's at eight," he said to me over a well-rounded shoulder as he walked away. "Don't be late."

Chapter 13

Dinner was served in an octagonal room that jutted out from the east side of the house with a splendid, panoramic view of the seemingly endless plateau that surrounded us. When I walked in, Uncle Lawrence and Maheesh were standing arm in arm at the window, their backs to me, Uncle Lawrence's head resting on the ledge of Maheesh's narrow shoulder. It was to be the three of us. No Alex Canyon and, thankfully, no Grette Gauntlus. Well the three of us, two serving staff, a kitchen person and a many-titled, much-sought-after chef, all of whom were flown in at the owner's pleasure. Fortunately his pleasure was to host us in style.

When they heard me behind them, they turned and greeted me warmly, as if we were simply three men on holiday together, meeting for dinner after a happy day at the beach. Although the sun still shone bright, at the touch of a pad Maheesh dimmed its intensity by half as the windows frosted over, throwing the room into a pleasant dusk. Then, like a family, we took our seats around a spectacularly set round table in the centre of the room. We began with fresh Arctic char sushi, followed by a creamy French Canadian pea soup served with fresh-baked breads, then grilled musk ox accompanied by fantastically flavoured oven-roasted vegetables mixed with semi-sweet local berries. Each course was paired with a magnificent wine.

It wasn't until we were savouring the last of the musk ox that Uncle Lawrence finally seemed prepared to continue with his tale. He was the type of man who felt that the conversation during a meal affected its taste as much as the seasoning used in its preparation and the wine you imbibed with it. I tend to agree, and, by that point, I'd learned not to push either man into telling a tale they weren't yet ready to tell.

"Maheesh has told you about the night Akhilesh Batten was killed," he began.

I nodded. "I know that he was there that night,

and that Sereena killed her husband in a fit of rage after learning he'd abused and killed their daughter."

"I cannot dwell on this part of the story too long," Uncle Lawrence said quickly. I guessed he'd used the time since our walk to have a rest; he looked better than he had earlier, refreshed. "But I will say that I too was there that night. I must tell you that, because it was the cause of my own 'death.' You see, Maheesh and I were staying with the Battens at their house near Delhi after our ski trip." The infamous ski trip. "We'd had a pleasant evening together, dinner, conversation, a few laughs, perhaps too much to drink. Maheesh and I were in our bedroom when we heard the commotion. It was horrid, the screaming, wailing…almost…inhuman. But, just as Sereena was too late to stop Akhilesh, we were too late to stop her. By the time we arrived at that hideous scene, it was all done. Sangita was dead, and so was Akkie."

Maheesh laid a comforting hand on his lover's shaking one and continued for him. "Fortunately I know much of life in India and how things work in this country, Russell, particularly in matters concerning the police and matters concerning the Batten family, both powerful authorities in their own ways, you understand?

"There was, of course, every chance the police would demonstrate a certain amount of leniency to-wards Sereena. She had obviously been driven insane by the transgressions of her husband against their own daughter, but the same could not reasonably be expected from Akhilesh's family."

My face reflected my disdain at what I'd just heard. "Are you saying they would have neglected the fact that their son was a child molester who killed their own grandchild, and blamed Sereena for what happened?" I asked, stunned at the thought.

"They simply would not have believed her, you see. Akhilesh had told his lies well. He'd been hinting for ages that Sereena was the unstable one, and he said he worried that *she* would harm Sangita. Akhilesh was their golden son. In their eyes, he could do no wrong. Regardless of how the facts appeared, they would believe Sereena was somehow responsible and that with her actions she had murdered their future, their reputation, their very livelihood. They would seek revenge. And possibly, I must admit to you, the authorities would turn a blind eye."

"What are you saying?"

"They would shame her, humiliate her, and then, Russell," he added afer a pause, "they would have her killed."

He said the words so calmly I found them doubly wretched. Finding words of my own to express the outrage I felt escaped me. I sensed the gentle eyes of my uncle on me. I turned to face him.

"It's true, Russell," he said. "Of course we don't

agree with it. We knew we had to do something."

"But...but what can we do?" I was reacting as if the horror of it all were unfolding as we spoke, not something that had already happened six years ago. My God, I thought to myself, what a tragedy it was. Sereena...my uncle...it was...it was nearly too much to take in.

"We had to act," Maheesh continued. "Quickly. We talked about a plan. Poor Cand...Sereena was in such a state she barely knew what was happening. The best we could do was finally separate her from the body of her child, and when we finally told her of our plan, she was compliant, I'm sure without really knowing to what she had agreed."

"The police were called," Uncle Lawrence kept on after a sustaining gulp of red wine. "We complained and caused much ruckus over the phone, saying we'd called earlier and had no response."

I shook my head, in a daze. "I don't understand. Why did you do that?"

"Two reasons. First, it took us some time to concoct our final plan and we did not want to arouse suspicion as to why we hadn't called the police immediately. They would know that sort of thing when they examined the bodies. And secondly, we needed to give my body time to disappear."

We kept quiet as one of the servers entered the room, cleared plates and refilled wine glasses.

Maheesh went on. "The police were told that

the three of us together, Sereena, your uncle Lawrence and I, discovered Sangita defiled and dead, obviously at Akkie's hands. Lawrence, driven by an understandable rage, attacked and killed Akkie. Then, in a fit of remorse and guilt at taking another's life, Lawrence threw himself off the balcony into the river below.

"Of course, the police immediately dispatched a crew to find Lawrence's body, but because of their unexplainable lack of response to our first emergency call, it was certain the body was long gone and might never be found. Which, indeed, would be the case. When the police processed the scene, we made sure that Lawrence's fingerprints and DNA were in ample evidence. Sereena's were no problem, as it was her home."

I turned to my uncle in disbelief and horror. What kind of madness was this? "You...you took the blame for the murder? You faked the murder and your own death? But...?" The questions in my mind were coming so fast they threatened to overcome me.

"Oh, my boy," he answered. "The most important thing was to save Sereena's life. Too many had already been lost that night. The only way we could be assured of doing that was if the police—and the Batten family—believed that it was not she who killed Akkie. And if it wasn't she...it had to be me or Maheesh."

I swung a heavy-lidded faze to Maheesh with

one thing on my mind: Why not Maheesh? This monster, Akhilesh, had been *his* friend, they were in *his* country, wouldn't *he* have had a better chance of surviving this...this execrable, ridiculous plan? And by the look on Maheesh's face, he knew exactly what I was thinking. He had thought it himself.

"Russell," my uncle said sternly, even though I had not opened my mouth. "It had to be me. Maheesh begged me not to do it, but it made the most sense. You see, I simply had the least to lose. If Maheesh had faked his death, he would have lost all his wealth and prestigious position in Indian society."

I made a face as if to balk at that. Who cared about Maheesh's place in society?

"Don't judge what you don't yet understand. If Maheesh did this thing, he would, without doubt, lose everything. If I did it, it was possible that I could lose nothing. At the time, we thought that, with Maheesh's help of course, I would stay in hiding for a while..."

"That was when we were told you had died in a skiing accident?"

He nodded. "Yes. Even the authorities agreed to that. They wanted to make as little a deal of things as possible, to save the Batten family the international controversy. And they were told my family would be devastated by a suicide. We wanted the story of my death leap from the balcony to be as sound as possible. It was a horrible thing to have to do, I know, but it was necessary. And we thought eventually I would be able to sneak back to Canada and take my life…or something like it…back."

"But you never did," I countered, as if it was I who'd been denied the rest of my life. "Why?"

"Several things happened we did not expect, and, most importantly, Maheesh and I were in love. Even if we had to live in secret, it was better than to be torn apart with no hope of ever seeing each other again." At this Uncle Lawrence gazed fondly into his lover's eyes and his face reflected the great love he saw there. "As time went on, it became disturbingly apparent that certain members of the Batten family were not buying our ruse, or if they were, they still felt some inclination to make life for Sereena as miserable as they could. The loss of Akhilesh was a heavy burden for them."

"So," Maheesh added, "it was decided that it would be Sereena who would go away, not run, just leave behind an uncomfortable situation with as few clues as possible as to where she was going. Enough time had passed, you see, that to most, the idea of Sereena wanting to leave the home and country that held such miserable memories for her would not raise much suspicion. For us it was a sad day, especially for dear Lawrence, for you see, Sereena was his only companion, she was the only one, besides me of course, who knew he was alive."

"And that's when she came back to Saskatoon?"

The two men nodded and Maheesh said, "After Candace legally became Sereena Orion Smith."

"She chose the name herself," Uncle Lawrence told me. "Using the initials of SOS was her idea, an allegorical reference; she felt in desperate need of help…emotionally, physically, every way possible."

"And, more so, it was an homage to Lawrence, her savior," Maheesh pointed out with pride.

Uncle Lawrence shook it off and mumbled something about the foolishness of such sentimentality. I sat there in dumbfounded awe; of the story, of the nearly impossible-to-believe circumstances these people had found themselves in and the incredible way in which they had decided to extricate themselves from it. My uncle's ultimate sacrifice—his life…or if not his real life, certainly his livelihood and lifestyle. That Sereena would go along with it…did it really make sense? But I knew it had been too much information to take in at once to even consider whether any of it made sense, or was it all just another fantastic deception? Deep down, I knew it wasn't.

"You are wondering about Sereena," my uncle said, still, after all these years, reading me so well.

I nodded solemnly. "Yes."

"She never wanted any of this. In the state she was in at the time, she would have more than gladly thrown herself off that balcony, for real, and might have done so on several occasions, that night and for months afterwards, if it wasn't for Maheesh."

"In many ways," Maheesh said contemplatively, deflecting any credit for himself, "I think Lawrence saved her life. Knowing what he'd done for her, that he'd made such an extreme sacrifice to save her, made her beholden to him. She owed him her life…she owed it to him to keep herself alive. Because for her to have killed herself—as she so much wanted to do in the unimaginable depths of her agonizing grief over her lost child—would have been to slap Lawrence's face. It would have been to say that all he'd done, all he'd gone through, was still going through, meant nothing. That alone kept her alive, kept her going."

"There was no reason for her to stay in India, what was done was done," Uncle Lawrence insisted. "I couldn't free myself from hiding unless I too went away from India, and I was unwilling to do that because I would not leave Maheesh. And Sereena's life was misery there. There was nothing for her there, whereas I had everything."

"Except freedom," I said.

"Bah," he retorted as if it meant nothing. "When she finally relented and agreed to leave the country, I demanded one favour, which she gladly granted." He leaned into me and said, "To return to her home, my home, and keep watch over you. Of all the people I'd left behind, my boy, it was you who I felt most guilty about leaving. I had abandoned you, unhappy with your work, with a family who did not understand you and no one to see to it that you were all right. So I sent you my dearest friend."

I smiled at that. Sereena had been my uncle's present to me. And what a wonderful gift she had turned out to be.

"Thank you," I croaked, my throat growing tight.

"Things are better now, yes?" He searched my eyes for the non-verbal answer.

I produced a wide smile. "Yes. My life is…" I stopped there, and even though I knew what the next word would be, I wanted to enjoy the great revelation of it, "wonderful."

Uncle's Lawrence's eyes sparkled, as they used to do before all this, and he exchanged a happy, paternal look with Maheesh. "I am so very pleased."

The servers brought in a fresh berry sherbet and aromatic coffee, and for some minutes we basked in the glow that follows a wondrous meal and the warmth of the mood surrounding the table. Yet although it was lovely, I hadn't all the information I wanted and eventually found myself breaking the spell. "So what's with the Alex Canyon and Grette Gauntlus show? Why did you send them after me now? Has something changed? Did something happen?"

My uncle's grey-streaked eyebrows rose high upon his forehead. "You happened, my boy."

Uh-oh.

"And Sereena," Maheesh added, shooting his

partner a look. "To be fair, Lawrence."

"Yes, yes, and Sereena," my uncle agreed.

"What about us?"

"I suppose, in the end, it really is my fault. Ever since I 'died' and went away, I've been desperate to see your face, to make sure you're all right, to remind me of home. Fortunately Maheesh has plenty of money, which allows me to escape my Indian hideaway from time to time. It's a risk, but I do it. Over the years, Sereena has kept me up to date on your travels, and when I could, I followed you, just for a glimpse."

I was struck dumb, yet, if I was to be completely honest, this was not a total surprise. Somehow, somewhere in me, I suspected it all along.

"She told me about your cruise last year and it was I who arranged that our yacht, the Kismet, would rendezvous with yours. Unfortunately, you spied me spying on you."

I recalled the fleeting vision of a man on the upper decks, looking down at me when I'd first arrived to come aboard the boat. "But I didn't know it was you."

"Still, you began your research. You found out about A&W Corporation."

How did he know about that? How di…oh maaaaaaan. "But why was that a danger? Why did Sereena have to disappear?"

"With Sereena's departure from India, suspicions

certainly abated. At first. But some of the evidence we'd planted at the murder site was being re-examined by a private firm hired by the Batten family—some of whom never bought the story of someone unknown to them, me, committing the murder, committing suicide, and the body conveniently disappearing. Although we've no concrete knowledge of what has been found, current rumours are not good. Maheesh has been threatened and it has been made clear that if ever it is discovered that he was involved in duplicity surrounding Akhilesh's death or if I was found to be alive, retribution against us and against Sereena would be swift and it would be severe."

I gave Maheesh a startled look. "Your life has been threatened? Are you in danger?"

He patted my hand and said, "It's nothing, really, nothing."

"Sereena began to worry that if you persisted in your research…after all, I've heard stories of what a great detective you've become," my uncle said with undisguised pride, "that eventually you would uncover her past and, by association, me and this entire story. If that happened, if we were revealed, we could easily find ourselves at the not so tender mercies of the Battens."

"So she decided to leave?"

"Yes. In the hopes of dissuading you." He chuckled then. "Of course, if only she'd known you as I do, she'd have realized that such an action would only serve to spur you on. But by then it was too late; she'd already made good her disappearance."

"So you sent Alex and Grette to stop me."

"At first more to see what you were up to and to ensure that any leads you discovered were...dealt with. I imagined there would be no stopping you until you had answers as to Sereena's whereabouts. So that is why I brought you here: to give you your answers."

"I'm sorry, Uncle Lawrence, to have caused you such trouble, but this simply is not good enough. There has to be another way. Now that I've seen you, know you're alive, I want you back. There has to be some way."

"No, Russell. There is not."

"But..."

"Never, Russell," he said harshly. "I will never come home."

Suddenly I was angry. "Why won't you even try?" My voice was a tortured, tearing whine. Why, why, why? I hated how I sounded, like a petulant child being denied, but the feelings were real and coursing through me like venom. He had abandoned me. I'd needed him so much. He was my guide in a strange and unfamiliar life I was just coming to accept and understand, the ruler by which I measured my success, the only person I could find comfort with when things got rough.

"Haven't you listened to a thing I've said?" Uncle Lawrence was visibly upset and the spark I'd seen earlier in his eyes was now but a faded glimmer beneath a dull, angered glaze. "This...this thing I've done...it has been the greatest achievement of my life! Why won't you let me have it?"

God, I wished I could better understand what he was saying, but it was as if he was speaking another language. He'd left me all alone, to hide. To hide from a crime he didn't even commit. At my expense!

Yet as soon as I heard the words reverberate through my feverish brain, I knew how wrong they were, how wrong I was. Uncle Lawrence had done a selfless deed, and all I could think about was myself, what *I* had lost. He'd found himself and those he loved in a disastrous situation and he made a difficult decision in the hope of making it better, in the hope of saving the lives and livelihoods of others. He had paid the ultimate price, not me, and maybe...maybe I would have done exactly the same thing.

He tried to explain. "I have enjoyed the greatest love of my life with Maheesh, and I have saved one of the dearest people I've ever known, Sereena. I am proud of both those things. I cherish that. I will not let it go. You will go home tomorrow morning, Russell, and I know I cannot ask you to forget me or forget this time together—and I wouldn't want that either—but I want you to never look back and to never search for me again. To do so endangers all that I hold dear." His voice smoothed into gentler tones as he added, "So you see, it's just a selfish request from a tired old man, but perhaps, perhaps, my boy, I have earned that from you?"

After many embraces and promises of a last farewell the next morning, we parted ways. I left the dining room as I'd come into it, at the sight of Uncle Lawrence and Maheesh, arm in arm, gazing out the window.

The knock at my door was so soft I almost missed it. I called out to whoever it was to come in.

"We'll be leaving at six tomorrow morning. That okay with you?" Alex asked in a tender voice I'd not heard from him before.

I was so tired, washed out like a year-old dishrag, feeling as if every bit of energy I'd ever had had been wrung from me. I nodded from where I was propped on my bed and told him I'd be ready.

"You look sad," he said.

I shrugged my shoulders. "I guess maybe I am. There's still so much I don't understand. And why won't he at least let me try to help him?"

Alex stepped into my room and closed the door behind him. His movements took me by surprise and my face must have said so.

"There are a lot of things about this you'll never

understand, Russell. You have to accept that."

I was sick of hearing it but too tired to argue. "I suppose so."

"But there *is* something more," he told me solemnly. "Something you don't know, and I think you should."

Chapter 14

Maheesh and Uncle Lawrence were fully dressed and in the kitchen sharing bagels with lox and cream cheese when I dragged myself downstairs at five-thirty the next morning. No sign of Alex or Mighty Aphrodite. Alex was probably warming up the plane or something, and Grette, well, Grette was probably killing her breakfast down by the river's edge. The men rose when I entered the room, all smiles and hugs.

"The staff prepared you a lovely breakfast picnic basket and thermos of coffee to take with you,"

Uncle Lawrence said and then, glancing at Maheesh, added, "I'm sure that plane you're on will be able to offer you the same and much more, but take it anyway, won't you?"

"Of course," I answered. I hadn't realized I was leaving quite so soon.

"No time to dawdle," Uncle Lawrence chirped gaily as he puttered around the kitchen cleaning off surfaces with a dishrag in his hand as though if he didn't do it, no one else would and the whole place would fall into disrepair. "Maheesh and I are off this morning as well."

"Oh," I remarked as casually as I could. "I thought you were staying on here for a while."

"Oh no, this was just temporary."

"So where are you off to?"

He stopped what he was doing and gave me a look. "I promised I'd say goodbye this morning, Russell, but I can't have it go on for too long. I just can't take it. Do you understand?"

After what Alex had told me last night I understood only too well. "So this is it then?"

We stood rooted to our spots, not quite knowing what to do next. None of us wanted this to end, to say goodbye forever, but we knew we must. Maheesh was the first to step forward. He embraced me like a father would a long-lost son. For someone I'd never set eyes on before yesterday, I felt inexplicably close to this man. My story with him, I somehow sensed, was not over. Over his shoulder I laid eyes on my uncle, who was watching us closely. Sadly, my story with Uncle Lawrence *was* over. I knew this goodbye would be forever. Final.

When Maheesh pulled away from me his eyes were damp. With a gentle pat on my chest he walked out of the kitchen, leaving my uncle and me alone. We stood there staring at one another, trying to commit to memory every inch of each other, the colour of hair, the shape of hands, the curve of lips, the look in the eyes. For so long I had a memory burned in my mind of the uncle I'd lost. Now I had to replace it with this newer, older, different version, a version of a man who, as Alex Canyon had confided in me, was dying.

Why didn't Uncle Lawrence tell me himself? Even talkative-as-a-stone Alex thought I needed to know this before I left the Arctic, before I left my uncle for what would truly be the last time. He didn't think I should have to go through the frustration of believing I could have helped my uncle, saved him, brought him in some sense back to life, when that was impossible. Alex felt I deserved the truth, the knowledge that this goodbye…unlike the one at the Saskatoon airport six years earlier…truly was the last. How many people get that chance? But my uncle wanted something different. And I was not about to take that away from him, regardless of whether or not I understood his reasons. This would be *my* gift to *him*.

"I'm glad this happened," I said to my uncle. "I know it has caused you some grief, and I can't pretend not to be disappointed that this isn't the beginning of something more, but I feel so blessed to have had these hours with you."

"You are happy, aren't you, Russell?" he murmured with a contented look on his face.

"Yes. Truly."

"And Kay, your mother, and dear, dear Anthony? How I miss them both."

"They are happy too, I think. My mother has come a long way from—well, from when you knew her. She even spent Christmas with me, spoke to lesbians too." He laughed his wonderful, hearty laugh, for that moment just as I remembered it. "And Anthony is with a marvellous man named Jared Lowe...but of course you met Jared, didn't you?"

"Yes, yes. Met him and most definitely approve. The perfect match."

Quiet.

"Russell...Russell you know you can't tell either of them about this, don't you?"

I nodded. I hated it. But I knew he was right.

For now.

"Can you tell me where you're going?"

"India, of course. Maheesh has many responsibilities there and I have much more hiding to do. It's not difficult to do: India's a big country and it's really quite glamorous you know, the life of concealment, a recluse from the world. And every so often, I use a great deal of Maheesh's overabundance of money and sneak away, to places like France, New York, the Mediterranean islands." All places I had travelled over the past years, places where, wholly unknown to me, I'd been under the watchful eye of my beloved uncle. He gave me a raised eyebrow and let out a scallywag laugh. "So you must be ever vigilant of what you do when away from home, my dear boy, for you never know who may be watching." His face went serious and he laid a gentle hand on my shoulder. "I'll always be watching out for you, son. I'll always be with you."

There it was. Now I understood. This was the reason Uncle Lawrence did not want me to know that he was filled with cancerous cells eating away at almost every organ in his failing body. He wanted me to believe that I would always be under his protection, his watchful eye. Wherever I went, whatever I did, he would be there.

And indeed, he would be.

We fell into one another as if we were two parts of one whole and stayed that way for many minutes. Like a warrior fighting against insurmountable odds, I barely held back the hard, back-shuddering sobs that threatened to overtake me.

When we parted, Uncle Lawrence looked deep into my eyes and said, "If you don't go now, my boy, my heart will surely break."

And so I did.

The Cessna rose swiftly into clear Arctic air at exactly six a.m. that Wednesday morning in July. Alex Canyon accompanied me the entire way. He read me well, as if he'd known me better and longer than he had; he knew I needed companionship but little conversation. I asked only one question.

"Where is Sereena?"

I had fully expected, the first second I set foot aboard that small jet, that I was on my way to see Sereena Orion Smith. But that desire (wish? fantasy?) remained unfulfilled. I didn't know what I'd say to her if I did see her, even less so now that I knew so much more about her dramatic, shocking, sorrowful past. She had survived spectacular highs and terrible lows. I, and scores of others, had imagined them— half-believed her stories of fairy tale proportions— but in reality, doubted their veracity, only because they were too big, too bold, to fit into our own much smaller, regular lives. Sereena'd told us little of herself because she knew we, frankly, couldn't handle it. And as I sat there that day, next to the man who'd taken me to the end of the earth to learn the truth, I knew she might be right.

Alex Canyon did not answer my question.

Lowering myself into the cracked leather seat of my Mazda, which was patiently waiting for me in the West Wind Aviation parking lot, I felt as if I'd been away a month. But it had been less than thirty-six hours—thirty-six hours that, for now, I wanted to forget, for a little while. That is my habit with big things. I need to put them away for a time, let them percolate somewhere in the back of my head before I decide what to do with them. If I hadn't done that, my first impulse would have been to go back on my promise to Uncle Lawrence and imme-diately call my mother to tell her that her brother was alive. And Anthony? Wouldn't he want to know that his former lover and greatest friend was not lost beneath a massive pile of snow on some unnamed mountain slope? Didn't my brother and sister have a right to know they still had an uncle?

Instead I dug out my cellphone and called the Saskatoon Police Station. I was told Constable Kirsch had left for the day. I looked at my watch. Almost seven p.m. I dialled his home number.

"Hello, this is Griffin Kirsch speaking." The voice of a wee boy, one who'd obviously been well trained by his parents on the social graces involved in answering the telephone.

"Hello, Griffin," I responded pleasantly. "Is your daddy home?" The words sounded funny in my head. Our playfully combative professional rela-tionship rarely goes beyond the workplace, so to hear the voice of someone who calls Darren Kirsch daddy, sits on his knee, plays ball with him, is tucked into bed by him, was an unexpectedly odd sensation.

"May I tell him who's calling?" the youngster inquired politely.

This was always a problem. If Darren knew it was me, he might take my call, he might not, depending on his mood. "My name is Russell." I gave it a shot.

I had to jerk the phone away from my ear when the little tyke, pleasantries dispensed with, yodelled for all of Canada to hear, "Daaaaaaaaaaaddy, someone wants to taaaaaaaaaaaalk to you!"

I heard Darren's shushed voice as he approached the phone. "Grif, you don't have to yell."

"I'm not yelling." The petulant reply.

"Who is it?"

"Don't know." Good boy.

"Hi, it's Darren," he said pleasantly into the receiver.

I seldom call him Darren out loud or hear him refer to himself as Darren. Gosh, I was feeling close to him. "Darren, buddy, it's Russell."

"Insert swear word here," he said, obviously restricted from giving in to baser instincts by the presence of his young son. I had to give him credit, he was getting much better at the pithy retorts.

"Cute kid," I remarked, meaning it. He was, I

was pretty sure, a good dad.

His voice softened. "Yeah, he's a pistol that one." Then hardened. "So what do you want?"

"The Pink Gophers, the choral group I asked you to check up on. Did you find anything yet? Any suspicious characters amongst the bunch?"

"All your gophers check out, Quant. None of 'em have more'n a parking ticket."

I heard something more in his voice and decided to push further. "Buuuuuuuuuut....?"

"Well, none of 'em have *made* trouble, but several of 'em have reported trouble to the police over the past six months or so. Nothing serious, just petty disturbances, irritations, crank calls, tires being slashed, that kind of thing."

"More than you'd expect from a random group of people?"

He hesitated then admitted, "Yep." Then he added, "A lot of the complaints came from one person... I don't have the file here at home, but it was a woman, Kim something, I think."

Kim Pelluchi. One of the two Pink Gophers I'd yet to track down. "One more thing, Kirsch. Just because none of the Pink Gophers currently has a police record, doesn't mean there isn't a rotten apple amongst them, right?"

He grunted in the affirmative.

"Thanks, Kirsch."

"Don't call me at home ever again."

"Why would I?" I promised, without meaning it.

I reached behind the driver's seat for the Saskatoon phonebook I keep there and looked up Kim Pelluchi's number. I had a list of the choir's phone numbers given to me by Jared, but it was at home and I wanted to get back to work on my case immediately. I'd been away from it far too long. I dialled but got no answer. Back into the phonebook I found a number for R. Caplan, which, according to the address, I confirmed belonged to Richie Caplan, the other Pink Gopher I'd yet to talk to.

"Yeah?" came the unexcited-to-hear-from-me answer.

"Hi," I said. "Is this Richie?"

"Nah, he's got a show tonight. I'm his roommate."

Show? "Oh, right, where's that at again?"

"The tent thing, dude. On the river, the Shakespeare thing."

I was guessing the roommate hadn't spent much time reading Shakespeare, but he'd told me enough for me to know what he was talking about. Shakespeare on the Saskatchewan is a summer-long series of presentations of Shakespeare classics-with-a-twist. They've done everything from *A Midsummer Night's Dream* on a golf course to a punk rock *Hamlet*, a heavy metal *Richard III* and *King Lear* as a business magnate. Over the past twenty years the festival's huge, boldly coloured tents, erected every year upon the banks of the South Saskatchewan River, have become a welcome harbinger of summer in the city.

"Right," I said to the fellow, "and what time does he go on again?"

"Eight or something like that, dude."

"Thanks, dude. Buh bye."

"Uh…buh bye."

To take advantage of the beautiful summer night, I lowered the roof of the Mazda (which involved getting out of the vehicle) then pointed the car in a direction that would take me just out of downtown to the Shakespeare tents. Overlooking the river, the tents have a beautiful spot between the Mendel Art Gallery and the University Bridge. Across the river to the south one can see the sprawling grounds of the RUH and U of S campus, to the north is Spadina Crescent and beyond it, Kinsmen Park with its popular kiddie rides, all just 70¢: a merry-go-round, Ferris wheel and a CN/CP Rail station with a fully operational, miniature, six-car train including a black engine and red caboose.

I pulled into a nearby parking lot at 7:50 and, leaving the top down, dashed down a paved pathway to a small, shack-like, A-frame ticket kiosk handily situated just outside the main stage tent. I was in luck, they weren't sold out and in I went. The interior of the big tent was just what you'd expect from such a venue, with bright blue folding chairs set up around three sides of a staging area that had been admirably decked out to look like some kind of forest setting. I hadn't even bothered to ask the ticket seller what I was about to see but saw by the program I was given that it was *As You Like It*, done as a soap opera. Fitting, I thought, as I found my seat and tried to recall a few bits about the play from having read it for a university English class eons ago.

I just had time to check the cast list before the show started. Richie Caplan was listed as one of the major players, portraying Orlando, the youngest son of Sir Rowland de Boys. And it was Richie who first appeared on stage...

"*As I remember, Adam,*" he enunciated mightily to an older man, "*it was upon this fashion bequeathed me by will but poor a thousand crowns, and, as thou sayest, charged my brother, on his blessing, to breed me well: and there begins my sadness.*"

And there began my boredom. I've never been a fan of Shakespeare. I've tried. I've read the plays, watched the plays, listened to the plays deconstructed by those more knowledgeable than I am. But whatever it takes to appreciate this, no doubt fine, art form, I do not possess it. So I sat there, intently watching my prey. Even made up as Orlando, I was certain I'd seen Richie Caplan before. Of course I'd seen his picture in the group shot of the Pink Gophers, of which he was a member, but that was a small photograph and I could, at best, only get a passing sense of what each person looked like. But in real life Richie Caplan looked a lot like…like…damn, who was it?

At intermission I gratefully retreated outdoors for a leg stretch and bum massage (those hard plastic chairs were not meant for long-term sitting). The milling-around area consisted of wooden-slat pathways through combed gravel, several picnic tables and a small, decorative water fountain. I meandered about with other theatre-goers who, judging from snippets overheard as they too walked about, visited the outhouse or headed into the yellow-and-white-striped refreshment tent for a beer or bottled water, were loving the show. So whadda I know?

Along the back edge of the main congregation area was a long, narrow trailer, which I guessed was used as a change room/staging area for the actors. On its side was posted the usual theatre stuff: a sponsor wall, welcome signage and details about the theatre company itself and the production, which ran on the alternate nights between *As You Like It* and an Old West version of *Romeo and Juliet*. But what caught my eye in particular was the wooden awning over the slat pathway that led into the performance tent. I'd just passed through it, twice in fact, but I only now noticed that it was covered with photos of all the actors and production staff involved in the show. I gently elbowed my way through a small crowd admiring the artfully arranged display and quickly found the 8 x 10— sans makeup—I was looking for: Richie Caplan. I was right! I did know who he was, or at least where I'd seen him before. Richie Caplan was one of the ruffians who'd attacked me at the Exhibition fair-grounds a few days earlier.

Caught ya!

I sat through the last half of the performance with considerably more interest, not so much in the show but in its star, who, as much as I hated to admit it, was a rather talented actor. I hoped he'd be as anxious to do some talking once he was off stage. I couldn't wait to hear how he would explain why a member of the Pink Gophers had followed and attacked me, a detective looking into the death of one of his fellow choir members. Or would he just keep on acting and read me some lines? I'd have to have my bullshit meter set on high.

As soon as Rosalind's epilogue was done, I snuck out of the performance tent and made my way around to the back, listening to the applause as I passed by several serious-looking "No Admittance" and "No Public Access Beyond This Point" signs. By its thunder I guessed the production was getting a standing ovation. The cast's exit corridor, a dirt path running between the tent and a chain-link fence directly to the dressing trailer, was not hard to find (out on a river bank there ain't too many places to go). I stood back against a flap in the tent, in wait for my Orlando/Richie. I didn't have long to wait as the first of the troupe emerged, but in the excitement of it all as the actors left the stage and headed for the changing area, Richie and the others charged right by me, leaving me in the dust of their exhilaration. Gosh, I had to wonder, did I really want to spoil this night for him?

Damn right I did.

So I headed back to the public area and waited. I knew eventually Richie would come out, changed out of his costume, makeup off, ready for a cold drink and warm adoration from the gushing fans awaiting him and the others. In about ten minutes I got my opportunity. I caught up to Richie as he headed for the refreshment tent, a big smile on my face, all innocent looking. "Good show," I offered.

He stopped and turned to me with a goofy grin, "Thanks, I'm glad you liked it."

Richie was sandy-haired, probably twenty-four, with a friendly-looking, oval face and a toothy smile. His pale skin showed smudges of makeup where he'd neglected to clean it off, in too much of a hurry to join the rest of the cast and crew in post-show celebration.

"Yeah," I said. "I especially liked the part where you tried to kick my ass behind the Ferris wheel with a bunch of your buddies."

He'd obviously not taken a real good look at me, thinking me just another nameless fan I suppose, but he did now. As he registered my face, he slowly began to back away from me, a frightened look building on his own.

"Shit, man, you leave me alone. Get away from me."

I matched each of his steps back with one of my own forward.

"Just stop right there," he warned me off.

"Richie, I just want to talk with you."

"Yeah, I bet. I want you to bugger off, right now, man."

By this point, we had made our way, in our weird backwards dance, away from the refreshment tent to near the ticket kiosk.

"Leave me be," he ordered, slipping on a bit of loose gravel.

"I just want to talk. Is there somewhere we can go?"

That's when he whipped around and took off, racing by the ticket booth and out the entrance gate at such speed he seemed to be a blur. I took that as a no and zoomed after him.

Richie flew by the powder-blue porta-potty building and up the paved road into the parking lot. It was dark out now, but as he weaved his way through the parked cars, I was able to keep an eye on him in the beams of the headlights of departing theatre-goers. Did any of them recognize him as "Orlando" and wonder why he was being chased and if perhaps they'd mistakenly left before the final act was over?

The way to the street was up a slight incline, which I hoped would slow Richie's pace, but he seemed to be in pretty good shape and set on making a clean getaway. When he reached Spadina Avenue he caught some luck with a break in traffic and sprinted across the two-lane road directly into Kinsmen Park. Did he have a car waiting for him somewhere? Should I go back for the Mazda? Unfortunately I only had a few seconds to consider my options while I waited for traffic to clear before I could follow him. I decided to keep at it on foot. If I went back for the Mazda, I'd surely lose him for good. At least this way I had a chance.

By the time I got across Spadina, I had temporarily lost sight of my quarry. I scanned all directions, my eyes doing their bit to adjust to the dark. Finally I spied a figure moving swiftly over the grassy field to my right. It had to be him; he was making for Queen Street. I took after him like a wolf on a rabbit. I didn't have time to think about why he was running, why he was so scared of me, but I did note that Mr. Thespian wasn't nearly so brave now that he didn't have his buddies around to help rough me up.

At first, despite the lack of lighting in the park (I guess city authorities didn't want to encourage late-night traipsing around), the going was fairly easy. Nothing lasts forever, I reminded myself as I fell, slipped, hit my head on a rock and rolled down a gulley. Suddenly the terrain had turned treacherous. I scrambled to my feet and looked around. Where was he? Where was I? With no lighting, ambient or otherwise, I couldn't make out where I was (except for the bottom of the gulley thing), but I could most definitely make out that something was climbing up my leg—something wet and cold. I made tracks scrambling out of the gulley that I now knew was filled with about two inches of water, sludge and unidentifiable creatures. Lovely. Out of instinct I ran to the right, following the gulley bed toward Spadina, thinking Richie might have circled back to the road. Instead of the road, I found myself confronted by a creepy-looking bridge spanning the crud-filled gulley, not unlike the one from *Three Billy Goats Gruff*. Somewhere along the way had I fallen through Alice's looking glass or been transported to the land of Oz? Was this still Saskatoon? Was there a troll under that bridge?

A shuffling noise behind me got my attention. I searched the area, barely able to make out the trees for the dark forest that lined that side of the gulley, but I was sure someone was there (which was okay because I was happy to have an excuse to leave behind that scary-ass bridge). I found a dirt path that led into the trees and tried to bully from my mind that song from *Wizard of Oz* where Dorothy and her companions are on the Yellow Brick Road (*...we're off to see the Wizard...*). This just wasn't the time, and really, I was more about wanting a pair of ruby red shoes to get me back home.

There was definitely someone in front of me, making their furtive way through the trees. I kept going until my foot caught the edge of something hard and I fell to the ground for a second time, scraping my right knee. I swore under my breath. When I pulled myself up I saw that what I had tripped over was the jagged edge where the dirt path abruptly turned into pavement. Jolly good. Now I'm sure this so-called park is a very picturesque and charming and lovely place to be—in the day-light—but not so much during a high-speed foot race at night. In an attempt to regain my bearings and catch a good sighting of my pursuee, I scanned the area surrounding me (mostly differing shades of black). Where'd he go? Where'd he go?

I swatted at a small swarm of mosquitoes who'd decided to perform an impromptu blood donor drive on my neck and became aware that, other than the whirring of the pesky insects, it had grown eerily quiet. I heard no footfalls nor other obvious signs of Richie, or anyone else for that matter. I crept forward along the paved path, searching the unfamiliar landscape for any clue. Eventually, again not unlike Dorothy on that yellow brick road of hers, I came to

---

a fork in the road. Super.

Directly ahead of me, between the two paths and near some rather scraggly-looking pine trees, I could just barely make out the silhouette of a small log building with a decrepit stone chimney propping up one end. Against it was the black blob of a lone figure, standing very still, perhaps hoping not to be seen. I pulled myself behind a nearby obliging ash tree. It had to be Richie. Had he seen me? I watched the blob for a while, waiting for him to move or make a run for it. He did neither.

I lowered myself to a crouching position and began a closer study of the area. At best, I was hoping to find a way to sneak up behind Richie, to catch him unaware, but I soon concluded it would be difficult, even in the thickness of night, to sketch out a route I might follow and still remain undetected. I considered a nearby clump of trees to my left and wondered whether or not I could make it from here to there without being spotted. Instead I noticed something else. There was something moving in those trees. My eyes strained to see what my brain was trying to convince me was there. I was finally able to discern the black-on-grey shapes of at least two people. Then I heard a noise. My eyes whipped to the right. There, next to a huge rock, was another person. And over by a collection of maple bushes— another one! My face felt hot as my brain screamed a taunting warning: You're surrounded, sucker!

Chapter 15

How had Richie Caplan managed it? He couldn't
have known I would be at the show tonight. Or
could he? Had his roommate figured it out somehow
and warned him? Nevertheless there we were, Richie
and I, along with his posse of rapscallions ready to
have a second go at me. Including Richie there
were five of them this time: Richie by the log cabin
in front of me, two more in a clump of bushes to my
left, one behind a rock on my right and another
further off in a maple grove. What to do? I swatted
at another mosquito and rubbed the spot to stop the

itching as I considered my options: fight or flight?

There's the big-ol'-jock-dummy part of me that always hollers, "Fight, you wuss!" and the big-ol'-wuss part of me that yells back, "Catch me if you can!" I couldn't be sure whether any of these guys had spotted me yet. If not, then I had one more option available to me: do nothing. I could sit there, clinging to a tree, and wait them out. Sooner or later they'd get tired of waiting for me and head off for their lairs or dens or wherever badasses live.

Another mosquito bite, at the ankle bone this time where it'll itch forever. That did it! I wasn't going to sit there like some kind of blood buffet.

I began with another scan of the facts. By this time, my eyes had adjusted nicely to the dark and I could see the figures a little more clearly. The guy by the log building wasn't moving, but the two guys in the clump of bushes to my left certainly were—back and forth, back and forth, back and... hey...wait a sec...what the hell is going on here? I recognize that! It appeared that Richie's hoodlums were...yup, they were having sex.

Out of the corner of my right eye, I caught some movement and turned just in time to see big-rock guy amble over to maple-tree guy. Was this to be more sex? What was this place? The two men spoke for a short while, sneaky-like—or so I decided, given the circumstances—after which big-rock guy pulled something out of his pants pocket and handed it to maple-tree guy; maple-tree guy looked at it, then pulled something out of his pants pocket and handed it to big-rock guy, and big-rock guy took off and then maple-tree guy took off. That's what they call a drug deal. I shifted my gaze back to the clumpers, but they too had disappeared. Not much for after-sex chat, I guess. I checked on the figure by the building; he was still there. I stared at him and could have sworn he was staring right back at me. And he must have been because about then he started coming right for me. Fight or flight? Big dummy or big wuss?

I held my ground.

The man who approached me was not Richie Caplan. He was wearing a snug T with cut-off sleeves—more to show off powerfully built arms and shoulders than to keep himself cool—and full-length jeans (must have had spindly legs). In the low lighting, I took him to be about forty, attractive in a buttoned-down-professional-gone-wild-for-the-night kind of way, except for his perfect helmet-head hair and a too-small mouth. And I knew exactly what was going to come out of it: "How are you tonight?" or "Do you have a light?" or "You got the time?"

"Wazzup?" he asked instead.

I had to stifle a laugh. He'd obviously been watching too much YTV circa 1990s. I gave him a friendly smile, told him I was peachy cool and walked away.

Kim Pelluchi lived in a gaily painted wartime house on 7th Avenue not far from City Perk, a popular neighbourhood coffee joint I'd been to several times. Except for the two who'd moved to New Zealand, Kim was the only Pink Gopher I'd yet to have any contact with. It was after eleven p.m., and I was a little weary from my foray in Kinsmen Park, but I'd had no luck getting in touch with her at any other time of day, so there I was, sitting in my car outside her house, plotting a good cover story for when I knocked on her door. Mary Kay representative? Nah, my car wasn't even pink. Election enumerator? Had possibilities. I caught a flash of movement in my rear-view mirror.

Nope, nothing there.

Girl Guide cookie seller?

A thump.

Still nothing.

Nosy neighbour? Maybe. How about Russell Quant, intrepid private detective? I had about settled on that when I heard another thump. What the hell?

I turned in my seat to check if perhaps a cat had hopped up onto my trunk.

Then all hell broke loose.

I had no time to react. They had planned their ambush well. The next thing I knew, the Mazda's door was wrenched open and I was being pulled forcibly from it and slammed into the dirty, hard pavement. All I could make out was a jumble of feet, mostly in trainers, some in flip-flops, as they shuffled around me in great agitation, the male voices grunting and calling out muffled instructions to one another like, "Get him down," "Get his hands behind him," "Where's the blindfold?" Gulp. Flight! Flight! I've changed my mind! I choose flight! Let me up, goddamn you!

At least one of the bunch was following instruction, and I was dutifully blindfolded with what I think was a man's shirt and my hands were tied behind my back. Someone yanked me to my feet and began pushing me along in front of the group. They neglected to warn me about the set of steps I was meant to scale, causing me a painful crack to my lower left shin before I figured it out myself. I was being taken into Kim Pelluchi's house. No need for a cover story after all.

"Oh shit, oh shit, oh shit," I heard a female voice warble as my captors shoved me inside the house and down into a half-sitting, half-lying position on a saggy-cushioned sofa.

"What's going on here?" I called out to whoever cared to listen.

For a second there was stunned silence, then a man's voice, "Who forgot to gag his mouth? Where's the friggin' gag?"

Oh for crying out loud. "Come on, guys! No gag, okay? How are we gonna communicate if I can't talk?"

"We don't want to communicate with you, you piece of shit!"

Piece of shit? I had never been called that particular name before and, as high school as it was, it stung. Ridiculously, the singsong verse of "Sticks and stones can break my bones but names can never hurt me" filled my head. I didn't want to test its legitimacy, particularly the sticks and stones part, but really, who the heck wrote that stupid song?

"What are we going to do now?" the woman questioned her cohorts. "Call the cops?"

Interesting. The kidnappers were turning themselves in?

"And tell them what?" a voice that sounded very familiar answered. "We've already talked to the cops. We can't prove anything, so they can't do a thing."

"But now we've caught him," she replied, her voice at a reedy pitch of anxiousness.

"Yeah, sure, caught him doing what? Sitting in his car outside your house. It proves nothing." Same guy. I just about had it, he sounded like…

"But he was chasing you! You can tell them that!"

There we go, it was Red Cap *aka* Shakespeare's Orlando a.k.a. Richie Caplan *aka* bastard creep jerk.

It was time for me to get into this verbal fray. "What is going on? Why don't you untie me and we can discuss this? There's no need for this blindfold.

I already know it's you, Richie and you, Kim. And the other guys are the same ones who jumped me at the Exhibition." I was guessing on the last part.

I took it they were deliberating over my request with their eyes, as I heard no voices until male number two finally came out with, "Forget that, man. I don't want him seeing who I am."

Male three and four quickly concurred.

"Why?" I asked. "What are you planning to do with me?"

"We're gonna teach you a lesson, you shitass punk!" Male three, I think.

I didn't like the sound of that. "Lesson about what?" I wanted to know. "Yes, I was sitting outside Kim's house tonight. I've been trying to get in touch with her for days. And yes, I was chasing you tonight, Richie, but only because you were running away from me. I just want to talk."

"Talk? Talk about what? Talk about how you can't wait to scare the shit out of us again? Huh? Is that what you want to talk about? Talk about how you're going to keep on ruining our lives? Is that what you want to talk about?" This from a frustrated-sounding Richie.

"I haven't done any of that stuff. You've got the wrong guy here. I'm not who you think I am. I'm not the boogeyman."

"There! If you're not the boogeyman, then how do you know about him?"

"Besides," added three, "we know you've been after these guys."

"It's a mistake," I told them. "Yes, I've been looking for Richie and Kim. I've been looking for all the Pink Gophers."

"The Pink Gophers? What do they have to do with any of this?" Kim asked.

And herein was the problem. Since the choir disbanded for a prolonged break, no one knew what had been happening to the others. Most of them had gone their separate ways and not kept in touch. They each believed the "boogeyman" was only their problem, their own horrifying reality, when in truth, all of the Pink Gophers were under attack. The question was, why? And by whom? They thought it was me.

"I was hired by Tanya Culinare's family," I said.

"You were hired by her family?" Richie said as if repeating it somehow made it more unbelievable. "Why?"

"She's dead."

That bought me some silence.

The next thing I felt was a hand unfastening the shirt that covered my eyes. And not a moment too soon; one of the collar buttons was really beginning to cut into my skin. When the blindfold dropped into my lap, I saw before me five frightened faces, Richie, Kim and males two, three and four (who I was happy, for the time being, to have remain nameless—just easier that way). Kim was a pleasant-looking gal in her late twenties with thick, dark hair and Raisinette eyes that stared out from behind artsy, dark-rimmed glasses. The guys were wearing nondescript jeans and wrinkled shirts and Ts, while Kim was in head-to-toe black. We were in a cramped living room, and judging by the bolts of fabric and proliferation of sewing notions scattered about, I guessed Kim or someone who lived there was a seamstress.

"How about my hands?" I suggested hopefully.

"Maybe later," Richie said with a still-distrustful glint in his eyes.

"How do we know he's not lying?" Three wondered. Good question, nimrod. "We should call her."

"Call Tanya?" Kim said.

"Yeah. Who's got her number?"

They exchanged glances. No one had her number.

"It doesn't matter," Richie mumbled. "It's true. She'd dead."

"Wait a minute," Kim began. "A girl jumped off that building on Broadway a couple weeks ago. I think that was where…" She looked at me. "Was that Tanya?"

I nodded. "It was."

"Oh my God. Poor Tanya. Oh God." She glared at Richie, aghast. "You knew about this? You knew she was dead? Why didn't you tell me?"

He nodded ever so slightly. "Duncan told me."

Interesting. Duncan didn't know about Tanya until I told him over the phone before I flew to Vancouver to find him. Richie and Duncan were obviously in close contact.

"And? Why didn't you think to tell me? Why?" Kim was demanding to know.

"Kim, I'm sorry, it's just that I knew you were already freaked out about everything else that was happening. I didn't want to get you more scared. I thought it was this guy." He indicated me with a point of his chin. "Duncan told me about him. I thought I could take care of it. I started following him, and then me and the boys took care of him at the Ex."

Yeah, right. You got run off by a wailing gnome named Jane Cross. Forget that part of the story, did you?

"You're a fucking gay actor!" she yelped at him. "Who do you think you are, Puff Daddy?" She turned on males two through four. "Get outta here! Scram, you losers!"

I have to say she was right about those guys. Now that I was seeing them in the light of day without their faux gang-wear, all they had going for them was the intensity of rangy youth but little real threatening presence at all. Yet they had been protecting their friend against a frightening predator (or so they thought), so I had to give them props for that. They looked at Richie and he at them.

"Go!" she screamed, falling next to me on the couch, burying her face in her hands and beginning to weep.

"Can Richie stay?" I suggested in a gentle voice. "I think it's important that I ask both of you some questions."

"Whatever," she burbled as she pulled her face from her hands and removed her glasses to wipe away the tears.

"I'll see you guys later, and thanks," Richie said to his compadres as they filed out of the front door, looking more relieved than anything. Once they were gone Richie sidled up to me, and I righted myself and turned my back to him so he could untie my hands. Even though the binding wasn't tight, my wrists felt sore and I rubbed them to promote normal blood flow.

"I just can't believe it," Kim said, once she'd controlled her crying. "Poor Tanya. I can't believe it." Then she turned to me with a look on her face as if a horrible thought had just come to her. "Was it…was it murder? Is that what you were hired to find out? Did he do it?'

"He? Who's he?"

"The boogeyman! You know who I'm talking about! You brought him up!" She was becoming unglued. Richie moved in beside her to lay a comforting arm around her shoulders. The couch was getting a little crowded. "Oh God! It was him, wasn't it? But why? You think it has something to do with the Pink Gophers? First Tanya, now us."

"And Duncan," Richie told her. "And Tanya's girlfriend, Moxie: she's dead too."

I laid my gaze on Richie's face. I was willing to bet that if I hadn't been blindfolded when I first mentioned the Pink Gophers, I would have seen that he knew more about this than he was letting on—to me *and* to Kim. And still was.

"M-M-Moxie...dead...oh...and Duncan...oh God, Richie, Duncan's dead?"

Richie shook his head. "I don't know. He called me after he first heard from this guy." Why does he keep calling me "this guy"? Was it kinda like Marlo Thomas' *That Girl*? "And I haven't heard from him since." He gave me another surly look, no doubt compliments of an acting coach.

Kim gave me a once-over, her mouth twisted into an I-just-ate-a-rotten-egg grimace. I couldn't really blame them for being distrustful of me. It didn't look good. If Richie and Duncan had begun to make the connection between the choir and the harassment and, possibly, the deaths of Tanya and Moxie, I could see how they could become paranoid and afraid of their own shadows. A guy snooping around their lives would seem like a viable threat. That's why they both had acted so scared of me. Although that doesn't mean you should try to beat me up when I'm out for an evening with my mother—

but whatever.

"I'm not the boogeyman," I told her. That's not a sentence I use every day. "I'm here to help you."

"He *is* a detective," Richie finally said. "I checked him out after I talked to Duncan. He has an office and everything, on Spadina."

They looked at each other for a while, then at me. Kim whispered in a hushed tone, as if afraid of anyone else hearing her, "He's coming after all of us, isn't he?"

Richie stared at me too with little-boy eyes. "Is he?"

"I don't know. I do know that many of the members of your choir have been having weird things happen to them; the level of severity seems to vary. I know that Tanya and her girlfriend, Moxie, are dead. Duncan Sikorsky has disappeared and two women have moved to New Zealand. All the others are still here in Saskatoon and most have reported of being harassed to the police."

"By the same guy? Who is he?"

"I don't know. That's what I'm trying to find out. That's why I've been trying to find and talk to the two of you." And you haven't been making it easy, I added to myself.

She nodded, looking numb-faced. "What do you need to know?"

"Obviously the two of you have also been experiencing harassment. Tell me about it."

"Mine hasn't been as bad as Richie's, but you better believe I've been reporting all of it to the police, every single time. I've been getting weird phone calls and letters slipped into my mail slot."

"Weird how?"

"One time, it was just some guy laughing, maniacal-like, you know, like he was crazy or something. Another time, it was a whispering voice saying, 'The boogeyman is going to get you.' One day someone left a dead bird on my doorstep." She visually quivered at the memory.

"There was the broken window on your car," Richie helped her out.

She nodded. "Yeah, that's right. It was in the winter and my car got filled with snow. Oh and he called my mother…I have no idea how he got the number, phone book I guess…and told her I was a sloppy lesbian slut and, well, a lot more than that, but I think my mom couldn't bring herself to repeat it word for word. I called the police and they were really nice about it, but other than changing phone numbers and trying to lift some prints from the car, which they were never able to, there was nothing else they could do. It's really been bad. I know some of the stuff seems piddling, but when you put it all together and have it happen day after day after day, it can really get to you, you know. But like I said, I didn't have the worst of it. Poor Richie has had all of what I got plus way worse."

"Worse how?" I asked.

"Someone tried to kill him."

I looked at Richie following Kim's unexpected revelation. He wasn't denying it.

"I've been getting calls too," he began his tale. "Mine started off *really* bad, threatening to slice the smile right off my face or cut my dick off. And then came the hoaxes. My power and phone and cable were cancelled. My landlord was told I was giving notice. If he hadn't called to confirm my moving out date, I'd never have known until it was too late. I get these huge food deliveries to my house when I haven't ordered anything. Someone spray-painted my car, with the word 'fag' on one side and 'boo' on the other. And it just keeps getting worse and worse and happening more and more often. Every day there's something more. Some days…it's almost too much to bear, man."

"He's almost been run over *three* times!" Kim exclaimed. "While he was on his bike."

"Is it always the same driver? Can you identify the vehicle?" I questioned.

"No, always different. I've been knocked over so many times there's barely any paint left on my bike; it used to be red, but it ain't anymore. The first time it was an old half-ton truck that came after me. Then there were two more times with a different car each time. They catch me by surprise. I have to swerve wildly to get out of the way; twice I actually toppled off my bike. Before I can get a good look, they've taken off. I thought it was coincidence the first two times, but I don't anymore."

"And tell him the rest," Kim urged but didn't wait for him to comply. "He was leaving his house to go to work one night and his doorstep was covered with marbles. He could have broken his legs or something horrible. And his house was broken into but nothing was missing. Then, two weeks later, he was taking some cold medicine and thank God his nose wasn't plugged up and he could still smell because the cough medicine bottle was filled with bleach! Imagine if he had downed that!"

Richie continued, shaking words floating on a tremulous voice, "I feel like I'm being followed all the time. I know he's been in the audience at the Shakespeare tent, watching me...the audience gets comment cards to fill out after the show is done, and one night someone had filled in each blank with the word

, so I know I'm not imagining it. I hear weird noises in the middle of the night, like someone's knocking at my door or scratching at my windows. It's, it's, it's driving me nuts."

I did not doubt it. My own stomach involuntarily contracted as I listened to these ghost stories, ghost stories that were true. I could also appreciate that what Richie and Kim and the others were living through was hard to empathize with; much of it was difficult, if not impossible, to prove, with little solid evidence to take to the police. It was unrelenting: the constant presence of evil taking little bites out of their psyches, eroding their lives until slowly but surely they'd all become helpless balls of fear. Whoever this boogeyman was, he knew what he was doing; he was someone who had studied fear and how to instill it in others. To think that such a character was out there, roaming the streets of Saskatoon, was a frightening thing.

"When did this start?" I asked.

"February, I think," Richie told me.

"I didn't really notice anything until late March, April maybe," Kim said.

It fit. Everything that had happened to this group of people happened after December, after that fateful trip to Regina when they were snowed-in in Davidson and had their picture taken.

"So why us?" Kim questioned. "Is it a gay thing? Because we're a gay choir?"

"It could be," I said. "But I think it's more than that."

"What? What could it be?"

I decided to share my latest theory with them. "I think it has to do with a photo that was taken of the Pink Gophers."

Richie pasted a frown on his face. "A photo?

What are you talking about?"

"Before Duncan disappeared, he left me a photo. It was a picture of the Pink Gophers and Moxie Banyon, Tanya's girlfriend. Moxie wasn't a member of the choir, yet before she died, she too was suffering the same kind of harassment as the rest of you."

"So you think this has something to do with who was in the picture?" Kim clarified.

"Yes. Moxie was a target of the boogeyman just like the others, and the harassment began shortly after the picture was taken."

"It makes sense," Kim said, looking at her friend for agreement. "Don't you think, Richie?"

He simply nodded.

She looked back at me. "If that's true, then... you think the boogeyman is one of us, don't you?"

"It's a definite possibility."

"But I thought you said every one of us has been a target for this guy. If that's true, then..." She stopped for a moment, gave it some thought then reached the obvious conclusion: "Ohhhhhh...you think one of us is lying about being harassed?"

"Possible." It was best for me to stay as quiet as I could here, listen to what these two had to say.

"Richie, what do you think?" He said nothing and she kept on. "That's crazy though. I know these people. They may not be my best friends or anything, but we've spent a lot of time together, at rehearsals and concerts; we've partied together. None of them are capable of this kind of crap. No way, right, Richie?"

"Yeah," he said, breaking a rather long silence. "No way."

"There's another possible suspect," I said, not sure if I yet agreed with them.

"Huh? Who?" Kim asked.

"Who took the picture?"

They stared at me.

"There were eleven members of the choir plus Moxie. That makes twelve. There are twelve people in the picture. Who took the picture?"

Kim glanced at Richie for help then back at me. "I...I can't remember. It must have been...well, gosh...who did take that picture?"

"You have a choir director, right?" I suggested.

"Frank," Kim answered, her brow knitted. "Frank Sadownik."

"Okay. So where was he? Was he the one who took the photo?" I asked.

"I...no, it wasn't Frank. He should have been there with us on the bus, but he wasn't. He stayed behind in Regina to visit with relatives. He'd made the trip down with his own car."

"The bus driver." This flat statement came from Richie.

"That's right, that's right!" Kim excitedly agreed. "That guy who drove the bus. He hung with us for a bit that night. He was just as stuck as the rest of us.

But again, I can't really believe he'd do any of this shit; he seemed like a decent guy, didn't he, Richie? We barely knew him, I suppose...what was his name? Guy, I think. He's French."

"Yeah," Richie chimed in. "Guy."

"How about anyone else in the hotel that night, someone you might have met or had contact with or an altercation of some sort?"

They both shook their heads, then Richie said, "Well, I guess there was the hotel staff, but why would they hate us so much?"

Kim shook her head as if the idea didn't hold water for her either.

"Did you go out that night?" I suggested. "Leave the hotel for any reason?"

"No. We ate dinner in the hotel diner then hung out in our rooms a bit, had some drinks, then went to bed," Kim said. "We left early the next morning. Not much chance to get into trouble. Maybe you're wrong. Maybe all this has nothing to do with that photograph. Maybe it's someone we met at the concert in Regina. Maybe it's someone from one of the other choirs...oh my gosh...do you think? Maybe one of the choir members we were competing against, or one of the choir directors, or maybe a relative of one of the singers got pissed off because we did so well and they decided to get some revenge!"

"But then why Moxie?" Richie asked. "She

wasn't in the choir."

"Even criminals can make a mistake," Kim announced in Nancy Drew fashion. "Maybe he included Moxie just because she was with us that weekend." Her eyes rolled around in her head a bit, and then she came out with, "Or maybe it's a disgruntled former member of our choir? Maybe it has nothing to do with Regina at all! See, Richie, you should have told me about this before. Now that I know this may be tied to the Pink Gophers, I can think up a million suspects."

Oh great.

"We have no disgruntled former choir members," Richie countered. "Anyone who can open their mouth and make a sound can join the Pink Gophers and stay as long as they want. That's why we're not that good."

"Well, yeah, I suppose, but, well, just give me a minute to think this through." She shot him a hurt look. "I think we're pretty good."

I was getting the feeling that if I allowed Kim Pelluchi much more time to dwell on this, she'd somehow find a connection between this case and the office of the Prime Minister or Buckingham Palace. I stood up. "You've given me some good ideas, Kim," I told her. "Thank you. If you come up with any other plausible ideas for why this is happening or who the boogeyman might be, please give me a call." I handed each of them one of my business cards and made a move to leave.

"But what now?" Kim asked in a whimpering voice. "What about us? What are we supposed to do? How do we protect ourselves against this madman?"

It was a valid concern. Unfortunately I had no easy answers for her. "Just keep on doing what you've already been doing," I suggested, giving Richie a meaningful look. "Watch each other's backs."

Chapter 16

I felt bad about leaving Richie Caplan and Kim Pelluchi, knowing that the boogeyman was real and somewhere out there on the streets of Saskatoon, waiting to get them. But what could I do? I wasn't a one-man security service or a caped crusader with nothing better to do. I couldn't protect everyone. I had my own client's interests to look after. It still felt rotten.

I'd had a long, long day—from Nunavut to Shakespeare on the Saskatchewan to a high-speed pursuit through Kinsmen Park and being kidnapped—

it was time to go home. When I parked the Mazda in the garage behind my house well after midnight, I was bushed. For a moment I laid my head against the car's well-worn headrest and closed my weary eyes; the Arctic Circle, seeing my uncle, meeting Maheesh, learning Sereena's saga, it all seemed like a vision I'd had, a hallucination, but it wasn't. It was reality.

I entered the house through the back doors directly into the wet-nose welcome of two happy-to-see-me schnauzers. Errall would have been there earlier to let them out, feed them and pat their heads, but I still felt a need to spend some quality time. I poured myself the dregs from a bottle of Cave Spring Pinot Gris I found in the fridge and led the oft-repeated parade to our favourite room in the house in which to hang out together: the den. It was too warm for a fire, but we still piled up on the couch that faced the fireplace and got in several good minutes of ear scratches and belly rubs. As I did that, I sang them their favourite song: "You're two little teapots, short and stout; here are your handles and here are your snouts!" Brutus was the first to call an end to our menagerie à trois by dropping to the floor with an audible "oof." Barbra stayed with me a little longer, more, I think, to promote her primary claim to me and mine to her than any real desire for prolonged petting. When that was over, I reached for my wineglass and downed a healthy swig. Ahhhhh, that tasted good, peachy I think. I picked up the nearby phone to check for any messages that had come in since I'd been away. There were three.

The first message was a reminder from Espirita Salon about a haircut appointment; the next was a hang up; the third was Doug Poitras. The real one. "Russell, ah, hi, it's me, Doug Poitras. I'm a friend of Anthony's. We met at your birthday party…well sort of met… I wasn't really sure what was going on there? Something about you thinking I was somebody else? Anyway, I was just wondering if you'd be interested in trying that again, maybe just the two of us this time, maybe a movie and drinks afterwards?" A little hesitation, then, "I'd really like to get to know you better. You can call me at 555-7411."

The computer voice gave me my options: respond, save or delete. I hit delete.

I must have made a sound within the expanded range of dog hearing because Barbra, who'd gone to lie down next to the dark fireplace, looked up at me with her soulful, understanding eyes. I swear that animal can read my mind. She knew that, as nice as Doug Poitras might be, the only man I could think about right then was Alex Canyon. Even though he'd left me that same morning on the tarmac outside Hangar 10 without so much as a backward glance, off to the other side of the globe, he was more present to me at that moment than any other man I could ever remember meeting. Without even trying, I could recall his scent, his voice, the heat that filled the air between us whenever he was near me. I laid my head back against the soft toffee leather of the couch, closed my eyes and summoned a vision of his handsome face. He had sat on this very spot, only days ago, during that hot, steamy, stormy night, and I could easily recall the smell of his damp skin as it dried in the heat of the fire. His eyes: so intense, so serious, so beautiful. I ached to reach out and touch him. Why had I let him go so easily? Why hadn't I said something to him, let him know how I felt?

How *did* I feel?

I forgot to close the blinds. The end-of-July sun peeked over the horizon and into my bedroom sometime after six that Thursday morning. I attempted to roll over onto my tummy, away from the scourge of light, but found I was wedged between two lumps of immovable canine. I kept my eyes resolutely shut, but the bright new day had other ideas, burrowing through my eyelids with cheery sunshine that grew in intensity with each passing minute. By a little after six-thirty, my brain, with no encouragement from me, began to list off the numerous things I should do that day and I gave up any chance of going back to sleep.

"This has to stop," I mumbled to the dogs as I

began to nudge them awake. "You cannot sleep on this bed. You have perfectly good mats on the floor."

With that, Brutus hopped off the mattress, as if he'd been awake the whole time and was offended by my uncalled-for diatribe, and went to stand by the French doors that led to the backyard and his morning ablutions. Barbra was a little slower going. Her head rose from slumber and she stared at me as if to ask, "You're sure about this?"

I stumbled out of bed and—thanks to well-planned (and slightly overgrown) backyard foliage—I was free to follow Barbra and Brutus outside without bothering with a robe to cover my nakedness. It's not that I didn't have one within easy reach, but this is a rite of summer that simply needs doing every now and again. The dogs ran off to take care of business while I luxuriated in a mile-high stretch, grasping at a pure-blue sky. Through squinting eyes I regarded the offending ball of sun, but who could be mad at such an irrefutably joyful sight, like a giant piece of lemon candy on a peaceful blue background, promising to only get sweeter and yellower as the day progressed. There was nary a breath of wind and my skin felt toasty after only a moment outdoors. It was a day meant for gardening or swimming or lazing about on a lawn chair, but none of those activities were on my schedule that lovely mid-summer's day.

By the time I reached PWC around nine, my

head was filled with what-abouts, what-ifs and how-comes. Although I suspected that Kim Pelluchi had been tossing her net too wide, I couldn't help but wonder if maybe she'd been right about some of her possible scenarios and suspicions. Suppose everything that happened had something to do with the competition the Pink Gophers had attended in Regina, an event I knew very little about. Who had been there? Were there any sore losers? And what about the choir director, Frank Sadownik, and the bus driver, Guy somebody-or-other? Were they potential suspects? Were all the members of the choir innocent, or was one of them the true culprit? I had a lot to do that day, and to top it off, I couldn't help but think about my secret voyage to the Arctic Circle: my uncle was alive and Sereena hadn't disappeared: she was in hiding. What would happen now? Could I really go on as if I knew nothing? Would I be able to keep these secrets from Anthony? From my mother? The only help for me was to keep busy, and that would be no problem.

I spent the morning collecting information, sometimes by good old-fashioned research, sometimes by cajoling, sometimes by trickery and fakery (my personal favourites). By noon I had a plan of attack in place and was heading out of town in the Mazda with a takeout meatloaf sandwich from Colourful Mary's and a bottle of Dasani on the seat beside me. Martensville is a small town twenty minutes northwest of Saskatoon, and Frank Sadownik—the Pink Gopher's choir director—lived on the outskirts, farming in summer and teaching school in the winter.

I stopped in town only long enough to track down someone to give me directions and soon found myself motoring along a dusty gravel lane that led off the main road (also dusty and gravelly) into the Sadowniks' farmyard. The yard itself was a collection of buildings in various states of disrepair and dilapidation, except for a neat row of three, steel-sided granaries that looked shiny and new. There was a stand-alone garage that appeared in better shape because of a fresh coat of barnyard-red paint but upon closer inspection was just as old as the other buildings around it. Surrounding the yard was an aged windbreak of dead or nearly dead ash trees, forever-thriving poplar trees and spindly-looking caragana. As I pulled up in front of a single-storey house I was greeted by several laying hens, one rangy-looking rooster and a very old dog who reminded me of a miniature wooly mammoth.

Unsure of the mammoth's intentions and biting habits, I gingerly stepped from my car, ready to hop back inside at the first sign of aggression. The animal regarded me with weary eyes and attempted a bark but did not quite succeed, instead letting forth from a jowly snout, a sound reminiscent of a coughing cow, along with a fair bit of graying froth.

His nose went right for my crotch, no doubt trying to get a bead on Barbra and Brutus's scents, and I pulled away, shy as Billy around Captain Highliner. I swung around at the sound of something landing on the car's ragtop. It was a scraggly-looking tabby who mewed at me plaintively, as if hopeful that a being of matching mental superiority had finally come to rescue it or at least have intelligent conversation.

"You can have her if you want," a voice called out to me.

I spotted a young boy, maybe eight, standing near some trees and fingering a toy tractor in his dirty little hands.

"Don't you want to keep your cat?" I asked stupidly. I was raised on a farm, and if this place was anything like most farms I knew, for every cat you saw, there were probably six more.

He decided the question was rhetorical and instead went right to business (I liked that about the kid): "Mom told me to come out here to see who it was. Who are you?"

"My name is Russell," I told him, glad the wooly mammoth had finally grown bored of my crotch and lumbered off in search of other things to sniff. "Is your daddy home?"

"How do you know who my daddy is?"

I wanted to ask, "How do *you* know who your daddy is?" but that was just nasty. Instead I went with, "Is your daddy's name Frank Sadownik?"

"He's on the field."

"Oh."

We stared at one another for a bit until I suggested we go talk to his mother. The boy, whose name turned out to be Gerald, led me behind a line of bushes and through some thick undergrowth down a well-worn path to a break in the windbreak where a woman and another child, a girl of about four, were toiling in a large garden plot. It was scorching hot out there, away from the protective shade of trees and buildings, and although the garden seemed plentiful, it looked dry. Bordering the garden was an endless field of maturing wheat, and every so often a light breath of air would cause the green-yellow heads to ripple ever so slightly, sending us a whiff of their yeasty sweetness.

The woman, who was on her knees amongst several rows of vining peas, looked up when Gerald announced our presence with a "Hey, Mom!" She raised the back of her left hand to her brow to push away a stray curl of dark hair and at the same time shade her eyes against the blaring sun. She gave us a wide grin as she gracefully pulled herself up into a standing position. Immediately I wished I had an easel, canvas and palette of paints, for here was a sight that begged to be painted (even though I am not an artist and I am as gay as a Christmas carousel). Stella Sadownik was gorgeous. She was a traditional prairie beauty, the kind of girl seen on the wheat fields of Saskatchewan, dairy farms of Iowa and steppes of Ukraine. Her complexion was pure as fresh milk except for a slight ruddiness from a little too much wind and not enough sunblock, her eyes were sparkling marbles, her lips were full, as were her hips and bosom. She had an unblemished, unadulterated country loveliness that could effortlessly have convinced Hugh Hefner to settle down to a life of hard work, hearty meals and a house full of straw-haired children.

"Hullo!" she called out as she made her way to where I stood at the edge of her garden. Gerald had already abandoned me in favour of squishing potato beetles. She was wearing a faded housedress that had seen better days (or maybe not) and a pair of ancient sneakers with the laces missing. Her knees and hands were earth grey, and under one arm she cradled a chipped, enamel-coated bowl. When she got near me she reached into the bowl, pulled out a handful of peas and handed them to me as if this were as natural as shaking hands. "New peas, sweet as baby's breath."

I used my thumbnails to open up a pod, rolled out the barely-there peas into my palm and tossed them into my mouth. She was so right. They tasted like miniscule beads of juicy sugar. It was a taste from my childhood; the first peas of the season, too small for anything but raiding from the garden and melting down one's throat. I smiled at her and nodded my appreciation.

"Good, right?"

As I tossed back a few more of the tasty green morsels, we introduced ourselves. When that was done I glanced around to check if either of the two kids was within overhearing distance. They weren't. "I'm a detective and I'm investigating the death of a woman named Tanya Culinare."

Stella Sadownik gave me a blank look.

"I believe she was a member of the choir your husband directs?"

"Oh dear," she said with surprising sincerity. "Frank will be so sad to hear about this. Is there anything we can do, something for her family?"

This woman was as sweet as the peas she dispensed. "That's very kind of you. I was hoping to talk to your husband about Tanya and the rest of the choir."

"Of course. He's on the field right now, doing summer fallow on the hill piece. I usually take lunch out for him after one o'clock, but he never complains about an early meal. If you can wait a few minutes, I'll put it together and take you out there."

"That would be terrific, thank you."

While Stella went inside the house to fix her husband's lunch, I opted to remain outside and enjoy the beautiful weather. I found a shaded spot on an old but sturdy-looking swing set and spent the next ten minutes or so swinging to the songs of meadowlarks and robins and watching Gerald and his younger sister, Sara, chasing after chickens. The wooly mammoth deposited his bulk next to me. He must have been unbearably hot under all that fur and fat. As I sat there commiserating with the dog, I reflected on how this was turning out much differently than I'd anticipated. I had erroneously expected the director of a gay choir to be gay. I expected Stella to be Steve, and Gerald and Sara to be Snickers and Cuddles, pet Pomeranians. I was obviously way off-base and chided myself for giving into stereo-typical thinking.

Stella, a cardboard box firmly under her arm, marched out of the house, followed by an as-yet un-seen third child, a girl, older, maybe twelve and sullen. Frank's wife led the way to the back of the garage where a rustbucket Dodge was parked. She handed the container of food to the older children, who hoisted it and themselves into the box, then climbed into the cab with Sara. She arranged herself behind the wheel and I pulled myself into the pas-senger seat. It was tight quarters, with the three of us squished together like canned cocktail sausages, yet somehow Stella had room enough to expertly manoeuvre the on-the-floor stick shift and propel us out of the yard and onto the gravel road that would take us to the "hill piece." I know from my own days in the country that farmers often have names for each separate piece of land they own, like "the back forty" or "north of the slough acres" or "granddad's quarter." The names rarely make sense to anyone other than the people who farm them, and I fully expected the "hill piece" might full well be as flat as a chalkboard.

Several minutes later, Stella took us off-road (finally, here was someone who actually needed an ATV but did just fine without) into a pasture, complete with mooing cows and a once-majestic windmill now far beyond its prime. We wheeled around a few bushes, through a dried-out slough, onto a deeply rutted road, then over a set of abandoned railway tracks. Eventually we stopped long enough for Gerald to hop out of the back to open a barbwire fence gate, which allowed us access into the "hill piece." Shortly, just after we topped a rather modest hillock, we spotted a cloud of dust where Frank Sadownik, in a red and white, 806 International tractor, was pulling a disker—not the cutting edge of farming technology—round and round the field, plowing under the latest crop of pesky weeds. Stella drove us to a spot a little ahead of where the tractor was working and, while we waited for her husband to reach us, began a non-stop gay chatter about this, that and the other thing, mostly about people and events she simply expected I'd know about but that of course I'd never heard of before. My mother does the same thing. To some farm people, the world is a small place where everybody's business is everybody else's business too.

Eventually the tractor came to a stop next to us, the mighty motor grinding to a halt. As Frank Sadownik climbed down from the cab, his three children rushed to greet him as if they hadn't seen him in forever. Stella watched with a beaming smile on her pretty face.

"This is Russell," Stella told her husband as he approached the Dodge, wiping his brow and hands with a soiled rag he'd pulled from his Mark's Work Wearhouse dungarees (the blue-collar version of wonderpants).

Frank Sadownik was a big man, big everywhere: head, shoulders, gut, thighs, feet, hands, nose. He was fortyish and beginning to lose his light brown hair, except for a thick thatch on his chest. I couldn't help but wonder if this was to be my fate. Despite paying it little attention or care, I like my hair and want it with me for a long, long time. Damn birthday. Farmer Frank reached out for a handshake, his crooked smile filled with crooked teeth. When he said hello, I had no doubt this unlikely character was not only a choir director, but could probably sing like a songbird himself: his voice surprisingly soft and melodious for such a big guy.

"I'm here to talk to you about one of your choir members, Tanya Culinare," I told him.

"Oh yes?" he said as he laid a smooch on his wife's rosy cheek.

"Frank," Stella said in a sad tone, "this Tanya girl has died."

"Tanya?" he said, surprised, both eyebrows reaching in vain for his hairline.

"Russell, I hope you enjoy horseradish," Stella said. "I put it on the hamburgers, gives them a special zing."

I looked to where Stella had set out Frank's lunch on the lowered tailgate of the half-ton, and next to his plate of hamburger on a homemade bun, homemade fries, sliced-in-half radishes and a thermos of steaming coffee was another plate of the same. For me.

"Oh my gosh, Mrs. Sad—"

"Stella, please. We're all friends here."

"I didn't expect lunch, really. You should have it. I have something in the car."

"Oh no, no, this is for you. Really. Enjoy."

And so I bit into the best hamburger I have ever tasted.

"Mr. Sa...Frank, can you tell me what you know about Tanya?" I asked, chewed and swallowed.

"Well, not much really. I don't usually get to know any of the choir members that well. You see, I farm in the summer and in the winter I pick up some substitute teaching jobs, but that still doesn't keep me as busy as I'd like. I used to sing in church choirs quite a bit when I was younger but not so much lately. Then Father Gowsky approached me about directing this choir."

"Father Gowsky?"

"He's the minister from the church where the Pink Gophers do their rehearsing. I guess he listened in a few times and thought they needed help. He knew I liked to sing and had done a little choir directing in school, so he asked if I'd be interested in directing these kids. I said sure, I'd give it a whirl, as long as it was in the evenings and in the winter when I'm not too busy here on the farm. Doesn't pay hardly anything, but I enjoy it. Although, as I said, I don't really get to know the singers. In that way it's a pretty professional group, most of them are there to sing, not use it as some kind of social party place, if you know what I mean. We show up, we rehearse, we go home."

"But you do have some social get-togethers, travel as a group to concerts and competitions?"

"Yes, that's so," he got out, between munches of hamburger. "But even at that we don't interact that much. They're all a fair bit younger than me. Not much in common really, other than music."

"I see." I looked at him hoping for more. I didn't get sniffed up by your dog for nothing, mister.

He complied. "Now Tanya, all I know about her is that she was pretty quiet. Serious type. Kept to herself most times I noticed her. She had a girlfriend with her this past year, Moxie somebody I think her name was. Moxie was a friendly girl. Liked to laugh. Probably loosened Tanya up a bit, but I can't really say. Now look at that." Frank had craned his head back and was staring heavenward. Stella and I followed suit in time to catch a glimpse of a massive flock of geese, hundreds, passing low in the sky overhead. As if they noticed us noticing them, they chose that moment to offer a greeting of cacophonous honking. "Beautiful birds, those are." We nodded in agreement. "Kids, you see that?" he called out to the children, who dutifully looked up to watch the disappearing birds. "How did Tanya die?" he asked me then. "Some kind of accident? That's just terrible."

Again I checked for the whereabouts of the children. They'd gone back to roaming the field, looking for who knows what, safely out of earshot. "The police say she committed suicide. Her family is not so sure."

Stella let out a gasp and Frank just stared at me.

"If that's so," I said, thinking it was time to rattle the bushes a bit. "If Tanya was killed, there's a possibility it might have something to do with her involvement with the Pink Gophers, specifically the competition in Regina last December and the bus ride home during which they became stranded in Davidson."

He nodded and tossed a radish into his mouth. Not quite the reaction I was looking for.

"I understand that although you were at the competition in Regina, you were not on the bus that took them home, is that right?"

"Yes, that's right." He continued to look at me as if I was reading him a story that had little to do with him but he found curious nevertheless.

"I wonder if you can think of anything that happened at the competition that struck you as odd, maybe disagreements or fights between the various choirs or even members of your own choir? Was everyone getting along? Were there any disgruntled singers, perhaps jealousy over the Pink Gophers' success at the competition, anything like that?"

"You mean somebody getting mad enough to want to kill Tanya?"

"Yes."

"I don't think so, Russell. That's not the kind of people we're dealing with here. And everybody in our choir got along just fine from what I noti…" He hesitated. Good sign.

"What is it, Frank? Do you remember something?" I pushed.

He swallowed some coffee to wash down the last of his burger. "No, not really. It's just that Jin sometimes made a fuss about things. Small things, like the time of rehearsals, or how long they were, or the colour of the shirts we wore at concerts, that type of thing. It was always something with him and it turned some people off."

Having met the makeup-savvy Jin Chau, I did not find this hard to believe. He struck me as the type to regularly get under people's skin. But how deep? "Did it turn *you* off?" My intent was clear and I hated to ask this in the way I did to the husband of the hand that was feeding me the best hamburger in the world, but it was my job.

Frank looked me squarely in the eye, then replied slowly, "I really didn't get to know him well enough for him to turn me off." He turned to his wife. "You bring out supper around six then?"

She nodded and that was it. Frank shook my hand perfunctorily and told me he had field work to get back to, in case it rained.

The forecast for the next few days was for continued sun and hot temperatures.

Chapter 17

The odour was unmistakable.

Pig.

Lots of 'em.

The second thing I noticed when pulling into the farmyard—not five kilometres from the Sadownik homestead—was the endless rows of cars and trucks and combines and tractors and every other motorized vehicle created by man, each long past its best-before date, lined up like broken toy soldiers waiting for repair that would never come. Most of them were sitting on rims, gutted of their motors and other usable parts, the colour of rust and dirt mixed together. My Mazda, although twenty years old herself, looked like Cinderella's glass slipper in a closet full of worn-out, dirty workboots. Making my way through the metal carcass graveyard, I inched the car up to the nearest of seven humongous, low-slung barns, no doubt housing the source of the offending aroma that permeated the air like oil in water, coating it and choking it with its overwhelming, almost tactile consistency.

Maybe this wasn't such a good idea after all, I thought to myself as I stepped out of my automobile and approached the door of the pig barn; my farm-boy nose had obviously become citified over the past decade and a half and was not enjoying its current circumstance. I slid open the door of the first barn and a fresh waft of the stuff assaulted me like an exploding water balloon. I persevered and entered. Welcome to Pigdom Come. The barn was huge, wide and long, with a continuous row of end-to-end pens running down each side from which I could hear the grunting, squealing, guttural, unmistakable song of swine. Marvellous. Sensory overload for both nose and ears. Yet, despite rumours to the contrary, and upon closer inspection, these pigs seemed to keep their room pretty darn neat, nary a spill of slop or mess of manure to be seen. So then where the good hell was that smell coming from?

I gingerly took a few steps forward until I was

close enough to lean forward and sneak a peek into the first pen. Yup. Pig. A little further. Another pig, this one as big as a house, lying on her side like a beached whale with about three million little wriggling pink things suckling at her three million little teats. The mother seemed oblivious to all these piglets feeding off her, and I swear she was staring me right in the eye, her pink ones meeting my green ones with a certain degree of animosity and…wait… what was that…did I hear chanting? It sounded like…"Four legs goooooood, two legs baaaaaaaaad." I was outta there.

I fared no better in the second barn, but in the third I found what I was looking for: a human.

"Excuse me, sir, hello," I called from the door, hoping he'd come to me and I wouldn't have to go to him.

"Whatever you're selling, I don't want," the pig farmer's voice called back.

Oh geez, I'd have to go to him. I entered the barn and, without acknowledging the sows and boars and their countless progeny on either side of me, I approached the man, who was busy doing pig farmer stuff about halfway down the barn's length, three-tine pitchfork in hand. He was a rather attractive man in his late thirties, balding, average height, soulful eyes, powerful chest and baseball-slugger arms obvious beneath the cotton of his one-piece jumper (I'm sure that's not how he referred to his outfit, but that's what it was).

"Lot's of cars and things out there," I started out in an amiable tone.

His face took on a friendlier expression. "That what you're here for? You looking for parts? What kinda vehicle? I can see what I got. Got most everything. And can I ask how you heard about me? Was it newspaper ad, referral, the notice up at the post office, my website?"

Quite the entrepreneur. "Actually I'm not here for parts."

Less-friendly look.

"I'm a little lost," I kept on. "I'm looking for a fellow name of Frank Sadownik? I think he lives around here? I'm Arnold Ziffel, the superintendent of the Prairie Lilly School Division, and we're looking to hire Mr. Sadownik. Just coming out to meet him in person."

"Oh, I didn't know Frank was thinking about getting back into teaching full time," the man said. "Sure, he lives around here."

"Maybe we could go outside and you could give me directions." And an oxygen mask.

"It's not far," he began, not moving from his spot. "Just head west as soon as you leave the yard here for about two miles till you come to a crossroad. You'll notice a big pine with a crooked top—you probably seen it on your way out here?—well, you turn right there and head another coupla miles until you see a yard with three newer-looking grain bins. That's his place."

"You been neighbours with Frank a long time?" I asked, pretending to have committed his directions to memory.

"Yeah, I guess."

"Good guy then?"

"Yeah sure, I guess. Likes his religion more'n I do, but he's okay. You never know nowadays with neighbours, do ya? It's a roll of the dice who you're gonna get, even on the farm, so many people coming and going these days. Used to be you were neighbours with the same folks all your life, and then your kids were neighbours with the neighbour's kids, and on and on. Now, ya never know. Game of chance."

I thought that was an odd comment on things, but maybe pig farmer guy just liked to wax philosophical. Regardless, I had to get him back on topic. "So you get along with Frank then? You think he'd make a good teacher?"

He frowned a bit. "I guess you'd know that better than I would."

"So you'd trust him with your kids?"

More frowning.

Maybe I needed to give him a little more reason to confide in me. "It's important in my line of work that we find out as much as we can about the teachers we hire. I like to talk to people like you, neighbours and acquaintances, kind of like getting references."

"Did Frank give you my name as a reference?"

Where was the toothless, big-bellied, grade-school-educated, all-trusting, gossipy pig farmer of days gone by? "Ah no…I'm just lost."

"Well, I've given you directions then, haven't I?"

Yep.

There are only a few bus charter and rental businesses in the Saskatoon *Yellow Pages* and I called them all until I found one that recalled being hired by the Pink Gophers—luckily for me, a name that tended to stick in people's memories—for a trip to and from Regina last December. That was the easy part. Getting the last name and address of the bus driver was a little more work—but not much.

I identified myself as Frank Sadownik (Jared had told me that, as the group's pseudo leader, it would have been Frank who arranged transportation to the competition). When I outright asked for the bus driver's information, the woman who answered my call had refused—and rightly so—until, that is, I told her how the Pink Gophers and Guy, the bus driver, had bought some lottery tickets as a group to commemorate the night they were stranded together in Davidson and that, surprise of all surprises, they'd won some money. The group simply wanted Guy to have his share. This, not surprisingly, is everyone's dream come true and the woman quickly acquiesced to my request. She revealed that Guy—last name Marcotte—had only been a part-time employee in the first place and, coincidentally, had not worked for the company since that December trip. She said his cheques went to a post office box but that she was pretty sure he lived in a trailer somewhere near the Circle Drive freeway and a railway because she remembered him complaining about the noise keeping him from a good night's sleep one day when he was late for work. After that it was as simple as studying a map of Saskatoon to find the right trailer park. I didn't have an address yet, and there was no listing for a Guy Marcotte in the phone book, but I was on his scent.

I pulled into a land where streets have no names and immediately felt ill at ease. I thought I knew Saskatoon pretty well, but here was a place I did not know at all. Sure, like any other city around the world, Saskatoon has its good parts and its bad parts, parts that are safe and parts less so; parts primarily inhabited by one specific segment of the city's varied demographic or another; parts for loud, parts for quiet; parts for richer, parts for poorer; dirty parts, clean parts; parts you visit and parts you don't. And this was one of those parts that kept itself well-hidden until you took a wrong turn. It was like stumbling upon a room in your house you never knew was there.

North of 115th Street, just off where the communities of Sutherland and Forest Grove don't quite intersect, is a triangular patch of land that hugs the CPR rail line, and therein lay the trailer court Guy Marcotte called home sweet home. I didn't even know if the place had a name.

I directed the Mazda off Central Avenue, down to the end of Powe Street, and the first thing to catch my eye was a flat-roofed building, boarded up with cheap plywood, with a sign above a set of barred front doors that identified it as Hagar's Confectionery. I couldn't even be sure whether or not the place was closed for business or just poorly—very poorly—kept up, and I certainly wasn't inclined to stop and find out. Nevertheless, Hagar's seemed a fitting sentinel for this hidden enclave.

I decided to case the area before making any other moves and slowly wound my way up and down the short, narrow, bland streets of the trailer park neighbourhood. As I did so, I marvelled at the countless types of trailers in every shape and size imaginable: skinny, fat, metal, wood. Some had decks and built-on extensions, others had barely enough nails to hold them together; some were freshly painted in bright hues, while others sat dejected and unloved in sickly yellow, pale green and industrial grey. The yards were uniformly small, but the similarity ended there: some were alive with cheerful pots of marigolds and pansies swinging from eavestroughs, healthy patches of lawn and pretty little outdoor sitting areas, whereas right next door the plots grew thick with weeds or had been left unattended for so long that all that was left was a scabby parcel of dead earth. Hagar's Heath—as I'd fondly come to think of the place—was where massive satellite dishes, souped-up cars and plastic yard ornaments went to live after the rest of the city's population had tired of them.

There was a lakeside-cabin-y feel to the whole place, with un-pruned, unruly tree limbs hanging low over trailers that pointed end-out at an angle toward the street, somewhere no one would ever think to live year-round but certainly would consider sufficient for a summer weekend getaway. Trailer parks are odd places in general; the homes are meant to be mobile, yet usually the only transient thing about them are the people who live in them.

After a few minutes of driving back and forth, I was beginning to get noticed by locals, many of whom seemed to be milling about as if in search for somewhere cooler than the un-air-conditioned boxes they called home. I wasn't sure if it was my sporty Mazda RX-7 with its top down that was seizing attention or the fact that a suspicious stranger had come to town, but I was definitely as foreign to them as they were to me. And this was their turf.

Finally I pulled to a stop in front of an off-white trailer with a massive bay window. Below it was a long-abandoned flower bed where two stalky delphiniums had managed to poke up through crackled earth so dry it was almost white. I waited until two young women on a leisurely walkabout, pushing three separate baby carriages, were about even with my car and called out a friendly, "Hello."

They slowed down, did not stop, stared at me but otherwise did not respond to my greeting.

"I was wondering if you could tell me where Guy Marcotte lives?" I asked in a pleasant voice.

They kept on truckin' and never looked back.

Okay.

Maybe they speak another language here in Hagar's Heath, I mused to myself.

I moved along until I found a guy working under the hood of his monster truck. The thing sat so high off the ground, on wheels that had to be twice normal size, he needed a stepladder to reach the motor. Again I pulled up and called out a greeting and asked for directions. The guy gave me and my car a careful looking-over then told me to get lost. So I did. I tried this tactic twice more until I finally found a more talkative resident. She was old, ninety if she was a day, wearing baggy trousers, a Hawaiian shirt and dirty white sneakers. Her blowsy hair was dyed red—about ten years ago—and her face was as wrinkled as a Shar-Pei hound.

"Why you want to find him?" she asked me from her perch on an ancient, wooden kitchen chair she'd positioned in a slice of shade next to the front (and only) door of her trailer.

Regardless of her cantankerous demeanor, when I realized she would actually talk to me, I got out of the car, came to within two metres of her and her chair and stopped, not wanting to push my luck and thinking it wise to stay close to the Mazda in case I needed to make a quick escape (this place was really giving me the heebie-jeebies). "I have something for him," I told her, not quite prepared to spin a fanciful tall tale (you see, I had thought I'd ask someone for directions, and they'd give them to me; that's how this kind of thing is supposed to work).

"Oh yeah? What's that?"

Fortunately I can be quick with lies if pressed. "I'm from the bus company where he used to work."

"Oh yeah." She began picking her teeth with a toothpick. Just finished a late lunch of Spam, I thought.

"I have his final cheque."

"Couldn't mail it?"

Patience, Quant, patience. I gave a little laugh. "Well, we misplaced his address." I knew what the next question was going to be, so I cut her off at the pass. "But I remembered him saying he lived out here, so I thought I'd deliver it in person."

"Mighty nice of you to do something like that outta the goodness of your heart." Was that sarcasm I heard?

Enough of this. "Do you know where he lives?"

"Don't know if I should tell you. That's private information, now isn't it?"

By this time, a neighbour, a skeletal-looking man in overalls, who'd been doing very little to hide the fact that he was listening to our conversation, gave us a harrumph. The woman looked at him and said, "This guy wants to give money to Guy Marcotte."

That seemed to be enough information for him. He waved his hand in a dismissive way, as if we'd interrupted his life in a most rude way, and ambled off with a sideways gait.

"He's down there," the woman said, her voice suddenly tired-sounding. "The brown one on the end behind all those damned lilacs."

Finally. I chuckled. "You don't like lilacs?" Everyone likes lilacs.

"Smell of the flowers drives me bonkers. And they attract bees! Bees everywhere, all spring long until those damn flowers die."

I nodded in empathy and thanked the woman and returned to my car. As I drove off I felt her eyes, and the eyes of several more of Hagar's peoples, on the scruff of my hot neck.

I pulled up in front of Guy Marcotte's home,

mostly hidden from the street by several large, globe-shaped lilac bushes. I got out of the car again and picked my way down a gravelled walkway through the bushes, noticing an abundance of brown, dried-out blooms. They were long done emitting their sweet, bee-attracting aroma; now they simply smelled...brown. The trailer was shabby looking and all the windows in my sight were covered over from the inside, no doubt in an attempt to keep the sun's rays from treating the metal box like a microwave oven. I mounted three steps to the door, rapped my knuckles on it and waited, taking a quick survey of the surrounding area and detecting the unmistakable scent of marijuana. It took a second knock before the door finally opened.

Now Guy Marcotte was what is known in gay lexicon as a Bear, and a cute one too. At well above six feet, he had about three or four inches and forty pounds on me, some of it muscle, some of it gut and butt. Although his head was shaved, you could tell it wasn't because he was trying to hide male pattern baldness, but rather he was going for a look. He hadn't shaved for a couple of days and dark bristles were poking up everywhere. His Tom of Finland face was tanned and he sported a mighty, dark-brown moustache that turned up at the ends like a happy face smile. He was wearing a leather vest (in this weather!), snug jeans and lace-up boots. He smelled of man.

"Yeah?" he grunted as he stepped out of the doorway, shutting the door behind him as if he was just leaving. I guessed I wasn't going to be invited in for dainties.

"Hi," I said, backing up and down the steps as he stepped into my personal space, either as some sort of intimidation tactic or, like some people, he just didn't understand polite speaking distance. "My name is Russell Quant and I wanted to talk to you about a job you did last December for the bus company. You drove a choir called the Pink Gophers to Regina?"

He nodded and shrugged his mighty shoulders. "Yeah, so what?" He clumped down the steps so he was now on ground level with me.

"I'm investigating several cases of harassment against the members of that group and I was wondering if I could ask you some questions about that particular trip?"

"Well, whatever, guy," he said. "But it can't be now. My girlfriend will have my ass if I don't pick her up at the mall in like five minutes ago. So some other time, huh?" He nodded, not unfriendly-like, as if to seal the deal and began to head down the path toward a dusty old Chevy parked in a makeshift driveway. I followed. "You can call me if you want."

Yeah, sure, heard that one before. "Your number's not in the book."

He cocked an eye my way as he slid into his car then rambled off a number that I committed to memory.

"Whenever," he said as his car's engine rumbled to troubled life. "Just not now. Sorry, guy," he added with a smirk. "I guess I'm whipped, eh?" And with that he backed out of his stall and sped off in a putrid puff of exhaust fumes.

I waved a jaunty so-long and headed back to my car. I was thinking about making a stop at the YW for a much-needed workout when my cellphone rang.

"Yo," I answered, trying out a new greeting.

"Russell," it was Errall. "We've been trying to find you for hours. Don't you ever check your...oh God, never mind that."

Suddenly my back went stiff and my veins filled with ice. There was something in her voice that demanded I pay close attention. Something bad had happened.

"Russell, we're at RUH..." The most heart-wrenching sound escaped her lips and I feared (wished?) she wouldn't go on. But she did. "Jared has been...oh God, Russell, Jared has been attacked...I think...he's dying."

Chapter 18

The seven-wing, seven-storey Royal University Hospital is located adjacent to the University of Saskatchewan campus off College Drive near the top of the University Bridge; it serves as the main trauma centre for the entire province. The interminable journey from Hagar's Heath to RUH was an exercise in sheer mental agony. I could not bear not knowing what was happening to Jared, the partner of my mentor, Anthony Gatt, and a man for whom I harboured an intense but inappropriate love, but above all, a dear, close friend.

Leaving the car in a parking lot, I sprinted to the Emergency Room entrance. I burst inside and immediately caught sight of Errall in the waiting room to the right of the doors, standing at the far end of the tiny room, on the phone, her back to me. I studied the other faces in the small area, none were familiar. I walked up to her and gently placed a hand on her left shoulder. She turned around with a jerk, as if expecting some sort of attack. When she saw it was me, she immediately hung up the phone. I'd never seen her eyes look that way before. Errall is known for the clarity and sharpness of her impossibly blue eyes, but at that moment they were dull, watery, bloodshot and unfathomably sad.

"Errall," I whispered. "Tell me."

"Let's get out of here," she hissed. "I've just gotta get out of this fucking place." A couple of the other people in the waiting room stared at her, not with distaste at her choice of words, but with empathy, for they understood only too well where she was coming from.

She led me through the ambulance bay and outside, the same way I'd come in, and immediately lit up a cigarette with unsteady hands. I wanted one too. Instead I put my hands on her shoulders, glued my eyes to hers and said, "Errall, what the hell is going on?"

"Anthony was at the store when he got a call from the hospital saying they'd found his name and number in Jared's wallet as the person to contact in case of an accident."

"He was in an accident? Is that it? What? For God's sake, Errall, what happened to Jared?" I fought a reckless temptation to throttle the information out of her.

The words came out of her mouth as if each was laden with spurs, causing her physical pain to say them. "It was no accident. Someone threw acid in Jared's face."

I was stunned. For a moment it was as if I hadn't heard her, as if the world had stopped communicating to me and I was in a bubble of oblivion, so quiet, serene, no sensory stimulation at all. But then, all too soon, reality exploded in my brain and I felt as if I might disintegrate.

"How? How, how, how?" was all I managed to get out.

Errall took two deep drags of her cigarette in quick succession. "I don't know. Anthony called me on his way here. He said he'd been trying to find you but couldn't. I told him to leave it to me." Her dark circled eyes grabbed onto mine as if they were drowning and looking for rescue. "It's bad, Russell. I think it's really bad."

"Where's Anthony now?"

"He and Jared's parents are with Jared, or as close as they'll let them get. They won't let anyone else in right now. I've been fucking alone with no one to talk to in that fucking stinking waiting room filled with snot-nosed kids and guys with fucking cuts oozing blood on the fucking floor..."

"Will you watch your fucking mouth?" I told her in a pressing tone. She was about to lose control—I was too—and this wasn't the time. "This isn't about you, Errall! Have you talked to Anthony at all? Do you know how this happened?"

"Barely," she said, surprisingly not striking out with a sharp tongue or fingernail to impale me for telling her off. "All Anthony told me on the phone was that Jared was attacked in their apartment. Someone must have come to the door. Afterwards Jared was able to get to a phone and dial nine-one-one. Whoever it was who called Anthony from the hospital said someone had thrown a substance in Jared's face and they thought it might be acid. They didn't know if...if his body could survive the trauma...Russell, oh God, Russell, why would this happen to our sweet, sweet Jared?"

I had the sinking feeling I knew the answer to that. Or at least part of the answer. "Do they have a suspect?" I questioned. "Are the police involved? Has someone been caught?"

"Why are you asking me all these questions I don't know the answer to?" she spat at me. "I hate that!" She tossed aside her spent cigarette with great disdain and reached for another.

"Errall, you know this case I'm working on."

"Yeah, yeah, yeah," she said. Her face took on the look of someone desperate for a change of subject.

"I think Jared is involved somehow."

"What are you talking about? How? Weren't you hired to find out why that woman jumped off the Broadway Condos building?"

"Yes, that's how it began, but it's become something much different. One thing led to another and then another..."

"But how is Jared involved?"

"I think the boogeyman is after him."

When Errall could smoke no more, I led her back into the waiting room. I didn't want to be far should Anthony or a doctor come out with news of Jared. Thankfully emergencies in Saskatoon that Thursday evening hit a slow spell and we mostly had the uncomfortable seats and bad coffee to ourselves. We spent some time going over what we didn't know and eventually fell into private silences, contemplating the fate of our friend.

"Russell," came a familiar voice.

I looked up from where I'd slouched down into my seat. It was Constable Darren Kirsch. Both Errall and I jumped up and, forgoing greetings of any sort, barraged him with questions.

"I thought I'd find you here," he said in a calm, professional voice.

Two men in their forties pushing an eighty-year-old woman in a wheelchair entered the waiting room about then, and Darren shepherded us into a corner where we sat in a tight group.

"Have you seen him? Have you heard anything?" I asked him.

"Although Jared was lucid enough after his attack to call nine-one-one, by the time the emergency response team arrived on the scene he was unconscious. They had to break down the door to the apartment. He's been slipping in and out of consciousness ever since. We've been unable to talk to him to find out exactly what happened or if he knew his attacker or attackers."

"But you've been to the apartment, where it happened?" I said. "You have some ideas, right?"

Darren eyed me carefully and then Errall, I guess to assess our mental stability at this highly emotional time. We must have passed muster, because he went on. "There was no forced entry—other than the ERT—so it would appear that Jared let his attacker in."

"It was someone he knew!" Errall exclaimed.

"Not necessarily. It just means Jared didn't suspect a threat from this person." He took a breath before continuing. "It appears that the attack took place right in the doorway. A substance was tossed into Jared's face. We're quite certain now that it was some low-grade form of acid."

Oh God. Oh God. Oh God.

"Is it...is it bad?" Errall croaked out.

The big cop only nodded.

All I could think of was Jared's face, a thing of such great beauty it had graced the cover of almost every major fashion and entertainment magazine in North America and Europe. People were awestruck by the curves and edges of a face put together in such perfect proportion that it defied easy description or conventional definition; the olive skin that gave him the exotic look of an untouchable stranger, the golden green eyes of a gentle lioness, the thick lips that when turned into a smile lit up a room. I did not know if *I* could live without Jared's face: could he?

And then one other thought. Acid was also used to desecrate Duncan Sikorsky's artwork in Vancouver.

"I spoke with Anthony," Darren told us.

"How is he?" Errall and I both asked at once.

"As you might expect. I spoke with him about whether he had any idea who might have done this. He didn't. He said everyone loves Jared." He looked at me then. "But Jared told him about your experience at the Berry Barn—I read the police report—and that you thought Jared might somehow be tied to the case you're working on. I need you to tell me what's going on, Quant." It wasn't a request.

I glanced around the room, and except for the two men and their mother/mother-in-law who were commiserating quietly amongst themselves, the place was empty. "It began with Tanya Culinare," I said in hushed tones, "the woman who jumped off the Broadway Condominiums building. That led to me to discover the death of her ex-girlfriend, Moxie Banyon."

"Another suicide?" Errall asked.

"Accident, or so it seems—to some."

"I asked the Moose Jaw cops some questions, like you asked, Quant," Darren said. "There really wasn't much of an investigation. It seemed like she drowned, no cause for suspicion."

I strongly disagreed with that assessment. "What about now?"

"We'll be looking into things a little deeper."

"I don't know how, but I think Moxie Banyon was murdered, maybe unpremeditated, but murdered nonetheless."

"Quant, what the hell…?"

"Just listen to me. As I dug into the recent past of Tanya and Moxie I found a disturbing similarity, a pattern of extreme, unrelenting harassment, as if someone wanted to scare them to death."

"You think Tanya Culinare and Moxie Banyon were scared to death?" He sounded incredulous and, really, I didn't blame him.

I nodded. "First off, Tanya Culinare was not the

most stable person to begin with. Then all this shit begins to happen, first to Moxie, then to her. They end up breaking up, or maybe they decide to part ways for a while until things return to normal—I'm not sure which. Moxie moves to Moose Jaw, then she—not a swimmer—ends up in a pool, fully dressed, and drowns. The barrage of harassment against Tanya escalates. I'm not a therapist, and I don't know if Tanya was unstable enough to be the type of person already at risk to kill herself, but given this constant environment of fear and mental torture, I think that's exactly what happened.

"I think the night she died, she'd been driven to the limit and finally cracked. For months she'd suffered almost daily doses of harassment: threatening phone calls, things that go bump in the night, mysterious packages showing up on her doorstep, constantly being watched or followed, all petty irritations that when added together were driving her around the bend. She had no family here, no friends to speak of, her lover had left town...and then died... She'd been to see a therapist, but it wasn't helping; he may not have even believed that what she said she was experiencing was real. Her only real friend, her boss, Victoria Madison, didn't believe her.

"Then that last night, she was hiding out in her apartment as she often did, alone, scared, as she often was, and then once more she heard noises, as if someone was trying to get in her apartment.

Maybe the phone was ringing too. Desperate and frightened, she tried to reach out for help. She knew that if she couldn't put an end to this, she'd go insane. She'd already tried the police. Her boss had given her the number of a private detective: me.

"So she calls me. It's two-thirty in the morning. She tells me that someone is coming to get her, that he wants to hurt her. She sounds like someone who is frightened to death. It's too much for her. She hangs up. She's all alone, no one to turn to. Someone is there, wanting to hurt her, perhaps kill her like they killed her girlfriend. She can't leave the apartment because she believes this boogeyman is behind the door, so she escapes to the balcony. Someone is still trying to get in, scratching at the door, phone still ringing. She feels all alone, helpless, terrified, desperate. She jumps."

For a moment the three of us sat there in silence, somehow sensing that my scenario was not far off from what really happened to Tanya Culinare that sad night.

I added an extraneous thought, "It could be that whoever was carrying out this systematic harassment didn't necessarily expect Tanya to kill herself."

Errall completed my gruesome hypothesis. "But it was a welcome result?"

I nodded and continued to unfold the steps of my case. "Then I met Moxie's best friend, Duncan—a man terrified of his own shadow. I found out he's been suffering the same kind of harassment from the elusive boogeyman character."

"Boogeyman," Kirsch stated flatly. "How can you be certain it's the same guy doing all of this? And why 'boogeyman'?"

Good questions. "I guess I can't be one hundred per cent sure, but whoever this person is, he or she loves nothing better than to send the victims little love letters. And they all say the same thing: Boo."

"God, Russell, this is giving *me* the creeps," Errall admitted.

"So then Duncan disappears, but before he does he leaves me a photograph of a group of people, and one of those people is Jared." I gave Kirsch a pointed look. "The list of names I asked you to check out was a list of people in that photograph."

He nodded. "Most of which had made complaints about being harassed." He was beginning to take me a little more seriously now. "So you think this boogeyman character is after everyone in the photograph?"

"Why else would Duncan give it to me?"

"Could he be wrong? Or could *he* be the boogeyman, trying to mislead you?"

Sheesh. I didn't want to consider that. But it didn't feel right. Duncan's fear was so palpable I doubted he could have faked it. "Maybe, but I don't think so."

"Quant, I think you're jumping to some mighty

big conclusions here." A typical cop response. They want to be the only ones who jump to the big conclusions. "There's a whole hell of a lot of difference between harassment and scaring someone to death, or worse. What you're talking about is murder."

"I know, I know. What I don't understand is that for some reason the boogeyman is treating some of the people in the photo differently than others. Some are only getting threatening notes and irritating calls, while others are ending up dead. It's like he hates them all, but some more than others."

"Or…"

I stared at Kirsch and waited for it. Despite his usual inclination to disparage most of what I say, Kirsch is—I hate to admit it—a smart cop, and he knows when something fishy is more than just an unpleasant smell.

"Maybe he's new at this," he began somewhat slowly. "Maybe the boogeyman is only just now beginning to acquire a taste for murder," he said, eyes narrowed in thought. "Something you said earlier—about how maybe he didn't intend for Tanya to kill herself. What if he just meant to harass these people for some reason and then, whoops, one of them—Moxie was the first—dies. Suddenly he's a murderer rather than a simple troublemaker getting petty revenge for something…and he finds that he likes it. So he steps up his efforts and, with Tanya this time, it happens again. Russell, this guy could be developing into a real maniac, ignited by his own actions, becoming…a serial killer."

All three of us shared a collective gulp. Could it be true? Had we stumbled into something this huge, this dangerous, this potentially fatal for everyone in that photograph?

"And now Jared," Errall said, looking at me with moist eyes, her mouth a grim line across a blanched face.

Darren stood up. "I'm going back to the station, dig deeper into those names on that list from the photo. Maybe something else's turned up." He stared at me, his face a piece of granite. "What about you? Is there anything else you should tell me?"

There've been times when I've held out on Darren, not told him all I knew, but not this time, not with Jared's life hanging in the balance. I gave him the names of the choir director and bus driver and a description of my brief meetings with both men and then he was off.

My phone rang. Oh crap, no cellphones in a hospital. But the way things were going today, I had to answer it.

"Mr. Quant?" a quaking voice came across the line. "It's Kim Pelluchi. You gave me your card with your number? You have to help me. Richie is gone!"

Despite her desire for more smokes, Errall agreed to stay behind in case word came of Jared's condition while I took Kim's call outdoors.

"Tell me what happened," I said to the woman in as calm a voice as I could manage. God, I wanted one of Errall's cigarettes.

"Richie and I had this big argument after you left last night," she said. "He told me that something *did* happen the night we were stranded in Davidson. He said he couldn't tell me about it but that he was going to put an end to all our hassles once and for all. Then he just took off on his bike." Oh shit. "And I haven't heard from him since. I tried reaching him all day today, but nothing, and none of his friends have heard from him either." The bike. Oh shit. "Mr. Quant, I'm scared something bad has happened to him, and you told me to call if…"

"Oh shit." I said it out loud this time.

"What was that?"

"Nothing, nothing. Kim, I think I may know where Richie is. I'll call you." And I hung up. No time to explain.

I ran back into the hospital, where Errall sat waiting and looking wholly miserable.

"Anything?" I asked her.

She shook her head. I'm guessing that by the look on my face, she knew something was up.

"I have to go."

She glared at me as if I'd lost my mind. "What

the hell is the matter with you?"

"I may know who's behind all of this, and if it's the same bastard who did this to Jared—"

"Go."

Chapter 19

I had recently seen a bike, a ten-speed, with flaking chips of red paint clinging to its battered frame. At the time I didn't know who it belonged to, but it all came together with the call from Kim Pelluchi. The bike, just like the one Richie described to me as his own the night before, was leaning against Guy Marcotte's trailer. Could it be a coincidence? Absolutely. But I didn't think so.

By the time I made a left off Central Avenue into the bowels of Hagar's Heath, the sun had set on this dreadful day and darkness covered the Mazda like a heavy cloak. Without signs to follow, I slowed my pace as I searched for the street I'd visited earlier that afternoon. My eyes were drawn to an unearthly glow, and even though the top was up and the windows were closed, I could smell smoke. What the hell is going on? I wondered to myself, my suspicions running amok. An alien craft landing? Someone being burned at the stake? What were these people up to?

My car trembled over the rough road surface and eventually I came to an empty lot…well, empty except for the bonfire. In the middle of the lot—I'm sure contrary to numerous city ordinances—was a large group of people forming a circle around a blazing fire pit. Were they swaying? Chanting? Wearing hoods? My stomach tightened and prickles of fear dotted my neck. Was this some kind of cult? Was something being sacrificed here? There was a smell, something familiar. But this was a matter for another time—in daylight, with a police escort. Maybe. I just wanted to get away unnoticed with my head and hide still attached to my body. I released the clutch and kept moving.

As it turned out, Guy Marcotte's trailer was at the beginning of the next street over, less than half a block away from where the fire-gazers were doing their spooky bit. I pulled up behind his empty faux driveway, thought better of it and moved the car further down the street. My gun was still safely stored in a box in my garage. Crap. Why did I even bother? No matter. If this guy was responsible for Jared's attack, I'd take him down with bare hands if I had to. I swung open the door of the car and slipped out with as little noise as I could. That's when I heard the growling.

I froze.

Dog!

Big dog? Little dog? Hungry dog? Stray dog? Tied-up dog? Pit bull? Chihuahua?

The growl continued, lasting an impressive fifteen seconds until the darn thing had to take a breath, and then another fifteen seconds, another breath, another fifteen seconds, and so on and so on. This was one inhospitable place, and I promised myself that after tonight I'd never return to Hagar's Heath. My current options however were few: get back in the car or track down someone who might be responsible for Jared's critical condition. Only one option counted. I began to walk. The growling continued but grew fainter the further away I got from the car. Tied-up dog. Phew.

It helped that I'd been to Guy Marcotte's trailer before. I knew the lilac bushes fronting the structure would afford me good cover, but only so far. I also knew most of the windows were covered over. I'd originally thought it was because of the heat, but now I had a new theory: something bad happened that night in Davidson, between some or all of the members of the Pink Gophers and the bus driver, Guy Marcotte, and Richie knew about it. Richie'd come here to confront Guy and instead had been taken prisoner, at least until Guy could figure out what to do with him. Earlier this afternoon when I had seen the red bike, Richie was probably already inside. Guy had pretended to be leaving, to lure me away from the scene of his latest crime.

My hope was that one of the windows at the rear of the trailer, facing away from the street, might have been left uncovered. I needed to get a look inside, either to prove my theory wrong or, alternatively, give me an idea of what I was up against.

Crouching low, I crab-walked across the open space between the lilac bushes and trailer. I made it without being spotted, I hoped, and plastered myself against the trailer wall, listening for telltale sounds from within. There were no screams for help or threatening epithets, but I could discern a light buzz of conversation or maybe a TV or radio. The window coverings—some sort of cheap vinyl blinds—were opaque, but through the thin material I could tell there were lights on somewhere inside, so despite the empty driveway, someone was home. The flaking-red-paint ten-speed bike was in the same spot I'd seen it in earlier, leaning against a tree trunk. Careful not to make a noise, I slid down the length of the long rectangle of the trailer, across the back and up the other side, checking each window along the way. No luck. Every one of them was covered. Great. Now what? Knock?

Yup.

I'd run out of patience for this cat-and-mouse game. I abandoned all appearance of stealth and marched back around to the front of the trailer and up the three steps to the door, rapping on it with a force of authority. I wasn't sure of my plan, but I had to find out if Richie was in there and in trouble. I'd force my way in if I had to.

Guy Marcotte, now in a red polo and denim cut-offs, answered the door with what seemed to me anticipatory speed. He appeared surprised to see that his guest was me and not someone else.

"I...I...well, I didn't expect to see you," he bumbled.

That much was obvious. "Where is Richie Caplan?" The direct approach seemed appropriate. "I know he's here. I want to see him. Now."

"What? I don't know what you're talking about. Who's Richie?" This guy would never win an Academy Award, or even a grade school amateur talent contest for that matter.

"I'd like to come in," I said, taking a half-step forward so that we were now uncomfortably close. He either had to kiss me or step back. He wisely chose the latter. Using the space he created, I slid by the large man into his home. Inside it was hot, smelling of cooked meat and in a general state of bachelor disarray. I wondered where the henpecking girlfriend was—if there really was such a person.

"You can't just come in here. You're not the police or anything," he reasoned absolutely correctly. Thankfully he failed to notice that with our relative sizes—he much bulkier than I—he could easily have tossed me outside onto my butt. Instead he stuck with verbal threats. "I'm gonna call them. I'm gonna call the cops if you don't bugger off right now."

"Go for it," I said. "That's a good idea." It really was. "They'd like to know where Richie Caplan is too." Well, not completely true. "Now where is he?"

I scanned the inside of Guy Marcotte's home. I could see everything except the bedroom and bathroom, which were at the far end of the long, narrow space. "Is he back there?" I asked, using a voice deep with bravado.

"He's not here right now."

Aha. "I thought you didn't know who he was?" Oh well, no time to get into that now. "Where is he?" I demanded to know. "What did you do to him?"

"Do to him? I didn't do nothing to him. I…"

"What?"

"Never mind. I told you, he's not here right now. Now get out."

I strode to the back of the trailer and stuck my

nose into the bathroom (gross) and bedroom (better, but not by much). No Richie. Guy kept to the same spot throughout my search. I walked up to him, put my face into his and murmured menacingly under my breath, "His bike is outside. Now tell me where the hell he is."

"I borrowed him my car." Huh? Indeed the Chevy I'd seen Guy driving earlier that afternoon was not out front.

"What for? Where did he go?" You let your kid-nappee borrow your car?

Guy looked away and shrugged his mighty shoulders.

"You're lying. I know what you're doing, Guy. I know you've been terrorizing the Pink Gophers. Richie knew it too. He figured it out last night and he came here to confront you and make you stop." I was desperate for him to say something that would make all this make sense because, right about then, nothing did. "What did you do then, Guy? What did you do to Richie Caplan to keep him quiet?"

As Guy's dark eyes met mine, I got the feeling that although I was on the right train, I was definitely on the wrong track. In a heavy voice, as masculine as he could make it, Guy said, "I'd never hurt Richie. I..." He stopped.

"What? You what?"

"I...I like the guy, okay?" He looked down at his big feet.

Oh boy. I did not see that coming. He was either being very clever, leading me on with this line, or else he truly was this big ol' galoot of a guy who had the hots for another guy and was bashful about admitting it. But if that was true, then where was Richie? Was he safe? Or had he been lying to his friend Kim? Was *he* the boogeyman? Had *he* attacked Jared?

"How long has Richie been gone?"

"I don't know. A couple hours I guess. I thought it was him when you knocked. I'm worried about him."

"Why? Where did he go? I want you to tell me exactly what is going on between the two of you."

"Nothing, really, man. Richie and I have been hanging out for a while." Hanging out—also known as dating, unless, that is, you're a gay guy still pretending to be straight. "We met during the bus trip to Regina, and, well, you know."

Yeah, yeah, yeah. "You're sleeping together." Keep the story going, buddy.

"Trying stuff out, man." The manly-man voice coming out of Guy Marcotte was deeper and gruffer than ever.

"That's beautiful, man. I'm happy for you." Perhaps a little smarmy. Then louder, "Now tell me what's going on!"

"Richie did come over here last night. It was really late. He'd had some kind of fight with Kim.

She's a friend of his. He said there was some kind of detective who...hey...that was you, wasn't it?"

Stellar bit of deduction. I just stared at him.

"All along, Richie has been trying to figure out who this boogeyman fuck is who's been doing all this shit to him and Kim. Then he heard from this other guy, Duncan, that another two girls they knew were dead and that some guy, pretending to be a detective, was after him. Then Duncan disappeared. This really scared Richie. He thought this detective—you—was the boogeyman. So he tried to get you before you got him and Kim. Then last night when you turned up, he began to believe that you weren't the boogeyman either. But if you weren't him, then who was? I guess you started talking about who could be responsible, and you brought up the bus driver—me—and the choir director. Well, Richie knew it couldn't have been me."

Oh really? I wasn't quite so convinced of that myself yet. "So Richie thinks Frank Sadownik is behind all this?"

Guy nodded. "At least he did when he got here last night. He was really freaked out when he got here, and I settled him down and finally I got him to sleep."

"He slept here last night?" I wasn't trying to embarrass the guy, just confirm suspect locations.

He nodded. More toe studying.

"When I came over this afternoon, was Richie

here? Why all the 'going to pick up my girlfriend' garbage?"

He shrugged a little, abashed. "Richie was here. I was just...I'm just a little shy about this stuff, eh?"

"So are you saying Richie borrowed your car to go see Frank Sadownik? And he's still there?"

Guy shook his head. "No. That's what he wanted to do. But after we talked about it, he realized it didn't make sense, that you were wrong."

Ah, wait a sec, I wasn't wrong about anything. Yes, I brought up Frank as a possible suspect, but I was just rustling bushes, that's all, looking to see what might fall out; that's how this detecting shtick works sometimes. I didn't need to explain myself to this guy. Instead I just scowled mightily and let him speak.

"But the idea of the whole boogeyman thing being related to that night in Davidson, when we were all stranded in that hotel, made sense to Richie. You see, something did happen that night."

According to Kim Pelluchi, that's exactly what Richie told her last night before he stomped off. Something happened that night in Davidson that he couldn't tell her about. I was beginning to think that "something" was his hooking up with the butch bus driver. But maybe that wasn't it at all. Had something else happened that night?

Guy kept on in his lightly French-flavoured

voice. "He didn't think much of it at the time, kind of forgot about it actually, until you brought up the possible connection between the harassment and that night in Davidson."

"Tell me what happened," I instructed as a teacher might a not-too-bright student. "I want you to start at the beginning, when you realized you'd have to pull off the road and stay the night in Davidson."

"You wanna beer?" Guy asked, moving toward the fridge.

It was broiling in the trailer. I did want one, but I was feeling paranoid. Did he have a gun in there? Richie Caplan's head? I shook my head no and watched carefully as he pulled open the fridge door, reached in and pulled out a can of Great West. He pulled back the tab and took a deep pull before continuing on.

"We all had supper together in the hotel restaurant, with drinks, lots of drinks for some. They invited me to join them, which was nice. After all, I wasn't part of their group, just the bus driver. Afterwards, someone, I think it was Kim, suggested we all go to one of the rooms and play a game."

"Game?"

"Tequila Pigs."

My stomach lurched at the memory of a game I know well—or rather, used to know, in my younger days. The entire game consists of three bright pink plastic pigs with red hooves, each no more than two centimeters long and one high. I was first introduced to Tequila Pigs by Pat, one of my more mischievous, bad-influence, university-era friends. It is, simply put, a drinking game. The players sit in a circle and each takes a turn tossing the porcine trio. Depending on the positions in which the pigs land, points are accordingly awarded and the player with the highest roll downs a shot of tequila. The names of the various positions in which these pigs can land are rather inventive: Rashers, Pork Bellies, Back Bacon, Rooters, the Canadian Bacon Lean and, everyone's favourite, Makin' Bacon. It's a silly, immature, hoot-hollering, sooouuuuuu-eee good time, and often ends with one or more players having to excuse themselves for a quick dash to the bathroom or nearest potted plant.

"It was fun at first," Guy told me, "but people were drinking way too much and way too fast. Some people were getting high too. So someone came up with the idea to change the rules. If you won a toss, you could either drink or pick someone to play truth or dare with."

Truth or Dare. Another potentially dangerous game (and a fairly decent Madonna documentary). The Pink Gophers were definitely playing with fire that night.

"At first it was pretty innocent. People were asked about stupid things they'd done when they were younger, childhood fears, dreams, stuff like that. But then things started to get personal, too personal. On one of Richie's turns he chose Duncan for truth or dare. Duncan chose a dare, and the dare was for him to French kiss the nelly guy."

"Jin Chau?"

"Jinny, yeah, that's him. Everybody began to hoot and holler, and Jin was playing it up, all coy-like but puckering up, getting ready for it. Duncan got all mad and refused. Then right after that, one of the gals wins a toss and calls on Jin, and he chooses truth. It was one of the dead girls, I think…"

"Tanya? Moxie?"

"I guess. Anyway, one of them asked Jin who in the circle did he most want to sleep with. He chose the model dude."

"Jared." Just saying his name gave me a pang of sorrow. How was he? What was happening at the hospital? I realized how grateful I was for the distraction of the case and that hopefully, I was doing something that would bring his attacker to justice. "He's a friend of mine," I whispered.

"Yeah, Jared, nice guy. Well, anyway, everyone just about fell over, pissing themselves laughing, particularly those two girls, Tanya and Moxie. Not your friend. I must say, he was pretty decent about the whole thing. But Jin, oh man, that guy just went cold. He got up and walked out. That pretty much brought the evening to an end, right there."

"What happened then?"

"Well, we decided it was time to go to bed. A lot of travellers were stuck in Davidson that night, so there were only four hotel rooms amongst the thirteen of us. So we had to split them up as best we could, based on whether the rooms had two beds or one and who wanted to sleep with who. Everyone else kind of doubled up, but no one wanted to sleep with Jin, and he ended up in the same room as Richie and me. There were two beds in the room, and even though Richie knows Jin, he asked if he could sleep in my bed."

I gave Guy a look that was meant to say, "Who do you think you're fooling?"

He had the sense to blush. "There was something sorta going on between us already," he admitted. "During Tequila Pigs, when Richie was asked who in the circle *he* wanted to sleep with, he said me, even though I was straight. So I kinda figured he liked me, and when we got into bed and the lights went off…well, we sorta did stuff."

"In front of Jin?"

"Well, he was in the next bed, asleep we thought… or hoped. I guess we didn't much care at the time, and like I was saying, we'd been drinking and toking."

Jin. He'd been humiliated by the game; the others laughed at him, his lust for Jared was revealed and turned into a joke, and then, to top it off, like curdled icing on a sour cake, he'd had to endure the lovemaking of two of his tormentors in the bed next to his. Just the thought of it was horrible. I could empathize with the feelings of mortification and self-loathing and hatred that must have begun to fill him, but to seek systematic revenge against the perpetrators in the way that he had, that was an act of pure lunacy. Was Jin crazy? Was he taking revenge on everyone who'd humiliated him that night? When I'd gone to his apartment, he'd certainly come off as a colourful character with strong opinions about how the world should work, but was he a psychotic killer, desperate for justice as he saw it, seeking harsh judgment against those who'd shamed him, rebuffed him, made a laughingstock of him? I could not answer that. I'd only spent a short time with the man. All I knew was that if he was the boogeyman, he was also a masterful liar and schemer.

When I stepped out of Guy Marcotte's trailer that night, I was grateful for the slight breeze that had come up while I was inside, adding a cool edge to the sweltering hot summer night. The air was still pungent with smoke from whatever ritual madness the locals were undertaking half a block away, and the darkness hid a million crickets who serenaded me with their cyclical song as I hurriedly made for my car.

I slipped into the low-slung driver's seat and

locked the door behind me. I had felt an unmistakable sense of foreboding when I'd first arrived in Hagar's Heath, and my time with Guy Marcotte had done little to quell the sense that I was not safe—and neither, I feared, was Richie Caplan. He'd borrowed Guy's car to go over to Jinny's apartment, to confront him with his suspicions, to try to put an end to the harassment once and for all. At least that's what he told Guy and what Guy told me. I didn't know who to believe at that point, but before I went galloping off to find the truth, I needed to cover my ass. I used my cellphone to call the police department and was routed through to Darren's office. It was late, but he was still hard at work. I asked if he'd had any further news of Jared's condition. He hadn't. I told him what I'd learned from Guy and that I was now heading over to Jin Chau's apartment and invited him to join me there if he felt like it. He did. I hung up and got set to start the car. I turned the key but nothing happened.

The silence in place of the expected whizzing of the Mazda's rotary engine coming to life was deafening. This had never happened before. Sure, the car is old, but it's as reliable as the day is long. Had it finally given up the ghost?

I unlocked the door and swung it open. I pulled the hood-release latch and stepped out of the car. It was hot, dark, quiet. Even the crickets were taking a break. I took a step toward the front of the vehicle but stopped when I saw something unusual out of the corner of my eye. It looked like a big, red donut on the hood of my car. I frowned and moved closer. What the heck…? It looked like…paint…someone had painted a big, red circle on the hood. Stupid Hagar's Heath hoodlums! But wait, next to the first red circle was another and…I began to twist my head to see the design more clearly. That was when the dog began to growl, maybe even the same dog as before. The crickets resumed their chirping madness, fast and furiously loud. I froze, not from the night creatures' warnings, but something much more sinister. To the left of the second O was another symbol, a letter, also blood red. The letter B.

BOO.

I heard the whistle of something moving swiftly through air and then nothing.

Chapter 20

I awoke with a weight on my chest so oppressive it felt as if my lungs were clogging up with cotton batting and even one more breath might be the last I could manage. My brain screamed: What's happening to me? Is this a heart attack? Am I in a hospital?

The truth was worse.

I was still in Hagar's Heath. Still hot, still dark, still the growling of the dog and crazy cricket chirping. But something was different. I wasn't standing by my car anymore. I was on the ground. I'd been moved—dragged?—into a narrow, dank corridor, somewhere between two trailers and behind one of those big, black, plastic garbage disposal bins. I knew I must have been pulled by my feet because my shirt had ridden up to my shoulder blades and my back felt tender from where the skin had rubbed off against gravel and who knows what else. I was lying on my back. My hands were tied together, as were my ankles. Definitely not in a hospital. The weight on my chest pinning my arms was a person. A person I recognized. A person who was staring down at me and, seeing that I was awake, smiled a broad smile and whispered, "Boo."

I beheld the face of the boogeyman.

It wasn't until I'd collected my thoughts and an appropriate four-letter-laden comeback that I realized I was also gagged.

"Helloooooo, handsome," Jin Chau purred. "Happy to see me?"

Jin was wearing skin-tight jeans and a white top that looked more like a blouse than a shirt. His face beneath the gaudy orange-pink of his hair was a mushroom-coloured canvas made perfect thanks to thick layers of concealer and dim lighting. He was wearing too much of a nose-choking, flower-scented perfume. One of his slender hands was poised coquettishly on his sparrow chest and I saw that his long nails were freshly painted luminescent silver.

"You couldn't keep your big nose out of my business, could you? Well, if you get into my business, sister, you gotta pay the price," he told me with the ringing conviction of someone who can only see things one way: his own. "I just wanted to get these dumb bastards back, that's all, but you started poking around, so you're gonna have to go down too, pretty one.

"Myyyyyyyy, you *are* happy to see me!" Jin had reached back with his other hand and had begun massaging my crotch. I became uncomfortably aware that, at some point during the time I was unconscious from a blow to my head, my attacker had undone the zipper to my pants. "Guys like you…you and Jared Lowe, and those fucking laughing hyenas Duncan and Richie, and the bus driver—did you know they're fucking each other by the way? Richie and the bus driver—guys like that, guys like you…you never even look at guys like me. You never give me…us a chance. Well, honey, you really should, just let Jinny give you some loving…and you'll never wanna go back to those vanilla clone-boys."

I stared up at him; I tried to wriggle my thighs and hips, but with the full weight of Jin—slight as he was—on my chest, hands and ankles bound, and my head buzzing like an electric saw, I was pretty much immobile. Jin blew me a kiss and began to shuffle his way down the length of my body, like a bear climbing down a tree, taking his time as he moved over my hips, pushing himself against me, thrusting his hands under me, massaging my butt cheeks. I had never been in this kind of situation before: completely helpless, being molested. I felt as if I might vomit, from my predicament, the bonk on my head, the molestation or maybe all of the above. I heard Jin's feminine laugh and then, with surprising strength, he flipped me over. My stomach lurched and again I had to swallow bile that burned in my throat.

From my new position, my left cheek thankfully cushioned by a stray clump of grass, I saw a large stick off to one side from where I was lying. It was too dark to make it out for sure, but I thought one end looked wet, sticky…with my blood?

Jin laughed some more and then began doing what I hoped most he would not. I felt the scrape of fingernails against the skin of my bare hips as he slid his be-ringed, taloned fingers beneath the waist of my pants and Calvins and began to pull down.

"Jinny is going to show you what you've been missing, what all the boys like you have been missing." His voice had lost its feminine purr, replaced by something rough and raspy, overflowing with naked desperation.

My mouth gagged. I heard screaming inside my head. I had to resist this. I had to buck upwards or roll away or do something! I tried to force my body, but my head, it hurt so bad…

When I came to, I think only seconds later, Jin had been successful in pulling my pants and underwear down to my knees. He was now on top of me, rubbing the length of his slim frame up and down my own.

"Are you ready? Are you ready for me?" his hateful voice gurgled near my ear.

I wanted to fight. I wanted to yell out. I wanted, God help me, to kill this person. This person who had done the unspeakable to Jared. This person who was responsible for the death of two women, maybe others. This person who was about to rape me. Kill. I wanted to. But my body was not responding. My head seemed unconnected to the rest of my body. Had he knocked the sense out of me? Was I paralyzed? No, I couldn't be, I could feel every inch of him on top of me. I could feel his hands exploring me, everywhere. I could feel the tears beginning to form in the corner of my eyes. There would be no help for me, no rescue. I'd sent Darren and the cops to Jin's apartment. They'd never find me here.

Again I woke up. How long had it been this time? Not long, I thought. Jin was still on top of me and as far as I could tell, nothing had happened. Yet. I was falling in and out of consciousness...one more time and who knew...?

"You're going to love this, I promise," Jin told

me, his breathing growing laboured with his ministrations.

I could feel his clammy skin against my own. No.

No!

"Noooooo...!" Jin screamed.

In my disoriented mind I chuckled thinking Jin's pleasure had peaked too soon.

But then he screamed again and there was nothing pleasurable or orgasmic about it. Jin was in pain. I felt him roll off me, yelp some more and then hop to his feet. I didn't have enough strength to get onto my back, so I tried to move my head as much to one side as I could to see what was happening. And there, surrounding us like a pride of angry lions circling for the kill, were the fine folks of Hagar's Heath, most brandishing either a flaming torch or weapon of some sort—shovels and rakes and what appeared to be long, narrow sticks with blackened ends, which I only recognized in the seconds before I passed out once again: they were threatening Jin Chau with the sharp, poker-hot ends of wiener roast sticks.

The people of Hagar's Heath kept Jin on the wiener stick, so to speak, until the cops arrived for him and an ambulance for me. I was treated for concussion and kept overnight in the hospital. If I'd been more in control of my consciousness, I'm sure I would have balked at the idea—as tough-guy PIs are supposed to do—but instead I spent a carefree, happy, drug-induced night of sleep at RUH. Early the next morning I was back to playing tough guy and was changing from the drafty hospital smock into my own clothes (which I'd found in a Sobey's bag at the bottom of my room's closet) when the door swung open to reveal Constable Darren Kirsch.

"Quant," came the gruff greeting as he walked into the room in his big he-man way.

I looked away at first, an unexpected jolt of embarrassment and shame passing over me like a hot flash. Kirsch knew what had happened last night, knew what had been done to me by that creature. For all I knew, he was the one who found me there, laying on the ground, naked from the waist down.

"Quant?" he said again, this time with surprising gentleness. He closed the door behind him so that now it was just the two of us in that overbearingly small, stifling hospital room. I felt a hand on my shoulder. "You're okay, you know. When we arrived you were unconscious, but the locals, they took good care of you."

My chest heaved with a deep sigh. I wasn't exactly sure what Kirsch meant; I could only hope that maybe the Hagar's Heath villagers had covered me up, pulled my pants up, so when the cops arrived—guys I'd once worked with—they hadn't seen me lying there like that, a helpless victim. Maybe, maybe I realized too that I'd been very wrong about the people of Hagar's Heath. I'd promised myself I'd never go back there. But I would, to thank them.

I turned to face the dark-featured Kirsch, a contrived look of calm plastered on my pale face. "Tell me," was all I said. I knew the cop would understand.

He took back his hand and walked a few steps away to a safer, manlier distance. "They found something called a 'Hate Journal' in Jin Chau's apartment. In it was a list of everyone who'd been on that bus stranded in Davidson several months ago. The names were ranked in order, starting with who he hated the most to who he hated the least.

"The names were cross-referenced to another list of all the means of harassment he'd come up with to seek his revenge on them. He was very organized about the whole thing. But why these people, why the harassment, why he hated them so much, we're not sure yet. He hasn't stopped wailing and railing yet."

"I know why," I sad flatly. I told Darren about the seemingly innocent game of Tequila Pigs and Truth or Dare that unwittingly began the devolution of Jin Chau's damaged psyche. "He wanted vengeance and retribution for the ridicule he suffered during the game and…I'm betting if we were to ask Beverly or some other brain-studier-type person…during his entire, sad lifetime.

"I'm guessing Tanya Culinare and her girlfriend, Moxie Banyon, were somewhere near the top of his list?"

Darren moved his shadowed jaw up and down. He'd obviously not been home to shave since sometime the day before.

I explained, "Tanya and Moxie had singled him out during the game of Tequila Pigs. We'll never know exactly how it happened, but there were copious amounts of alcohol involved, drugs too, and I can imagine that Tanya and Moxie, perhaps a bit out of their usual characters and blissfully unaware of how their actions were affecting Jin, acted cruelly towards him, set him up for embarrassment, then laughed at him. From what I knew of them, neither of those two women were the type of people to be intentionally cruel, but in those circumstances, maybe they were. Maybe to a regular person their actions wouldn't have seemed as devastating, but to someone like Jin, a damaged soul, someone who lived his life in constant defence of who he was and couldn't help being, it was, simply, the final straw that broke the camel's back."

"That was why he went after them so aggressively?" Darren asked.

I nodded. "And Richie Caplan for suggesting Duncan Sikorsky French kiss him, and Duncan himself for his public revulsion at the thought and refusal to do it."

Kirsch continued to nod. He told me, "Next on the list were Kim Pelluchi and Guy Marcotte—who Jin referred to in his journal only as 'the bus driver'—so he possibly did not even know the guy by name."

"That's explains why Guy Marcotte didn't experience or report any incidences of harassment; Jin didn't know his name or where to find him."

"Makes sense," Kirsch agreed.

"But wait." Something did not add up. "If that's true, what was Jin doing outside Guy Marcotte's trailer last night if he didn't know his name or where he lived? Was it Richie? Did Richie tell…oh my God, Richie. He was going to see Jin…is he okay? Did Jin…?"

"Richie Caplan is fine," Kirsch assured me. "He actually never got to see Jin. By the time he got to his apartment, Jin had already left."

"But then how…?" Eureka. I love moments like this. "I think I have this figured out."

"Care to share it, Sherlock?"

"In a way it *was* Richie's doing that Jin found Guy—and me. During the course of his harassment, Jin'd been tailing Richie, and as luck would have it, he followed him right to the doorstep of—guess who?—Guy Marcotte."

Darren looked doubtful.

"You see, Richie and Guy had sex that night in Davidson, in the room they were sharing with Jin.

Guy insists they thought Jin was asleep, but I kinda have my doubts about that. Apparently it was Guy's first time with another guy, and neither he nor Richie was in the mood to wait for a better time or place.

"Imagine Jin's excitement at having found the man who belonged to the unknown name on his hate list. Could be that last night he was checking Guy out, no doubt planning how he'd exact his revenge on his new subject."

Darren finished up for me. "When along comes Russell Quant, troublemaker." Grrrrr, "Getting too close for comfort, and another one of those unattainable kind of gay guys who habitually scorn him. So, no dummy him, Jin decided to capitalize on opportunity and went after you."

Not my luckiest day.

"What about the other Pink Gophers?" Kirsch wondered. "They were lumped together at the bottom of the list. They suffered the least at Jin's hands: mild harassment, hang-ups, that type of thing."

"They were probably included just because they were there that night during the Tequila Pigs game. I'm sure they smirked along with the others and did nothing to protect Jin or stand up for him, so that qualified them to be on his naughty list."

There was one person we hadn't talked about, and I wondered where he was on Jin Chau's Journal of Hate list. "What about Jared? Was he on the list?"

"Jared's name was all alone at the bottom of a well-worn page, written in caps, with the 'a' shaped like a heart." He gave me a lopsided look. "I suppose that means he was in love with Jared Lowe?"

"Yep. During the game, Jin announced that he wanted to have sex with Jared."

"Oh Keeee-rist!" Kirsch's face contorted. "What the hell kind of screwed up game is this?"

I ignored that, knowing that Darren Kirsch was just the type to have kissed a few maidens in his younger days during illicit late-night games of spin-the-bottle or naked Twister. I knew, as sure as I know my name is Russell Quant, that Jin had fallen in love with Jared—I could attest that this was not a difficult thing to do. But somewhere along the way, Jin's bruised and battered and diseased mind turned that love into hate. It consumed him, threatened to wreck him and, in self-defense, all he could think of to do was destroy it—and Jared along with it.

"We've learned more about Moxie Banyon," Darren informed me. "Her doctor had diagnosed a heart defect shortly before she died. We can't be one hundred per cent certain, but the police were able to trace Jin's whereabouts and they know he was in Moose Jaw around the time of Moxie's death. And they know he had access to a gun." Man, a lot happens while a guy's taking a nap in the hospital; the cops had been admirably busy. "The theory right now is that Jin figured out Moxie's schedule, knew she'd be alone in the pool after closing that night and confronted her, probably using the gun to get her undivided attention. None of the people who were at the pool around closing time could identify Jin, so he may have been in disguise. When he was certain no one else was around, he used the gun to force her into the deep end of the pool. Even for a strong swimmer, treading water can be difficult for prolonged periods of time, but for Moxie, who was probably frightened out of her wits, a poor swimmer and had a weak heart, well, it would have quickly become near impossible. Jin couldn't have known about Moxie's heart condition, but it worked in his favour."

"Maybe," I mumbled.

"Whassat?" Darren asked, confused.

Jin had begun small, with phone calls in the middle of the night, slashed car tires and petty irritations. He was probably taken by surprise at how delectable the taste of revenge could be and soon graduated to break and enter and property destruction, then bodily threats and other more serious personal harassment. "Moxie Banyon was Jin Chau's first fatality," I said, "but what if he didn't plan to kill her? He wasn't a killer—not yet—and he probably only intended to give Moxie a good scare, otherwise, why bother with a disguise? If he intended to kill her, there'd be no need to keep her from seeing his face, knowing who her tormenter was, and actually you'd think he'd have preferred that. But no, Jin expected to walk out of that pool with Moxie still alive and unable to identify him. He just wanted to scare her. Instead her poor heart gave out and she went under and drowned."

Darren gave me a half nod as he considered my theory. "Unplanned, possibly," he allowed, "but a murder nonetheless."

"Yes," I agreed wholeheartedly with that. "It was murder. And it tasted good to Jin. So he again upped his tactics of terror as he pursued enemy number two, Tanya Culinare. Jin isn't a big man or a strong man and, really, not a man of great physical violence, but he discovered he was a master at feats of mental violence, capable of driving a person to their own demise, in effect scaring them to death. So he used this as he went after Tanya and the others. He became their boogeyman. In his mind, this seemed a fitting sentence for those who'd made his life so miserable." I added, "And truth be told, neither Tanya or Moxie—really none of the Pink Gophers—were specifically to blame for the greater woes of life as lived by Jin, but they were handy scapegoats."

Tanya Culinare was a woman of compromised mental strength. I would have to report to her family my findings that indeed she had taken her own life. She had, of her own volition, taken the steps to that balcony and leaped over the railings that sad summer night. But I'd also report that were it not for the cruel mental manipulations of Jin Chau to which she'd been unrelentingly subjected to for months, she might still be alive today.

"The question will always be," I put to Kirsch, "would Jin eventually have killed them all?" Were the deaths of Tanya and Moxie enough? And what of his final act of love/hate against Jared? Here was a beautiful man who would never return his love. By all reports, Jared did nothing to encourage Jin and treated him with kindness, but that wasn't enough. It could never be enough for someone like Jin. And the only way he could think of to fix his pain was to remove the object of his passion. Jared wasn't leaping to his own death, he did not have a weak heart to do him in, and Jin did not have the physical strength to physically kill Jared, so he did what came to mind. He destroyed the object of his affection: Jared's beautiful face.

"Tequila Pigs, huh?" Darren said, giving me a look as if I'd invented the game myself.

"I swear," I responded, a little indignant. "It's a real game—three little plastic pigs, red hooves."

He turned thoughtful. "Who would have thought that three plastic pigs could cause all this trouble?" He made a move toward the door.

"It wasn't just the pigs," I said. Something told me Jin Chau had had many fearful boogeymen of his own to deal with in his lifetime.

We hugged for a very long time, saying nothing, just touching one another and trying to give each other and take from each other some measure of strength, love, encouragement, whatever we had, whatever we needed. Finally we pulled apart.

I was taken aback by my friend's face. It was as if, with the loss of his lover's beauty, so had his own faded. Anthony's skin had grown pale and blotched and slack at the jowls. His eyes were pale reflections of what they once were and his hair was lustreless. He stood in front of me with a bit of a stoop, looking inexplicably shorter than I knew him to be. My heart broke for him and I pulled him once more into my arms.

Again we parted and sat next to one another on my rumpled hospital bed.

"How's the news?" I asked.

"Not good, I'm afraid," he told me through dry lips. "The damage to his face is severe. Even though he'd tried to wipe it away with his sleeve, the acid was in full, prolonged contact with his skin. But he will survive. In many ways, most ways actually, Jared will return to normal. He'll be able to eat, speak, see, hear…thank the sweet Lord that none of those abilities were taken from him…he could have lost an eye or had acid in his mouth or…well, never mind that…he will be normal, except…except he will never again look like Jared."

"I'm sure they can do miracles these days with

plastic surgery and...and...and other treatments." I was desperate to dispense some sense of hope to this broken man.

He nodded weakly. "Yes, yes, of course. As soon as Jared is able, we'll pursue some options." His face seemed to brighten a bit. "That is what we must focus on now, puppy. The things we *can* do."

I nodded too and mindlessly rubbed Anthony's back, and as I did so I couldn't help but think about the man who came before Jared in Anthony's life, my uncle Lawrence. Would it help Anthony now, at this horrible juncture in his life, to know that Uncle Lawrence was alive? Would he want to seek him out, for advice, support, encouragement, as he had so many times during the course of their strong relationship and even stronger friendship? Or would it be cruel of me, knowing what I knew—that Uncle Lawrence was dying—to give Anthony this hope which one day soon, too, would be taken from him, a second time. Oh God! What should I do? This was too difficult to figure out. I'd had no time to reflect on any of this, to make sense of it, to come to some closure about Uncle Lawrence, his life, his relationship to Sereena, his illness and his impending death. I needed time. But Anthony did not have that luxury. My friend needed help now. Did I have it to give—in the form of Uncle Lawrence; by withholding it, was I making a conscious decision to leave Anthony in pain?

No, I decided. I *did* have help to give my friend, but, for now anyway, it would have to come from me, only me.

"How are you, puppy?" This was so like Anthony; despite the hell he was living in, he still thought of others. "I know you went through significant unpleasantness out there last night." He gave me a worried look. "Are you okay?"

I patted his thigh with what I hoped was convincing reassurance. "I'm fine, Anthony, really."

"Russell," he began softly. "I know what…what that monster tried to do to you. You need to talk about it."

Something caught in my throat. No, I did not need to talk about it. I did not want to think about it. I…did not…no. I had nearly been raped. I could barely think the words in my head, never mind say them out loud. It seemed…untrue. It didn't fit with my reality, my view of life, which is, generally, pretty sunny-side-up, despite the crap I sometimes deal with in my line of work. But this…this would take time to work through.

"Perhaps later then?" He laid a hand on my arm and rubbed it slowly, his sign of abiding affection, telling me he'd be around when the time was right.

"Perhaps."

"He's awake right now," Anthony said, searching my face with his all-knowing eyes.

My skin shifted yet again and my heart began a

rhythmic thrum. "Let's go," I whispered and smiled weakly.

Anthony spoke of meaningless minutiae as we made our way via elevators and endless drab hallways from the ward where I'd been recuperating to where Jared lay in Intensive Care. He needed to talk, mutter, make normal comments on normal things. I tried to join in when I could, but I was reeling with the thought of what I was about to do, about to see, and wondering: How do you react when you first encounter the destroyed face of a friend you love? What could I possibly say? What should I allow my face to show so as to spare Jared's feelings?

The hospital corridors were echoingly empty that time of the morning, the light of a summer day surprisingly grey and cool against the green-tinged hallways and stainless-steel gurneys and carts we passed along the way. Every so often I could hear gentle moaning or whispered prayers from behind doors of rooms I did not want to enter, and hoped did not belong to Jared. As we got closer, my mind began to spin with doubt, with fear, with uncertainty that I could do this. Coupled with an unceasing nausea, I could feel more acutely every scratch, every bruise, every bit of bodily damage I'd suffered at the hands of the same monster who'd put Jared in this hospital. I felt sick over what happened to Jared, over the fact that I'd failed to protect my friend from this. If only I'd worked faster, smarter, figured things out sooner, maybe none of this would have happened.

My pace slowed and finally Anthony, several steps ahead of me, stopped and turned to gaze at me with soft eyes. I stopped too and looked up from the nondescript mottle of the tile floor and saw... salvation. Only then did I know I could do this. I just needed a little help. Beyond the shadow cast by Anthony was Sereena, her face silently beckoning me forward. And behind her, almost a blur, another figure: Alex Canyon. My heart swelled with something new.

I entered the hospital room of my beloved friend. To me he was as beautiful as ever, with lips stained the colour of sweet summer berries.

Excerpt from

Sundowner Ubuntu

the fifth novel in the Russell Quant mystery series

Chapter 1

Murder.

There are many reasons to commit it.

Mine? My mother asked me to.

The snow was crunchy underfoot as I approached the weathered house where he lived. Although in my head I knew it was impossible, I had a feeling in my sour gut that he knew I was coming for him. As I hesitated outside the door, I passed the knife from hand to hand, feeling its unfamiliar heft in my sweating palms, then tested the glistening blade's sharpness against my thumb.

My eyes crinkled against bright morning sun. "Quant," I muttered under frosty breath, "what the hell are you doing?"

But, disgusted as I was, I could not turn away.

The door shuddered, then made a scraping noise as I slowly pulled it open, wrecking my hope for silence so as not to announce my arrival to Mr.

Crow—or anyone else—inside. Not that it mattered much; my course was set. I poked my head inside and was instantly assaulted by an acrid scent; eau de ammonia. Cloying warmth encircled me. As my pupils adjusted to the darkness, I heard sounds of burbling disturbance and discontent. Our eyes met. And so it began.

I quickly circled behind him, grabbing him and locking him in my arms. Surprisingly, he barely struggled as I took him outside. He knew. I splayed him on the white ground beneath my greater bulk, my knees and thighs keeping him in place, and shivered at the thought of what I was about to do. I began to entertain wild thoughts of alternative courses of action.

It was too late to turn back now.

I pulled back his head, revealing his vulnerable neck to the nippy air. Only then did he make gurgling sounds of protest. Maybe he hadn't really believed I'd be capable of this until right then, in that last, defining moment of his life. But it was too late for Mr. Crow, way too late. This had to be done.

Tightening my grip around the wooden handle of the knife, knuckles white, I pressed the sharp cutting edge of the instrument against his throat. I was surprised by the ease with which the knife did its evil duty. I was even more surprised by the amount of blood and how it spurted and spewed. The body underneath me shook with a death fury that unhinged me with its intensity. Although he was no match for me in size, I felt myself being bucked off; I fell back, slipping on an ice patch as I attempted to get a grip with my Timberland boots and pull myself up.

Dumped on my ass, the first thing I noticed was the knife, still in my hand. It looked perfectly clean, as if I'd wiped it off, yet I hadn't. The steel had been cold, the blood hot; the two did not stick together.

The second thing I noticed was the headless body of my victim rising to his feet.

My face contorted in horror as I realized that Mr. Crow was not dead.

He turned a full three hundred and sixty degrees, swayed left, then right, hopped from one foot to the other, then he turned again.

I haltingly made it to my feet, the knife falling to the ground, burying itself beneath reddened snow. Mr. Crow made a jarring move towards me.

Then he charged.

I turned and ran for the hills, a scream burning in my throat.

"Dat's goot, uh huh?" my mother, Kay Quant née Wistonchuk, asked for the millionth time as I forked another heap of her home cooking into my mouth.

March had come in like a lion, a roaring storm

chasing me from Saskatoon to Howell as I'd headed for my mother's homestead farm for what was supposed to be a two-hour visit. That was two days ago. I'd been storm-stayed—and desperately trying to shovel my way out ever since.

"You haf no chicken?"

Damnation, she'd noticed. I thought for sure that with all the other meats—meatballs, beef slabs, veal cutlets, farmer's sausage—she wouldn't.

"You don't like de chicken, den? It's goot." She passed me the platter, heavy with deep-fried, golden pieces of Mr. Crow, and urged me with her eyes. "Have the letka."

"My plate's full right now, Mom," I begged off on her offer of the drumstick, the leg of the same chicken that had tried to chase me down in that bloodied field of trampled snow, even after its owner had lost his head. "Maybe later." Like never.

I just couldn't bring myself to eat it, and perhaps I will never eat chicken again. Each time I see a leg or some other readily identifiable chicken part, I picture the Braveheart battleground of Mr. Crow's last stand. Sure, he'd come to his execution willingly, with uncommon dignity even, but things got ugly after that. That damn Mr. Crow, named—by my mother—after his morning ritual, seemed as capable of living without a head as he was with one (at least for several, horrifyingly long minutes, and he'd made the best of them). By the end of his pursuit, during which he'd demonstrated an uncanny sense of where I was (sans eyes to see me with), the previously pristine landscape surrounding the henhouse—once gleaming white from the storm's snowfall—was splattered a grisly crimson, as though a game of paintball had gone dreadfully wrong. I had taken refuge atop a nearby grain seeder turned flowerpot, amongst brittle stalks of long dead delphiniums and shasta daisies, and watched in utter horror as Mr. Crow danced headless to his slooooooooooow death.

"Vell, ve go to town tomorrow, and I buy odder meat mebbe, uh huh? You tell vhat you like and I buy," my mother offered.

I finished chewing a tasty pickled beet before giving the reply I knew she'd been dreading. "Mom, I'm going home tomorrow morning. I've been here two days, and I really have to get back to work."

"Not two days," she argued back. "You vant cream in coffee? Vhat for dessert? I heat up some *nalesnehkeh*."

"Yeah, Mom, two days."

"But de roads, not safe yet. You vait one more day, dey be much better den, uh huh."

I knew it wasn't the roads she was really worried about; it was loneliness, the result of cabin fever that commonly sets in with farm folk, particularly near the end of long winters. She wanted me to stay. She always does, as a matter of fact, winter or summer. It makes me feel wanted, for sure, but it's difficult being a detective from a desolate farmhouse, nestled in the hills that surround Howell, Saskatchewan, population too low to count.

When it comes to where I prefer to lay my head at night, I am much like my mother: stubborn. If at all possible, I want to be in my own bed, in my own house, with my dogs and things surrounding me, in the nest I've worked a lifetime to build. I want running water that is hot consistently, rather than on a whim as it is on the farm. I want it gushing from the shower head, not dribbling out between globs of rust. I want to flush the toilet with careless abandon, rather than with bitten lip in fear of the septic system acting up, as it so often does. I want Internet access and more than three channels on the TV. I want 7-Eleven and Mr. Sub and a gym to go to rather than an exercise routine that includes a few laps around the barn with a mouldy German shepherd-husky cross nipping at my heels and looking at me as if I'm crazy for running around with nothing to chase.

I do not want to murder my supper.

Clara Ridge was half an hour late for her appointment, which was going to make things tight; I had to be at the airport by five.

"I'm very sorry," she apologized as she lowered

herself into the chair in front of my desk, pulling off black leather gloves by their fingertips. "I hate being late."

Usually a statement like that is followed by an explanation, but when it became apparent none was forthcoming I moved along. "Are you sure I can't take your coat? Would you like a coffee or something else to drink?"

She shook her head and I noticed her hair, styled to within an inch of its freshly dyed life, moved along with it, without one follicle falling out of place. "Thank you, but your receptionist already offered. I'm a little chilled, so I'll keep my coat on."

Clara Ridge was a handsome woman in her mid fifties who'd obviously gone to some trouble to appear in my office looking well-groomed. Along with the too-perfect hair was a spotless makeup job and fresh manicure complete with bright red nail polish. Her coat was dark fur, real fur; don't see those around much anymore.

"I saw your ad in the *Yellow Pages*," she told me. "I hope that's okay. I haven't been referred or anything. You know how it is with doctors—specialists especially—if you haven't been referred by another doctor, they simply won't see you, no matter how long you're willing to wait for an appointment. Are private detectives like that? I don't know, that's why I'm asking."

I smiled. "Not this one."

In fact, I wasn't too picky at all about how my clients came to me. Being a detective in Saskatoon, a small prairie city, has its challenges. There isn't a mysterious dame (or dude) smoking a long, slim cigarette, wearing a jaunty hat low over worried eyes, silhouetted against the frosted glass of my office door at midnight, nearly often enough to keep a private dick like me in continual work. I'd been lucky of late though, working fairly regularly, usually on rather pedestrian cases, affairs of domestic or financial distress, but they pay the bills and allow me a few indulgences (nice coats and scarves in winter, bedding plants in summer, shoes and good wine always).

"How can I help you?" I asked the woman.

"I want you to find my son. Can you do that?"

Immediately my mind went to some likely scenarios: runaway, druggie, custody battle. I nodded. "I can certainly give it my best, Mrs. Ridge." I reached for a pad of paper and pen. "Let's talk about details. What is your son's name, and when did he go missing?"

"His name is Matthew and he's been missing— or rather I haven't seen him—for about twenty years."

Holy Amelia Earhart! And you're just realizing it now? Not a very observant parent. "I see," I said with little conviction. "How old was Matthew the last time you saw him?"

Mrs. Ridge was staring straight at me, eyes wide, as if waiting to be led into telling a story she didn't want to tell but knew she had to. "Sixteen."

"Can you tell me what happened?" I was betting on a runaway.

"He didn't run away from home," she said, guessing my thoughts. (Either that or I'd said it out loud and didn't know it.) "He was...taken."

For a split second I had an unsettling feeling that aliens were going to come into this story, but I brushed it off. More likely a divorce custody arrangement gone bad. "By whom?"

"The police."

Although I wrote the two words on my pad, I didn't quite comprehend the connection between the cops and a missing kid. I stayed silent.

"You see, Matthew was a good boy; he really, really was."

Uh-oh, the deluded—and usually misguided—parent's refrain. How many teachers and police constables and social workers and babysitters and detectives had heard that one before?

"He was such a beautiful boy, too; tall, with the most gorgeous blond hair, like straw, and a sweet, sweet smile. He enjoyed school, did well, loved sports and had lots of friends. And we tried our best with him, but you know how it is, you get busy with life, work and all. We had a struggling business, a corner grocery store that my husband and I ran;

we had no other employees to help out. Matthew seemed so well-adjusted, and well, we just didn't realize he was having problems; he got in with the wrong kind of kids, I guess.

"By the time he was thirteen he started getting into trouble with the police. At first it was petty vandalism, bullying kids in school, that kind of thing, not serious really. Even so, my husband, Clement, would punish him, severely. We thought it helped, but I guess…well, I guess it didn't. Things got worse. By the time Matthew turned sixteen he had started stealing things, getting involved with drugs." She seemed a bit flustered and began to peel off her fur. "I'm hot now. Perhaps I will take off my coat. Could I have a glass of water, please?"

While Mrs. Ridge de-furred herself, I poured a glass of water at my office sink and found ice cubes in the bar fridge that holds up one end of my desk. She accepted the drink and downed half of it, her eyes glued to the ceiling.

"Was Matthew arrested?" I queried to get her going again. "Is that why the police took him away?" I knew at sixteen Matthew Ridge would have been a minor and subject to different laws than an adult, but even so, there was punishment available for serious crimes committed by a teenager.

She nodded. "Yes. The summer after he completed grade ten. He got caught one too many times. He had multiple charges against him, a long history with the police by that point, so they decided—and we agreed—he needed to be rehabilitated. He was sent to reform school."

I do not know a lot about reformatories, but I was pretty certain they weren't in the habit of cutting off all contact between parents and their children. So then why had the Ridges never seen their son again? "Did Matthew escape from the school?"

"No," she whispered. "I'm sorry, Mr. Quant," she said, dabbing at her upper lip with the cocktail napkin I'd given her with her drink, "this is very difficult to talk about." She dug around in her purse and pulled out a neatly folded pile of tissues, no doubt softer than the napkin. Withdrawing one from the pile, she dabbed at the area under her eyes.

"Take your time," I said, touched by her obvious torment. There was something she wasn't telling me yet, but I could almost see it on the tip of her tongue. "Can you tell me why you didn't see Matthew after he went away? Did something happen to him at the school?"

"That's not it," she said. "You see, Mr. Quant, we hadn't seen Matthew for several weeks before he was sent away to reform school." She wrung her leather gloves and tissue together into a twisted rope of leather and…whatever it is tissues are made of. "You see, grade ten was a difficult time for Matthew, and he got into a lot of trouble. When it continued into the summer, my husband finally got fed up. He kicked Matthew out of the house and told him never to come back. Matthew's actions were affecting our business; most of our customers were local, friends and neighbours, but no one wanted to shop in a store owned by the family of Matthew Ridge, the biggest troublemaker in the area. People knew he was into drugs, and they thought he might be a dealer—although I'm sure he wasn't—and they didn't want their children anywhere near Matthew or his bad friends.

"I know it sounds stupid, I know it," she said, her voice growing hoarse with sorrow and despair. "We should have tried to help Matthew rather than put him out on the streets, but I was powerless against my husband's wishes. I told Clement it was better to have Matthew at home where at least we could watch over him, try to teach him some sense. I begged. But there was nothing I could do. When we heard that Matthew had continued to get into trouble and had been arrested, that was just the last straw for Clement. He washed his hands of him, as if he had no son. They sent him away. Matthew never called us; we never visited him. I don't..." she sobbed, "I don't even know if he ever got out of that horrible place, if he even survived it. I don't know what became of him. Oh God, Mr. Quant, I feel so horrible. I've been a terrible mother."

And she cried.

I offered her a box of tissues even though I knew she had her own stash somewhere in her lap. She took one and gazed pleadingly at me through a curtain of tears. "Can you help me?"

I looked at her, not immediately answering, wondering what happens to a middle-class but troubled sixteen-year-old boy abandoned by his parents and left to fend for himself in the world.

"There was nothing I could do twenty years ago, but there is now," she told me, her voice suddenly strong, belying the tears.

"Has your husband had a change of heart?" I inquired.

"In a manner of speaking," she said. "My husband had a heart attack."